BREEZE FROM
THE RIVER MANJEERA

Hema Macherla

To

Monica Ali, you inspired me —
so much

I admire you a lot
I loved Brick Lane,

Hema Macherla.

Email - hemamacherla @hotmail.com

Tel - 01708 471249

The Q

D1350500

Published in the UK by
The Linen Press
75c(13) South Oswald Rd
EDINBURGH
EH9 2HH
www.linenpressbooks.co.uk

First published by The Linen Press, 2008

ISBN 978-0-9559618-1-6

Typeset and designed by Initial Typesetting Services, Edinburgh
Printed and bound by Bookforce Distribution Ltd

ACKNOWLEDGMENTS

Firstly I am indebted to my husband, Radhamanohar, for his faith in me. Without his continued support it would not have been possible for me to write this book.

My gratitude to John Farley, creative writing tutor at Fairkytes, who made me write the first page at least three times and gave me invaluable feedback. He also nagged me to send my book to Richard & Judy.

To Russ, who volunteered to nit-pick my grammar.

My thanks to Frances, Jean, Maureen, Peter, Bill and Alice for their helpful comments and honest criticism.

Special thanks to my daughter Smitha, who read and edited the first drafts of my book with utmost patience. To my son-in-law Matt for his enthusiasm. To my son Littoo (Vamshi), for refusing to read it unless I got it published, and my daughter-in-law Sandy for her interest. To my cute little Leo and Sophia for filling my writer's-block spaces with fun.

Many thanks to Lesley Horton for her constructive criticism and Maggie Hamand for her helpful suggestions.

To my large, loving family in India and the USA for their eagerness to see the book in print.

Heartfelt thanks to my excellent editor and publisher Lynn Michell for her patience and guidance and making my dream a reality

For
Amma, Nanna and *Pedda bavagaru*

With love and respect

CHAPTER 1

Sleep seemed frightened of her nowadays just as she was frightened of sleep. Blessed or cursed she didn't know, but she must have slept lightly for a few minutes, just long enough for the nightmare to wake her again. When she opened her eyes, the room was dark apart from a faint streak of light from the street lamp that threw the shadows of the trees onto the pale blue walls. Neela felt a chill down her spine. Whether it was because of the English winter, the fright of the nightmare, or the emotional turmoil inside her, she didn't know but she longed for the warmth of her own bed in India.

A rush of wind that leaked through the gap at the bottom of the window made the calendar flutter. Neela saw the bold letters and numbers. The date was the seventh of March 1985.

A year ago, exactly, she remembered the noise and commotion as her parents turned the house upside down, cleaning and scrubbing every inch of it. The furniture was moved from the front room to the shed. In her grandparents' time it had been the finest and most beautiful of its kind, delicately carved with lotuses and swans, but now it was threadbare and the surface veneer was peeling off in ribbons. Her parents borrowed modern furniture from their neighbours to transform their front room.

She could still hear her mother's anxious voice.

'Neela, quickly, hang up those new curtains; they will hide those hideous rusty iron bars on the windows.'

After arranging the curtains neatly, Neela went to the back yard and gathered a few *mandara* flowers, their leaves shiny and dark green. She arranged them in a copper vase which she placed on a *tea-poi* in the middle of the room. She looked around, satisfied. The linen curtains, the natural cane furniture with its yellow cushions, and the red *mandaras* complemented one another nicely in that whitewashed front room.

In the kitchen, her mother, Sharda, prepared *samosas* and onion *bajjis* for starters. For the main course, *aloo biriyani*, soft *naan* breads, and crispy *parathas*, accompanied by spiced lentils, deep fried tender okra and stuffed baby aubergines. The tender *rasamalai* and sweet Mango *halva* were the after dinner delicacies.

Parvati, the old *Dadima* from next door was astonished to see so many dishes for so few people. '*Hai-Ram*! How much are you preparing, woman?' she said. 'You can feed a king and his army with all that food. Today is only the bride-viewing day, not the wedding day!'

The memory of that dear old lady brought a smile to Neela's lips. She was certainly a *Dadima*, a grandmother to everyone in her village of Gangapoor.

'I know, *Dadima*,' her mother said, 'but since they are coming from London, I have no idea what foods they like, so I decided to make a variety so that they could choose.'

'I know what you mean, Sharda. But I warn you that if you make this much now, they will expect much more for the wedding,' said *Dadima*.

'Yes, you are right,' sighed her Maa in agreement. 'But this is nothing compared to the happiness we will get if they agree to marry our girl.'

Neela remembered the excitement, happiness and hope reflected in her parents' faces. At last, a well-educated man from London was coming to view their beloved daughter.

2

Chapter 1

They had approached so many suitable boys for Neela, but not one had agreed to marry her. Neela loathed the visits of these potential bridegrooms who came over with their relatives, mostly women folk, and examined her as if she were an ornament. She remembered the humiliation she suffered from the scrutinising stares and the intrusive questions.

'So Neela, since you haven't studied much, have you learned anything else?'

'Can you cook at least?'

'What about the housework? My son can't stand a messy house.'

'Um . . . anything else? Can you sing?'

'Can you do embroidery?'

'Nowadays, these young girls can't do a thing.'

'Oh, drawing and painting! That's a surprise! But what use will that be? It's a waste of time and money.'

While his family watched, weighed and compared her qualities to see if she would be a fit wife for their son, the would-be groom would sit ogling her with greedy eyes. Neela sighed. She knew that in this game of arranged marriages anyone from the boy's side, even the dog, would rule the girl's family. When the Interrogation session ended, the real anxiety began, but in the end the results were always the same.

'Sorry, our boy wants a fair-skinned girl.'

'Sorry, the dowry you are offering is not enough because your daughter is not a beauty.'

'We all enjoyed your hospitality . . . but if only your girl's skin tone was a little lighter . . .'

'We will think about it but only if you double the dowry.'

She had been through many of these encounters in the last four years and more and more wished that she had gone to college like the wealthy girls in the cities, but with her village school education she could only get a job in the *Charminar* cigarette factory. How many times had she asked her father to let her work there? At least then she would be independent, even if she didn't get married. But his answer was always the same.

'Only after my death. As long as I am alive I won't let my daughter work for her living.'

In her community it would be a disgrace for any parent to let their unmarried daughter work. She knew that she would never be independent. It was impossible.

Just when her parents were losing hope, the miracle had happened. Ajay Pattwar had arrived from a foreign land seeking a suitable girl for marriage. Of course, if she were lucky, and he liked her, she would have to leave her beloved parents and her dear friends. She would have to leave India. Her parents told her it would be worth the sacrifice.

Now, as preparations were well underway, Neela was surprised to find the excitement rubbing off on her. Her thoughts focused on this bridegroom: how would he look? Would he be like a film star, perhaps tall and handsome? If so, would he like a girl who was considered dark and plain? *Pundit-ji,* the marriage broker, had said, 'It's not that they can't find a match, no-no.' He clucked his tongue. 'They just want a girl from your cultural background and her personality is far more important than her looks. That's why they are coming from so far away.' He chuckled. 'You never know, you might be in luck.'

The day arrived. A taxi stopped in front of their modest house, causing a stir in that small village. Neela, hearing the commotion, went to her bedroom window and opened its wooden shutters, just a crack. A crowd of children, men and women were gathered around the taxi. She knew that they had followed it from the main road because it was big news when a taxi came to Gangapoor. Her parents, aunties, uncles, and neighbours rushed out to welcome the new guests and invite them in.

Ajay stepped out of the car but remained hidden behind his lavishly-dressed mother, Durga-devi Pattwar. Neela's eyes boggled at the sight of her. How did that bright green, chiffon sari circle her bulging light brown flesh and non-existent waist line? No wonder she was blocking any view of her son. Neela gasped to see that the woman's huge neck, wrists, fingers and even her hair – which was twisted in a high bun – were overflowing with gold and emerald jewellery. Through the gate she sailed in slow motion, followed by the long trail of her loud relatives.

Neela's anxiety rose. Her tiny room was like a hot oven. The small table fan, even twirling at high speed, didn't help to cool her. There she stood, surveying her room, so cluttered now with heaps of colourful saris in silk, cotton and chiffon. There was no room left to move; even her bed was laden with jewellery. Gold, silver and pearl necklaces, bangles and earrings, all glittered in half-opened boxes. Her aunties, and her friend Suji, had brought their entire jewellery collections and all their saris so that she could choose. The window sill, used as a dressing table, was overflowing with *Ashoka* face powder, Eyetex *kajal*, a new *Vicco turmeric* vanishing cream, and a bottle of red liquid *vermilion*.

Neela had already sifted through a pile of saris that, one by one, she patiently tried on, standing in front of a full-length mirror. Her aunties and Suji decided how suitable each one was for this bride-viewing occasion. They concluded that the dark colours didn't suit her; pale colours made her look darker, and the bright colours were too loud and distracting. Eventually they settled on a subtle, dusty-pink, silk sari with black brocade and delicate silver embroidery. They teamed it with a matching blouse adorned with tiny black and silver beads. She chose her late grandmother's coral necklace and earrings from the box of jewellery which she and her mother shared.

'You look so elegant. This sari really suits you and shows off your slim figure,' cooed Suji, arranging the sari *pallu* neatly on Neela's shoulders.

'Look at your eyes, they are sparkling already,' Aunty Jaya smiled, looking at Neela's reflection in the mirror as she clipped into her long hair garlands of fresh jasmine flowers.

The delicate fragrance wafted around her. Neela was in turn excited and nervous. At any moment now they would call her out to the drawing room to introduce her to Ajay, who, if she could reach his expectations, would make her his wife and take her across the seas to that far away wonderland where he lived . . .

'Neela, come, come quickly. They want to see you now.' Her mother came rushing in. 'Take these *jelabis* to offer them.' She thrust a tray of pastries into her hands before pausing to examine her daughter and to check whether she was presentable for these potential customers.

Neela felt a wave of exhilaration. Her steps faltered. Beads of perspiration broke on her forehead. The tray rattled in her hands. Her quickened heartbeat made her breathless so that she had to stop. Putting the tray down on a table, she leaned on the wall for a moment, dabbing her sari *pallu* on her forehead to wipe away the droplets of sweat. Then, taking a deep breath to compose herself, she took the tray again in her hands. With her eyes downcast, she hesitantly entered the front room where everyone fell silent as they turned towards her. Though she was looking down at her feet, she was aware that all eyes in that room were on her. The guests from London and their relatives sat on the borrowed chairs while her parents and family sat opposite on straw mats on the floor.

'This is Neela, my daughter.' Her father stood up, introducing her to the guests.

Neela tried to steady herself again but it was impossible to stop trembling. Carefully placing the tray on a *tea-poi*, she greeted them, '*Namastay*,' with her palms folded together. She kept her head down modestly as she lowered herself to sit between her parents. Suji came and sat behind her for moral support. Patting Neela's arm, she whispered, 'Don't be shy. Look at the bridegroom.'

Neela lifted her eyes slowly and shyly towards Ajay. The first thing she saw was a pair of highly polished shoes shimmering like black glass. Then she noticed his navy suit, white shirt and blue tie. He appeared to be business-like or one could say 'London-like'. He was of average height and medium built. His complexion was one or two shades lighter than her own, and his features were thick and wide in his round, clean-shaven face.

'Please have some more almond *burffi*. Neela specially made it with pure *ghee*. She saw the recipe in a magazine,' said Sharada.

Neela heard in her mother's voice the desire to impress the bridegroom with her daughter's culinary skills and literacy.

'No thanks. I've had enough,' Ajay answered in English and looked at his mother.

'He doesn't like Indian sweets. Don't force him,' his mother supported him.

'Would you like to ask Neela anything?' Uncle Das interrupted.

'He can't understand much Hindi,' Durga-devi smiled proudly at her son.

Neela looked up at Ajay curiously while Uncle Das repeated the same question in his strong, Indian-accented English.

'No, not really,' Ajay said in a dry tone, taking at least a minute to answer.

'Neela loves to draw and paint. Did you see those patterns on the threshold? She painted them.' She heard Aunty Jaya's voice and glanced again eagerly at Ajay.

His gaze was fixed on an empty space on the wall. He didn't turn towards her or to the threshold. Was he shy, or was he nervous like her? wondered Neela. Perhaps wearing that dark coloured heavy suit was just too uncomfortable. The day had been scorching hot and unbearably humid. The single ceiling fan wasn't making much of an impression either. It squeaked noisily, as if saying that it was getting old and couldn't go on turning round and round for much longer.

'So, Ajay, it must be completely different from here, the way you do business there, in the UK?' Uncle Das was trying to engage him in conversation.

'Definitely, Das-*bhayya*. Do you think they have little tiny shops and weigh things with old fashioned scales and stones like we still do? No, no . . .,' Uncle Madhu tried to show off his knowledge but was stopped abruptly by his older brother's dismissive hand gesture.

'Actually, what sort of business do you do, Ajay?' Uncle Das continued his conversation with Ajay.

'He runs a newsagents business. It's going quite well,' Durga-devi answered, glancing round at everyone. 'He is always busy with the business, his hobbies and what not.' She looked in the direction of Neela and her family, saying, 'He hardly ever has time to relax or eat properly.'

'It's good to have hobbies, otherwise life would become dull like ours.' Narayan Swaran, Neela's father, looked appreciatively at Ajay. 'Most of us don't have time for any other activities. We only work, eat and sleep.'

'May I ask what sort of hobbies they are?' Suji asked suddenly.

Neela looked at Ajay's well-fed figure and thought that either his mother was lying about him having no time to eat, or his metabolism must be very low.

'Oh, he likes going to car shows and football and shopping. Of course only in designer shops,' Durga-devi replied.

'That's wonderful. You play football!' Uncle Madhu was excited.

Ajay squirmed uncomfortably in his chair.

'And you said shopping . . .?' Suji enquired.

Could shopping be a hobby? mused Neela.

'Uh, I told you already, he only shops for designer clothes,' Durga-devi tried to smile.

What on earth does 'designer' mean? Neela wondered.

Neela couldn't help but notice that while Durga-devi was talking proudly about her son, Ajay was staring at the ceiling and walls, uneasy, oblivious of Neela's replies. Why wasn't he saying anything.

'Is he mute, or what? I wish that queen ant would go and sting him hard. Then at least he might open his mouth to scream,' whispered an annoyed Suji, looking at a giant red ant coming out of a tiny crack in the cement floor near Ajay's chair. The image amused Neela so much that she had to cover her mouth with her hand to stop herself giggling. 'Neela doesn't speak much English but she will learn quickly. She is a fast learner,' pleaded Sharda.

Durga-devi waved her hand in the air and said, 'My Ajay doesn't speak much Hindi so your daughter will have to speak English to him. And what she doesn't know, I am sure he will teach her.'

Neela's family continued to treat Ajay and his family as if they were royalty as they invited the guests to eat.

'Please come in.' Her father escorted them into their tiny dining room. 'Sorry we could only offer you these modest seats,' he gestured towards the borrowed, laminated chairs and table. 'They might not be as comfortable as yours in London.'

'Don't worry. It can't be helped. We'll have to adjust.' Durga-devi looked at Sharda and added, 'I know you won't have proper cutlery, but do you at least have some spoons?'

'Oh, I am sorry, I didn't realise! Please forgive me. I will bring them in a minute.' Sharda was tripping over her sari in her haste and panic to reach the kitchen.

'You sit, Maa.' Neela steadied her mother. 'I will go and fetch them.'

'I don't know how you will like our food . . .' Sharda continued worrying.

Neela gave Suji a meaningful look, shaking her head, and Suji in return looked up, and shrugged her shoulders. The image of her parents, respectful in front of Ajay and his mother, their hands folded and their heads bowed like two worthless beggars, would stay in Neela's mind for ever.

'So what would you say, Ajay?' Uncle Das smiled, when the guests started to leave to go to their relatives in the city.

Ajay didn't answer immediately. Neela understood that he needed some time to think and make up his mind.

She knew that her parents didn't sleep for the whole week. Neela too needed some time to think because there was something about Ajay that didn't quite match his well tailored suit. Perhaps he was not up to her expectations? Expectations! She was surprised she even dared think of that. Was she allowed any expectations? She never really dared to imagine a stunningly handsome husband. But recently she had been secretly dreaming about a man who could cast a spell on her.

The day after the bride-viewing, as the evening was drawing in and cooling down the heat, Neela went and sat on the wooden swing on the veranda at the back of the house. She lightly pressed her feet on the stone floor, making the swing squeak gently.

'What are you doing out here on your own? Dreaming?' Suji came and sat next to her.

Neela looked at her friend thoughtfully but couldn't answer. Suji was newly married and seemed to be in love with her husband. It was Suji who had told her about those intimate magical moments between a man and a woman.

Suji knew what was on Neela's mind. 'So what do you think? Do you like him?'

'I don't know, Suji. Nothing happened to me when I looked at him. No magic or anything of the sort you talked about.'

'Don't worry. When you eventually get married, it will all come with that first touch.'

'Do I have to get married?'

Suji looked astonished. 'What sort of question is that? Of course you have to.'

'Why, what's wrong with the way I am now? I am happy. Why can't I live like this for the rest of my life?'

'Don't be silly, you can't live your whole life unmarried. Even if you are happy, what about your parents? How would they feel when people talked about you?'

'Who cares about people?'

'You don't, but your parents do. You know that people talk about unmarried girls over twenty as if they were really cheap,' she pressed her feet down on the floor to stop the swing and turned to Neela. 'If you wait another couple of years, they will throw mud at you and you won't even be able to hold your head high when you walk on the street.' She stopped for a moment and looked at her friend, 'It will break your parents' hearts.'

Neela went quiet for a while, staring at the grey clouds travelling across the sky.

'Is marriage the ultimate destiny for a girl?'

'It seems to be here.' Suji shrugged.

'I wish girls were free to do whatever they want. Study . . . work . . . fall in love and marry for love . . .' Neela said languidly, still looking up at the drifting clouds.

'Fall in love? Marry for love?' Wide eyed, Suji placed her hands over her chest. '*Hai-Ram*! How dare an unmarried girl not just think but utter that sinful word *love*? Your parents will hang you and then hang themselves in shame.' Suji tied an imaginary rope around her neck, stuck out her tongue and coughed.

Neela's dark mood dissolved, and the two girls both laughed until tears were running down their faces.

'The rule, my dear, is to marry first, and love later.' Suji said placing her thumb on her chest, 'Like me.'

'I don't think he liked me, Suji.' Neela halted the swing.

'Don't be silly. Of course he liked you. You looked so pretty.'

'Don't joke, Suji. Didn't you notice how he seemed more interested in the walls and ceilings than me . . . I suppose I can't blame him.'

'Now don't underestimate yourself. He is not used to this kind of culture . . .' Suji continued.

'Um.'

'Everything is everyone's business here. No wonder he felt uneasy about the whole situation.'

'I suppose so.'

'His Mum certainly enjoyed the attention and being treated like a queen.' Suji made a face.

'Yes, strange . . . very rude I thought.' said Neela.

'Aren't most mothers-in-law? I just ignore the rattle of my one.' Suji suddenly turned to face Neela. 'One piece of advice though, you will have to keep an eye on Ajay. His mother obviously rules the roost.'

'Yes, but . . . I don't know, Suji. In a way I am dreading their answer. I mean either way.'

Seeing Neela's eyes widen with fear, Suji laughed. 'Don't worry. I will give you some lessons later on how to manipulate your husband and how to keep the mother-in-law at bay.' She laughed, holding Neela's hands and pulling her up. 'That's enough for today. Let's go for a walk and watch the sun sink into the Manjeera.'

CHAPTER 2

The sun was rising like a fire ball. Although it was still early in the morning, the air was already hot and humid as the cool breeze had died away. The bright sunlight and the heat woke Neela. The flat roof top where she was sleeping was becoming unbearable under her skin, and the thin bed sheet gave her no protection. That summer, like all the others, was relentlessly hot. In another hour or so the ground outside would be as hot as a frying pan and inside the house would be like a sauna. It was impossible to even breathe without a fan. The only relief would come in the early hours of the morning, just before dawn, when the cool breeze would again break up the thick, suffocating night until the leaves of the coconut and almond trees rustled once more in a gentle lullaby before blissful sleep came to bless troubled souls. Neela longed for winter, when the weather would be comfortably warm during the day, and cool enough at night for blankets to feel cosy.

'*Namaste* Ma-ji.' A familiar voice below at the front gate broke into her thoughts. Neela quickly rolled off the thin mattress and ran to the low parapet wall around the edge of the roof. She glanced down in the direction of the voice. It was *Pundit-ji*, the marriage broker, talking to her mother in his loud sing-song voice.

'Your troubles are over, Ma-ji! Your daughter is going to be a bride soon.'

'What? What are you saying, *Pundit-ji?*' her mother's voice was choked with emotion. 'You mean . . . they have agreed . . .? Please come inside. Come and tell me everything.' Sharda was already wiping away tears.

The drumming started up in Neela's chest as she waited and listened.

'I will tell you everything and every word, Ma-ji, but first make my mouth sweet.' *Pundit-ji* was chuckling with joy. He sat comfortably on a rope cot with cushions heaped around him. As the messenger of much awaited news, he knew he would not only get sweets and his remuneration but an additional gift of money or whatever the household could afford.

Neela's heart raced with fear, joy and wonder. She ran down the stone staircase which led to the backyard, but there, overcome with shyness, she hesitated, and, instead of facing the household and *Pundit-ji*, she turned towards the well. Making as little noise as possible, she ran water into a small bucket tied to a rope over the metal wheel and drew up its coolness. Although the squeaking noise of the wheel drowned some of his words, she was listening keenly, and anyway *Pundit-ji*'s voice was familiar, even when he was munching pastries and savouries. Neela concentrated on the news.

She thought about Ajay and found it impossible to imagine him as her future husband. She couldn't even spell the word husband.

She poured water in to a round brass container and carried it to a jasmine creeper that wound round the steps leading to the balcony. Sitting on a small stool, she brushed her teeth and washed her face, arms, and feet. The cool water soothed her and extinguished the heat in her body. She poured the left-over water onto the leaves of the jasmine creeper and watched it sink through the cracks in the baked earth to its thirsty roots. Normally she would have stayed there, smelling the heavenly scent of the flowers, but that day she couldn't concentrate on anything.

'Neela, where are you, *beti*?' Her mother, followed closely by her father, came running towards her with open arms and embraced her.

Chapter 2

'Did you hear what *Pundit-ji* was saying? They . . . I mean Ajay . . . has agreed to marry you. Go and touch *Pundit-ji*'s feet and get his blessings.' Sharda wiped away the beads of water on her daughter's face with her sari's *pallu*. 'Your *Bapu* is going to the Hotel *Maha-Raja* this evening along with your uncles to see the Pattwars and to discuss the wedding.'

Neela noticed her mother was talking non-stop without pausing for breath saying the same thing over and over again. Her face glowed with happiness and tears of joy rolled down her cheeks. Her father was speechless but just kept smiling at her. His eyes glistened.

'Congratulations, *batie*,' he had said at last. 'God blessed you . . . us,' he said in a voice that was breaking with emotion. 'We are lucky.'

Not once had anyone asked her if she liked her prospective husband or if this was what she wanted. She knew that it hadn't even occurred to them. And if they had asked her, would she have had the courage to reject him and so remain a spinster for the rest of her life? How would her parents face society? How could they bear the shame? Unanswered questions popped into her mind like mushrooms sprouting up in the wild. But looking back, she knew that she had no choice but to go with everyone's wishes. She could ask no questions of them, or of herself.

The Pattwars were in a hurry because Ajay didn't have much time left before his return flight to London, so the astrologer set the wedding date for the following Friday, exactly ten days later.

'Congratulations!' Suji came running with her arms wide open and hugged Neela.

'I know you are going to be very lucky.'

'Am I?' Neela lifted her troubled eyes.

'Yes, of course.' Suji squeezed her hand. 'Haven't you heard about England from the people who've been there? You know . . . the clothes they wear, and the makeup. Apparently everyone owns a car, *puglee*.' Suji's face was dreamy.

There was so little time and so much to do. Neela's parents borrowed Uncle Das's huge four-bed roomed house, with polished floors and European sanitary facilities to accommodate the VIP guests. *Muhurtam* (the most auspicious time for the wedding) was set for 11.30 pm. Yet from Monday the house was buzzing with hundreds of guests, relatives, and friends. Invited or uninvited the whole village was there, to get a glimpse of the preparations for this most special of celebrations. The place was filled with colour and the atmosphere was electric. The *Shahnai* played the sweet traditional melodies of wedding songs.

They started the preparations a few days before the big day. The entire backyard of their house was cleaned from end to end and sprinkled with water to settle the dust, and then covered with straw mats. A temporary roof, thatched thickly from palm leaves and supported by strong wooden poles, was erected over the area to shade it from the piercing sun. At the far end, near the well, a temporary kitchen was built with huge rocks as stoves, and lit with long, thick pieces of wood. Vast pots and pans, filled to the very brim with all kinds of delicious curries, bubbled and spilled over red flames. Three professional male chefs were hired and they cooked the rice, the breads and the sweet pastries. The delicious aroma of spices, ghee and sweet *jaggery*, mixed with the scent of the firewood and burning coal, filled the air.

A marquee of a jazzy-coloured canvas was raised over the front yard of the house. Underneath, in the centre, was the wedding stage – a raised wooden platform with a canopy of inter-locking coconut leaves artistically woven into an arched umbrella. Amongst the leaves were fairy lights, fresh jasmines and *kanakambara* flowers that filled the air with their delicate scent. The stone floor around the stage was covered with colourful rugs and row upon row of steel chairs. Those with the cushions were reserved for the VIP guests. All through the wedding day the entire street echoed with the vibrant sounds of the wedding band playing lighthearted love songs and old traditional wedding songs. A few young men and women danced in front of the house while Neela's parents graciously and affectionately received the guests. Excited conversations, polite greetings and infectious laughter competed merrily with the wedding band. Young unmarried boys and girls playfully sprayed one another with *Attar* from elegantly carved silver *attar-dan*. When the women arrived, their richly-coloured silk saris, bordered with gold and silver thread, rustled across their turmeric smeared feet. The gold bangles on their wrists, the anklets, the silver rings on their toes, and the fine chains around their waists jingled with every step they took. And the men, in their crisp cotton *dhotis, lalchies* and silk *kurtas,* stood around laughing and joking. The helpers hurried in and out to finish their tasks in time. The air was filled with the intoxication of joy and excitement.

In the middle of the vibrant chaos, Neela, having bathed in warm water mixed with turmeric and sandalwood powders, sat in the prayer room worshipping the '*Devi*', the goddess of married bliss. Her bridal outfit was a white cotton sari soaked in turmeric, dried to a light auspious yellow. Its colour brought out a subtle beauty in her. Her red, green and gold bangles matched the border of her sari. When her mother fastened her late grandmother's coral and pearl necklace around her slender neck, Neela remembered how much she missed her *Nani*, who had adored her and often said she was her favourite grandchild.

It took Aunty Jaya, *Dadima* Parvati and Suji almost two hours to get her ready. Suji painted a delicate lotus-shaped traditional wedding *bindi* with liquid *vermilion* on her forehead. She lined her dark, oval eyes with the paste of homemade *kohl* and painted her lips with new red lipstick. *Dadima* Parvati smeared her already henna-patterned feet with a paste made from turmeric, and put a dot of *kohl* on her left cheek to protect her from *drishti*, the evil eye. Aunt Jaya braided her hair into a long plait, entwining its length with delicate jasmine flowers and tiny red roses. The scent of the flowers mingled with the sandalwood paste, the camphor and the incense sticks.

Her head felt as heavy and painful as her thoughts and she wondered if it was because of all the flowers in her hair or the sleepless nights over the last few days. In a few hours' time she was going to marry a stranger who wouldn't even look at her properly or utter a word to her. Everything had happened too quickly and there hadn't been enough time to prepare herself. In the days leading up to the ceremony, Neela still felt numb, but deep under the veneer of calm lay the unanswered doubts and fears like heavy stones beneath water. She doubted whether Ajay liked her. She had doubts about liking him. She had no idea what to expect of her future.

Her noisy young cousins and their friends burst into her room and interrupted her thoughts. For a moment, she stared mutely at them. Shankar, Uncle Das's son, was entertaining the others with stories about the new guests from London who were staying with them. He was oblivious of Neela's growing discomfort. Suji tried to shoo them all out, but they wanted to hear more.

'No, no, not yet. Please let Shankar finish,' they chorused.

Enjoying the attention, sixteen year old Shankar didn't pick up Suji's hints – or chose to ignore them – and so continued his tale. 'We gave them breakfast this morning, oh my God!' he shrieked. 'I can't believe that his Mum . . . Durga-devi or *Girga-devi* . . . whatever her name is,' he looked at Neela, 'she ate everything – you know – our Indian breakfast, the *puris* and the *bajjis* or whatever you people sent over from here. And then she still moaned that we hadn't served her any toast!'

'What is toast?' interrupted Neela, dragging her thoughts back to the present.

'Toast is a sort of roasted bread. Don't you know what an English breakfast is? Do you think they eat *puris* and *upma* like we do? No, no, they have cereals like cornflakes with milk, and then toast with butter and jam . . .' he displayed his knowledge, explaining how Durga-devi made his mother toast bread on a hot griddle on their modest two-ringed gas stove. Making a whistling noise and wiping the sweat from his forehead with his index finger, he started up again. 'Anyway, in the end we had to send our servant boy, Hanuman, to the other end of the town to get the bread, only to be scolded by that woman for being too late.'

Listening attentively, the audience shook their heads from side to side, saying 'Cluck, cluck.'

Shankar turned to Suji. 'You know what? After all that, she complained that it wasn't fresh.' He stopped for a second, looking at everybody. 'You should have seen poor Hanuman's face after walking two miles in the hot sun without any shoes and proudly presenting the loaf of bread to this new rich lady of London or *Gindon*. Poor Hanuman expected to be praised and hoped that the rich lady would throw him a few of her English coins.' Clapping his hands and spreading them widely, he exclaimed, 'Oh, no, no, her hand was too large and it wouldn't fit in her purse! Hanuman was so disappointed.'

Neela knew Shankar was fascinated by these people from London. He had been observing them closely, their way of gesturing and their body language, ever since they had come to stay in his house, and he couldn't stop talking about them.

'As if that wasn't enough, Suji-*behn*,' he continued, 'that *Girga* . . . oh no, Durga-devi-the Great . . . wanted instant Nescafé. She didn't like the taste of our usual *chai* or coffee. Since we couldn't find that particular brand anywhere, I had to go ten miles into the city on my bike early in the morning to get it for her.'

'Hmm!" sighed Neela. She remembered overhearing a worried Suji approaching her mother. 'Even though her life is going to be comfortable, how on earth is Neela going to deal with that dragon? Suji had asked.

But Neela had watched her mother shrug it off, saying, 'It is a miracle that they have agreed to marry my daughter so don't spoil things now with any unfounded doubts.'

'But Aunty . . .'

Sharda had raised her hand to hush Suji. Then she had lit an oil lamp in the prayer room, and had said quietly, 'Whatever is in Neela's *karma* will happen. Who are we to change it? Only the God Almighty can do that!' With eyes closed, Sharda had bent to a small statue of Lord *Ganesh* on the shrine, and stayed there, still and silent.

Back in Neela's room Shankar's sister, Rekha, was nudging her brother with her elbow. 'Shankar, Shankar, tell them how scared Ajay was yesterday when he went with you on your scooter.'

'Oh my God!' Shankar hit his chest with his palm. 'Ajay was so scared. I bet he'd never sat on a motor bike before.' He looked at Neela and smiled, 'He was clutching my waist so tight with both his hands that it hurt and then he started shouting and screaming his head off," Shankar mimicked Ajay; 'Be careful! Watch out for that rickshaw! Look, look the bus is coming!' Shankar laughed. 'He was rabbiting like that non-stop until we reached home.' The rest of his group laughed loudly with Shankar and even Neela was having trouble controlling her giggles. Suji, feigning annoyance, responded, 'Don't laugh so much. No wonder Ajay was frightened to death. Who wouldn't be the way you drive so stupidly fast?'

Aunt Jaya rushed in carrying a huge basket of flowers and tinsel. 'Come on children! Come and decorate the car. We have to send it to fetch the bridegroom soon.'

That did the trick. Shankar and party dashed out, full of enthusiasm for their new task of decorating the rented white Ambassador car. At last the room fell silent.

'Don't worry, Neela. Everything will be fine. Just remember that you will be in London in a few months' time.' She looked into her friend's eyes, tucking a loose strand of hair behind her ear. 'Did you

Chapter 2

ever think in all your life that you would end up going to that great
country?'

Neela squeezed her friend's hand, her throat tight with emotion.

'I never thought you would,' Suji continued. 'It's so strange . . . but
I am so happy for you.'

Neela was grateful for her friend's reassurance and affection.

'Look how excited they are,' Suji smiled, pointing at Neela's little
cousins Kitty and Bubloo, who burst into the room like a fresh breeze.

'Neela *behn*, Neela *behn* . . . Bubloo is saying that you are going
very far away and also in an aeroplane. Is that true?' Kitty asked with
wide-eyed concern.

'Look, Neela *behn*, she won't believe me. You are going by aeroplane
aren't you?' Bubloo looked at her. 'She thinks you won't fit in. But my
Dad said aeroplanes are very big.' He stretched his hands wide.

'Are you going forever and ever?' worried Kitty.

'No, no, of course not. She will be visiting us soon.' Suji tried to
console Kitty.

'But . . . but, Neela *behn*, are you going to wear those little English
dresses? And those stick-heeled shoes?' Kitty wondered.

'Um, that's a good question,' Suji made a face. 'Answer it, Neela,'
she teased, and then looked at Kitty. 'What do you think, should she
wear them or not?'

'No. Yuk, please don't wear them Neela *behn*. They won't suit you.
And all the boys would laugh at you,' frowned Kitty.

'Imagine trying to balance in those stilettos while trying to pull
those skimpy little dresses down to hide your knees." Suji's laughter
was infectious. They all laughed until the *kohl* from their eyes ran
down their cheeks.

Suddenly the noise from the wedding band rose to a crescendo – a
great vibration of sound that shook the whole house and announced
that the bridegroom had arrived. Neela could hear people rushing out
to receive Ajay and his party.

'Come, come and look,' Suji pulled Neela to her feet and dragged her to the window. Ajay, in his new cream suit, and his mother, in her expensive peacock silk sari, both gifts from Neela's parents, were getting out of the gleaming white Ambassador which the children had decorated with fresh flowers. Every one clapped and cheered and showered them with *attar* and fresh rose petals.

Minutes later, a group of older women burst into the room. 'Come, Neela, the auspicious moment has arrived.' They pulled her gently to a standing position without any physical effort on her part, and sat her in a big rounded cane basket. Uncle Das and Uncle Madhu lifted it up and carried her slowly towards the *Mantapam* – the wedding stage. Neela's heartbeat matched the drums outside. She felt peculiar, dazed and out of control as she got out and let them lead her by the hand to take her place next to Ajay.

He was already seated on a velvet chair instead of the traditional low, flat, wooden stool. The priest positioned Neela to face Ajay for the beginning of the marriage ceremony. Her mother started pouring water slowly from a silver pot while her father placed Ajay's feet on a silver tray and washed them. These were signs of respect towards the man whom they had carefully selected to receive their beloved daughter as his wife. Neela's parents then took their places on either side of their daughter, took her delicate, henna-patterned hands, and placed them in Ajay's, offering her to him as a gift. For the first time Neela was aware of his touch. His hands were warm, damp with sweat and, like her own, trembling.

As the band reached another crescendo, the priests chanted the *Veda-mantras* faster and louder. A small group of married women had already prepared the *mangal-sutra*, a sacred thread, by smearing it with turmeric and vermilion powders and threading it through two gold pendants. Ajay placed the *mangal-sutra* – the wedding necklace – around Neela's neck and tied the three knots, signifying unity. The band kept playing while the priest knotted the end piece of her sari with the robe on Ajay's shoulder. The ceremony concluded with the two of them taking seven steps together around the holy flame, the *Agni*.

The fun and games continued, but Neela was present only in body because she was living again the moment in the wedding ceremony when her hands had been placed in Ajay's, and her parents' gentle, trusting voices had given her to him with their tears and with their hearts. 'We brought our daughter up like a flower, with love and care.' She had heard her father repeating the priest's words. 'Now we are placing this delicate flower in your hands. From now on she is entirely yours. Whether you drown her in milk or water, it is up to you. Now she is your responsibility but please treat her gently with love and affection. Respect her as a friend and look after her as if she is a part of your body. We promise that she won't bring you or your family any pain or shame.' And with those words, she knew that she was tied to Ajay for life and nothing could change that. From now on she was not Neela Swaran. She was Neela Pattwar.

CHAPTER 3

Ajay was due to fly back to the UK on the day after the wedding, but at four o' clock the house was still buzzing with the guests who had stayed on, and who had taken a nap after the heavy festive lunch. A small reception was arranged in the front room where a table was heaped with wedding presents. Neela wore a saffron- coloured sari with a thin brocade border of navy and gold, and was still adorned with garlands. She was sitting next to Ajay on the sofa and someone was serving them tea in silver cups. From the corner of her eye she could see Ajay switching the cup from one hand to the other as he struggled to drink from hot metal that burnt his fingers. When beads of perspiration shone on his face, she hid her smile by pressing her lips together.

Uncle Das waited until all the guests had left the room before conveying Sharda's urgent request to Ajay.

'According to our tradition, Ajay, the newly-married couple should spend at least three nights together. So if you could spend at least one night here, we would be delighted.'

Neela looked at Ajay curiously.

'Sorry, I can't. I have to go,' he said abruptly.

'It's all right, Sharda,' her father said consolingly. 'We don't need to force our old traditions on Ajay.'

Neela was glad and relieved that he wasn't staying. She had been dreading it.

Uncle Das looked at his watch and said, 'Look, it's only six o'clock and there is plenty of time left before we set off for the airport. Neela, why don't you take Ajay to the river Manjeera?' He turned to Ajay. 'It's not very far, Ajay, and the evening air from the river will be cool and you can relax a little before the long journey.'

And off he went to arrange a car without waiting for an answer. Neela understood he wanted to give them, the newly-weds, a chance to be alone. Having been instructed by Uncle Das, the car dropped them off at the banks of the river and returned to the main road to wait for them. The hot summer sun had evaporated most of the water, exposing the fine, white sand that glistened in the orange glow of the sunset. A cool breeze blew from the mango groves making the air much fresher than in the village. Despite her earlier misgivings, Neela felt romantic and elated, seduced perhaps by the beautiful setting and the sinking sun. Ajay just stood there looking at the river.

'It's still hot,' he complained, wiping his brow with a hand-kerchief.

For a long time, Neela didn't know what to say though there were so many questions that she still wanted to ask him. Moments passed until the silence was so solid that she could almost see it. She forced herself to break the shell of her shyness to ask him, 'Would you like to go for a walk along the river?' Her voice sounded strange even to her own ears.

'No, it's too hot,' he said in broken Hindi.

'We can sit here then, in the shade.' She took a rug from her basket and spread it under an ancient Banyan tree.

'I think we'd better be going. I have a lot of packing to do,' he said in English, glancing at his watch.

She read the restlessness and boredom in his face, but her need to spend more time alone with him was too urgent and made her bold.

'Please, can't you stay for a few more minutes . . . I want to talk to you.'

26

Chapter 3

He looked at her with a frown and muttered, 'What is there to talk about?'

Neela watched the sun sink beyond the horizon until the world was painted with darkness, as if it couldn't bear to witness her disappointment.

Almost the whole wedding party went to the airport to see Ajay off. Neela watched her new mother-in-law trailing behind him like a shadow.

'Say, Bye to your wife,' she whispered as if he were a child.

He obeyed his mother, but his voice was dry and hard, his eyes without emotion.

'His mummy-*ji* should have brought a cardboard cut-out of him instead,' hissed Suji.

Neela waited in case there was one last farewell glance from him, but it didn't happen. Her heart sank further.

'Didn't you ask him to stay when you went to the river?' Suji enquired.

Irritated, Neela shook her head.

'Don't be shy. You are very quiet. At least talk to your mother-in-law. She is looking at you now.'

Neela didn't feel like interacting with anyone. The only person she wanted to talk to and the only person who could answer her questions was Ajay. But it was clear that he didn't wish to. She forced a smile in Durga-devi's direction and attempted the look of a shy and happy bride. It was suffocating being with all these people who imposed on her, expected things of her.

As Ajay's plane tilted up into the sky, Neela acknowledged that a different phase of her life had just begun. And another had come to an end.

Climbing into the waiting Ambassador car to sit next to her mother-in-law, Neela wondered why Durga-devi wasn't going back to England with her son. She wanted to ask her own mother but didn't get the chance. She craved privacy. She needed to think properly and to try to understand her own complex, troubling feelings.

The village was silent and sleeping except for the occasional dog barking and the buzzing noise of a ceiling fan. Normally at this time, Neela would retreat to the caressing night breeze on the terrace of the roof top where she could relax and listen to the radio. She loved losing herself in the *ragas* of the divine *sitar* or the melodious voice of *Latha*. Instead here she was making up a bed for her new mother-in-law in the better of their two bedrooms.

It was then that the wind carried the words from the hall.

'I can't stay here for ever Narayan *bhayya*. You have to settle the money soon. The solicitor said he won't be able to register the house in my name until he receives the total amount.'

Neela froze. Her hearing became sharper.

'Give me just a few days please, Durga-devi-*ji*. I will somehow manage to pay you every *paisa*,' her father pleaded.

But Durga-devi's voice was hard. 'All right, fair enough, but what if you can't manage? You said the same thing before the wedding but I trusted you and let you get on with it. Don't forget how much we compromised for your simple village wedding.'

'But you know, Durga-devi-*ji*, how it is here in India. And everything happened so suddenly that there wasn't time to organise that sort of money. The expenses for the wedding were twice as much as we expected.' Sharda's voice was a whisper.

Neela had to move nearer to the door to hear. She understood that her parents had no intention of letting her know anything about this. How much dowry had they promised the in-laws? She felt a strong urge to burst into the hall and confront her parents, but she managed to control it.

It didn't take long for her to discover that her mother-in-law's demands had cost her parents their entire house and two acres of rice fields.

Chapter 3

Late at night, when Durga-devi was asleep, Neela confronted her parents.

'How could you do that? Why did you sell your entire property for her? At least you could have told me before you went ahead with that greedy woman's wishes.' She was furious that her parents had sacrificed so much.

'It's nothing if our daughter is going to have a happy life. Don't you worry . . .' Sharda smiled and hugged Neela.

'Yes . . . always our daughter's happiness . . .' she mocked, wriggling free from her mother's embrace. 'And don't you care about my feelings? You think I am so selfish that I don't worry about you?' She turned to her father and said, 'Whatever happens, Bapu, I am not letting you sell this house.'

'Don't make it more difficult for us, Neela. What is a house? Bricks and mortar and nothing else,' her father replied.

Overcame with emotion, Neela hugged him tight. Where were they going to stay after they sold this house? It might be old and crumbling but it was their home. The feeling of loss was so overwhelming that she had to leave the room. She went up to the terrace of the roof top where, in the faint light of a crescent moon, she could think and analyse her situation.

Durga-devi stayed on for another week, enjoying their hospitality, while she squeezed every last penny of the dowry from Neela's parents. Just before she left for London, she said to Neela, 'We will send you the necessary documents for your immigration, and meanwhile, if you want, you can write letters.' Durga-devi smiled and handed over a piece of paper with her address.

Neela knew that there wasn't much point in writing to Ajay. He wouldn't be able to read Hindi and she couldn't begin to write in English.

In the months that followed, so much changed. Her parents sold the house and moved to a smaller, rented place to pay off their debts. It saddened Neela so much even though her parents seemed to be happily adapting to their new surroundings. She knew that it was nothing for them as they would do anything to give their daughter a better life. Her heart went out to her father when he took another evening job to raise more money towards her air ticket.

Neela lost count of the sleepless nights when the same haunting questions came to rob her of sleep. Did Ajay really like her? Why hadn't he talked to her? Did he marry her just to please his mother? Unable to find peace, she would reach for a jar of *Amritanjan* and rub a smear of the pale yellow gel into her temples to try to find some relief from the ache in her head. She closed her burning eyes, deeply inhaling the strong scent of mint and eucalyptus.

Strained and exhausted with endlessly thinking about Ajay, one day she finally confided in Suji.

'Why don't you write to him?' Suji suggested. 'He might respond, and it will give you a chance to communicate and get to know each other.'

'That's not a bad idea but how? He can't read Hindi.'

'Hmm, that's a problem . . . but I have another idea. Why don't we ask Shankar? He knows how to write in English,' said Suji.

'Are you mad? How could I ask a boy, let alone a teenage boy like Shankar, to write to my husband?'

'Don't worry, you can write your very own personal love letter later when you learn English,' Suji laughed, teasing her friend.

'Don't you dare impose that task on poor Shankar. He will be baffled and shocked.'

'Oh, really?' Suji pretended to be serious. 'Let's see then.'

Later that day Shankar was reading out loud the letter which had been dictated by Neela and edited by Suji.

'Dear Ajay . . .'

'No . . .' hesitated Neela, 'Please, don't write like that.'

'Like what?'

Neela blushed and lowered her eyes.

'Oh, I know.' Suji turned to Shankar, wagging a finger at him and said, 'Neela doesn't want to write that 'Dear' bit yet so cross it off.'

Shankar laughed. 'It doesn't mean anything for English people. They always start a letter with *Dear.* It's like when I send my teacher a letter of apology. I write, *Dear Sir.* It doesn't mean I love him dearly.' Shankar was enjoying displaying his convent school knowledge.

'OK. OK, get on with it then. It should go in the five o clock post today,' Suji said.

Dear Ajay – Shankar spoke every word out loud – *It has been nearly two months since we got married. And I have been waiting for your letter ever since. Hope you haven't forgotten me. Please give my regards to your mother, brother and sister-in-law and please give my love to their children. It's important that we should keep in touch with each other, so please write to me. Waiting eagerly for your reply,'* Shankar looked up. 'Shall I write here, *With love from Neela?'*

'No, don't you dare!' screamed Neela.

He laughed and said, 'OK, OK, don't shout so much. I will write, *With respect from your wife Neela.* Is that all right?'

'That's better. Now write the address carefully and make sure you post it by four o'clock. Don't you dare forget!' Suji wagged her finger at him.

Neela waited for the postman every day and ran to the door as soon as she heard the familiar *'Patha'.* Months went by but nothing came. At last, when she had nearly given up, an aerogramme arrived with a foreign postage stamp. Of course her heart was pounding when she rushed to her room and shut the door firmly. Her hands shook as she opened the envelope.

'So! What did he write?'

It was later in the evening when Neela and Suji sat together on the banks of the Manjeera.

Neela went very quiet. She drew patterns in the sand with her finger.

'If you don't want to tell me, it's OK. I am only asking because . . .'

'It's all right. Read it.' Neela opened her bag and took out the letter from London.

'Oh, blue paper, how romantic! Are you sure you want me to read it?'

'Go on, Suji,' Neela flung the flimsy paper into Suji's lap, and then watched impatiently as Suji unfolded it.

'Is that all . . .?' Suji said after she had skimmed the contents.

'Yes, that's all.'

'Not from Ajay?'

'No. Not from Ajay.' Neela stared at the short formal letter from Durga-devi which contained only the necessary travel information. However much she searched, there wasn't a single mention of her letter to Ajay. Despite her hopes, she knew that the long awaited reply from Ajay would never come.

Chapter 4

It took more than six months of anxious waiting, and a dozen letters from her father to Durga-devi, before Neela eventually received the go-ahead for her departure from India. It would be her first journey by air, but it was so much more than that. She was about to embark on the strangest experience, the longest step, the biggest adventure she had ever taken.

The preparations started a week before she left with her mother packing the suitcases, adding a new item every day. She packed so many snacks that you might have thought her daughter was travelling to a desert, and sent her husband to the city to buy a couple of fashionable saris and cardigans.

'You must wear one of them for the journey because you are going to London you know . . .'

'But mum, all my saris are fine. Why spend so much money?'

'It's fine, *Beti*. My daughter is going to London. What's money?'

Dadima Parvati came round with gifts of a new sari and guava fruits. She hugged Neela tightly and said, '*Sada suhagan raho*. Have a long married life. *Suputra praptirastu*. Have a beautiful baby.'

On the day Neela left, the whole village came to send her off and many people followed her up to the main road as she travelled with her parents and Suji in a bullock cart along the dusty track. They would travel to the city and there catch a train to Bombay.

'Take care of yourself.' the villagers called after them.

'Give our regards to your husband.'

'Don't forget we are here for you.'

'You are not only the daughter of your parents, you are the daughter of this village.'

Neela, moved by their affection, waved back until she couldn't see them any more because of the tears in her eyes.

When the cart reached the outskirts of the village, Neela could hear the jingling sound of the River Manjeera. Her heart became heavy as she craned her neck to catch a last glimpse of the flowing blue ribbon. How could she live without seeing it every day?

'You might find another river in England where you can go for walks with Ajay,' Suji suggested.

'Suji . . .'

In reply Suji took Neela's hand in hers.

The river glinted in the sun, greeting Neela as the cart stopped at its banks and she and Suji climbed down to stand one last time on its shores. It was difficult to bid farewell to her dear childhood friend. They stood together for a few moments silently staring at the river. It was so hard to part.

It was even more difficult for Neela to leave her parents at Bombay airport. Her mother clung to her like a child, hugging her and kissing her. Her father, trying to be brave for all of them, wiped Neela's tears and said, 'Be happy, my dear, you are going to your husband's house and also to London. Sharda, your daughter is going to a famous city. You should be happy and proud.'

'Yes, I am happy, *Beti* . . . but . . . it's so far, and I don't know when I am going to see you again . . .'

'Maa. . ., Bapu,' Neela hugged them tight as they kissed her goodbye.

As the Air-India plane climbed higher and higher, so did Neela's emotions. The hardest part had been leaving her parents whose tear-stained faces remained with her throughout the long, emotionally-charged journey. Although she felt confused and very upset, there was also curiosity as she considered her destiny. Where was she going, sitting in that strange container, shooting up and up through the sky and over the clouds? How could a vehicle this big lift into the sky as effortlessly as a bird? And how extraordinary that a simple village girl like her was heading for the world's greatest city – London! Would she be like the smallest insect on a great big plain? Would she fit into the new household, her family from now on? What would happen to her?

'Would you like a drink, Madam?' the air hostess's voice broke into her thoughts. When she looked up, confused, the lady next to her smiled and showed Neela how to open the tray that was attached to the seat in front of her.

'Is this your first time on a plane?' the woman asked.

'Yes, *behn-ji*.' Neela smiled in relief at the sound of Hindi.

As the the cool, tangy-sweet orange liquid slid down her throat, Neela felt a bit calmer. She closed her eyes to settle down for a nap.

When Neela woke, the plane was already on its descent path and she could see the landscape below. She was amazed to see everything on such a minute scale. The houses, trees and cars looked like doll's houses and toys. And so, finally, the plane landed at Heathrow Airport, ending her ten-hour journey. Her heart missed a beat at the thought that she was in England and thousands of miles away from her tiny Indian village. A giant aircraft with big bold red letters spelling British Airways was on parade on the tarmac.

After completing the formalities at Customs, Neela made her way towards the exit. Lost and utterly alone, she searched for a familiar face in the waiting crowd. There were people holding name cards or bunches of flowers, smiling, waving, hugging and even crying. It was incredible to see so many nationalities in one place. Pushing her luggage trolley, she moved forward, slowly and hesitantly. What if Ajay hadn't come? She began to search in her handbag for the piece of paper on which was written Ajay's address and phone number.

But there was Ajay. He was waiting at the far end of the lobby sipping coke, not scanning the crowd eager to find her face, but staring casually around, observing others who packed that place. Dressed in casual jeans, a sweat shirt, and a blue denim jacket, he looked different. His face seemed rounder, fuller, and with an extra chin. The shirt under the unbuttoned denim jacket didn't hide his protruding stomach as the suit had done when he came to see her in India. Had he put on weight? She watched him. There was no sign of his mother. Had he come on his own to collect her? It was a small ray of hope, but it withered immediately because seated next to him was a smart, bobbed-haired woman in a beautifully cut, knee length, crimson dress which complemented her golden complexion and showed off her curves and tiny waist. Draped loosely over her right shoulder was a white fur coat. A matching handbag hung on her left shoulder, and she wore shiny red, high-heeled shoes. Neela was astonished to see an Indian woman in those clothes, but at the same time acknowledged that they suited her Hindi film-star looks. The woman was nudging Ajay and pointing in her direction. He turned finally and looked at Neela. She saw on his face the familiar frown, the same sombre look, but now his gaze lingered a little longer. Self-conscious and flushing a hot crimson, she managed an awkward smile. She kept walking, and at last reached them with her trolley. Ajay took it from her without a word.

'Hello, I am Yamini, Ajay's sister-in-law,' said the fashionable woman in a very awkward, English-sounding Hindi. Then she introduced her husband Suraj, who was standing opposite. He looked completely different from his younger brother Ajay, much smarter with his square jaw and tall, trim figure. Their two children, twelve year old Ritu and nine year old Rakesh, smiled at her.

'*Namaste,*' Neela greeted them. Remembering the Hindu custom, she bent down to touch all the elders' feet in the traditional gesture.

'Don't be silly. No one does that nowadays! Where do you think are you – still in the eighteenth century?' Yamini laughed as she pulled

Neela to her feet and whispered, 'Save this for Ma-ji and you will make her very happy.'

'Go and get the car,' she said to her husband. 'We'll wait outside.'

As they all set off for her future home, Neela felt shy and timid, sandwiched between Yamini and her two children in the back seat. She felt peculiar, different, and detached from the real Neela.

'How are you?' she wanted to ask Ajay, who was sitting in the front passenger seat reading a map, but instead she asked Yamini. Her voice sounded strange even to her own ears

'Fine, thank you.'

'Don't pull my hair,' Ritu shouted at her brother. Neela, sitting on the edge of the seat between the brother and sister, felt their hands and elbows bumping her back as they wrestled with each other.

'Look, Mum, she is poking her tongue out at me,' Rakesh complained, leaning over Neela to get his mother's attention but he stopped when he caught Neela smiling at him.

'No school today?' Neela attempted to start up a conversation with Ritu in Hindi.

But the girl just stared at her before turning to her mother to say something in English, and suddenly the whole car shook with loud laughter. Neela turned her head and stared out of the window.

Night was falling, robbing the day of its last light. She wondered what time it was here in England. She looked at her wristwatch – a wedding gift from her friend Suji. It was showing the Indian time of 9.30pm. She tried to calculate the time but however many times she did the sums, she worked it out at four in the afternoon. She was surprised to see the enveloping darkness outside. In India at 4 p.m., the hot afternoon sun would be beating down and people at home would be waking up from their afternoon naps ready to have their tea. The ice cream *walah* would have started his rounds in the village, calling, 'Ice cream, iced fruit, sweet and cold . . .' and the school children, on their way home, would engulf him.

Despite the heating in the car she shivered and pulled her new Kashmiri shawl tightly around her shoulders. Comforted by its warmth and softness, she traced the gold leafy design on the dark maroon soft wool. Her mother had insisted on buying it for her.

There was so much to hold her attention as she was driven through the traffic of London – the twinkling cats'-eyes in the middle of the roads, the endless procession of cars that whizzed past, and, best of all, a sprinkle of snow that glistened on the ground and on the bare twigs of the trees. It was outlandish and magical. She was still staring at all that was new and surprising when the car jolted to a stop at some red traffic lights, and she saw that everyone in the car, except Suraj, was asleep. And so, as he drove steadily on, Neela too sank deep into her seat and closed her eyes, immersing herself in her own thoughts.

At last the long, tiring journey was over. The car stopped in front of a smart detached house. Neela got out of the car and stood shyly by while Yamini unlocked the oak door with its decoration of leaded glass. She led Neela inside, calling out loudly for her mother-in-law. The men unloaded the luggage and Neela thought quietly about what was inside all the carefully wrapped gifts that her parents had sent to everyone in her new family, each one thoughtfully chosen as appropriate for its recipient.

'Hello, Neela, come, come,' Durga-devi came out of the kitchen, wiping her hands on her sari *pallu.*

'*Namaste* Ma-ji,' Neela stepped forward.

'Stop, stop! Don't you know you have to put your right foot first when you enter your in-laws' house for the first time? *Hai-Ram!*' She smacked her brow with her fingers. 'Do you want to bring bad luck to the house?'

Neela trembled, and cursed herself for not remembering the custom. She took a step backwards. She paused before cautiously putting her right foot first and bent down to touch her mother-in-law's feet with both her hands.

Chapter 4

Durga-devi grumbled her blessings, 'May you have a very long married life and be the mother of a hundred sons.'

'Oh, what a journey, Maa! So much traffic,' said Suraj, rubbing his forehead as if he had a headache, and disappearing straight upstairs.

'The traffic was horrendous and I was cooped up in that back seat. Can you imagine being squeezed in between two fighting children and her?' Yamini gestured at Neela, wrinkling her nose, 'Uh! I don't know what was in her bag, but the whole car smelt of some peculiar spice. I need a shower.' She too rushed upstairs after her husband.

Neela watched Ajay shift his weight from one leg to the other, as if he was standing on hot coals. Looking restless and uncomfortable, he mumbled something to his mother and opened the front door. Then he too vanished without even glancing at her.

'Hmm! everyone has disappeared just like that.' Durga-devi flicked her fingers. 'In seconds, as if their duty has finished.' She shook her head.

Neela stood in the brightly-lit hall, very aware of her new surroundings while Durga-devi's eyes swept over her, up and down.

'You haven't changed at all. You look the same,' she said dryly.

Her scrutinising gaze made Neela wretchedly self-conscious so she lowered her eyes and stared at her crumpled cotton sari.

'Take your shoes off and come in,' Durga-devi guided her into the living room and gestured towards a sofa. 'Did you have a nice journey?' she asked, very matter of fact.

'Yes thanks, Ma-ji,' Neela replied in a small voice, 'My Maa and Bapu sent their greetings to you.'

'Um . . . how are they?' Durga-devi turned abruptly towards the staircase, without waiting for Neela's reply, and called, 'Ritu . . . come down and show your Aunty Neela the bathroom. Now you wait here. Ritu will come and show you the bathroom.' She pressed her hands on the settee for support and got up slowly, 'I have to see to dinner . . . *Hai-Ram* . . . no one bothers with anything in this house except eating and I am not getting any younger . . . *Hai-Ram* . . . my legs are killing me.' She bent down and rubbed her hands over her arthritic knees before leaving the room.

Ritu took her time coming down, so Neela took a few deep breaths. At last she had a few minutes to herself. Sitting on the very edge of the brown leather sofa, she looked around the room. The soft light from the chandeliers cast a peachy sheen on the walls and furniture, and the flames from the gas fire made everywhere warm and cosy despite the wintry air outside. China ornaments – a swan and a dancing lady – a flower vase, and a couple of family photographs in silver-plated frames occupied the mantelpiece. An oval mahogany-framed mirror hung over it. A huge Sony television and a video recorder stood in one corner. Neela had never before been inside a house like this one, nor seen a television this big, not even in films. It was an entirely new experience for her Indian village soul. She touched the peachy carpet with her fingers to feel the softness of it. How could she walk on that velvety surface with her dust-encrusted Indian feet? While she took in the splendour of the room, she forgot all about Ajay. How and from where did they get fresh air? She looked at the closed doors and the windows behind the net curtains.

At dinner time everybody returned to the dining room.

'Come, come, we are waiting for you,' Yamini called to Neela.

Feeling refreshed after her shower, Neela followed Yamini and took the only remaining empty seat at the huge, oblong dining table, next to Ajay. She observed that the room was smaller than the living room, but just as nicely decorated with its cream walls and chintz curtains.

'Ajay, you have been very quiet since your wife arrived. Are you feeling shy?' teased Yamini.

'No, no, *Bhabi*, I am fine, thank you.' Ajay gave an awkward laugh.

'Then see if she is eating properly,' Suraj said, looking at Neela's full plate where the food was untouched.

'Perhaps she doesn't like my cooking. Perhaps it's not like her Mum's!' sang Durga-devi.

'Oh no, Ma-ji, it's nice . . . very nice, only . . . I am not . . . that hungry,' stammered Neela. She felt uncomfortable eating in front of strangers and intimidated by the two whispering, giggling children. They were staring at her the whole time as if they hadn't seen a human being like her before.

'What's the matter with you? You will choke if you do that,' Yamini scolded them, pretending to be angry, but giving them the excuse to let their suppressed giggles burst into laughter.

A smile played awkwardly on Neela's lips. She understood why they were staring at her like that and was painfully aware of her traditional Indian looks. She was wearing a pale pink cotton sari with a purple border. Her dark, slightly curly hair, smoothed with coconut oil, was combed flat and braided tightly into a long plait that hung down to her hips like a snake. It swung from side to side when she walked. Her glass bangles, of which she had at least a dozen on each wrist, along with her silver anklets and toe rings, jingled rhythmically. Aware that she looked, talked and acted differently from anyone else round that table, she found it difficult to eat. Her throat felt tight and her mouth became dry until it was impossible to swallow a single morsel.

Later, when everyone had gathered in the living room for after-dinner coffee, Neela quietly reached for one of her suitcases. It was still standing in the corner of the room uncertain, like its owner, about where it belonged. When she opened the lid, the scent inside gave her comfort. Breathing deeply, she closed her eyes and with her fingers delicately traced the lid of a small cane box that her mother had given it to her as one of many Hindu traditions. It was something that every mother would send with her daughter as she left for her husband's house for the first time. It contained the white *chamantie* and *parijata* flowers, now dried, but still smelling wonderfully sweet. The auspicious vermilion, turmeric and sandalwood powders were packed in tiny pieces of torn newspaper. The dried dates and other fruits, and the aromatic camphor in plastic bags, smelled divine and nestled neatly in another small box. There were other packets and parcels in her suitcase, filled with Indian sweets and savouries for the family. Taking them one by one, she carefully placed them on the coffee table.

'Maa sent these for you,' she said to her mother-in-law.

'Uhm,' said Durga-devi. She was chewing *paan* and only for a second stopped to look at Neela before continuing her preparation. Spreading the green leaf with lime paste, she added betel nuts, fennel seeds and tiny droplets of coloured sugar. Even though she pretended that she didn't notice the presents, Neela knew her mother-in-law was watching every move she made.

'What are they?' Yamini asked, knowing her children were longing to know.

'They are the sweets and savouries.' Neela turned to the children. 'I have something else for you.' She smiled at them and un-wrapped another brown paper parcel. She handed a hand-made hessian shoulder bag decorated with coloured beads to Ritu, and a leather pencil case to Rakesh. They took them from her without a word of thanks.

'A sari for you,' Neela continued, handing Yamini a bright yellow chiffon sari, and wondering if this modern woman would ever wear it.

'Oh for me! Thank you very much. That's very nice . . . what a wonderful colour . . . so bright . . . it's almost . . . luminous.'

'You will glow in the dark if you wear that,' laughed Suraj.

'And then we won't have to switch the lights on,' Ajay joined in.

'Look, look, this is nice,' Suraj was looking at his own gift, a hand-spun Indian style shirt.

'Um, very nice,' Yamini mocked.

Durga-devi wrinkled her nose when she received a golden bordered, mauve *Gadwall* sari. 'Who is going to wear these Indian cotton clothes? Just look at the quality. So cheap! I don't know why your parents bothered sending them.'

Chapter 4

Neela was numb. She said nothing.

There was still one last gift in her suitcase which she had carefully chosen after frantically searching every shop in town in the pouring monsoon rain. She remembered how she struggled with a broken sandal strap held together with a safety pin. It was an ivory silk shirt with gold buttons and had matching cufflinks. She was excited at the thought of presenting it to her husband, but she couldn't do it now, not in front of everyone. She would wait for that special moment when she was alone with him.

'No gift for Ajay?' Durga-devi's shrill voice again.

Neela hesitated for a moment, looking at her mother-in-law's *paan*-stained red teeth and mouth. Knowing that she had no choice, she dug her hands into the suitcase to take out the shirt. Pushing back a few tendrils of hair from her forehead, she went over to her husband and shyly put the packet in Ajay's hands. He received it in silence, and, without turning his gaze from a blonde girl on the television, he passed it straight to his mother. Neela was stunned. She stared at his mouth rhythmically chewing gum, looked at his mother's mouth chewing a triangular bundle of *paan* leaf. It was Ajay's indifference that hurt her, and she had to blink hard to hide her tears. Fortunately no one noticed, or, if they did, they pretended they didn't. Meanwhile Durga-devi fingered the material. She rubbed it between her thumb and fore finger and shook her head dismissively. Neela knew that she was trying to guess what it had cost and her heart fluttered like a leaf as she waited for the verdict.

'*Hai-Ram!* Only this cheap shirt?' She pushed the bundle of *Paan* leaf to the side of her mouth with her tongue, making her cheek swell. She lifted her head and looked at everyone before continuing. 'Not even a gold ring or a chain for my son? I knew this would happen. What are we, beggars? Do we look that cheap to them? How dare they insult us like this?' While Durga-devi's harsh voice barked its disappointment, slowly, discreetly, one by one, everyone left the room. The first to go was Ajay.

Neela couldn't and didn't understand why anyone would be so obsessed with gold especially as the supposedly distressed old woman was already weighed down by a ton of it on each and every part of her body. She knew what the woman had been expecting. But there wasn't even a grain of rice to eat in her parents' house, let alone a grain of gold.

Though Neela was tired and jet-lagged, she was too restless to sleep on this, her first night in a strange, new country. Lying awake on a narrow folding bed in a tiny room, Neela stared at the pale blue walls. Faint light from a street lamp leaked through the thin curtains and cast strange shadows that danced like ghosts on the walls. There were two old tea chests stacked in the corner, like the giant body of a monster. Her new brown resin suitcases, which sat on top, looked like a double head. Their silver handles were mouths and their buckles eyes. She smiled because they looked so out of place. Her Bapu had bought them for her, spending nearly half his month's salary but of course not telling her. The dark blue polyester curtains, patterned with light blue rabbits and orange carrots, glowed in the slanting light of the street lamp. She traced some more of the rabbits and carrots on the matching duvet while she waited for Ajay.

Now that finally she was alone in her room, to her surprise she longed for Ajay. Would he come to her now? Maybe just to ask how she was? She had left everyone and everything and had come all this way across the ocean just to be with him. Would he talk to her until she felt more comfortable with him? As the minutes turned into hours, it dawned on her that the bed was for her alone. Instead of anticipation, she felt the lack of familiarity of that small store room, that big house, the people in it and longed for her parents, her own bed, and the roof top of her house under the stars. She yearned for the cool breeze from the river Manjeera, and the rhythmic rushing of its fast-flowing water.

CHAPTER 5

A persistent banging on the door woke Neela. She tried to open her
eyes but they felt heavy. Where was she? Still disorientated, she felt for
the softness of the pillow and the mattress with her hands to make sure
that she wasn't dreaming. Was it true she had travelled so far and come
to London? After forcing her burning eyes open and squinting against
the daylight, she raised herself up on her elbows and looked round,
absorbing the reality. The room seemed a little better in the light of
morning but still strange. Apart from her two suitcases, nothing was
familiar. In one corner, an old rusty bike leant against some boxes that
were brown and small, just like her. She smiled at the thought.

Another impatient knock on the door forced her out of bed.
Shivering in the icy chill of the room, Neela pulled her sari *pallu*
around her shoulders before going to open the door.

'Grandma wants you to come down,' Ritu said impatiently and
ran off.

As Neela turned to go into the bathroom, she saw Yamini rushing
out of her room.

'Wait a minute,' Yamini shouted. 'Last night I told you to keep the
shower curtain inside the tub but you didn't, did you?' She pushed
open the bathroom door. 'There was water all over the floor. 'It was
like a swimming pool in here and I nearly slipped.'

'Oh, no! But where . . . water?' Neela looked from Yamini to the
bone-dry floor.

'You can't see any water now! I had to mop the floor twice last night, uh.'

'I am very sorry.'

'What is the use of that now? Can't you understand a simple thing like having a shower?'

'How can she? She's never seen one before,' said Durga-devi, arriving on the scene with a bucket and a mug.

'From now on don't even try to have a shower, just have an Indian bath,' Yamini hissed, grabbing the bucket and the jug from her mother-in-law's hands.

Shaken that she was already in the wrong, but grateful for the bucket, Neela, followed Yamini's instructions. She placed it carefully under the taps and climbed into the tub. She crouched down and pulled the shower curtain around her, making sure that it was tucked inside the tub. After filling the bucket, she began pouring the warm water over her head and shoulders, using the jug, and slowly her body relaxed. Her half-opened eyes were still heavy with sleep but the scent of the sandalwood soap, brought from India, roused her and reminded her of the bathroom in her parents' house.

It was a tiny, mud–walled, roofless room next to the well with a rusting tin door that creaked loudly whenever anyone touched it. In summer she used to enjoy the buckets of cool water freshly drawn from the well and in winter the hot water from a cylindrical copper boiler which had a flute in the middle through which flames erupted from the burning chips of wood and coal. The bath water ran out through a small plug hole at the bottom of the wall into the flower beds, the vegetable patch, and the roots of coconut, mango and almond trees. She remembered the jasmine creeper, near the back veranda that produced flowers in abundance. She took a deep breath as if she were inhaling its delicate fragrance. A wave of home-sickness washed over her.

What a contrast! Last night she had been too tired to notice the sea-green tiles with patterns of white sea-shells and the matching tub, the pedestal basin, and the toilet. Thank God Ritu showed her last night how to flush the toilet, otherwise she wouldn't have known. What a frightening noise it made! But how did they keep it so clean? It was impossible to clean the dirty hole in the ground in India, and oh, the stench. You could only get rid of it by throwing gallons of water mixed with at least a bottle of phenol. Would the people in her village believe that a bathroom like this even existed? Neela decided there and then that if ever she went back to India she must take a photo to show them. She climbed out of the bath and carefully placed her feet on the cork mat. Her heart stopped as she saw a few tiny droplets of water from her hair on the light green vinyl floor. She grabbed a hand towel from the rail and frantically wiped them dry.

Dressed in a cream-coloured, cotton sari with a maroon border and a blouse, she dusted some *Ashoka* talcum powder on her face and after placing a small red *bindi* between her eyebrows, she dipped her ring finger in the *Eyetex* pot and lined her eyes with *kohl*. She combed her long hair until it was smooth and chose a *lovintokyo* hair band. Its glass beads matched her sari. Fastening it at the end of her long plait, she stood tall on her toes, trying to look in the small mirror that hung on the wall but it was too high for her. Feeling refreshed, she went down.

Yamini, dressed in a black and white outfit, Suraj, in jeans and a sweat shirt, and the children in their school uniforms, were sitting around the dining table having breakfast. 'Oh, Neela, you look fresh. Come here,' Yamini gestured at a chair. 'Do you want some toast?'

Neela looked at the browned slices of bread slotted neatly in a steel toast rack. It reminded her of Shankar's description of the drama over a piece of toast on her wedding day. A smile played on her lips as she said politely, 'No thanks. Can I just have some tea please?' Since her arrival in this new country she had lost her appetite. Yamini poured some tea into a mug.

Neela gasped. It was the largest mug she had ever seen, 'I only want a half cup please.'

'Don't worry, there is plenty left. See.' Yamini said, shaking the teapot.

She sat down shyly on the edge of the chair but she found it difficult to sip the English tea, so different from her sweet rich milky *chai* in India. It looked pale, watery, and was luke-warm with very little flavour. Her taste buds refused to recognise it as proper tea but she gulped it tentatively like a bitter medicine. Where was Ajay? Stealing a glance into the living room, she craned her neck over the heads of Suraj and the children and tried to look through the gaps in a beaded curtain. Realising that he was nowhere to be seen, she felt disappointed and stared at an empty chair at the table.

'Ajay didn't stay here last night . . . he went . . .' Yamini read Neela's thoughts.

'To see someone important,' said Suraj, hurriedly finishing the sentence.

The children fought all through breakfast, throwing cornflakes at each other. Yamini shouted and scolded them. Eventually she sent them upstairs to fetch their school bags.

'I tell you, they are hard work,' she told Neela, taking her anger out on the marmalade jar which she shook viciously.

Suraj pushed back his chair and stood up.

'I must go,' he said, leaning over Yamini and kissing her lightly on the lips. Neela turned her eyes away in embarrassment because it was the first time she had seen a couple demonstrate affection so openly in public.

Flipping her hair back and clearing her throat, Yamini stared hard at Neela.

'Did your father send the remaining dowry with you?' she whispered.

'What dowry?' Neela was puzzled by Yamini's abrupt question.

'You know what Ma-ji is like. Be careful not to give it to her because she swallows everything.' Yamini dragged her chair nearer to Neela's.

'Since you are staying in my house, it would be wise to give it to me. I promise it will be safe.'

Her bluntness and directness shocked Neela. Hands shaking, she put the mug down.

'It has already been paid into Ma-ji's account in India.'

'Really? What a liar Ma-ji is! She never said anything to me.' Yamini banged the table in anger and disappointment, but seeing Durga-devi at the door, she quickly composed herself and leaned back in her chair. 'Look, Neela, in this country no one sits around idly and chit chats. Everyone here works. Time is work and work is money. God knows how I have managed the house, the shop, and so many other things, and my children all this time.'

'*Huh, haa, Hai-Ram!*' Durga-devi sat down heavily, pulling her plate of toast towards her and pouring herself some tea.

'Of course, *you* help, Ma-ji, but you are not young any more and your arthritis is eating you up.' Yamini transferred her gaze to Neela. 'And now you have come, an additional mouth for us to feed. We will have to work even harder in the shop. So where will I find the time for housework?'

Neela understood exactly what Yamini was getting at.

'I will help you,' she said eagerly.

'Thank you,' Yamini gave Neela a *that's what I wanted to hear* look.

'I have to leave now.' She wiped her mouth and hands with a napkin. 'Ma-ji will explain everything to you.' Her domineering voice addressed Durga-devi. 'Tell her to start by clearing the table and washing the dishes.'

Neela couldn't help but notice how Yamini managed to change her expression according to the situation.

All the modern gadgets looked complicated and confusing, so it took Neela a while to finish all the clearing up in the kitchen. Then she brought out the vacuum cleaner to clean the carpet in the living room and struggled with the heavy, unfamiliar appliance. At last, after managing to clean downstairs, she dragged it upstairs to her mother-in-law's bedroom – a room crammed with two wardrobes and two single beds. Why would Durga-devi need two beds? She looked from one to the other, unable to tell which was the spare bed. They both looked slept in, with crumpled bed sheets. Who on earth was sharing her mother-in-law's bedroom, she wondered as she stripped the sheets from one of the beds.

Three weeks went by when she saw almost nothing of Ajay. He had come home only twice since her arrival and on both occasions had neither spoken to her nor come near her. Now she understood why there were two beds in her mother-in-law's room. Ajay slept in the spare bed. Strange, she thought, even after he is married? She shook her head, trying to dismiss him from her thoughts, but whatever she was doing, there he was, preoccupying her. She wanted to ask either Durga-devi or Yamini about his whereabouts but something about the way they treated her stopped her. Time and time again she tried to understand her situation but it defeated her.

The alarm buzzed but Neela didn't have to look at the clock to know the time. She felt sleepy, listless, and tired. She had never done so much work before, but then in India her Maa would never let her lift a finger. When she was little, Sharda would say, 'Go and play with your friends,' and when she grew older, it would be, 'Go and study,' or 'Go to the river Manjeera for a walk.' And in recent years she would say, 'There will be plenty to do when you get married,' and she would sigh, adding, 'Who knows what sort of in-laws and husband you will get? A woman here does donkey work all day without a minute's rest. But does she get any recognition for it? No, no, not a bit. You know what they say? It is better to be a tree in a forest than to be born a female.'

'I wish you wouldn't worry so much, Maa. Who knows, I might be lucky and happy.'

Chapter 5

'Yes, of course, I hope you get a good husband who treats you so well that you won't miss us.'

Neela sighed. In a way the housework gave her something to do with her time and some satisfaction in earning her keep. She didn't want to be a burden on anyone or a charity case. Though Durga-devi insisted theirs was a combined family home, she knew it was Yamini's house. Sometimes she woke before the dawn broke, stealing a few moments between the realities of night and day to allow herself to dream and hope. Not that she could dare hope for any romantic liaisons with Ajay but perhaps if she learned to love this woman, Durga-devi, as a mother figure, and this place as home, she might, one day, find a way to Ajay's heart and earn his love.

The sound of milk bottles at the front door dragged her back to reality.

'My God, it's nearly a quarter past five,' she gasped, throwing off her blankets. Her body shivered and her teeth rattled as the winter chill bit into her bones. She always felt painfully cold while no one else seemed to mind it as much. How on earth was she going to stay here for ever? The thought dampened her already frustrated spirits.

A month, which felt like a lifetime, had passed since her arrival. Her routine was pretty much the same every day. She rose at five and cooked three different breakfasts. The first person to come down was Suraj, who liked fried eggs on toast and grilled hash browns with a gallon of sweet coffee. Yamini, on the other hand, always dieting, would have just a slice of toast and a cup of tea. The children ate cereal and toast and drank hot chocolate while quarrelling and hitting each other. Neela made them packed lunches and saw everyone off to their respective destinations.

After clearing up the breakfast things, she replaced the stained table cloth with a clean one, and prepared a tray with a plate of onion *bajjis*, coriander chutney, and a pot of *masala chai* for her mother-in-law. The following day she might prefer an English breakfast, two slices of buttered toast, one with jam and one with homemade hot mango pickle with milky tea or coffee. Durga-devi liked to have a different breakfast every day after her bath and morning prayer. She said that in her younger days, when she was in Uganda with her husband, she never had to lift a finger as there were always servants, cooks and gardeners working for her all the time.

'My luck changed when we left Uganda to come here,' she blew her nose into a tissue. 'Now my arthritis won't even let me sit in the dining room.'

But Neela knew that she secretly preferred eating breakfast in the living room where she could watch television.

Neela's thoughts turned to Ajay. She still didn't know where he went each day. He would hardly ever wake up in time for breakfast during his rare visits home, and when he eventually woke, he always seemed to be in a daze or in a bad mood. His blood-shot eyes frightened her.

By the time Neela had tidied the house and hung the washing on the line, it was nearly half past twelve and time to prepare her mother-in-law's lunch which was always two chapattis, a vegetable curry, rice with *dal*, and a cup of sweetened yoghurt with honey or mango pulp. She had to serve it at *exactly* half past one in the afternoon. The thought of food made her stomach grumble because all she had had time for earlier that morning was a few gulps of tea. She boiled half a cup of milk and half of cup of water in a pan. Finally, seated at the kitchen table, she inhaled the delicious aroma of *chai* and ate her toast with butter. She never dared try Yamini's marmalade or Durga-devi's strawberry jam, but with hot mango pickle that she had brought from India, toast tasted delicious.

After she had served her mother-in-law's lunch, she started on the savouries and sweets that Yamini had ordered in the morning. She boiled and reduced the milk to a thick consistency, added pistachio powder, *ghee*, sugar, golden raisins, shreds of saffron, and a teaspoon of cardamom powder, then poured it into a tray to cool down and set. Next she started frying the flaked rice, soaked pulses, cashew nuts and coconut pieces to make the *chudva*. She hoped that Yamini would like it.

The house was quiet after Durga-devi went to her room for her afternoon nap. Yamini and the children wouldn't be back until four. That precious hour was the only time she had for herself during the day. She wanted to snatch a few moments to read again the letter that had come that day, before she prepared tea for everyone. Wiping her hands on her sari *pallu*, she sought the privacy of her boxroom. Lifting the pillow, she slid out the slightly crumpled blue aerogramme. Just the mere sight and feel of it filled her heart with happiness and nostalgia. She opened it gently and looked at the uneven handwriting stretched right up to the edges. It was written without a comma or a full stop. The home-made glue on the fold swallowed some of the words. The smudges of blue ink from a leaking fountain pen were everywhere. She smiled at the thought of how those pens back in India vomited ink from time to time. She stroked the paper lovingly, content with reminiscences provoked by its texture and smell.

> *My dear precious beti Neela, she read. It has been a month since you left and not only our house but our hearts also have become empty I can't tell you how much we are missing you Your father talks about you and nothing else We are very happy and proud of you Your friend Suji said that she would write to you soon The rudraksha plant which you planted last year is having its first flowers now Please convey our good wishes to Ajay and tell him and Durga-devi that we are always grateful and indebted to them for accepting you as one of them and most importantly Neela please give your undivided love and affection to Ajay in abundance and serve your in-laws with care and respect*
>
> *Awaiting for your reply with love your* Maa

'Maa . . . Bapu . . . It's been so long. I am missing you both so much,' she whispered, gently pressing the letter to her heart. Inhaling its scent again, she looked through the window and imagined her parents' house, the back garden, and those white, pink and yellow *rudraksha* flowers. She could almost see them swaying. She could almost feel the warm breeze on her cheeks.

'Neelaaa . . . !' A loud voice made her jump. Someone was calling her. Her name sounded different in that strange accent. Recognising the owner of the voice, her heart raced with excitement and she had to take a few moments to recover. Then she ran as fast as she could to the landing. There he was, standing in the doorway of his mother's room, holding out a shirt.

'I want you to iron this,' Ajay said in broken Hindi as he stretched out his arm.

'Yes . . . of course,' she took the shirt from him. 'When . . . when did you arrive?'

The effort of speaking to him made her stammer. He didn't answer but looked at her strangely for a second before turning round and going into the bathroom.

Had he only called her for that? Her excitement was damped down like a roaring fire extinguished by cold water. She didn't mind doing his chores but she did mind his silences. There was always a pressing reason for him to go somewhere, or a more important person waiting for him, and to spare a moment to stay with her and talk to her seemed of no consequence. She winced.

'Aunty-Neela . . . !' The shriek of Ritu's voice summoned Neela to the kitchen. The arrogant look on the girl's face surprised her.

'Why did you put tomatoes in my sandwiches? You know very well that I don't like them!'

'I forgot.'

'I don't know Hindi,' Ritu made a face. 'Say it in English.'

Neela looked at the girl blankly, not understanding.

'Oh my God, Neela, can't you understand what Ritu is saying? At least apologise to her,' Yamini said, arriving in the doorway.

Chapter 5

'*Sarry*,' Neela said meekly.

'What did she say, Mum? Sorry or sari?' Mother and daughter burst out laughing.

'You can't even make a sandwich without doing something wrong. Look, Ritu didn't even touch it,' Yamini sneered.

'Oh Mum, you didn't hear what she said this morning for *breakfast*, she said *beakfrost*.' Their laughter filled the room again.

Though she couldn't understand English, she understood the tartness of the words and stood there stunned until Ajay's voice thundered from upstairs.

'Mu . . . aamm . . .'

'Oh, no . . . !' Neela ran. Ajay was standing by the ironing board, fuming.

'I am sorry . . . Ritu . . . Ritu called me . . .' Neela, lost for words, looked at his furious face.

He ignored her at first and continued to call his mother but when he realised that she wasn't at home, he turned and looked hard at her.

'You have to remember. My chores come first for you,' he said, pressing a finger on his chest.

She nodded but the tears pricked and stung her eyes, shaming her into thinking that she couldn't cry for every little thing. Next time she would take their insults without tears.

On every alternate Thursday night it was Neela's duty to mix the *Super Vasmal* powder with coconut oil to massage into Durga-devi's hair while the older woman chewed her *paan-beeda*. Neela tried not to look at the red stained tongue and the black rotten teeth in the mirror in front of them. After she piled all the hair up and wrapped it in cling film and a towel to protect her clothes, Durga-devi would leave it overnight to soak the jet black dye into her grey hair. And on Fridays she would wake an hour early to wash the *Super Vasmal* out.

'Neela, Neela, where are you?' Durga-devi was standing at the bottom of the stairs in one of her special silk saris.

'Yes, Ma-ji, coming,' answered Neela, having cleaned the black smudges of hair dye from the bathtub. Every Friday Durga-devi went to the temple to do the *Pooja*. Neela had to accompany her, carrying a plastic wire basket containing coconuts, bananas, betel leaves, incense sticks, camphor, and crystallized sugar.

'*Hai-Ram*, I am not getting any younger,' Durga-devi complained. 'I have two sons, but what use are they? No one gives me a lift. I go to the temple only once a week and still they say they don't have time to take me. Look at my friend Sita. She has only one son but she is very lucky. You know her daughter-in-law is very nice. She drops her everywhere.'

It was a struggle for the old woman to walk because she was so heavy. Helping to support her, Neela couldn't help thinking that her mother-in-law should lose some weight.

'Is this your new daughter-in-law?' asked a woman of similar age.

'Yes,' Durga-devi sighed. 'Yes, Sita, her parents are very poor you know! But what can we do? We thought we would help this girl by offering her marriage.' She paused a little and whispered in her friend's ear, but quite loud enough for Neela to hear. 'You can see, can't you? Who would have married her? Not an ounce of beauty in her. But my Ajay has the kindest heart, God bless him.'

Neela felt Sita's sympathetic eyes on her. '*Hmm!* What can we do?'

'You know what Yamini is like, and now this girl is another financial burden to me.' Durga-devi whispered loudly to Sita.

Neela couldn't believe her ears. If Durga-devi hadn't liked her, why had she chosen her for her son? She wanted to ask her right there and then. She wanted to say she hadn't come over here because of her mother-in-law's charity. On the contrary, she had brought a sizeable dowry. She was a daughter-in-law in her own right and not inferior to Yamini. She was seething with fury at the insults to herself and to her dear parents, but she stopped herself from saying anything. This wasn't the right time or place.

Chapter 6

Neela was about to serve dinner when she heard raised voices from the dining room on the other side of the beaded curtain. She stood rooted to the spot.

'I can't take your tantrums and harassment any more. You are worse than those debt collecting bailiffs,' shouted Durga-devi, pulling a wad of notes from her blouse. 'Here, take the money.' She threw them angrily across the table in Yamini's direction.

'Don't throw them at me like a bone to a dog,' Yamini shouted back.

'You are barking like one,' Durga-devi hissed, flinging her hands at her daughter-in-law.

'Don't you dare talk to me like that for this measly amount of money.'

Hai-Ram! I am getting old. Where on earth do you think I could get that much money each month?' She rubbed her knees.

'Now you have brought her,' Yamini gestured towards Neela, 'we have another mouth to feed. We don't have money-growing trees in our back garden to feed every one for free.'

'You are not feeding us for free! You are squeezing money out of me every month. I have never ever seen a daughter-in-law like you before. Never in our community.'

'I haven't seen a mother-in-law as mean as you either. Thank your lucky stars at least I am letting you and your brood stay here.'

'This is not your house, you crafty little ... .' Durga-devi's fist banged the table. 'This is my son's house.'

'Oh! This is my son's house,' Yamini mocked, laughing and throwing her head back. 'Is it? Don't forget who brought the dowry to pay for it,' she spread her hands wide and rolled her eyes.

'Why are you shouting like that? I gave you the money and that's finished,' Durga-devi's voice became a bit weaker.

'Hang on a minute.' Yamini paused while she counted the money. 'You haven't given me the correct amount.'

'You greedy woman, can't you count?' Durga-devi wagged her finger. 'What about the extra fifty pounds that I gave you?' The old woman was becoming breathless with anger.

'That's not enough to feed an extra mouth for a month.'

Durga-devi shook her head. 'But Neela is doing all your housework, so I shouldn't pay you anything.'

'That's not on. Whether she does the work or not, the cost of keeping and feeding her isn't any different.' Yamini stared at Neela, who had come through the curtain and was standing with a bowl of chapattis in her hand. 'If she doesn't do the housework, what else is she going to do? Bite her nails? Don't use your mean tricks on me.'

'Whether you like it or not I can't afford any more than this,' said Durga-devi, signalling that Neela should serve supper.

'In that case why don't you ask your good-for-nothing younger son to pay for it or take his wife with him? She is his responsibility.'

'Mind your own business,' yelled Durga-devi.

There was no one in the house that afternoon. Even Durga-devi had for once gone out. Neela relaxed as the house grew hushed and silent. The sun was shining brightly outside and her room felt warm. She opened her bedroom window to breathe the fresh air. The tall poplar trees in the distance were swaying in the gentle wind; they always reminded her of the gigantic *rala* trees at the banks of the Manjeera in India. She could still hear those rustling leaves that sounded like bells jingling in chorus with the flowing river. She craned her head out of the window trying to listen to the faint music of the poplar leaves, but instead she heard a baby cry. Curiously she looked down to see a young mother on the pavement, pushing a pram, like one of the porcelain figurines in Yamini's showcase. She pushed her head further forward but saw only a wrapped bundle in a white laced blanket. The hood of the pram was hiding the baby's face. The English with their fine features and fair complexions fascinated Neela. In India she had heard so many stories about them from her grandfather. He used to be one of Mahatma Gandhi's followers and claimed that he saw the *Angrezi* in hundreds. It had never occurred to her that one day she would see them in the flesh. She loved the children with their pink complexions, red cheeks and light-coloured hair. But she had never seen an English baby.

What would it be like to soak in that sunshine and walk in those woods or in the park? Neela wondered. Once or twice she had wanted to but she didn't have permission to go out on her own, even to the shops. While the thought doubled her desire, the tranquil mood gave her the courage to do what she wanted. She could go and see those real life porcelain figurines and their doll-like children in the park and, if possible, talk to them. Perhaps she could smile at them. How she missed talking to people! Days and weeks had gone by without the need to utter a word since the entire household never required more than a nod from her. If her life continued like this, she might soon forget how to pronounce words, let alone hold a conversation.

Neela grabbed a full-length brown overcoat. Its sheen might have diminished over the years, but its softness and warmth comforted her. She was grateful to Yamini for giving it to her. Having fastened each button, she looked in the mirror and saw that the coat reached to her feet and swallowed her small build. She winced. How she wished she was taller and light-skinned. She knew the coat would look good on Yamini's tall shapely figure and suit her creamy complexion.

As she took the house keys from the hook, her eyes fell on Yamini's red high-heels. Maybe if she wore shoes like that, she might look a little taller. She took them out and carefully tried one on, but it was two sizes too big for her feet. Holding on to the wall, she put the other one on and then carefully took her hands off the wall and tried to walk to the mirror. The four inch high, pointy heels wobbled her feet making her slip and land on the floor with a thud. She tried to pull herself upright by grabbing hold of the cupboard door, but her twisted feet inside the shoes hurt badly. She wrenched the shoes off, wondering how on earth Yamini could walk so fast in them. She felt much better after pushing her big toe into the ring of her own brown Indian *cheppals*. She remembered the conversation on her wedding day when Kitty had worried about her wearing shoes with heels like thin sticks and little skimpy dresses. Smiling to herself, Neela stepped out of the house and pulled the front door shut behind her.

He was there at the gate.

'Where is Maa?' Ajay asked as she did an about-turn and struggled to unlock the door to let him in.

'She . . . she . . . went to see Sita, *masi.*' Neela's heart was beating too fast and she felt breathless.

'Oh shit!' He brushed past her.

Neela, not having expected him, didn't know what to do except to follow him back indoors. She stood in the hall while he took off his shoes. He had definitely put on weight since their wedding in India. Her eyes swept over his figure. Actually if he didn't have that bulging stomach and double chin, she thought, he might look all right. When he lifted his head and looked at her, Neela turned her gaze away, wondering if he guessed what was going on in her mind.

'I am hungry,' he grunted.

Relieved to have something to do, Neela fled to the kitchen to prepare some lunch for him. She knew what he wanted for his lunch, because since her arrival she had been instructed how to cook his food. In the beginning it had been difficult for her to make chips, burgers and roast potatoes, and, as a result, often he would leave the food untouched, which made his mother angry.

'What sort of a wife are you? Can't you cook for your own husband?' Durga-devi would wag her finger at Neela. 'Do you know how much money he is pouring down the drain by going to restaurants?' This mantra was chanted on a daily basis until Neela learned to cook the English food properly.

She heard the sound of Ajay's feet thumping across the landing and guessed that he was going to have a shower. Now, since there was no one else in the house, perhaps she should seize the opportunity to ask him all the questions that were bothering her. While she cut the potatoes, she planned. First she would ask him how he was, then why he wasn't talking to her, and thirdly if he liked her. And what else? She scratched her head. Now that she finally had the chance, she had forgotten all the other things she wanted to know about. Maybe she shouldn't ask too many questions at once. Perhaps she should just talk to him. Like a friend.

Neela rehearsed the whole conversation over and over while she prepared his lunch, and when she heard his footsteps on the stairs, she placed everything on a tray and waited.

'Your lunch . . . do you want it . . . in the dining room?' She cursed herself for being so timid.

'No, I will have it in the conservatory,' he said, pushing past her.

She liked the conservatory. Sun shone through the glass making the place warm and bright. She always wondered how it would feel, just sitting in one of those cane chairs and relaxing with one of her favourite books like Yamini so often did.

After placing the tray carefully on the cane coffee table, she cleared her throat. 'Sorry, I . . . was . . . I mean, I just wanted to go for a walk . . . I didn't know you were coming home,' she said in the hope of starting a conversation but he grunted something unintelligible while he switched on the television.

'How are you?'

'All right,' he shrugged.

'How is work?'

He frowned and turned up the volume. Noticing his expression change, her mind went blank and she forgot her words. As she stood there staring at him her inner voice shouted, *For goodness sake he is only your husband. Be bold and talk to him.*' She struggled to raise her voice over the drone of the television.

'Are you staying here today?'

He didn't answer but with the same grumpy expression continued to flip through the channels while he munched his food.

'I . . . I'd like to talk to you,' she said, twisting the end of her sari *pallu* nervously.

'Shush . . .' he shouted, and his eyes shot her a furious look before he turned back to the screen.

CHAPTER 7

Neela stood at the kitchen window watching the sky turn red and the birds fly home. Do they have families? She wondered. Do they ever feel lonely like her despite being in a flock? Here she was, surrounded by this whole new family, yet she felt totally alone and isolated. What was the point of getting married if one individual didn't love the other? In fact what was love? How did it happen between two strangers? Did it really exist in real life or was it only a fantasy invented by writers and poets? She knew her parents loved each other and Suji said she loved her husband, but she just couldn't imagine them like the lovers and soul-mates portrayed in books. Was it all an illusion? What about Romeo and Juliet? Were they real people? Her parents had done what every parent in India had to do; they had fulfilled their responsibilities and duties by finding her a husband. Now she was his property. She winced. Women always depended on someone else – a father, a husband, and later perhaps, a son? She wished she were educated and independent. What did her future hold? Would Ajay ever accept her as his wife? Would she ever come to love him? These thoughts swarmed like bees. Stop it! She shook her head vigorously and scrubbed the burnt saucepan with a Brillo pad in frustration. Her hands ached but the pan sparkled. She exhaled the deep breath that she was holding, and started to wipe the pan dry.

'Are you happy here?' a voice interrupted.

Neela, startled that someone had been reading her mind, spun round to see Yamini beside her.

'Are you?' Yamini probed again, taking a cup from the cupboard.

'Yes . . . of course,' Neela stammered.

'Really?' A sceptical smile played on Yamini's face. 'Do you like Ajay?' She took a tea bag from the container.

'Do I like . . .?' Neela repeated the question as if she did not know what it meant.

'Do you?'

'Ye . . . yes,' she stuttered.

'I was wondering why you don't want to go to his place.'

'His place?' Neela asked, puzzled.

'Uhum.'

'Does he have his own house?'

'Didn't you know?' Yamini exaggerated her surprise.

'No!'

'Now, listen,' she poured hot water into the cup, 'he lives in a rented room, not very far from here. Why don't you ask Ma-ji to send you there?'

Abandoning the pan and the tea towel on the worktop, Neela replied, 'But he hasn't asked me.'

'If you are waiting for him to ask, he certainly won't. It won't happen in your lifetime. Go and tell Ma-ji, that you want to go to your husband's house and don't stop fussing until she agrees.'

Neela looked at Yamini, confused.

'Don't look at me like that. You have to stand up for what you want sometimes. Otherwise . . .' Yamini waved her hand up and down the length of Neela's body, 'you will be here for ever.'

Stunned by what Yamini had told her, Neela stared at the damp patches on her sari left over from the washing-up. As she digested Yamini's words, she felt a faint glimmer of hope and dared to think that the puzzle of Ajay's strange behaviour might be solved.

Why on earth had no one mentioned Ajay's other accommodation before now? So that's where he disappeared to for days on end! He clearly had no intention of taking her there with him. She felt cheated. A familiar banging pain started up in her head and she pressed her thumb and forefinger to her temples. That night she tossed and turned on the rabbits and carrots as a jumble of thoughts disturbed her. Finally, she came to a conclusion. She decided that she would follow Yamini's advice.

The following morning, she waited until everyone had left the house before entering the living room. Durga-devi was sitting on a sofa listening to devotional songs on a tape and preparing her post-breakfast *paan*. Neela cleared her throat.

'Ma-ji!'

'What?' Durga-devi didn't look up.

Neela watched her mother-in-law's plump fingers, busily dipping into a small compartment of the silver *paan-dan* box. She wiped a couple of aromatic green betel leaves with her hand, smeared lime paste on them, sprinkled *khasu* powder, and added a few granules of mint before folding the leaves into a triangle and securing it by piercing a clove right through its centre.

'Why are you not sending me to Ajay's house?' If she hesitated now, the words might stick in her throat for ever and never be spoken.

Durga-devi looked astounded but seemed to remain calm. Neela watched her place one of the *paans* in her mouth and saw her push it with her tongue right inside her cheek. The old woman's eyes shot a long, hard glance at her. Despite her boldness, Neela felt like a frightened schoolgirl standing in front of a headmistress.

'So Yamini has been talking to you and trying to influence you, I suppose! I don't understand why she is so keen to send you away when she constantly complains about not having any help in the house! Who does she think will do the housework if I send you there?'

Talking with her mouth full, Durga-devi recounted the argument she had had with Yamini and how she loathed handing over so much of her hard-earned savings and pension money each month. Since her eldest son had become a hen-pecked husband, there was no way that she could afford a separate house even half as decent as this one, she explained.

In the beginning, she told an astonished Neela, it was Yamini who had suggested the idea of going to India to find a bride for Ajay. She had agreed that marriage might make him settle down and behave responsibly, and after experiencing Yamini's dominating nature, Neela seemed to be the ideal person for the role. Looking up, Durga-devi took a deep breath.

'I have to ask Ajay first. I am not sure whether he wants you there,' she paused, looking at Neela. 'You see, he is renting only one room and it's not big enough for two.'

'It's all right, Ma-ji; I don't mind . . . I will adjust.'

'You don't mind, but he might! Anyway I will try, but don't you dare get your hopes up, girl,' she warned Neela.

The previous evening, while collecting the washing from the garden, Neela had overheard Yamini complaining to her husband in the conservatory.

'I wish you had the courage to tell your mother to pack her bags and go to Ajay along with that mute little Indian mouse.'

'Are you mad? You want to throw away the extra income that Mum gives us? You know how Mum worries about Ajay, and if we send her there, just think what will happen to her pension fund! We won't get a penny.'

'Yes, I know, but sometimes it's just too much for me. The house is overcrowded and I can't breathe. I don't think I can put up with this much longer.'

'I know, my *pyari*, please be patient.'

'Don't *pyari* me, it doesn't work.'

Chapter 7

'OK, my love, if *pyari* doesn't work, can I say *darling*, in English?' Suraj tried to lighten up the mood. 'Mum is getting old . . .'

He never did finish his sentence. Neela heard him yell Ouch! What had Yamini done to interrupt him?

Two weeks had passed since she had spoken to Durga-devi and her hopes of going to Ajay's house were diminishing fast. She didn't know if Durga-devi had even mentioned it to her son. No one said anything to her. On the Thursday she prepared the head massage oil for her mother-in-law as usual. She pounded dried fenugreek leaves, *neem* leaves and hibiscus petals into a powder and mixed it with coconut oil.

After a half an hour of gentle massage, Durga-devi seemed satisfied and told Neela to sit down in front of her.

'I am sending you to Ajay's place tomorrow,' she said.

'Tomorrow?' Neela couldn't believe her ears,' Really, Ma-ji?'

'What do you mean, *Really*, Ma-ji?' Durga-devi mimicked. 'Go, hurry up and pack your bags, but first of all make sure you finish everything around the house.'

'Yes, Ma-ji . . . thank you, Ma-ji.' Controlling the urge to hug and kiss her mother-in-law, Neela ran upstairs, delirious with happiness.

Neela entered Yamini's room knowing that it would be the last time she vacuumed in there. She changed the bedding and went to wipe and tidy the dressing table. As always the contents of those tubes, jars and bottles of make-up dazzled her. She picked up one of the elegant bottles and held it in her hands, slowly reading the label, one letter at a time. It spelt *Poison*. Surprised by its name, she took off the lid and breathed in the scent. She was tempted to spray it behind her ears, like Yamini did, but she didn't have the courage. Would her new room be like this? She hummed a theme song from a Hindi film while twirling round and round, and almost dropped the perfume bottle.

CHAPTER 8

The next morning Neela heard Yamini arguing with Durga-devi at the breakfast table. 'Why can't Ajay come and fetch her? I am not a taxi driver.'

'You know his car gives trouble.'

'Can't he hire a cab or can't she go by train? How many favours must I do for you and your favourite son?' Yamini asked.

'He can't come for her today, and she doesn't know how to get the train. Anyway, you are not doing it for nothing, are you?'

Durga-devi pulled a small bundle of money, rolled securely in a handkerchief, from her blouse. She put the tip of her index finger into her mouth to wet it and started flipping the notes to count them. She pulled a few from the bundle and handed them to Yamini.

'*Maha Rani-ji*. Be ready by the time I come home. Don't be late, OK!'

'OK, Yamini-*behn*.' Neela nodded.

After changing into her favourite lilac sari, Neela carried her two suitcases down to the porch.

'You can't wait to get out of this house, can you?' shouted Durga-devi.

'Oh, no . . . it's not that, Ma-ji. Yamini-*behn* said not to be late . . .'

'Huh, she won't come home that quickly for you or anybody else,' Durga-devi glanced at the clock and frowned. 'The minute she finishes work she will head into town to buy more of those English outfits and handbags, shoes and makeup. She thinks she is English.'

Neela hid a smile behind her sari *pallu* because the old woman was moving her hips in a grotesque imitation of Yamini walking on stilettos.

'Or she will go and see her friends,' Durga-devi continued. 'You know why?' She poked a finger on her chest. 'To gossip about me,' and she wagged the same finger at Neela, 'and also about you.' She paused to take a breath. 'Anyway, did you clean the kitchen cupboards?'

'No, Ma-ji . . . I will do it now.'

'Until you do everything that you are supposed to do, you are not going anywhere. Understand?'

'Yes . . .'

After two claustrophobic months, Neela set off on her second car journey since arriving in the country and this time, a smile played on her lips. She was on her way to a home that she could call her own. She glanced out of the window as they drove through a more elegant part of town, stared at the shops and the hustle and bustle of the town centre. When the car stopped at a pedestrian crossing, she saw a young couple at a bus-stop kissing each other passionately. Embarrassed, she averted her eyes.

Throughout the hour-long journey Yamini kept up a continuous grumble. Firstly it was Durga-devi's demands, then Suraj not understanding her difficulties, and finally Ajay wasting her time when he could easily have collected his own wife himself.

'Ajay's car works perfectly well when he comes home for money. You know, it's his Mum's fault. She spoils him rotten. And if you carry on like this, soft as a pillow and as mute as a mouse, he won't change. Not in a million years.'

What did she mean, 'change'?

The smart side of town was soon left behind as they headed out towards the poorer suburbs where Ajay lived. Here, the High Street was full of sari shops, grocery stores and spice markets named after gods and girls. There were even some poky-looking restaurants named *Tajmahal, Maharajah Vegetarian* and *Kabir's Karai.* Neela whispered the names to herself. When they pulled up at some traffic lights, she could hear the soundtracks of Hindi films blaring from a shop that sold videos. There was a Hindu temple at the end of one road, a mosque on the other side, and a little church in the turning on the right. Asian people filled the streets, wearing their own dress, talking loudly in their mother tongues. Neela's spirits lifted. Where was she? In all its chaotic, colourful glory, here was a little India.

The car turned into a narrow street at the back of some shops where the houses were terraced, old, grey and dreary. Yamini was becoming impatient and cross with the narrow roads, the bad Asian drivers, and the children playing on the roads.

'Look at the state of this place! Can anyone believe this is Britain? People here live like frogs in a well and can't get out,' she complained.

Turning into an even narrower road, Neela wondered how any car could negotiate its way here, let alone Yamini's big BMW. They came to a halt in front of a small terraced house behind a short brick wall and a missing gate. The patch of lawn was brown and dry, the doors with window frames were painted an avocado-green. Tired net curtains fluttered out through the broken seal at the base of the glass pane.

'This is it, Number 163, Princes Road,' said Yamini, switching the engine off.

'What a battle it's been with Ajay and his mother to get you here,' she sighed.

Neela turned to her in surprise. Although she knew that for Yamini she was just a little Indian country mouse eating Yamini's cheese in Yamini's sophisticated house, she did not know that it had taken so much persuasion for her husband to take her. She was married to him after all, so what alternative was there?

'Princes Road. Ha, ha! Very funny! Come on then, *Rani-ji,* your prince lives in this palace,' laughed Yamini, opening the car door for

Neela. The two women were greeted by the smell of spices fried in ghee.

'What a stench. No wonder the locals have moved away from here.'

Smart Yamini looked quite out of place here, as did her gleaming maroon BMW among all the old bangers.

Neela stood behind Yamini as the door squeaked open.

'Hello, *namskar*,' a woman in her forties wearing a sari and with kind eyes greeted them.

'Hello, I am Yamini, Ajay's sister-in-law, and this is Neela, his wife.'

'Yes, yes, he told me this morning that you were coming today. Please come in.'

'Where is Ajay? Is he at home?' asked Yamini, gesturing to Neela to go in first.

'Yes, yes, he's just come in. He must be in his room upstairs.'

The woman walked to the staircase and called, 'Ajay *bhayya*!' with a note of excitement in her voice. 'Come and see who is here.'

Ajay came down the stairs smiling broadly as he greeted his sister-in-law, but the smile quickly faded when he turned to Neela. As usual his eyes were blank. His lips managed a dry 'Hello.'

'OK, Ajay! There's your wife,' Yamini pointed at Neela. 'I've brought her safely to you and you look after her properly. I must get home. It's almost time to take Ritu to music class. Neela, go upstairs to your room.'

Yamini spoke without taking a breath. She touched Neela's shoulder lightly. For the first time, and only for a fraction of second, Neela thought she saw a hint of sympathy in Yamini's eyes as she turned and walked away.

'All new brides feel the same, shy and nervous. Everything will be fine by tomorrow, you will see.' the landlady said, smiling at Neela.

'Thank you, *behn-ji*.'

'I am Anita. Are you taking her out for dinner tonight, Ajay-*bhayya*?'

'No, I don't have time.'

'Then in that case, come and have dinner with us.'

Neela didn't know what to say to the unexpected invitation so she looked at Ajay for guidance.

Noticing Neela's hesitation, Anita said, 'Don't worry, I have already cooked enough.'

'Thank you, but it's a trouble for you.' Neela replied in a small voice.

'No, not at all, it's a pleasure.'

'Thank you.'

'Don't just stare at her, Ajay-*bhayya*. Take your wife upstairs to your room and show her where everything is. I will call you when I have set the table.'

Ajay – because Anita told him to – took one of Neela's suitcases and started up the stairs. Carrying the other suitcase, Neela climbed behind him in silence. He stopped on the landing and opened one of the doors.

It was a small room with yellow and green floral wallpaper. In the middle was a double bed with a pink, lacy bed-spread which occupied almost all the floor space. An old, white melamine wardrobe stood against the opposite wall, leaving just enough space to move around. A tiny dressing table was near the window; although most of the polish on the mirror had worn away, there was enough of it left for her to catch a glimpse in it of a frightened Indian girl.

Neela stood with her eyes downcast, just inside the doorway. Ajay moved away to the other side of the bed where he sat down, picked up a newspaper from the floor and busied himself with its contents.

In the bathroom mirror, Neela stared at her reflection. With her oval face, brown complexion, black hair, oiled and tightly plaited she judged herself plain and unattractive, especially compared to the fair-skinned Yamini. No wonder Ajay didn't like her. How would he feel about living with her? Then she asked herself how it would be for her to live with him. Would she ever love him? Would love eventually come to them?

Anita called them for dinner, saving Neela from any further soul-searching. For the time being.

A man, whom Neela guessed was Anita's husband, was already sitting at the dining table which stood behind the sofa in the living room.

'Ah! Ajay! Congratulations on the arrival of your new bride!' He greeted Ajay, then turned to Neela and invited her to sit down, pulling back a chair for her.

'By the way this is my husband, Dinesh,' Anita said, as she came out of the kitchen.

'*Namaste*,' Neela greeted him with her palms together.

Seeing the way Ajay greeted Dinesh, she guessed that they knew each other well.

'Neela,' asked Dinesh, 'you must be feeling cold? It takes time to get used to this freezing climate.' He pulled a small electric heater nearer to her.

'I don't think I will ever get used to this cold weather. I am always freezing,' Anita said.

'So, Neela, I heard that you have already been here for two months and how do you feel? Do you like it here?'

'Yes, I like it here, *bhayya*,' she smiled.

'No one likes it in the beginning. Everyone misses India,' said Anita.

'It all depends upon Ajay. He might make her forget it.' Dinesh smiled at Ajay.

Ajay shrugged silently.

'Ajay-*bhayya*, a husband's love is the most precious thing to any woman. She forgets about herself in her love for him. That's why all parents in India plead with their sons-in-law to look after their daughters with more love and affection than they gave them themselves, so that they won't miss them.' Anita sounded a little emotional.

Neela's eyes searched Ajay's face, hoping for a positive reaction, but found nothing to reassure her.

The food was delicious. It was a welcome change for Neela to have dinner in someone else's house, dinner which she herself had not prepared. And Anita's easy hospitality reminded her of India where this would be the norm. Neela made a move to help her with the dishes but Anita wouldn't let her.

'It's your first night here in this house, so don't keep your husband waiting.'

'Actually I have to go out now. I am meeting someone.' Ajay was standing in the doorway of the kitchen.

Neela was unsure whether he was addressing her or the others.

'Are you joking? How can you leave your new wife at home alone on her first evening?' Dinesh's voice was jovial.

'I have to,' mumbled Ajay.

'Are you serious, Ajay? Can't you postpone your meeting till tomorrow?' Anita asked, wiping her hands on her sari *pallu*.

'Sorry, Anita-*behn*.'

'Don't say sorry to me. Say sorry to your wife!'

Ajay didn't say when he would be home. Neela wanted to ask him, but by the time she had decided what to say, he had put on his shoes and left.

'It doesn't matter, let him go. Some men like to work hard,' said Anita. 'Come and have some coffee with us.'

On the bed in the strange room, Neela stared into the darkness of the night. Nothing had changed in the past two months. She sighed and turned over, pulling the blankets tightly around her. She had never thought her life would be like this. She never had big ambitions or a wish for wealth, yet she had dared to hope for a little affection and love from her husband. Maybe dreams were sweeter than reality. It was clear that Ajay had married her out of duty to his mother.

75

Was she having a nightmare? Neela was dragged from sleep by the weight of someone lying on top of her and pinning her down. She smelt alcohol and tobacco on the breath of the person who held her and who breathed heavily into her face. She fought desperately to get free but his grip was determined and strong. His hands fumbled as he tried to open the hooks that held her blouse until he was tearing the fabric and bruising her flesh. Neela screamed. She tried again to push him off but it was impossible. Her slight body was no match for his heavy, fleshy one. Then he was hurting her, hurting her in a place that was too intimate to even have a name. Neela cried out in pain and humiliation. At last it was over. Ajay grunted and slid off her. He rolled to one side of the bed and passed out. Neela was aware of her fast-beating heart. She was aware of her body soaked in sweat, his and her own. She felt deep disgust. She felt dirty and cheap. She felt robbed of her self-respect.

Impossible to stay in the same bed when there was a snake lying beside her. She managed to get herself to the bathroom despite her legs giving way and the shaking that ran in waves from her head to her toes. The water was icy, making the pain where he had bruised her worse. She gritted her teeth, not caring if she froze. She scrubbed and scrubbed with a bit of soap, trying to clean herself, trying to wash away his filth. Even after dressing, her teeth still chattered. At the window, she looked out at the dark empty street and contemplated escape. Gusts of wind blew the branches of the leafless trees. Fear and nausea engulfed her.

Was it like this for every woman? Although she knew so little, her instincts told her that what had happened to her was wrong. She felt an acute sense of loss. She understood that a married woman should give everything to her husband but surely not like this. No, she could not accept this. A few minutes ago, she had lost everything to a man who did not even love her. So now what? Could she run away? Could she return to her former life with its peace and simplicity? She felt violated.

CHAPTER 9

Outside the wind howled, rattling the glass that was loose in the window frames. The chill bit into her bones through her thin cotton sari. Neela rummaged through the contents of the wardrobe, searching for blankets, but there weren't any, not even an extra bed sheet. Some of Ajay's clothes were hanging haphazardly on twisted old metal hangers, with other garments carelessly thrown over the rail, clinging on by a sleeve or leg. A pile of unwashed clothes was heaped in the bottom of the wardrobe. All his clothes were impregnated with the same smell which made her nauseous. She held her breath and closed the wardrobe door. Trying not to disturb him, she dragged her suitcase out from under the bed and pulled from it a couple of saris, but their light fabric did not offer her any warmth in that stormy night.

She heard Anita and Dinesh leave for work and noticed that the small clock on the dressing table showed eight in the morning. Ajay's snoring reverberated in the new silence. She noticed that with his limbs outstretched, he occupied the entire bed. He looked fierce and satisfied like a predator after making a meal of its hunted prey. She turned her gaze away, revolted.

Her body felt stiff and painful as she tried to get up from the floor. She had been sitting there the whole night, upright and still. Carefully, without making any noise, she lifted the lid of her suitcase and gently took out the beaded purse and unzipped it. They were there - the five one pound coins, shiny and new - and with them the image of her father lovingly embracing her and pressing the money into her hands. The memory of him bidding her farewell for the last time would never leave her and for a second she relaxed into its warmth and comfort.

'Why, Bapu?'" she had asked him. 'I don't need them.'

'I know, *Beti*, but just in case. You never know when you will need it.'

She could still see the concern in his eyes. She closed the zip and muttered, 'Yes, Bapu . . . you were right.' Wiping her eyes with her sari *pallu*, she walked softly out of the room and pulled the door shut behind her.

As she ran to the nearest phone box, she wondered whether Durga-devi would be awake yet.

'Hello,' Durga-devi's voice sounded unusually soft.

'Hello, Ma-ji,' Neela whispered.

'Hello, hello . . . who is it?' Durga-devi was shouting now.

Neela tried to speak up but her voice failed her.

'Why are you not saying anything?'

Neela held the receiver. How could she tell Durga-devi what had happened to her? How could she find the words?

'I know who you are,' she heard the old lady scream in a high-pitched tone, 'You must be one of those rogues, playing about.' There was a momentary pause before her voice thundered on. 'You think you will scare me with your heavy breathing? *khabardar*, I will call the police . . .'

Neela, fearing that her eardrums would burst at the ranting, held the receiver away from her ear and let it dangle. She swallowed hard and replaced it on the hook. How could she tell anyone what had happened to her, especially Durga-devi. What was she thinking? She walked across the street to a small post office and bought an aerogramme instead. For days the blue aerogramme was to lie on her dressing table because she could not bring herself to pick up her pen and write a letter. Not to anyone. Not to her parents. Not even to her friend Suji. She couldn't break their hearts.

Most of the time Neela shut herself in her room. Ajay's violent abuse continued. She dreaded the nights he was at home and their room became a torture chamber for her. Even though she managed to detach her mind from what Ajay did to her, a part of her died every time Ajay used her body as a rag doll.

'Are you all right?' Anita asked one morning, looking at Neela's swollen face.

'Yes, thank you, Anita-*behn*,' she replied, turning from the landing to go to into her room.

'No, I don't think so. You are not all right, Neela.'

The gentleness in Anita's voice stopped her in her tracks. Neela's enormous dark eyes looked up, hiding nothing, not even her shame. Anita's concern touched her deeply.

'Neela, what is it?' Anita came nearer as Neela bowed her head to hide her tears.

'There, there, don't you get yourself upset. Don't worry too much; things will get better in time.' Anita put her arms gently around her shoulders. The flood gates opened and Neela did not have the power to stop them. Anita held her close until her sobs subsided, then led her into the living room and sat her down on the sofa.

'Relax for a few minutes, Neela. I will make you a cup of tea.'

While Anita was in the kitchen, Neela wondered how she had let everything out like that to a total stranger. She suddenly felt silly and wiped her eyes with embarrassment.

'Don't be ashamed of crying!' Anita said, reading her thoughts. 'We are only human, not brick walls. We all have emotions and I know how terrible it is for you.' Anita said, handing her a steaming mug of tea. 'Don't worry too much, Neela. It's only a matter of time and I have a feeling that in the end everything will work out well.'

'I am so scared, Anita-*behn*, I just want to go home ... to my parents,' Neela's eyes filled again with tears, 'but I don't know how ... I have no money for the ticket and my passport is with my mother-in-law. You know, I tried to phone her several times but I just couldn't tell her anything.'

'I know it's very difficult to approach a mother-in-law, but please don't do anything like going back to your parents. I don't think that is wise.'

'But what else can I do?'

'Don't worry, we will think of something together,' Anita patted her on the back, trying to be reassuring.

It was soon obvious to Neela that Ajay didn't have a job or a business as his mother had claimed. He was living on unemployment benefit and spending it all on alcohol and women. He had a routine. Most nights he would go to a pub where he would pick up some woman. Neela soon became accustomed to the smell of cheap perfume when he returned. During the day he slept off his hangover, at least giving Neela a bit of breathing space.

Disgusted with Ajay's cruelty towards his new wife, and his irresponsible behaviour, Anita threatened to kick him out and told him that if it wasn't for Neela she would not tolerate him in the house. In Anita, Neela had a staunch ally.

'Would you like to learn English?' Anita asked Neela one afternoon at tea.

'English? Do they teach it here?'

'Yes, the school near the park offers evening classes for people like us and I think it would be useful.'

'I would like to, Anita-*behn*, but I don't know what Ajay will say.'

'Well, you don't know until you ask him, do you? It doesn't cost much, and he might agree. Who knows?'

'Yes,' said Neela. 'But he might say no.'

'Just try him.'

Chapter 9

For the next two days Ajay went out early in the morning and came home late at night and Neela was glad that he left her alone. Feeling slightly more relaxed, she spent most of the time talking to Anita and being part of her world.

'Are you not originally from India?' Neela asked her one day.

'No.' she took a deep breath. 'Let me tell you a bit of history here. Large numbers of Indians had migrated to East Africa in the late nineteenth century. They were employed by both the Indian and British governments to construct hundreds and hundreds of miles of railway in Uganda which was under the British government. After their work was completed, many Indians remained there. Actually they became extremely important to the Ugandan economy as traders and lawyers who gradually established themselves and grew successful. However, like many immigrant communities, their contribution to the country's wealth went unacknowledged and caused friction between them and the local population.' Anita stopped, and saw that Neela didn't know any of this. 'Have you heard about Idi Amin?'

'Umm, sort of,' Neela nodded, remembering the conversation her father had with Durga-devi when they came to see her.

'After he came in to power in August 1972, Idi Amin called the entire Asian population 'Blood suckers,' and forty eight hours later he issued an eviction order for all sixty thousand Asians, including those who held Ugandan passports. However a second verdict was also issued which stated that all those with professional backgrounds such as doctors, lawyers and teachers should not leave the country, and if they tried, it would be considered as betrayal.'

'Oh, no,' Neela was astonished.

'Yes. But when Amin asked the British for financial aid after he came to power, this was refused. His revenge was to evict the Asians so that the British would have no option but to take them in because they all had British passports. Some went back to India, some to Canada, but thousands flew into Britain.'

'That's how you came here?'

'Yes.' Anita smiled ruefully. 'You know how yesterday you asked how you would survive without any money, or without knowing any English. Well, let me tell you this, we landed in Britain penniless and with only the clothes on our backs because we had to leave all our businesses and properties behind. When we landed at Stanstead it was absolutely freezing and we didn't have any warm clothes at all. We went through health checks at the airport and then they ushered us onto a bus to Stradishall in Suffolk. It was a former RAF base. We slept and lived together in the same large hall. It was not comfortable but we were grateful to have a roof over our heads and glad that we were safe from the harassment. Food was scarce. We survived on whatever we could get from meal vouchers. As I said, we didn't have a penny but we were determined to re-start our lives.'

Neela was silent. Anita had paused for a while, recalling images and memories.

'All the children went to local schools and you know it was difficult to learn a new language and adapt to such a different way of life. As the children grew up, the problem of finding a match for them became a huge problem. For generations, arranged marriages were the norm. Now suddenly parents faced the frightening possibility of their children getting married to individuals who might not only be from a different caste, but from a totally different race.'

Neela listened curiously.

'Those who were academically or financially successful didn't have any difficulty finding a match here in their own community. But some parents went to extreme lengths, even returning to India in search of a traditional spouse, especially for their sons. It was also an easier way to find a wife for those who were not very successful, or divorced, or widowed.' Anita sighed. 'You know what it's like in India, Neela. Most people live in a dream world and so they had no way of finding out if these people were telling the truth or not. They see a British person from a rich, prosperous country and they regard them as a god. So for these men, a bride was guaranteed along with a substantial dowry. More often than not they wouldn't tell the girl or her parents the truth and the men who were married before pretended that it was their first marriage. The poor girls would eventually find out the truth, but only once they arrived here. Then of course it was too late.' Noticing the fright in Neela's eyes, Anita smiled and said tenderly, 'Don't worry, it doesn't happen to everybody. There are so many happy marriages and I am sure yours will be too. In time.'

'I don't know,' Neela replied.

'Don't agonise about it now. Come on, let's find out the dates of enrolment for your English class.'

CHAPTER 10

Neela was preparing Ajay's dinner from the groceries left over from the previous week's shop. She made four *chapattis* and a small bowl of potato curry. As usual, Neela carried the tray upstairs and placed it on a tiny bedside table in front of Ajay's chair. Wiping her trembling hands on her sari *pallu*, she asked hesitantly, 'Could I learn English please?'

'What?' Ajay reached out for his plate.

'I . . . I . . . want to learn English.'

'Why do you want to learn English?' he asked with his mouth full. 'What for?' His eyes crawled over her face like two spiders.

'I would like to learn . . . and it might . . . help me in the future.'

'How exactly?'

'I don't know . . . but I want to learn,' she said again.

'How dare you talk back to me?' he shouted, 'Who is putting all these rubbish ideas into your brain? Eh!'

'No one. I just thought of it and . . . it doesn't cost much.'

'Oh, doesn't it?' Do you know how much it cost me to bring you to this country? Are you listening, bitch?' She noticed how bloodshot his eyes were.

'But I can find some work . . .'

Even before she finished the sentence, he was on his feet, pushing back his chair and slamming his fist onto the table so that his food flew all over the floor. He strode towards her like a mad bull and hissed his foul breath in her face. Neela fled to the bathroom and closed the door, but under his blows, it rattled like a leaf in a storm. Fearing that he might break the door down, she opened it again.

'You think that by learning English you can go out with white men?' he shouted, dragging her back into the bedroom. 'They wouldn't even look at you . . . you ugly thing.' Panting hard, he slapped her across her face. 'Why are you crying? You look even more disgusting now. That's why I go out. The girl I had last night,' he leered, 'what a beauty! Worth more than the money I spent on her and I was happy until I came home to you . . .' His spit flew everywhere.

Neela made a run for the door but he reached out and grabbed her. He beat her. He beat her hard, with his fists inflicting blow after blow all over her face and body.

Neela didn't know how long she lay there but at some point the sound of heavy rain on the glass pane reached her through the silence. It was an effort to open her eyes. Her body was a mess of scratches, cuts and bruises. Hot prickling tears ran down her burning cheeks for the humiliation she had suffered, for the insults that had been heaped on her, and for the knowledge of her own vulnerability.

She lay motionless until two soothing hands reached out and held her shoulders. She didn't need to look round to see who it was. Instead, she buried her head in that kind embrace and let her grief shake her like a cyclone. Anita looked around the room, took in the broken glasses and shattered bottles. The drama of the previous night was obvious. Holding Neela close, she led her out of the room. In the bathroom she wiped her wounds with antiseptic.

'Don't worry, Neela. The wounds will heal in a few days' time. The water is hot; have a bath, and you will feel better.'

Neela obeyed, responding to the compassion and concern in her landlady's voice.

'That's better. You look fresh. Come and have some toast.'

'I am not hungry, Anita-*behn*.'

'How long are you going to go without eating?'

Neela worried that the previous night's commotion had disturbed Anita and Dinesh. She looked at Anita, ready to apologise, but the words wouldn't form in her mouth. Anita's gaze told Neela she understood. Neela took a piece of toast from the plate and finally managed a smile.

Neela slept most of the afternoon as exhaustion finally caught up with her but as the evening approached, she became tense and restless. Dreading Ajay's arrival, she went down to ask Anita if she could sleep on her sofa that night.

'Of course you can sleep here tonight but you can't avoid him for ever. Look, Neela, I hope you don't mind me saying this, but there are only two options in your situation. The first one means you forget all about your identity and your self-respect and you become a slave to . . . forgive me for saying this . . . that rogue of a husband of yours. You will spend your entire life numb like a stone, and without any feelings.' She paused for a moment. 'Now the second option is to go out and get a job, I mean any job, and become financially independent. As long as you are dependent on Ajay he won't change.'

'True,' nodded Neela.

'If you go out to work you will meet other people and see the outside world and that will give you the chance to think independently. Only then can you escape this rut and survive.'

Neela went quiet for a moment, tracing the arm of the chair thoughtfully before saying, 'No, Anita-*behn*, I don't want to stay here at all.'

Anita looked at her questioningly.

'I want to go back to my parents.'

'I thought you had decided against it.'

'I did but now I feel even if I earn money, he won't leave me alone. You know how he is, Anita-*behn*?'

'I know but Neela . . .?'

'I don't think I can bear it any more.'

'What about your parents? Think about them?'

'I don't think they want me to suffer like this.'

'No, certainly not, but do you want them to suffer?'

Neela looked at Anita, bewildered.' Of course not.'

'That's what you will be doing if you go back.' Anita poured the tea into a cup and handed it to Neela. 'Hopefully one day you might be able to go to your parents. Not as Ajay's wife, Neela, but as a confident individual of whom your parents would be proud. So take your time and think about it.'

While Anita's words showed her a new direction, Neela doubted that she was capable of taking it. Leaving everything and going back to her parents was a tempting option, but she knew in her heart that Anita was right. Not only would she be a burden to them, but they would be shattered knowing that their beloved daughter had been treated so horrifically by her husband. It would destroy them completely. And society in India would not allow her to live in peace. There would be no respect or sympathy for a woman who was separated from her husband. But the alternative was impossible for her. She wouldn't last long. In Ajay's hands she would definitely go insane or die.

In the midst of all this misery, Neela saw one small ray of hope. What about the second option? Why not? But with hope came defeat and panic. How could she find a job without knowing any English? Neela raced out of the kitchen to find her friend. 'Anita-*behn*, I can't speak English,' she called. 'How can I possibly find a job?'

Anita smiled at Neela's show of spirit, the first she had seen since the girl had arrived in her house.

'Haven't you heard what they say here? Where there is a will there is a way.'

CHAPTER 11

It was about a mile's walk to Mr Rusheed's sewing factory.

'Remember everything I've told you and you will be just fine.' Anita's voice was firm.

Though nervous, Neela nodded in agreement.

A kindly-looking middle aged man greeted them as they entered. Neela didn't need any introduction but guessed that he was the owner, Mr Rusheed.

'Hello, Rusheed-*bhayya*, how are you?' Anita beamed and introduced Neela.

'Pleased to meet you,' he said to Neela.

'*Namaste*.'

'Anita-*ji* phoned me about you, please come in.' He took them into his office.

'Only if you have a vacancy for her, Rusheed-*bhayya*,' Anita joked.

'Of course, Anita-*ji*. With Christmas coming we could do with an extra pair of hands.'

After Neela had filled in some forms and signed the papers, Mr Rusheed took them on to the factory floor and introduced Neela to each and every person there. The large hall accommodated several sewing machines and their operators were all women. In the middle of the hall some men and woman were measuring and cutting fabric on wide tables arranged in a row. People at smaller tables were hemming garments and sewing on buttons. A mountain of different fabric rolls were heaped on the other side of the room waiting to be transformed into dresses, skirts and blouses in those experts' hands. And in another smaller room men ironed the finished garments before others covered them with cellophane and hung them on a long rail – an endless line of garments ready to be dispatched to their marked destinations.

Neela had desperately wanted to tell Mr Rusheed that she didn't know anything about sewing or dressmaking before he offered her a job, but Anita had silenced her.

'Rusheed-*bhayya*, Neela is a very fast learner. She will learn the job in no time at all, you will see.'

'That will be good, my dear.'

'What are you saying? What if I can't learn?' Neela whispered in Anita's ear, but seeing Mr Rusheed looking at her, she nervously returned his smile.

He decided on an eight-hour day shift, sewing buttons and hemming, for two pounds per hour.

'That means sixteen pounds a day!' Neela couldn't contain her amazement.

After she had thanked Mr Rusheed, she threw her arms around Anita and hugged her tight, saying, 'I love you.'

'Well, don't choke me to death, girl,' Anita replied with a smile.

Anita took on herself the less exciting responsibility of telling the good news to Ajay. Neela listened from the kitchen where she was preparing dinner while her friend went up to tell him. There were a few minutes of stunned silence and the next thing Neela heard was a noisy peal of laughter

'Don't joke with me, Anita-*behn*. Who in their right mind would give her a job?'

'You should be proud of her, Ajay. You don't realise how lucky you are to have a decent wife like her,' Anita replied, annoyed.

'Ha! Ha! Very funny, ve . . . rry decent wife and I am ssooo . . . lucky . . .'

Chapter 11

Neela busied herself grinding cloves and cardamoms to drown out his sarcasm.

The next evening, as Neela got in the front door, the phone started to ring. She knew Anita wasn't at home, so she went to answer it, but Ajay had already picked up the receiver on another extension. When Neela put the phone to her ear, she could hear his voice.

'Mum, Neela has found a job.' Ajay sounded furious.

'What do you mean, she's found a job? Are you going mad or what?'

'No, Mum, really, Anita helped her to get a job,' his voice was shaking.

There was a silence for a while, and then Durga-devi wailed loudly.

'I knew this would happen. That girl . . . she looks as if butter wouldn't melt in her mouth and she can't speak more than a couple of words of English . . . *Hai-Ram!* . . . she has misled us. Oh my poor son, how much more must you suffer? And how can I live seeing you miserable like this?' There was a loud snort. 'I am telling you, she will boss you around the same as that shameless Veena did.'

Neela was puzzled at the mention of this new name.

'Why did you persuade me to marry Neela, Mum? You knew I didn't want to. And you seem to be blaming me for everything I went through with my first wife, that wretched Veena.'

Neela put her hand over her mouth in astonishment.

'Oh my God, he was married previously,' she whispered to herself. Then, 'No wonder she left him.'

'Well, we did discuss it . . . how much dowry you could get and how we could clear all your debts. But I know, neither you nor I were satisfied with the dowry that Neela brought. A measly hundred thousand rupees was far less than we needed. We trusted that marriage broker but he misled me telling me then that Neela would inherit her ancestors' precious jewels and heirlooms. It didn't take long for me to realise that there were no precious jewels, no heirlooms, and not even a speck of gold, only a chain of imitation pearls and corals. I knew then that the marriage broker had deceived us.' Durga-devi paused for breath. 'When I confronted him, he gave me a cheeky grin. He said, '*Don't you know, Durga-devi? What they say in India? Tell a hundred lies if you must, but get a girl married! Don't worry so much, Durga-devi. They gave you much more than they could afford, and Neela is a nice girl, worth more than all those precious stones and gold.* Oh Ajay, I can't tell you how he annoyed me, munching all those pastries and belching loudly. I remember him rubbing his stomach and saying, *Think that you have made a girl and her parents happy. It will do you good, Durga-devi. God will grant you a very long life.* Then he counted his remuneration and went happily to find another set of parents and another match.' Durga-devi's voice sounded weepy, 'My son, since Neela was the only child to her parents, I expected much more. But oh no, she came empty-handed, bringing misery and being a heavy burden on us. Now we have to bear this burden and dig more into my savings to pay that greedy Yamini. That's why I thought it would probably be better to send Neela to you. At least she could cook and clean for you.'

'What shall I do, Maa?'

'You still in doubt? Just make sure she resigns the job.'

'Are you mad, Ajay. This time it was Yamini's voice. 'Shouldn't you be happy at least that she is working? Don't you realise that you won't need to suffer for money anymore? Why do you worry? Neela won't go anywhere. She won't think that far ahead and she doesn't have anybody in this country like Veena had.'

'Ajay, *beta*,' his mother's voice again. 'Your sister-in-law is right. Don't worry, let her work. She can't go anywhere while her passport is with me. But make sure you take charge of the money she earns.'

Neela quietly replaced the receiver. Now she understood why Ajay had married her.

It was a few days later when the front door opened and there stood

Ajay holding a bunch of flowers. Neela stared first at him and then at the pale yellow chrysanthemums in disbelief. They were so beautiful, so delicate and vulnerable in his rough hands.

'They are for you Neela.'

Ajay had been treating her a little better. Although his routine hadn't changed, he was less volatile and hadn't laid a finger on her for quite a while, but she still felt uncomfortable in his presence.

Fetching a jug of water, he said, 'Go on, have a bath and freshen up.' He took the flowers from her hands and placed them in the water. 'Don't cook anything today, I will order a take-away. We could relax and watch television. What do you think?'

The warm water was heaven trickling on her tired body. Then a knock on the door, and Ajay's voice.

'Have you got any money for the take-away?' There was even a trace of gentleness in his voice.

'Yes, I have some in my purse. You can take it.'

The next thing she heard was the front door bang shut. She prayed, looking at the naked light bulb hanging from the ceiling, that her marriage would finally bring her some peace.

Dressed in a sky blue sari and with a small red *bindi* between her arched eyebrows, she looked into the worn old mirror and liked her reflection. The evening light gave her skin a glow. Feeling fresh, she turned on the tape recorder so that Hindi folk songs filled the room and seated herself on the bed to wait for her husband, her heart lighter than it had for a very long time with the strange new sensation of hope. Soon she was fast asleep.

The alarm clock woke her. The other half of the bed was empty. What had happened last night? Where was Ajay? She leaned on her elbow and, taking in the neat room, and knew at once that he hadn't come home last night. She jumped out of bed and looked in her purse. It was empty. A whole month's wages gone.

Ajay didn't come home for another three days.

'At least learn your lesson now. You need to look after yourself.' Anita told her.

'You know . . .' Neela lowered her eyelids.

'You are scared of him hurting you again, aren't you?'

Neela nodded.

'If he hits you again you should call the police.'

'Police?' Neela exclaimed.

'Why not? Just because he is your husband? His family has treated you like dirt and now he is treating you even worse, and you shy away from going to the police? What a typical Indian woman you are, Neela! Shall I admire and salute you for that?'

Neela bit her lip.

'You are letting him get away with murder, Neela, and it won't do you any good. What gives him the right to treat you so badly? You have to be assertive and firm with him.'

'Anita-*behn*, I don't know how.' Neela replied.

CHAPTER 12

On her way to work, Neela nearly always caught up with a young English couple who walked hand in hand and seemed very much in love. She named them *Anarkali* and *Saleem* and smiled when the girl tilted her head to gaze up at the man and he responded by drawing her close and kissing her lightly on her lips. Watching them brought conflicting emotions of joy and envy. At the railway station, Neela and the lovers parted company as she crossed the road to her workplace. One day, soon after leaving the young lovers behind, she caught a glimpse of her reflection in a shop window. An ordinary young woman stared back; a woman who was timid and gullible. There was absolutely nothing to be proud of. She didn't have the ability and confidence of Anita, nor did she have the beauty and charm of the young woman who walked the streets with a man's arms around her shoulders.

It was a Friday, and there was the usual end-of-week blissful urgency at work with everyone waiting for the day to end.

'Who wants to make tea today?' shouted Tahera from the other end of the room without taking her eyes from the garment that she was sewing.

Neela volunteered as usual. She was never in a hurry to go home. She loathed weekends. They were either silent and lonely, or noisy and violent. When she brought out the tray, Tahera was calling her name.

'Anita is here,' said the girl, making a gesture towards the door. Surprised, Neela turned to see Anita talking to Mr Rusheed. They both looked worried and when they started walking towards her, Neela knew that something was very wrong.

'Neela, you have to go home immediately.' Anita said gently, taking Neela's hand.

'What's the matter? Why?'

'It's . . . I am afraid your husband . . .' Mr Rusheed began, clearing his throat. 'Anita tells me that he is not well. I think you should go home.'

'But . . . but I can't leave the work now.'

'Don't worry about it, my dear.' He gave her a sympathetic look and took the tray from her hands.

She would be home in a couple of hours. Why couldn't Ajay wait? Neela wondered impatiently as she followed Anita out of the factory, but near the gate there was Suraj too, leaning against his car, looking grave and smoking a cigarette.

'Come on, hurry up. We have to get to the hospital,' Anita said, grabbing Neela's hand and starting to run towards the car.

'What's happened?' Neela asked, turning to Anita and then Suraj.

Anita climbed into the back seat next to Neela but said nothing. Suraj took a last puff of his cigarette, pushed the stub into the ash tray and fumbled with the keys as he started the engine. They drove on in silence. Neela knew not to ask.

Out on the open road, on their way to the hospital, Suraj finally half-turned to Neela in the back and said, 'Ajay has been in a car accident. He lost control . . . and the car hit a lamppost. Neela, I'm sorry but . . . .he is badly hurt.'

Ajay's family were already assembled at his bedside, and the looks on their faces as they turned to Neela told her all she needed to know. Only Durga-devi's noisy weeping broke the silence.

'Neela, be brave, my dear,' Anita said quietly. She had an arm around her shoulders as they walked slowly towards Ajay's bed.

His body was covered with a white cloth. Neela stared but her mind was blank.

Chapter 12

'You little devil, you witch, because of you my son is dead! Look at him! Are you satisfied now?' her mother-in-law screamed. 'I took pity on you and made him marry you. I didn't know your stars were no good. You are destined to be a widow. You killed him.' She wailed again, putting the sari *pallu* over her eyes.

Someone hushed Durga-devi and led her out of the room. Neela was aware that her head hurt and her ears were ringing from the screaming.

'You poor girl, how quickly your life has finished even before you had any children. *Hai Ram!* What is there in your life now but emptiness?' someone was saying.

According to Hindu custom, everything was now finished for her. Marriage was her destiny and her husband was her life and soul. Her duties as a wife were to satisfy her husband physically, and bear him children for his clan. But her life with Ajay had ended as abruptly and dramatically as it had begun.

After the cremation, some of the women led her into the bathroom. They sat her in the tub and, according to their custom, they poured bucket after bucket of cold water over her head. At last someone handed her a towel. She heard the women talking.

'She isn't even crying,' one of them said.

'Do you think she is in shock?'

'She doesn't care, does she?'

'It's sad, he never liked her.'

After the speculation came the questions.

'Where were you at the time?'

'Was he alone in his car?'

'Why was he drunk at that time in the afternoon?'

'Did you have a row with him?'

But Neela was detached from everything and everyone. None of this registered.

'Does she have to follow all these cruel ceremonies even here in this country?' Neela heard Anita pleading.

'You know how traditional our mother-in-law is so please don't upset her any more,' Yamini answered.

'*Pundit-ji*,' Anita asked again, 'Can't you skip some of the rituals? Please?'

'How dare you even ask?' Durga-devi shouted. 'My son is dead and you are taking sympathy on that devil?'

'But, aunty-*ji*, she is like a daughter to you.'

'Mind your own business,' Durga-devi panted. 'Who asked you here anyway?' She waved her hand and pointed at the door. 'Get out!'

'There, there, you are getting too emotional!' said one of the female mourners.

'Ma-ji, calm down, *Om, shanthi-shanthi-shanthi-hi,*' the priest chanted the peace *mantra* before turning to Anita. 'Look, my dear – I don't know your name – but Neela must follow these rituals. If we don't perform them properly it will be a great sin and she won't be forgiven by God or her ancestors. She will suffer a great deal not only in this life but also in her seven forthcoming lives,' he said, raising his hands in the air. 'What's more, Ajay's soul will not rest in peace.'

And so, despite Anita's attempt to intervene, the rituals went ahead. Neela vaguely remembered someone wiping the sacred vermilion off her forehead, someone else pulling off her wedding necklace. Her lovely green glass bangles were broken to remove them from her wrists. Her shimmering yellow wedding sari, in which she had been clothed, was ripped off and torn to shreds. She gasped for air as buckets of cold water were thrown over her head. Finally a plain, coarse, white sari was dragged over her. It felt like she was the audience, watching, not participating. For hours she sat motionless, obeying the priest and partaking in *karma*, the deeds and rituals for Ajay's *atma*, to reach *moksha*, the eternal heavens. This lasted for twelve long days.

And then it was over and everyone had gone. Neela lay on her bed in the dark and stared at the date on the fluttering calendar. Within a single year she had been married and widowed and still she was only twenty-five. A wry smile played on her dry lips. She could never again wear red vermilion or *kajal*. Colourful clothes or jewellery were out of the question. She would be forbidden to attend any auspicious ceremonies or weddings, nor could she celebrate any festivals. She was allowed one bland meal a day. Looking at a widow's face first thing in the morning was considered a bad omen in her community, therefore people would avoid her. She struggled to take it all in.

Chapter 13

'Why can't she answer? Is she deaf?' Durga-devi shouted downstairs.

Neela had heard her name being shouted but she had neither the energy nor the will to respond. Moments later her door was flung open with such force that it hit the wall with a thud. She opened her eyes.

'Can't you hear her yelling her head off? Do I have to come up here and tell you? There is a phone call for you,' Yamini said. 'Who is phoning you this early in the morning?' She made a face, slammed the door shut, and went thumping down the stairs again.

Neela tried to stand up but her legs felt weak. Wrapping her sari *pallu* around her shoulders she steadied herself and set off down the stairs as slowly as if she had forgotten how to walk.

'Here, take it.' Durga-devi almost threw the receiver at her.

It was her mother on the phone, sobbing.

'My *batie* . . . my *puglee batie!*' Her far-away voice was distraught and although Neela knew how hard this was for her mother, she could find nothing to say. She tried to tell her that she was fine, but no words came. Then her father's voice.

'I am sorry, my dear, I am awfully sorry! I know how difficult it is for you but please be brave, my child. Soon I will arrange for you to come home. Until then take care of yourself, *beti*.' His voice was breaking and she knew he was trying desperately to control his own grief. Still she couldn't respond to the heart-felt compassion in their voices.

Almost every day the whole house shook with Durga-devi's heart-rending wails. Neela understood that it was a devastating experience to lose a child and Durga-devi was no exception. She doubted whether the old woman would ever recover.

Where was Ajay now? Where had his aggression and anger gone? What had happened to his insatiable desire for alcohol and women? When she had seen him lying on the hospital bed she had found it impossible to believe that his personality had been extinguished because his threats and violence still haunted her. When asked if she missed him, she could never answer. It just wasn't the right question. She still thought about him, desperately trying to understand him, but she didn't know why she didn't just forget all about him. All he had done was hurt her and make her life a misery. Night after night she tried to make sense of it all, but in the end all she could do was shake her head violently from side to side, trying to empty the pointless thoughts.

Her life had been busy until a month ago. In spite of all the hard times with Ajay she had enjoyed her job at the factory and her friendship with Anita. Most of all she had lived in hope. She took a pride in whatever she did for her husband. Sometimes just cooking his meals, or washing and ironing his clothes, or doing the housework gave her a job-well-done satisfaction. But why did she do all that for him? Her relationship with him was that of a servant and master but without any reward.

Neela knew that Anita understood all this without explaining any of it to her. The thought of her friend was a great comfort and sometimes even made her smile, and now she felt a strong wish to be with her. It became a need. Just being near Anita would give her enough strength to live through the darkness. Many times during this bleak period of Neela's life, Anita would phone but the in-laws wouldn't let her talk to her friend. Neela's anger and restlessness increased until one day she picked up the phone and dialled Anita's number. Yamini, who always watched her like a hawk, grabbed the phone.

'What are you doing? Have you gone mad?' she asked angrily.

'I want to talk to Anita.' Neela replied, reaching out for the phone.

Yamini was taken aback by this forcefulness. 'No, you can't. Remember, Ma-ji already told you that you mustn't talk to anyone for one month.'

'Please, Yamini-*behn*, please. I beg you. Just for once let me talk to Anita. She will be worrying about me.'

'Oh, really?' Yamini made sarcastic clucking noises with her tongue. 'Ask her to pay the phone bill then.'

Neela turned away in disgust and wondered how on earth she had expected anyone in such a family to understand her.

The four weeks after Ajay's death passed like a prison sentence and finally the first month's ceremonies were over. Now one more task remained for the family and that was to decide what to do with his widow. Many discussions went on behind closed doors between family members and relatives. Should they let her stay or send her back to India? Neela didn't have any wish to leave her tiny, dark, shabby room; she liked it's grimness, and the comfort of being able to hide from everything and everyone. The sleepless nights gave her the opportunity to mull over her situation. She hadn't forgotten what Anita had said. After a lot of deliberation, she came to a decision. She wouldn't go back to her parents. If her fate had brought her this far, she would remain in this country. It was now up to God to decide what to do with her.

Life was hard for her but there was still one way forward and that was the chance of getting her job back at the sewing factory. This one faint hope kept her sane through those four long weeks. She was sure that Mr Rushid would be kind enough to understand her month-long absence. She could rent that same room in Anita's house and not be a burden to anyone.

Finally Neela was summoned. The living room fell silent as she entered and all eyes turned towards her. Holding the wall behind her for support, she took a deep breath. Although her eyes were downcast, she was perfectly aware of every one of the family members seated on those velvety peach sofas. It was like entering a courtroom with herself in the role of criminal.

Suraj broke the silence, stating without any kind of preamble:

'Neela, we have decided that you should go back to India. We have discussed the matter with your parents and they have agreed. Your ticket is booked. You need to get ready for a flight this Saturday morning.'

Her inner voice screamed in frustration. She was desperate to tell them what she had decided for herself. She lifted her head slightly. It was the first time she had looked at any of them since Ajay's death. The expressions on their faces, like the voices she had heard during the past month, were full of dislike and loathing. A month ago she would have gone to India happily but she felt differently now and was determined not to succumb to their orders.

It took a while for her to summon the courage to speak out. Ignoring her pounding heart, she lifted her chin, cleared her throat, and took a deep breath. Looking directly at her mother-in-law, slowly, in a small but firm voice, she said, 'I am sorry but I don't want to go.'

The room again fell silent.

'What? You don't want to go back?' Durga-devi and Suraj said together.

'But what can you do here?'

'Where will you stay?'

'Don't you know that Ajay is no more?'

'Have you gone mad?'

There was a pause as their puzzled faces sought one another for answers. Then she heard the hissing again.

'You can't stay here.'

'You have to go . . .'

Chapter 13

'Yes, you must go . . . go.'

The jumbled voices rattled in her ears.

It had taken so much courage and strength to do what she had just done, and now she had to struggle again to cope with their rejection. The humiliation was so great that she wished she was dead instead of Ajay. There in front of her were Ajay's people. In the midst of everyone, men and women, young and old, she, Ajay's new bride, widowed in less than twelve months, stood alone and helpless, yet not even the women seemed to understand her anguish and pain. Not one person had a kind word to say. For the first time since she had come to Britain, she felt more angry than sorry. She wanted to ask them why they were treating her like an enemy and what exactly was her crime?

She held back the tears and reminded herself that she had to take charge of her own life. Suppressing her fear, she looked at her mother-in-law and said, 'I want to continue my work at the sewing factory and live in Anita's house as before.'

Once more there was a stunned silence. Neela saw Durga-devi get to her feet, seething with anger. Her face burned and her finger wagged.

'Are you not ashamed?' she thundered. 'How can you say that you will live in that same room? Don't you have any feelings for my son, your own husband?' Her lips curved, and she sneered. 'Have you no shame? You can't do that. You are a widow. Remember you are a widow.' She shouted and stopped to look at everyone for support. She waved her hands and raised her voice still further. 'Don't you dare spoil my family name . . . you . . . shameless girl! How do you think I would be able to hold my head up in my community?'

'Now Ajay has gone, she is free, isn't she!' Suraj said with a sarcastic laugh.

'Since she started that work, she thinks she can do anything she wants. It has gone to her head,' Yamini shouted.

'She doesn't give a damn about your family or your family name

Maa !' Suraj said. 'I haven't got any more time to waste,' He looked at his wristwatch. 'Don't be silly and childish! Go and pack your bags.'

Determined not to be defeated, and ignoring Suraj, Neela looked straight into Durga-devi's eyes and said, 'In that case I will stay here with you.'

'With me . . .?' Durga-devi screamed. 'What are you saying, girl?' She looked round at everyone in the room and said, 'Did you hear that?'

'Yes, Ma-ji, I mean it,' Neela said, without taking her eyes from the old woman. 'You are the one who got me married to your son and I came here as your daughter-in-law. Since my husband . . . your son . . . is no more, am I not your responsibility? Is it not my right to live with you? How can I go back to my parents? They have already given me to your family and since I am carrying your family name, am I not a member of your family?'

Durga-devi and Suraj were speechless.

A few moments later Durga-devi started weeping. 'The worm has turned into a snake! *Hai-Ram!*' She placed her hands over her head. 'Oh, why did you put this burden on me, son? I am already dependent on my only remaining son, Suraj. Does she think there are piles of treasure stored away somewhere? Oh, God, help me!'

'Then accept what I have asked for.' Neela said her head high. 'Instead of being a financial burden to you, I will go back to work and be independent.'

''On one condition,' Yamini said unexpectedly. 'As Ma-ji said, you can't live with Anita and ruin our family's reputation but I suggest that we allow you to go back to work.'

What motive had made Yamini change her mind Neela did not know, but she was immensely grateful for her intervention.

'Yamini-*behn*, I agree to your conditions.'

And before anything else could be said, Neela ran out of the room.

CHAPTER 14

And so Neela slipped back into her old routine of doing the house work, cooking and colouring Durga-devi's hair every Thursday. Her old room looked the same with its Bugs Bunny sheets and curtains. She thanked Mr Rusheed silently for his kindness. Even without her asking he had kept her job for her. Neela didn't even mind having to get up at four in the morning to finish all the household chores before catching the train for the hour's journey to work. Her job was vital for her sanity.

Many weeks went by before Neela managed to phone Antia.

'Oh! Neela, how are you?' Anita sounded so anxious. 'It's been such a long time . . . *puglee*?' There was affection in her soft voice and she always called Neela *puglee* when she was concerned.

'I am fine, thanks, Anita-*behn*.'

'I have been worrying about you; I tried to phone you but . . . they . . . you know . . .'

'I understand Anita-*behn*. They don't like me talking to you.'

'Anyway, I am glad that you phoned at last. Is everything all right?'

'Not bad, Anita-*behn*,' Neela replied. 'Did you know they tried to send me back to India?'

'No! Really?'

'Even my tickets were booked.'

'And then what happened?'

'I told them that I wouldn't go . . .' she narrated the whole drama.

'Wow, congratulations! At last you have spoken up, and stood up for yourself.'

'It was you, Anita-*behn*, who inspired me to stick to my decision despite them all shouting at me,' Neela replied. 'And I can't express my appreciation in words . . .'

'Don't be silly. You have done it all on your own. I am proud of you and you should be too.' Anita cleared her throat, suppressing emotion. 'I was wondering how you would ever convince them to let you go back to work.'

'It was difficult, but my salary lured Yamini,' Neela laughed. 'I am so grateful to Rusheed-*bhayya* for taking me back.'

'That's good. Why don't you come over? It's been a long time.'

'I would love to, Anita-*behn*, but..' she hesitated.

They both knew that Anita wasn't allowed to see Neela.

'Are you still there?' Anita asked, understanding her silence.

'Yes I am.' Neela drew a deep breath and said, 'I am an outsider in this family and in this house, Anita-*behn*.'

'But you are paying rent so it's yours too.'

'My mere presence causes so much tension. I am scared even to breathe freely.'

'Don't be, Neela. Recent events have shocked you so much and it will take time for you to get over it. I am sure you will feel better soon.'

'Thank you, Anita-*behn*.' She paused for a moment. 'I have an idea. Can I come and see you tomorrow afternoon? If it's OK with you.'

'Certainly, my dear, but how will you . . . '

'I will ask Mr Rusheed to give me the afternoon off. I am sure he won't mind if I offer to make up the time later.'

'Please do that. It will be a pleasure to see you.'

It had only been eight weeks, but it felt like a lifetime since Neela had walked along those familiar narrow lanes from the station to Anita's house. The main road was busy and noisy as always with grocery and sari shops blaring out Indian film songs. She inhaled the delicious aroma from *The Taj, Taste of India* and *Chai-wala* restaurants. And as she turned into Princes Road, a group of children who were playing on the uneven pavements turned to greet her. She smiled at them and felt at home. Everything was exactly as she remembered it. How she missed this place. She stopped at the corner shop, looked in her purse, and counted her coins. There was just enough to buy a small box of chocolates for her friend. Since she had to hand over most of her monthly wages to Yamini, she was left with almost nothing for herself.

'How could you let them do that? They are personal letters. They have no right to read them,' Anita said with a frown, placing a tray of tea and *samosas* on the coffee table.

'My parents wouldn't write anything but praise for my in-laws.'

'For what?'

'For keeping me and looking after me. They always tell me to be grateful and obedient to my in-laws. Anyway . . . what have I got to hide from them?'

The look on Anita's face made Neela laugh. 'Don't worry, I always paint a good picture of them in my letters. You know I have to do this. I am sorry for burdening you with all this. Where would I be without you, Anita-*behn*?'

'You would be where you are now,' Anita laughed. 'Serving your dear old in-laws.'

'Do you know how much I love you?' Neela took Anita's hand in hers.

'Oi, oi, stop that,' Anita screamed, snatching her hand away. 'People will think we are a couple of weirdoes. Don't waste your sweet words on me, save them for that special someone in your future,' Anita teased.

'What!' Neela's face fell.

'I am sorry if I shocked you, but I am not joking. Even in India divorces and re-marriages are happening. It's only your in-laws who seem to be living in the last century. Why do you want to waste the rest of your life as Ajay's widow when he didn't even love you?'

Neela felt hot and uncomfortable; her mouth tasted bitter.

An uneasy silence danced between them for a moment. But Anita broke the tension with a love song which she sang tunelessly, making Neela laugh.

'Your song reminds me of our *Anarkali* and *Saleem*.'

'Oh, yes, looks like *Anarkali* is pregnant now.'

'Is she? That's nice,'

And so the rest of the afternoon continued easily, giving Neela the chance to talk about nothing and to laugh for the first time since Ajay had died.

That night Neela recalled Anita's words and felt uneasy. 'Someone special for the future.' Aware that she had been living in the past and simply reacting to the present, it had not occurred to her to give any thought to her future. She was afraid and had no idea what was in store. She expected that becoming a widow would be distressing and would turn her life upside down for ever, but she knew now that it wasn't how she had imagined it.

Despite what tradition dictated, Neela was aware that the loss of a husband had not upset her until one particular morning when she came face to face with Rakesh on the landing.

'Good morning. You're up early.'

'My God, no!' He screamed and covered his eyes with his hands and shouted, 'Mum! Mum!'

'What is it, son?' Yamini came running.

'Why does she do this to me?' the boy cried. 'Always showing her face first thing in the morning?'

'Don't you know his exams are starting today?' Yamini shouted, before turning to her son. 'Don't worry, darling. Go and pray to God and everything will be fine.'

As the boy ran downstairs to the prayer room, Yamini banged her door shut. Neela stood speechless on the landing.

Every morning on her way to work on the tube, Neela observed the commuters who thronged around her – the squabbling school children, the immaculately-dressed professional men and women, the factory workers in their casual clothes, and others still in their work uniforms. Some hid their faces behind newspapers, journals and books, while others stared out of the window, or discreetly peered at the reflections of faces in the carriage windows, deliberately avoiding eye contact. One morning she noticed a man in the seat across from her. He wore dirty ripped jeans and his greying beard and unruly hair covered his rugged features. He was smoking and swigging beer from a can. His red-rimmed eyes were half closed and she knew that in a minute he would snore like a lorry. That makes two of us, Neela thought. The ugly ones. The misfits. One drunk and one totally insane.

The sewing factory became her home. Everyone there had a story to tell, some amusing, some happy and some sad, but all with their share of hardships. She loved the women's energy and their ability to laugh at themselves. As Christmas approached, the workload doubled as it always did at that time of year, and all of them were rushed off their feet to get the orders completed for the deadline. Mr Rusheed urged everyone to put in extra hours in the evening and most people agreed. Neela was definitely tempted, but knew she would not be allowed – until her work mates urged her on. When she made the phone call, Yamini answered.

'It's up to you. Ma-ji is not at home.' she said, after a surprised pause. 'I don't know what she would say.'

'Could you please let her know that I need to stay to complete some urgent orders,' Neela informed her.

It was done. Mr Rusheed ordered a take-away for everyone along with a huge box of *Laddoos*. The old portable stereo shrieked Hindi film songs and almost everyone sang along and moved their hips and heads with the music. When Mr Rusheed was out of sight, young Raj took hold of Vimla's hand. She was old enough to be his grandmother but he twirled her round, singing, '*Roop thera mastana,* You are so beautiful. *Pyar mera divana,* I am going mad with love.' And Vimla scolded him, pretending to be annoyed. Neela felt the excitement and joined in the fun, while her hands worked away, fast and efficient.

By the time they had finished the work it was nearing midnight. Mr Rusheed arranged transport home for everyone and Neela arrived back dizzy with happiness and exhaustion. She let herself in quietly so as not to disturb the sleeping household. She wanted to hug her happiness to herself, to remember the pleasure the evening had given her. Perhaps there would be other evenings like that, whole days, even the rest of her life, who knows? Hope spread like a path of flowers before her as she closed the front door behind her and turned to go upstairs to bed.

The living room door opened and Durga-devi appeared. Neela stopped in her tracks, her foot already on the bottom step.

'I am sorry, Ma-ji, if I disturbed you,' she said quietly.

'What are you doing here, you whore!' Durga-devi had been waiting for Neela to come back and fall straight into her trap.

'I have been at work,'

'Why bother to come home? That Muslim boss of yours . . .' Durga-devi hissed. 'Have you no shame, you hussy? You are his kept woman, aren't you? I knew it.'

'No!' Neela was appalled. How could her mother-in-law even think such a terrible thing?

'You have brought shame to my family's name. *Hai-Ram!* I know you won't rest until you destroy the whole of my clan like you destroyed my son.'

'You are accusing me wrongfully,' Neela flung back.

'What have I done that God sends me this slut with an ill-fated horoscope which destined her to be a widow? Oh God, what do you want me to do with her?'

Neela watched as her mother-in-law beat her chest with her fists, wailing loudly. Woken up by the commotion, the family gathered on the landing and stared down. Neela again felt like a criminal.

'If you want, I will leave your house in the morning,' Neela said steadily.

'And go where?' Durga-devi shouted.

Where she would go, Neela had no idea, but she was surprised at her own bluntness.

'Where else but to her lover boss's house,' Yamini answered for her.

The next morning Neela faced a bombardment of accusations as she got ready for work.

'If you go back to work against my wishes, you will have to leave home.'

'And you are not going anywhere but to India.'

'That too, and with shame hanging over your head.'

'But how can I pay for my maintenance without working?' Neela asked in a small voice.

'Huh! As if you are paying us thousands. Don't worry, you are just a charity for us,' Yamini sneered.

'Jesus! She brings trouble after trouble,' Suraj said with a shake of his head. He took a last sip of coffee before saying to his wife, 'From tomorrow, send her to the shop. She can get on with the cleaning there.'

'But at least I have to inform Mr Rusheed that I am leaving.' Neela said in alarm at this new suggestion.

'Don't worry, I have saved you the task. I've already spoken to him. I gave him a piece of my mind and he didn't dare answer back.'

A sparkling white Christmas came and went but Neela hardly noticed it

CHAPTER 15

The days passed painfully slowly for Neela. She hated the house, she despised the people in it, and now she loathed the shop too. One morning, as she lay contemplating her future, she was disturbed by someone banging on her bedroom door.

'Come on, get up! Don't sleep like a lazy donkey. It's already seven o clock. Who do you think will do all the work? The tooth fairy?'

She covered her ears and forced open her burning eyes. Her head was heavy with pain and her throat hurt like the pricking of a thousand needles. Eventually she forced herself out of bed and somehow managed to cook breakfast for the family.

'Neela,' called Yamini from her bedroom, 'go and post these letters and make sure you weigh them properly and stick the right stamps on them.'

Neela took the letters, but when she opened the front door she was almost knocked over by a great gust of wind. 'Yamini-*behn*, it's snowing,' she called.

'So what? Put your coat and scarf on. It won't kill you.'

The snow was falling heavily, covering everything. The scene was spectacular, like one of those paintings that hung in the living room. It had snowed last winter, but this was something so magical that it looked like another world. Her teeth chattered and she shivered as she pulled her scarf around her neck. On any other day she would have been happy to run out and be covered with those feathery flakes but today not only her heart but her whole body ached with fever. She stopped and held onto the gate for a moment. Her shoes just couldn't cope with the snow. They soaked up all the damp through their soles and wouldn't grip the pavement. She had to hold onto a wall, gate or a pole to support her from falling as she walked on.

At last she reached the post office, stood in the queue, and posted the letters. She came out and waited to cross the road, standing at the edge of the pavement for the traffic to clear. The dark clouds parted revealing the bright sun and releasing streaks of light which hit the silvery, dazzling snow. The glare of the brilliant white blinded her and the world began to spin. Knowing that she was losing control, she moved sideways to hold onto the lamp-post for support but she slipped on the hard ice and blacked out.

'Come on, dear, wake up. You are going to be all right.' A nurse was smiling at her, and after glancing round, Neela understood where she was. 'You slipped and passed out on the road, dear, but luckily the car that was coming stopped in time and someone called an ambulance.'

It was strangely peaceful in the hospital that afternoon, and Neela relished the few hours of freedom from her prison. Here too was an opportunity to think. She also seized her chance, asked the nurse if she could use the phone, and dialled Anita's number.

'Anita-*behn*, I can't live this horrible life any more. I just want to die,' Neela blurted, her emotions freed from behind the dam of silence.

'Shush, Neela, calm down and tell me what has happened and where you are.'

Neela explained through her sobs.

'You should get out of that house now.' Anita said calmly and firmly.

'But how?'

'What about going back to your job at the sewing factory? I am sure Rusheed-*bhayya* would find something for you.'

Neela gasped. 'After all that drama, Anita-*behn*? Durga-devi and Suraj accused him, insulted him, and threatened him. I am so ashamed,

Anita-*behn*, how can I go back and ask him for another favour as if I haven't caused him enough trouble already?'

'Yes, I understand,' said Anita, 'But you have to find a job no matter what. Get yourself out of that hospital bed and go down to the job centre.'

'Yes, Anita-*behn*,' Neela said meekly.

The next time the nurse came round with a thermometer, Neela plucked up the courage to say in her broken English, 'Me no job. Work want. I no English.'

The nurse smiled at her. 'I am sorry but I don't understand what you are saying. Just give me a minute and I will call the interpreter.'

Neela sighed. She couldn't even communicate with the locals. The doctor who had seen her that morning was a south Indian but they couldn't understand each other either. He tried his best to talk to her in broken Hindi mixed with English. What she couldn't understand properly was the British accent and however hard she tried, her limited English vocabulary emerged as Hindi.

The interpreter though, could understand her, and was kind enough for Neela to have the confidence to tell her the truth.

'I just don't want to be a burden to them. I don't mind what kind of work I do, housework, looking after children, or cleaning . . . anything.' Neela noticed that the interpreter looked concerned and added, 'I am sorry to burden you with all this.'

'No, no, not at all. It's fine. I understand,' said the woman, touching Neela's shoulders lightly.

'I don't know how to find a job.'

'It's not easy. You have to have training to be a child-minder, but try not to worry too much. Give me your phone number and I will call you if anything comes up.'

'*Shukriya, behn*, I would be so grateful to you,' Neela said, giving Anita's phone number to the lady. She prayed to be ill a little longer but the doctor discharged her that evening.

On Yamini's insistence, Suraj gave Neela the afternoon off. No one was at home except Durga-devi who was having a nap in her room. Grateful for the blessed peace, Neela sat in her room, carefully stitching the hem of a pure silk purple sari for Yamini. The contrasting border of tiny flowers and leaves shimmered in golden thread. The silky softness of the fabric slipped through her fingers, making her task difficult. She pictured Yamini in the sari with her fair complexion and slim, curvy figure. How would it feel to wear such a beautiful garment? Neela couldn't resist draping it around her shoulders and walked across to the mirror. Her reflection shocked her. It wasn't just the married symbol of red *bindi*, but her face looked painfully empty and lifeless. The sparkle in her eyes was gone and in its place a blank stare. Her once soft lips were dry and cracked and she had forgotten how to smile. The purple silk didn't suit her. No, she corrected herself, she didn't suit the sari. She shut her eyes, unable to look. Her tears spilled on the silk, marking it with the ugliness of sorrow. She pulled off the purple fabric and dressed herself again in her faded cotton sari that matched her lost charms.

The phone rang, releasing Neela from her thoughts. Hearing Anita's voice she thanked her lucky stars that for once she was alone in the house.

'What a surprise! You answered the phone!' laughed Anita. 'Listen, remember you asked that Interpreter lady about work, well, she phoned me this morning and asked whether you are still interested?'

'Yes, of course!' Neela's heart leapt.

'Good, now don't you dare say no! Now listen, a recently widowed doctor has been left with two small children and needs some help. So basically your job will be to look after the children and do the housework.'

'Oh, that would be wonderful!'

'So?'

Neela went quiet for a moment.

'So, what do you say?' Anita repeated.

118

'I will take it . . . definitely but . . . I am just thinking . . . what if . . .'

'No *whats* and no *ifs* . . . you are just going to tell them that it is your decision and that's what you want. OK?'

'OK . . .' said Neela.

'Good girl! I wish you luck.'

However much she rehearsed her words and told herself to be brave and bold, when the time came it was very difficult. Eventually she broke the news at the dinner table.

'What?' A piece of chapatti dropped from Durga-devi's mouth.

Suraj's eyebrows went up and his hand froze on the spoon in the rice bowl.

Yamini rolled her eyes in a 'here-we-go-again' manner.

Even the children looked at each other in surprise as if they were hearing something beyond their imagination.

Then the cyclone hit.

'You are not going anywhere to work, even if Her Majesty the Queen asks you. Who do you think you are? A *mem-sahib*?' Durga-devi wagged her finger. Her eyes bulged, reminding Neela of Ajay. 'You think you can do whatever your dumb brain takes a fancy to?' she barked, waving her hands in the air.

'She thinks she is someone special, a right little madam,' Yamini said, spooning aubergine curry onto her plate.

'She seems to have forgotten how much shame she had already brought us,' Suraj said to his wife, throwing the spoon angrily into a pot of cucumber *raita* and making a mess on the cloth.

'*Hai-Ram*, she is bringing one trouble after another,' Durga-devi clucked. 'I can't even go to the temple without someone enquiring about the little witch. *Hai-Ram*! I can't take any more, Suraj, *beta*, and I might as well follow your father's example and run away from it all. What can we do with her?' She tapped her fingers on her forehead.

Apart from the noise of cutlery there was a deathly silence until

Suraj's deep voice rang out. 'If you step out of this house, that's it, you are out.' He stood up, pushing his chair back. 'And for good. Is that understood?'

Neela stood her ground while Suraj left the room and then faced her mother-in-law. 'Ma-ji, I really need to work and I am prepared to leave this house if you wish.' She was surprised at how steady her voice was.

The two fuming women seated at the table looked at each other in disbelief. Durga-devi got up and wobbled after Suraj, and then Yamini followed her.

Neela remained in the dining room, alone with her thoughts. The living room doors were closed but she knew that behind them the debate would go on amongst the trio late into night. Although Neela had made up her mind to take the job, and had said that she would leave the house, she had no idea where she would go. Anita had rented her room out to another lodger so that was no longer an option.

By the following morning, Yamini had successfully won round not only her husband but also her mother-in-law, and brought through the verdict.

'I supported your cause and we are kindly agreeing that you can stay here but on one condition – same as before – you have to pay for your keep.'

Neela nodded in agreement thinking that at least one problem had been solved for now and the rest could wait.

On the following Monday morning, Neela raced through her household chores and left to catch the eight o' clock bus. Warm sunshine streamed through the clouds, and made the previous night's dew glisten on the flowers and delicate buds. She tucked a strand of hair, loosened by the breeze, behind her ear, and wondered how other women kept their hair in place.

The bus stopped at the sixth stop and the lady next to her confirmed that this was where she should get out.

CHAPTER 16

The hospital building stood, solid with age, surrounded by green lawns inside a tall iron fence. Neela walked through the open gates with all the other visitors and out-patients. On the pathway she tried to interpret the signpost. Carefully separating the syllables she read: Ca..su..al..ty; Ur..ol..ogy; Gy..na..eco.. lo..gy; and Ch..est..nut.. wa..rd. But there were no signs for the doctors' residences. Bemused, she scanned the place until a man mowing the lawn at the side of the building caught her eye. He looked friendly enough to approach.

'Please, doctor house where?'

The gardener looked up and switched his roaring machine off so that they could hear each other. Shading the sun with one hand, and trying to straighten his back, he said, 'What can I do for you, love?'

She repeated the question, handing him a piece of paper with the doctor's address.

'The residences are at the back of the building, love. Go straight from here and turn right and you will see them.'

She thanked him and followed his instructions. The doctors' quarters were situated at the back of the hospital in a straight line at the end of the lawn. She searched for the white door with the number 28. Heart racing, she rang the bell.

The door opened within a few seconds and a man, who looked to be in his forties, stared at her with a mystified expression before it dawned on him who she was.

'Mrs Neela Pattwar?'

'Yes.'

'Please come in.' He opened the door wider.

Neela followed him into the lounge, wondering where the doctor was.

'Please sit down, sorry about the mess.' He started to pick up some of the children's books and colouring pens, and some washed clothes off the sofa to make room for her to sit down.

'Oh, sorry, I haven't introduced myself. I am Dr Vikas.' He stretched out his hand.

Hiding her surprise and wondering how a doctor could look this untidy, she said, '*Namaste*,' bringing her hands together.

Perhaps he remembered that some Indian women do not shake hands with a man, because he dropped his hand and said *Namaste* instead. He looked tired as though he hadn't slept for weeks. Of course . . . he had just been through a tragedy and was probably taking his wife's death very badly. She looked at him with sympathy.

'I just made myself some tea. Would you like some?'

'No thank you, sir,' Neela said nervously in Hindi, wiping her sweaty hands on her sari *pallu*.

When he emerged from the kitchen he was holding out a glass of orange juice and said, 'I hope you might like something cool.'

'Sorry sir, me, no good English,' Neela explained.

'Don't worry, Mrs Pattwar, your English is much better than my Hindi,' he replied, smiling kindly. And so they continued, his broken Hindi mixed with her broken English.

'You see, Mrs Pattwar,' he said, as he sat down on a chair near the window, 'my children are still quite young and in need of someone to look after them. My job doesn't spare me much time for that. As you know, most Indian men are quite useless at looking after children.' He laughed awkwardly as he gestured at the messy room and added, 'Or coping with the house on their own.'

Neela gave him an encouraging smile.

'Let me explain what I would like you to do. My children will need your help getting ready for school and . . . they are very fussy eaters . . . so it might take quite a while to feed them. And I will be grateful to you if you could be here when they come home from school. Once I come home from work you can leave.'

'Certainly, sir.'

'Thank you, Mrs Pattwar,' he said. 'Those are the main priorities and we would also appreciate it if you could do the usual housework and sometimes cook the evening meals. I hope that's not too much for you.'

'Oh, no, no, sir, I will try my best to look after your children, sir. And I don't mind the housework or the cooking, sir.'

'Thank you, Mrs Pattwar. And the other thing is, whenever I am on call, I might be home very late. Do you mind staying longer on those days?'

Neela didn't hesitate, even though she was aware of how her household would react.

'Of course we are desperately in need of somebody like you, but I do understand if you have other commitments.'

'No, no, sir,' she said hurriedly. She was determined to get this job no matter what. 'I don't have any commitments, sir. I will manage, sir.'

'Thank you very much, Mrs Pattwar. I am grateful.'

'Thank YOU, sir.'

Pleased with Neela's willingness, Dr Vikas then called upstairs to his children who were still asleep.

'Come on, Rahul and Pallavi, wake up! It's already eight thirty.'

He turned to Neela. 'They should be ready by now,' he said with a wry smile. 'You see, Mrs Pattwar, how disorganised we are!'

While he excused himself and went upstairs to wake the children, Neela took a look round the room, her eyes lingering over the photograph on the mantelpiece of a pretty woman who was probably his wife . . . his dead wife.

'These are my children.' The doctor was back, bringing two sleepy children with him. Seven year old Rahul and five year old Pallavi greeted her shyly.

'Hello, you can call me Neela.' She smiled and they smiled back.

'Neela will be looking after you from now on,' said Dr Vikas, sitting on the sofa with one child on each side of him. 'So you have to be good and listen to her, OK?'

They smiled at her again.

After sending the children upstairs to get ready, he said to Neela, 'Your friend Anita discussed wages with me but . . .,' he stopped and looked at her, 'I am just wondering whether what we agreed is all right with you.'

Neela felt awkward discussing money. 'It's fine sir . . . whatever . . . I mean, it is up to you, sir, I don't mind . . .'

'Well, this is the advance, Mrs Pattwar. A month's salary,' Dr Vikas said, handing her a sealed envelope.

'You are already paying me, sir?' Neela's eyes opened wide and her hand shook.

He laughed heartily this time.

Neela felt elated throughout the bus journey home. Thinking about her job at Dr Vikas's lifted her spirits. The doctor's gentleness and polite manners had surprised her and she hadn't felt at all like a maid in front of a master. She already warmed to the children and was amazed at how different they were from Yamini's two.

She started work the very next day. This time the children were up by the time she reached Dr Vikas's house. Rahul, the eldest, didn't need much help but Pallavi wanted Neela around for everything. After giving them breakfast, Neela packed their lunch boxes with sandwiches, fruit and a carton of juice and brought them down ready for school. Pallavi with her golden complexion, big eyes and dark ringlets looked as pretty as a doll. And Rahul, though a little darker than his sister, had sparkling eyes and looked very much like his father.

'Beautiful children. They are nice too,' she couldn't help saying to Dr Vikas.

'Thank you,' he flashed a smile, but it quickly faded. 'Come on, children, we are already late,' he said abruptly, guiding them out of the front door.

Neela went to the window and watched them climb into the car. Despite his sorrow Dr Vikas looked smart and dignified. What a beautiful family, she thought, yet it looked incomplete, imperfect, without the pretty woman in the picture.

CHAPTER 17

Instead of being preoccupied with her own life, Neela's thoughts increasingly turned to the new family that she worked for. When she had first cleaned the children's room, she had seen a second portrait of the woman in the photograph downstairs. She was hugging the children and smiling at them with eyes full of love. Neela took the picture down and wiped off the dust. She stood there staring at it before replacing it. The happy faces smiling at her through the sparkling glass tugged at her heart.

Her job was to clean the whole house except for Dr Vikas's room. She had been instructed not to go in there. Neela finished the cooking and saw that the clock showed three in the afternoon. She decided to stay until the children came home from school and settled into a chair near the window, noting how quiet the place was. The only sounds came from the birds in the garden. She looked through the window and saw sparrows searching for food in the lawn and naughty squirrels running around and jumping in and out of the plant pots. Much to the gardener's annoyance, and Neela's amusement, the squirrels dug up every newly planted bulb. They looked so cute carrying them away to their secret places.

When the taxi pulled up in front of the house, Neela went to open the door. She watched the driver help Rahul and Pallavi clamber out with their school bags and lunch boxes. When they caught sight of Neela, the children slowed their run to a walk and shyly returned her smile. She took their bags and helped them remove their shoes. Remembering the doctor's instructions, she beckoned them to follow her upstairs.

'Clothes . . . change,' Neela said, and her heart went out to them when they obeyed her.

Poor children, she thought, how they must be missing their mother. It was scarcely six months since they had lost her. How fresh and raw their grief must be.

'You all right?' Neela asked, looking at Pallavi who was staring at her with wide eyes and a thumb in her mouth.

Rahul put his arm around his sister protectively and Pallavi clung to him sobbing.

The sight tugged at Neela's heart. She could only guess at the anguish they must be feeling.

'Come here,' she said, longing to comfort them, and stretched out both her arms. But the children didn't move. Instead Rahul glanced at the portrait of his mother on the window sill. Neela knew that he understood that his mother would not be coming back but she wasn't sure about Pallavi who was only five.

'Please, no cry.' she stepped forward to wipe the little girl's tears.

'It's all right,' Rahul said, using his shirt to wipe his sister's tears.

As one child took care of the other, Neela thought about how quickly they would grow up after coping with such tragedy.

'What would you like to have for tea?' she asked in Hindi, forgetting for a moment that they couldn't understand. 'Sorry . . . I no remember . . . you Hindi no understand,' she laughed awkwardly. 'You . . . what . . . eat . . . your . . . tea?' She made signs with her hands.

Her broken English with its Indian accent broke the ice. Their drawn faces lit up with smiles.

'You don't say it like that . . . you should say . . .' Rahul corrected her.

But the lighter mood only lasted a few seconds.

'I don't want any, thank you.' Rahul said.

'Why . . . you . . . no . . . hungry?'

They both went quiet for a while and stared at her.

'Your Dad say, I give tea and you eat.'

This time they both looked at each other.

'I want Daddy . . .' Pallavi began.

'He will come soon,' Neela said, kneeling down in front of them. 'You something eat and your daddy happy.'

'OK then.' they both said at once.

'Can I watch the television please?' Pallavi requested.

'Of course,' said Neela, taking her into her arms. She was once more surprised by their good manners.

'Do you like cartoons?' Pallavi enquired.

'Oh, very . . . like.'

She cut some fruit and placed some biscuits and crisps on a plate and took the tray into the living room. 'Ok, eat . . . you, and I milk . . . shake . . . make.'

'Thank you,' they both said in unison.

She was amazed at the way they said 'please' and 'thank you'. She had yet to hear Yamini's children use those words

'Aunty Neela, would you like to watch Tom and Jerry with us?' Pallavi asked. 'It's very funny.'

'Aunty?' Neela murmured.

'That's bad, Pallavi. Remember what Daddy said? You have to ask their permission first. Some ladies don't like to be called Aunties.' Rahul was playing the big brother. 'Mostly we call all Indian women *aunty*, except Bindu *akka*, because she says she is too young to be called aunty. We can call you '*akka*' if you like,' he said.

'*Akka*?' asked Neela.

'"*Akka*" means "big sister"'.

'Oh . . . No *akka*,' she replied after some thought. 'Aunty . . . good . . . please . . . I . . . happy,' Neela said, moved by their kindness.

'OK, Aunty Neela,' the children said in chorus.

'Thank you, thank you very much.' And she gave them a hug.

Watching cartoons and laughing with them was a wonderful new experience, and later the children played games in the garden while Neela sat on a bench and admired their energy.

When they spotted their father, the children immediately threw down the bikes that they were riding up and down the garden and ran to him, calling, 'Daddy! Daddy!' Neela stood up hastily.

'Hello, my little angels, how are you?' He stretched out both his arms and embraced them, laughing. Sitting the children down on either side of him on the bench, he asked if they had been good.

'We had a lot of fun today, Dad. Aunty Neela made us nice sandwiches and milk shakes. And we watched cartoons. And she played games with us.'

'Oh, really?' Dr Vikas smiled at Neela. 'Thank you very much, Mrs Pattwar, for looking after them. They seem to have taken to you.'

'Thank you, sir,' she replied, not used to being praised.

Even though he was attentively listening and responding to his children, Neela could see that Dr Vikas was very tired. She deliberated before asking him if he would like some tea or coffee.

'Please,' he replied, pulling up a chair and gesturing for her to sit down too.

'How are you? It must have been a very long day for you.'

'I am fine, sir,' she replied, sitting down on the very edge of the chair.

'Looking after kids is a tough job. I hope they didn't give you too much trouble.'

'No, they are very nice children, sir. I have enjoyed looking after them.'

'Thank you very much for your help, Mrs Pattwar. The house looks tidy, after . . . after . . . quite a long time.' Neela heard the catch in his voice and stared at her finger nails, not knowing what to say.

'OK, it's getting late so I will drop you home,' he said looking at his watch.

'It's fine, sir. I will go by bus,' she insisted.

'See you tomorrow, Aunty.' the children called as she waved them goodbye.

Neela felt fulfilled that day. She already adored the family and thanked God and the interpreter and Anita for finding her this job. Even the thought of going home didn't depress her and she felt she had more strength to face the in-laws even though the housework and the usual spiteful comments awaited her.

The following morning, Neela woke early. She was looking forward to the day ahead and, after finishing her tasks, rushed towards the front door, but Durga-devi emerged from the lounge, blocking her path. Slowing down to a walking pace, she said, 'Bye, Ma-ji.'

Durga-devi just nodded. Her face didn't crease with her usual disapproval. What was going on?

'The doctor paid you a very substantial sum, didn't he? Good man! Keep him happy.'

Neela stopped in her tracks. How did she know about the pay? Instinctively she looked in her bag and saw that the envelope containing the money was gone. She retraced her steps and remembered that in her haste, the night before, she had left the bag on the hook in the hallway, where she had hung her coat and gone straight into the kitchen. She couldn't believe that her mother-in-law had searched her bag, and she knew that even if she asked about the money, she would never get it back. Feeling bitter and cheated, Neela went out, furiously banging the front door behind her.

The minute she arrived at the doctor's house she felt better. Even though the family was mourning their great loss, the atmosphere in the house was warm and loving. She contemplated the way people's natures coloured their surroundings. Her time in those surroundings always passed quickly and gave her the strength and energy to face the long miserable weekends at home. She would have loved to work weekends as well but Dr Vikas wanted to spend as much time as possible alone with his children. Though most of the time he hid his sorrow, she could sometimes see very clearly how painfully lonely Dr Vikas was. Why had God or Fate done this to him? Neela sighed, remembering an Indian woman who once said, 'God tests the good by making them suffer.' But why?

CHAPTER 18

The sun shone all day, drenching the world in a golden glow On her way home from the bus stop, Neela noticed how slowly the sun set here. She saw the tall poplar trees swaying and she heard the jingling music of their leaves. A pleasant breeze brushed her body, reminding her of those magical evenings at the River Manjeera in India when she would build dream palaces in her future, and watch the reflections of floating clouds go by as she counted the silver ripples in the flowing river. The memory didn't make her sad like before but rather enchanted her. It was refreshing spending time with the doctor's children. The suffocating veil of darkness was slowly lifting and at last she was able to see some pale rays of hope.

A few weeks ago Rahul had asked her why she hadn't learned English when she was at school.

'I really love the stories you tell us but I wish you could tell them in proper English,' Pallavi had remarked after listening to one of Neela's stories about a wise monkey and a selfish crocodile.

Neela scooped up the little girl, laughing. 'Sorry, I . . . no . . . learn, my . . . village school . . . no . . . learn . . . English But . . . I . . . A, B, C, D read, write.'

'Oh, that's great. Then don't worry, you can learn it now,' Rahul suggested.

'How? I, big now, and learn difficult.'

'It doesn't matter if you are big. We will teach you.'

'You, me, teach?' Neela's eyes widened with astonishment at their generous offer.

'Yes!'

'Real?' She put her hand over her heart.

'Yes, really!' they both shouted.

'Thank you, thank you.'

Neela gave them both a big hug.

So the 'school game' started. They lent her some of their books, pens and papers and became her teachers. Neela was a willing student and it was fun for the children.

The three of them laughed at her mistakes, and whenever she learned something new, the children would reward her with praise or a kiss. The exhilaration at her success lasted until she reached home, and even for some time afterwards. She was learning slowly, but there was definite progress. Even Dr Vikas noticed it and started leaving the shopping list for her in English instead of in Hindi. Neela smiled to herself, remembering how much she had yearned to learn like that in India, all those years ago, when reluctantly she had had to leave school.

It was on a Friday evening and she was about to leave when Dr Vikas called her back, saying, 'I am sorry, I almost forgot to tell you that your mother-in-law rang me last night and told me that you need some extra money to send to your parents but you were too embarrassed to ask me.' He looked at her. 'Please don't be.' He handed her a sealed envelope.

Neela was speechless, but he smiled again. 'And please feel free to ask me in the future,' he said.

Clutching the envelope, Neela walked to the bus stop feeling utterly ashamed. As she waited for the bus her body shook with anger towards Durg-devi. She couldn't believe the audacity of the woman, taking advantage of the doctor's good nature, and even involving her parents.

Boiling inside, she wasn't afraid to confront her mother-in-law and raced straight up the stairs to her room.

'Why did you ask the doctor for money?' she shouted, waving the envelope.

Durga-devi just smiled. 'What is it do with you? I asked him and he said of course he would give it to you.' She stretched out her hand for the money.

'Why did you tell him it was for my parents?' asked Neela, hiding the envelope behind her back.

'Do you think he would have given it to me otherwise?' answered her mother-in-law, chewing her *paan*-leaf.

'You know very well that he has already paid me this month's salary.'

'Has he? So how much does he pay you for the services that you provide for him?'

'You know very well how much! You are the one who took the money from my bag.'

'Tell him that if you worked as a call girl you could get ten times the amount he pays you in a single night.'

'Shut up! How dare you?' Neela shouted, but knowing that her anger would only provoke the devil in this woman, she controlled herself.

'Look, Ma-ji, there is no need to drag that decent man into it. Please don't do that. If you want the money, fine. Take it. But remember, I will pay him back every penny, so don't expect any of my salary next month.'

Neela threw the envelope containing the money at Durga-devi and ran to her room, where she burst into tears of anger and shame.

As the summer progressed, Neela picked up the news that Yamini and her children were going to India to her sister's wedding.

'Suraj can't afford to leave the shop, so we're going without him,'

Yamini told her while writing a list of gifts that she was going to take for her parents and sisters.

Neela thought about her own parents, and wondered whether Yamini would take a few gifts for them. She remembered a lamb's wool jumper she had seen in Marks & Spencer that would be suitable for her father now that winter was approaching. And the maroon china-silk sari that she had seen in Upton Park would look fabulous against her mother's complexion. She hoped that the remaining few pounds from her clothing factory wages would be enough to cover the costs.

But Yamini told Neela that she could carry nothing extra because her luggage was already overweight.

CHAPTER 19

One day Neela was sitting in the doctor's garden keeping an eye on the children while they played hide and seek with their friends, and contemplating the present, when the fragrance of freshly cut grass and watered earth brought back strong memories of India. What a change, she thought.

It was during the monsoon season that she used to smell the same fragrance in India. At the end of every hot summer when the clouds gathered she used to run out to catch the first drops of rain on her tongue before they hit the parched earth. Every drop that came from the heavens above was like nectar. Getting drenched and inhaling the distinctive scent rising from the satisfied earth was a thrill.

'Neela, that's enough, you will catch the cold.' her Maa would call from the kitchen window. 'Remember last year you were ill with temperature for three days.'

Neela's eyes misted at the memory. She smiled remembering her Maa's endless supply of hot, hot pakoras which she ate sitting on the swing on the back veranda while watching the torrential downpour. Later, when a hazy sun emerged from the clouds, everything would glisten and she would lose herself in the music of the tup-tup sound of rain trickling down the leaves, a drop at a time, into the puddles under the trees.

Rahul's voice jolted her from her reveries.

'Aunty Neela!' Rahul was saying a bit impatiently. 'I said, can you tell us the monkey and crocodile story again please?'

'Now, again? You hear it many times.' Neela replied, returning with a jolt to reality.

'Please Aunty, Mark and Julie want to hear it.'

'OK, then,' she smiled, shaking off the last of her memories as they gathered around her.

'Long time back in India forest a monkey live on a mango tree, near lake. Every day he eat mangos and throwing some in lake. One day a crocodile came up and say, 'Your mangos very sweet. Thank you. And every day, when his wife cooking, crocodile come up. Eating mangos, they talk and talk. Quickly they are friends. One day crocodile take mango home. His wife like it so much. She say, 'If mango is much sweet, monkey eating mango every day, his heart might taste sweetest. I want eat his heart.'

'Oh, no!' children said in chorus.

'Then what happened?'

'What happened?'

Crocodile very sad feel. But he scared of his wife, went crying, and said, 'Monkey, Monkey, my wife invite you for dinner.'

'Oh, nice. But I no swim.'

'Don't worry, you sit on my back. I take you safe.'

'Oh, no, poor monkey.' Pallavi held her head in her hands.

'In middle way monkey notice crocodile crying and say, 'Why you crying?'

'Sorry Monkey, my wife want eat your heart.'

Monkey so scared. He think and think and say, 'Oh, it's all right. I put my heart on mango tree. Go back, I bring it.

Crocodile take Monkey back.

'Stay here,' Monkey say. 'I bring my heart.'

He jump on the tree and say angry, 'You namakharam, you deceive me. I think you my friend. How you hear your wife? You no friend any more.'

'Wow!' the children clapped. 'Very clever monkey.'

'Can you tell us more stories tomorrow?'

'OK, I will,' Neela replied, pleased at her success at holding the children's attention.

And so the summer holidays gently unwound with Neela increasingly absorbed in the children's activities and in their lives. She was content, and so, it seemed, were they.

'We are going to Chessington, we are going to Chessington,' shouted the children one day the minute Neela got in the door.

'What is Chessington?' asked Neela.

'It is an amusement park.' explained Dr Vikas, coming through from the lounge.

'There will be rides and shows and all kinds of fun things for children. I am taking them there this bank holiday.'

'Are you coming, Aunty Neela?' Pallavi asked.

'Yes, it will be fun,' Rahul's eyes lit up. 'We can have a ride on the magic carpet like the prince in your story. Please come.'

'Me?'

'Yes,' said the children.

'I don't know,' said Neela looking at Dr Vikas.

'You are welcome. They want you to come,' he said.

'I would love to but . . .' her face clouded over, anticipating her in-laws' reaction.

'Please don't worry if you can't. We will understand.' Dr Vikas noticed her hesitation.

'Oh, no, no, sir. I will come.' It was too tempting. She couldn't refuse such an opportunity to be with the children. She knew excuses would have to come later but for now she just wanted to enjoy planning the trip.

'Good,' said the doctor.

Later, the cost of the trip crossed her mind. She had fifteen pounds, saved safely in her suitcase, but she wondered whether it was enough.

'Sir . . .,' she hesitated.

Dr Vikas lifted his eyes from the British Medical Journal.

'How much does it cost, sir? I mean the trip.'

'Oh, don't worry about it,' he replied.

'But sir . . .'

'Please. It doesn't cost much.'

'Thank you, sir.'

Neela found herself anticipating the trip with as much excitement as the children. When the day came, she packed the picnic hamper carefully so that the family would have everything that they needed. As the car started, she shivered with excitement. It was going to be her secret adventure, and she was quite clear she was going to keep it from her in-laws. She had never ever seen the rides that the children had told her about. She could watch all the fun. She had never been so far out of London and she was looking out of the window for the small villages which Rahul had told her they would pass through on the way. She always wondered what a British village would look like and now she would find out and be able to compare it with those in India.

Once they reached there, as she had half expected, the rides petrified her, but she loved the hustle and bustle. It reminded her of a *mela* in India. Children, parents and grandparents screamed as adrenalin pumped through their veins. If it wasn't for the obvious joy in their faces, she might have thought they were going through some form of torture. Rahul and Pallavi tried to persuade her to go on the rides with them, and then Dr Vikas encouraged her as well. On the magic carpet, she forgot all her inhibitions. On the roller coaster she became one of them, screaming and laughing away her pent-up emotions as loudly as any child. She almost forgot about the doctor but then he was busy taking photos and getting the picnic ready for them. He looked relaxed and happy as he watched them having fun.

It was ten o'clock by the time Neela was dropped back home. She crept in quietly, desperate not to wake her mother-in-law but while she was removing her shoes, she heard voices in the living room. Wondering who it could be, she stopped for a second at the foot of the staircase to listen. The living room door opened and Suraj appeared.

'Ah, Neela, you are back. Could you make some strong coffee for my friend?' he demanded.

Nodding in response, Neela went into the kitchen, made two mugs of coffee and took them through to the living room. She gasped at the state of the room. It was littered with beer cans, wine bottles, glasses, and crisp packets. Suraj and his friend Tariq were lounging around and laughing very loudly over the loud music and clapping their hands. They were obviously drunk. Because the sight of them brought back memories of Ajay, and because she found such ugliness intolerable, Neela looked away, but already Tariq was watching her and looking her up and down. Slowly, from head to foot. Very uncomfortable in the presence of these two men, Neela handed them their coffee and turned to go.

'What a beauty,' Tariq said, his words slurred.

Suraj banged his hands on the table, threw his head back and roared with laughter. He pointed his finger at Neela.

'Her! You mean that dark little thing? You call her a beauty?' He punched his friend on his shoulder. 'That's a good one!'

Tariq's eyes continued to drool over Neela.

'No, no, brother,' Tariq said, 'I am not joking. Look at her face.

141

Isn't it just so innocent? And her eyes! Aren't they beautiful? Who cares if she is dark. Look at that fantastic figure!'

Suraj stopped laughing and looked at Neela thoughtfully. 'OK man, if you say so.' His words were slurred too but Neela was sure she heard him say:

'I will give you permission but . . .'

'Since she is my brother's wife and I have to respect him . . .'

'She can only be your third wife but . . .'

'There is a price.'

Neela moved towards the door, meaning to get out fast.

'Wait,' ordered Suraj. 'Bring me the cigarette case.'

Neela obeyed with legs that would hardly carry her.

'Yes, why not, brother?' Tariq took another sip from his bottle. 'I won't disappoint you . . .' He belched. 'I will make you and,' he lifted the bottle towards Neela, 'her . . . very happy.'

'How many wives are you allowed in your religion?' Suraj chuckled. 'You have one already back at home, one in this country, and she will be wife number three.' He laughed.

'How much?' Tariq asked, ignoring the counting.

'Bid.'

'Five hundred pounds?'

'You must be joking.'

'Seven hundred?'

'No way.'

'All right, brother. My final offer. One thousand!'

'Done.'

The men shook hands and raised their glasses.

Neela was fixed to the ground with one hand to her throat. Tariq moved closer. The pungent smell of alcohol on his breath made her feel sick.

'Come on, sweetie.' The words wobbled out of his mouth.

Go on! Run! Her instincts told her to get out of there fast but her legs felt like jelly and her steps faltered. Then she felt the weight of his arms on her shoulders. She struggled to shrug him off but his grip was strong. He was trying to pull her sari *pallu* off her shoulders when she let out a piercing scream. She looked at her brother-in-law for help but he was slumped in a chair semi-conscious. She hoped Durga-devi would come down, but no one came to her rescue.

People had trodden all over her when she was young and vulnerable and she wasn't going to let it happen all over again. Somehow she had to survive this. She sank her teeth into his arm, scratched his face, and after what seemed like an eternity, she managed to push him off with what strength she had left in her. At last she wriggled free but her sari *pallu* remained tight in his fist. As Tariq pulled it hard her whole sari came off, unwinding into his hands. Grateful for her underskirt and blouse, she ran for her life, up to her room, and slammed the door shut.

Shivering like a leaf and breathless, she hid inside the wardrobe, but Tariq's feet were thumping up the stairs and then he was banging on every door.

'Open the door, sweetie. Let me in,' he called repeatedly.

Neela waited for the door to give way under the strong blows from his fists. She wriggled back as far as she could into the corner of the wardrobe and prayed.

Just as she expected, the door swung open and Tariq came in, calling her name. She peered through a tiny gap in the wardrobe doors, and tried to quieten her breath. He stood there in the middle of the room, narrowing his eyes to see through the darkness, and then he looked under the bed and lifted up the covers. She pressed herself further back and held her breath. Thankfully God seemed to be on her side because he turned, grunted, and walked out to try another room. The banging and shouting eventually ceased.

Although she knew he had gone, she was unable to move. She sat for hours in the same position in the wardrobe with her eyes wide open. In the early hours she must have nodded off into an uneasy sleep.

The alarm went off as usual, not attentive to the previous night's events. Neela's eyes felt heavy and painful, and she reached to stroke her throbbing head. Had it been a nightmare? No. Last night's drama was real and its aftermath worse because of the humiliation. But she remembered Dr Vikas and his children and got up. She needed to call them to tell them that she would be late. Looking down at her under-skirt, she remembered Tariq's brutal attempts to lay his hands on her. She grabbed a sari – any sari – from the pile of clothes and wrapped it around her body. The daylight made things easier.

The living room door was wide open, and she could see it was just as chaotic as the previous night with the addition of more bottles, empty cigarette packs, stubs, and crisp wrappers. The tape from the hi-fi had finished, leaving a low buzzing noise. The TV was still on but the screen was flickering. It was like a scene after a cyclone. Tariq was lying on the floor with his arms and legs wide spread and Suraj was propped up against the sofa, his legs stretched out in front of him. Both men looked ugly and monstrous. Their mouths were open, and they snored loudly. She was revolted. And there in the middle of the littered floor lay her abandoned sari.

She tiptoed across the floor and grabbed it. The phone was at the far end of the room. Would she be able to step over Tariq and walk around Suraj to reach it? She turned back and left the door slightly open behind her so that she could hear them if they came out. Feeling weak and shocked, she climbed back up the stairs. Her mother-in-law's door was slightly ajar and she pushed it a little wider to see if she was in. The room was empty and the bed looked as though it hadn't been slept in. Where was she? Oh yes. Neela remembered it was *Vinayak chaviti* last night, and she must have gone home with her friend Sita *masi*.

She felt far from safe without her mother-in-law, but was glad that the coast was clear so that she could get into Yamini's room and plug in the phone. She lifted the receiver, dialled, and heard the doctor's polite, husky voice.

'Hello, sir,' she said very quietly.

'Oh, is that you Neela? Are you all right? I was wondering what had happened to you.'

'I am not well, sir.'

'You must be very tired. It was a long tiring day yesterday.'

'I am sorry; I can't come today sir . . .'

'That's OK,' he said quietly. 'You have a rest today.'

But . . . the children, sir?'

'The children will be fine,' said the doctor. 'Divya is taking them swimming in a few minutes anyway and they will stay there until evening, so you needn't worry. We will see you soon.'

'Thank you, sir.'

If only all men were like Dr Vikas. She sighed and replaced the receiver.

As she went back to bed, she felt Tariq's touch still burning on her skin like a hot iron rod. The ordeal brought back painful memories of Ajay and she gave thanks to the gods that she had escaped this time. But there would be a next time. Tariq would try again. Knowing that he would be back, she got up and pulled tea chests and suitcases against the door.

Someone banging on her door woke her. Hearing Durga-devi calling her name, she got up and dragged the tea chests and suitcases away from the door.

One glance at Neela's swollen face and red eyes, and Durga-devi frowned.

'What's happened to you?" She was clearly puzzled as she looked round the room and at the fallen suitcases. Neela said nothing. Her mother-in-law repeated the question and Neela decided to tell her what had happened.

'Ma-ji, forgive me for telling you all this, but you are also a woman and I hope you will understand. Try and imagine yourself in my place and tell me how would you feel and what would you do?'

'Are you sure all that happened?' Durga-devi asked.

'How much more evidence do you want than this?' Neela peeled off her sari *pallu* and showed her mother-in-law the scratches and bruises on her shoulders and on the back of her neck.

'If you don't believe me, Ma-ji, go and see the state of the living room yourself.'

'Let me talk to Suraj and if he says everything you say . . . I mean, if what you are telling me is true, I will have to make sure that Tariq doesn't come to this house again.'

CHAPTER 20

The following evening Neela heard Durga-devi confront Suraj while she cowered on the landing.

'It was very kind of Tariq to propose marriage to that girl.' Suraj said. 'He wanted to give her a new life and another chance for happiness.'

What cunning lies. Neela could hardly believe her ears.

'And Mum, she is only young. In this day and age so many widows and divorcees get married again, even in our community. And since we live here in England, I thought why not give the poor girl an opportunity?' Suraj continued.

'But Suraj, I saw the scratches on her shoulders and *Hai-Ram*, the state of the room!' Durga-devi replied, not convinced.

'Mum, listen to me. Why am I being accused of wrongdoing when my intentions are good?'

There was a long silence.

'And Mum, do you really believe her? She could say anything to spoil my name. Maa. Can't you see?'

Their voices faded as they walked towards the lounge. The door closed. How naïve she had been. Of course a mother like Durga-devi would always believe her son before anyone else.

A couple of weeks went by without Suraj bringing his friend home. This was something to be grateful for, but Neela desperately wanted to talk to her mother-in-law again and convince her about what had really happened. However, the habitual look of disgust in Durga-devi's narrowed eyes kept her at arm's length. God only knew what else Suraj had fabricated for his mother.

It was the middle of the night when Neela woke up hot and breathless. Thankful for the tiny window, she got out of bed to open it. Behind the curtains, the full moon in a cloudless sky mesmerised her and a gentle breeze cooled her anxiety. But who was chatting outside at this hour? When she leaned forward to peer out, a movement caught her eye, down below, at the gate. No! She gasped. Why were Suraj and Tariq out at this time? It must have been the sound of the car that had woken her.

With the night so silent, Neela didn't even have to strain to hear their conversation. She heard her name mentioned once. And again. She listened all the more keenly.

'I have the money ready now. I can take her with me right now. What is the problem?'

'No, Tariq. She will scream her lungs out and wake the whole street. Besides this has to be done quietly. I have to think about our reputation. Listen . . . tomorrow I will collect her from the doctor's house and tell her that I was just passing by. She might be surprised but she won't have a clue and I will bring her straight to your house.'

'Brilliant, Suraj! Thank you. Here is the advance . . . tomorrow when you bring her I will give you the rest of the money.'

'Oh my God!' Neela put her hand to her mouth. There were beads of sweat on her forehead. Her first thought was to run away. The room was spinning as she staggered over to the bed and lay down, burying her face in her hands. What could she do now? Where could she go? She had to get away.

However harshly she had been treated, she had always thought that the house would shelter and safeguard her. Never did she imagine that it would become a trap. She looked around her tiny room, a frail bird-cage surrounded by wild animals. For a long time she was numb with fear, until the noise of a car engine brought her to her senses. Tariq was driving away.

Restless and frightened, she packed a few of her clothes in the smaller of her two suitcases and waited until dawn broke. When the birds began to sing at first light, she tiptoed quietly down the stairs, moved silently through the kitchen, and opened the back door. Without a backward glance, she walked through the gate and out into the alley-way. She checked over her shoulder then headed briskly towards the station.

The road ahead was empty. Only an occasional car passed her and a dog barked in the distance. Neela kept glancing over her shoulder, fearing someone might be following her. She was running now, desperate to escape, running all the way to the station. At the ticket counter, she emptied the contents of her purse and asked for a ticket.

'To which station?'

She stared at the person behind the counter.

'Ticket please.'

'Where are you going, love?'

'Oh, sorry,' she paused. She hadn't thought about where she would go. The only thing that mattered was to get away from that place as fast as she could. She glanced anxiously at the list of the stations on the board next to the counter, and stuttered, 'Wimbledon.' The last station on the list.

'Single or return?'

'Single, please.'

She took the first train that came to the station. It didn't matter where it went as long as it took her away from that Tariq-infested area.

The train was empty. After several more stations the seats started filling up and only then did the panic ebb away a little. She gazed at her ticket. What would she do once she reached Wimbledon? Where would she go? What could she do now? As she stared out at the station names, she thought of Dr Vikas. She was sure that he would be kind and understanding if she told him what was happening to her. But how could she put him in the position of possibly having his name dragged through the mud by her in-laws? In fact, how could she carry on working at the doctor's house if she was living far away? Through tears, and to distract herself, she started counting the stations on the map. The only glimmer of hope was her friend Anita. Hers was the only shoulder she could lean on.

She didn't wait for Wimbledon. At Upton Park she jumped out, ran to a phone box, called the doctor to ask him to give her a few days off, and then phoned Anita.

'I am sorry, Anita-*behn*. I am so sorry to burden you with this.'

'Don't worry. Just come here at once.'

'I think you'd better go to the police,' Anita said the minute Neela stepped into the house.

'Oh no, Anita-*behn*. I just don't have the strength to cope with the tangle of legal procedures.'

'But you have had the strength to bear all this from your monstrous in-laws!' Anita replied.

They were standing in the hall, Neela's suitcase on the floor.

'Relax,' said Anita as the phone rang, and Neela jumped.

'Yes, she is here. I will give it to her.'

'Oh no, why did you tell her I am here?' Neela was waving her hands, trying to push away the phone that Anita held out for her.

'Talk to her,' Anita hissed, but seeing the fright in Neela's eyes she shouted back into the receiver, 'One minute, aunty-*ji*,' and pressing the mute button, she pulled Neela to her side.

'Why do you panic so much? You haven't done anything wrong.'

'Yes . . . but . . . they will come and take me away.'

'You must give her the impression that you didn't know anything about your brother in-law's plans. He probably hasn't dared tell her a thing. Just play it cool and tell the old lady that you have come to see me for a few days.'

'Hello, Ma-ji,' Neela's voice trembled.

'How dare you go like that without telling me?'

'Ma-ji . . .'

'I searched everywhere for you. What shame! Eventually I had to phone the doctor to ask if madam-*ji* is taking some time off. You didn't even have the decency to tell me where you were going. And may I ask why?'

'No . . . yes . . . it's not like that . . . I only . . .'

'Shut up. What do you think you are doing, disappearing like this?'

'Ma-ji . . . I . . . I . . .'

'You ungrateful *sytan*! I won't tolerate your behaviour any more. Come home at once.'

'I want to stay here with Anita for a few days.'

'Well, you can't. Suraj says he will come and fetch you home.'

'No,' Neela cried.

Anita, listening to everything, grabbed the phone back from Neela.

'Look, aunty-*ji*, you are older than me and I respect you for that, but is this the way to treat Neela? She is your daughter-in-law and not your slave. Leave her alone otherwise I will call the police and complain that you and your family are harassing her.'

Neela's eyes widened with astonishment.

'Oh no! Durga-devi won't take that kindly.' Neela said after Anita had banged the phone down.

'I strongly suggest you leave them for good and get on with your own life.'

And with those unflinching words from her friend, Neela felt a wave of relief, as if something was finally over. Anita had given her the strength to carry on.

Chapter 21

That night, as Neela lay on a sofa bed that Anita had made up for her, she thought about her friend's unwavering compassion. The small house, with only one bathroom and a tenant upstairs, was already overcrowded but Anita showed not the slightest sign of resentment. Even so, Neela knew she couldn't take advantage of Anita's kindness for very long and it would be better for everyone if she could find somewhere else to live. As long as she continued to work for the doctor she could afford a cheap, rented room. Whatever happened, her job gave her modest financial independence and security. Then she would remember Tariq. How could she leave the house and move freely around London with him searching for her everywhere?

Having talked all of this over endlessly with Anita for the last three days, Neela made up her mind that she would not let Tariq cripple her freedom. She had to go back to work as soon as possible, and with a little more vigilance and care, she would be fine.

Although she dreaded her first journey back to work, because the train was full of people it wasn't as bad as she had anticipated. Curiously her in-laws had not phoned the doctor, nor attempted to make any contact.

After searching the local paper, Neela finally found a one bedroom flat to rent. It was on the third floor of an ex-council block, three stations away from Anita. When Neela went to inspect it, a woman named Gill Martin introduced herself and showed her round. A narrow corridor, which separated the two rooms, led to a tiny kitchen and a small bathroom both of which she would have to share with Gill who was in the bigger of the two rooms – probably the living room before the flat had been converted. Neela's room had flowery wall-paper and contained a single bed, a wardrobe and a chest of drawers. Though not particularly appealing, it was tidy and habitable, and most of all, affordable. She was comforted in the knowledge that it was only an hour's train journey to the doctor's house, and miles away from her in-laws. Without hesitating, she paid the deposit.

Neela didn't have much to carry but Anita insisted on accom-panying her to her new home. Soon Neela, Anita and Gill were sitting in the kitchen, gulping weak tea and nibbling digestive biscuits. Neela listened intently while Gill described her new neighbours.

'Since you are going to live here, my dear,' Gill said, looking at Neela, 'you should know a few things.' She flicked her ginger curls back from her forehead and leaned forward. 'You know the couple opposite? I don't know where they are from but they are weird! There is definitely something sinister going on in this house.' She took a gulp of tea, maintaining the suspense.

'Oh really,' Anita replied.

'She is big, you know, and screams and shouts like hell. And the man is puny and has a terrible stammer. He is definitely a battered husband.' Gill shook her head dramatically.

'Poor man, it must be hell for him,' Anita said. 'Doesn't he go out at all?'

'I hardly see him out except with her.'

'Oh.'

'And if you think that's bad, wait until you hear the noisy family downstairs.'

'Oh, you mean that young family?' Anita asked, while Neela sat mute.

'Yes, but..,' Gill gulped the remaining tea, ' . . . oh my good God, you should hear the noise those kids and parents make. Sometimes they won't let you sleep. Each one of them is as bad as the next. And their language! It's foul!'

'Never mind, there are people like that everywhere,' Anita replied, looking anxiously at Neela. 'Don't worry, love.'

'There are some good ones as well but I haven't told you about them yet.' Gill continued. 'The man upstairs lives all alone but is very decent and keeps himself to himself. I can guarantee that he will be the one to jump to help if anyone is in need. The other one on the top floor is different. You know the educated sort! I have seen him in summer sitting under those elm trees in the park reading poetry.' Gill said, pointing at the trees they could see from the window.

'Who lives in the flat next to him?' Anita asked.

'The elderly couple . . . must be Punjabis. You know he wears a turban or whatever you call it. They are very nice though, always smile at you, and ask you how you are.'

Gill paused to light a cigarette and held it between her fingers. 'I must warn you though about the landlord. Have you paid your deposit yet. Because he demands the rent on the first day of every month otherwise he barks like a mad dog.'

'Thank you very much for all the information and your hospitality, Gill.' Anita stood up and shook hands.

'You are welcome,' Gill said, then looked at Neela. 'Are you all right, love? You haven't said much.'

'I am fine, thanks,' Neela smiled.

'I was concerned about Neela living alone, but after meeting you I feel much better about it,' Anita said, as she turned to go. 'I am sure you two will get on well.'

Gill saw tears in Neela's eye as Anita took her leave.

'Don't worry, love, I am here.' Gill said, and patted Neela on her arm.

CHAPTER 22

That first night in her own room was hot and humid. Humming to herself, Neela opened the window because the room smelt musty and she liked the way the light from the street lamp poured in and played hide and seek through the fluttering curtains, making patterns on the ceiling that were as crazy as her thoughts. This was the very first step that Neela had ever taken on her own.

One difficult task remained. She had to collect the rest of her belongings from her in-laws' house, and in particular her passport. Her heart ached remembering her grandmother's coral necklace and earrings that were still with Durga-devi, but she doubted if she would be able to retrieve them. And if she went back to the house, would they ever let her leave again? As much as she wanted to solve her own problems, she knew that, confronted by her in-laws, her courage would fail her, and their anger would get the better of her. It wasn't until the small hours that she finally made a decision. Though she didn't want to see Durga-devi ever again, she decided to go and confront her, but she would ask Anita to go with her.

They took an afternoon train so that they could catch the woman on her own.

Durga-devi might have lashed out at Neela on her own, but seeing Anita at her side, she invited them both in.

'You came home at last! *Ayiye, ayiye Maharani!*'

Neela lifted her head and looked directly at Durga-devi.

'I've just come to collect my things. I'm moving out,' she said.

Durga-devi's jaw dropped.

'Yes, Ma-ji, I am moving out.'

'What do you mean moving out?' Durga-devi's anger was quick to surface. She turned on Anita, wagging her finger. 'I knew you were the one behind all this. You have been brainwashing her. You can't take her with you. She belongs here,' she shouted.

'No, Ma-ji, no one is taking me anywhere, and please don't blame Anita. I am moving out to be on my own. I am not moving in with Anita.'

Durga-devi looked from Neela to Anita, her mouth open.

Neela took a deep breath and continued, 'I am renting my own room.'

'What? And with whom, may I ask?' Anger made the older woman breathless so that she had to pause. Sitting down heavily on the sofa, she lifted her flabby arms in the air and screamed, 'I know you're living with him, that rogue of a boss of that clothing factory. Isn't that it?'

'Ma-ji!' shouted Neela.

Anita pushed Neela behind her and stepped in front.

'How does your mind work, Durga-devi! I don't think you will ever come out of that dark cocoon of yours, will you?'

'I am only concerned about Neela, Anita. How on earth is she going to live on her own in this strange country? She can't even speak the language,' she screeched, smacking her forehead.

'Don't worry, Ma-ji. I will be fine.'

'I supported you and helped you so much. How could you forget all that so quickly? You never told me you intended leaving home.'

'I am sorry, but I think it's better for everybody if I move out. Please be happy that I won't be a burden to you any more.'

'Oh, you are not a burden to me, uh, *Hai-Ram!* What are you talking about? You are an ill-fated girl and that is my *karma*. I lost my son

158

because of you. Oh, God! Why have you brought me this heartache?'
Durga-devi played the same old record.

'That's why you should let me move out, Ma-ji, and we can both live
in peace,' Neela said calmly.

'Did you hear that? After all I have done for her, she is not even
grateful, is she? Now she is accusing me of not giving her any peace.
What will everyone in my community think when they know that she
has moved out and is living by herself? Who will respect me now that
you've destroyed my family's honour?" She covered her eyes with her
sari *pallu*.

'Look, Ma-ji, I am not going to do anything that destroys your
family's honour or bring you any shame. I am just going to live my
own life quietly."

'Go, go, and live wherever you want to or with whoever you want
to, but what about the money we spent on feeding you and clothing
you and giving you a roof over your head for nearly two years? Who is
going to repay all that?" Durga-devi dabbed her eyes with her sari *pallu*
and blew her nose. "How can you throw all that money into someone
else's lap?

'Some people are just so selfish, Ma-ji!' Anita retorted with biting
sarcasm.

'Why stand there wasting any more time, Neela? Go and bring your
things down otherwise we will be here all day.'

'But she has all my things,' Neela whispered.

'Oh, my God,' Anita muttered under her breath, and automatically
her hand went up to her head.

It was all a bit of a struggle but finally Neela had most of what she
needed. Durga-devi threw Neela's passport after her as she dragged
her stuff down the stairs.

'If you will just give me back my jewellery, then we will get out of
your way,' Neela said, picking up her passport and putting it safely in
her bag.

'Jewellery? I don't know anything about jewellery.' Durga-devi replied.

'But, Ma-ji, you took it from me when I arrived. You said that you would look after it for me,' Neela said firmly.

'Did I? I don't remember. Maybe Yamini has taken it with her.'

'But it was my grandmother's jewellery. She gave it to me,' Neela cried.

'Come back later and ask Yamini.'

It was a bitter decision to take, but in the end Neela decided she would have to compromise just to get away. And so she left behind her most beloved possessions. As she stepped out of the house for the last time, she knew that she might never see her grandmother's jewellery again.

CHAPTER 23

Neela was woken by the morning light which streamed through the window panes and turned the fading yellow flowers on the brown wallpaper to a sparkling gold. She felt totally free. She had done it. She had finally moved out of her in-laws' house. Her sense of achievement was so overwhelming that it made her laugh out loud. For the first time in her life she was not afraid of being alone, nor worried that someone might frighten or harm her.

Gradually she got accustomed to the new place, along with all the noises from the flat above. Every night, the man who lived there would have one too many and shout abuse at the top of his voice, sometimes all through the night. In the beginning it disturbed her but Gill assured her there was no need to worry and that he was harmless. Neela noticed that sometimes Gill too would get drunk. Women in India did not drink so this was a new experience for her. She had seen Yamini having a glass of wine occasionally, but she was never intoxicated. Neela found Gill amusing when she was drunk and quite enjoyed the way she talked nonsense. It was during these drunken episodes that Neela learnt about Gill's background and how her husband had left her for a younger woman. When Gill was sober she was a completely different person, bubbly and compassionate, and she never mentioned her divorce.

The elderly couple on the first floor and a young couple on the third floor exchanged polite greetings with Neela. The Punjabi couple opposite talked to her too and enquired about her background and family. But the noisiest family on the second floor ignored her smiles. The parents were often either drunk, or hurling abuse at each other. The neglected children would fight with each other, and threw rubbish all over the steps, balcony and onto the pavement. At first, Neela didn't understand the names they were calling her but she knew that they were scornful. She guessed it was because she was the only one in the block who wore a sari. Whenever she climbed down the steps, they would stop playing and shout, 'Paki go back! Paki go back!'

At first she ignored their comments and just smiled at them. She soon realised that there was no point explaining that she wasn't from Pakistan but from India, as she did when she first arrived, because it made them laugh at her even more and that hurt her. She finally understood that it wasn't anything personal. They just didn't like foreigners.

Apart from that, life continued in a surprisingly normal and smooth way. Working at the doctor's house remained the same as before. Although the children obviously missed their mother, time seemed to be easing their pain and they became closer to her. On good days Dr Vikas came home early and spent time with his children, and on other occasions he would go straight to his room and stay there behind closed doors until one of the children needed him. Sometimes Neela was surprised at how vulnerable he seemed. His red-rimmed eyes and the tears on his eyelashes didn't escape her sympathetic gaze. He very rarely talked about his wife, even with his children, and never to her. She knew that he was trying hard to get used to life without her but she wondered whether time would ever heal his pain.

Now that Neela didn't need to rush home like before, she often stayed on a little longer. The children would give her their old story books while they did their homework. When she discovered a new word or a new rule of language she would try it out and use it in her conversation, but often incorrectly, making them laugh and correct her. As she became more competent, they gave her harder and harder tasks. She learned how to use a dictionary and began to understand more complex words and sentences. They even played the exam game; she had to learn new words, meanings, and even spellings and then they tested her. Rahul gave her a book, *Little House on the Prairie* by Laura Ingalls, saying, 'This is your real test, Aunty Neela. If you can understand the first chapter, you will pass your exams with grade A.'

She brought it home with a little dictionary and diligently read for a few hours each evening before she went to bed. Gill laughed at her studying hard for her 'exams' until late at night.

'I must admit I admire your determination. If you study like this, no doubt you will get a university degree soon,' she said.

At the beginning, learning English was a very slow process because she had to look up the meaning of every other word, but gradually she didn't need the dictionary nearly so much. And she was learning new words all the time from their context as she began to master whole sentences. Soon she was able to follow the story and found herself actually enjoying it. There was so much satisfaction in being able to read and in understanding English, and her achievements gave her an incredible sense of accomplishment. The children's ability to teach her, and her own capability for learning, was far beyond anything she could ever have imagined, even in her wildest dreams, when she was in India. Talking to Gill helped too, and soon Neela's spoken English was much improved. Her vocabulary was still limited, but now she managed to be understood.

It was seven-thirty in the evening with the July sun still shining. Neela was setting the table for dinner under the canopy in the garden at the doctor's house.

'Aunty Neela, Aunty Neela,' Rahul and Pallavi rushed towards her. 'We are going to India for the summer holidays.'

'You are going to India!' Neela stopped, cutlery in her hands, and looked at Dr Vikas. 'Really?'

He smiled at her and nodded. 'Their grandparents are desperate to see them.' He ruffled Rahul's hair affectionately.

'Oh, that's wonderful. You are going to see your grandparents.' Neela said to them.

'It's also important for them to see their grandparents.'

'Of course, sir . . . How long are you going for, sir?'

'Six weeks.'

'Six weeks!' Her heart became heavy as she contemplated being without them for so long. She looked at the children, who were talking about running through mango groves, and how they would play with their cousins. They were too excited to eat.

'Have you been to the lake *Bhadrakali*, Aunty Neela?'

'No, I haven't,' she answered, summoning up a brightness she did not feel 'Oh, why don't you come with us? Shall we take aunty Neela, Dad?'

Neela's heart swelled at the little girl's affection.

'Maybe next time.'

'You must come next time. You will love it there,' said Rahul enthusiastically.

"Oh, yes, remember, Dad, Grandpa took us for an early morning walk near the lake as the sun was came up? Wasn't that beautiful?'

'Yes, I remember,' smiled Dr Vikas. 'It was as if the sun was rising up from the lake itself.'

'I remember the boat trip, that was nice, wasn't it, Dad?' Pallavi interrupted.

'Yes, it was darling; it was wonderful in the still waters of the lake.'

'And you know, aunty Neela, I love the things they sell on those little carts,' continued Pallavi. 'My God, how they shout at the top of their voices? She cupped her mouth with her hands, imitating the vendors, "*Mirchibajji, Pakoras, Panipuri, Masala vada.*'

'Have you seen how they balance the fruit and flower baskets on their heads?'

Chapter 23

'It *was* fun, wasn't it, dad!'

'Yes. It was fun,' their father's voice trembled as he replied.

The next few weeks raced by and Neela realised how desperately she had been clinging to Rahul and Pallavi for her own emotional security. As the day of departure approached, the children couldn't sleep because they were so wound up with excitement. Rahul was particularly interested in the journey itself. He had a passion for planes. The huge jets that flew in the air like birds amazed and fascinated him and he had a collection of aircraft books, models and toys in his room. From the day his father booked the tickets, Rahul talked endlessly about jumbos, tri-stars and airbuses. In the end his only remaining faithful audience was Neela who listened intently, wondering how a child of that age could have acquired so much knowledge.

The night before they left, Neela stayed up late with the children, talking to them while they packed. She didn't sleep, but tossed and turned, dreading their departure. Early the next morning the taxi arrived. Neela longed to go with them to the airport just to see them off, but to ask would be presumptuous. Neela's eyes filled with tears when she kissed the children goodbye.

'It's only six weeks and the time will fly, just like that,' Dr Vikas said, clicking his fingers. He knew what Neela was feeling. 'Have a restful holiday from these rascals.' He handed her the house keys. 'Please keep them with you in case of anything.' Neela was grateful for his trust.

She stayed on the doorstep, waving, until the taxi turned the corner and disappeared. Six long and empty weeks stretched endlessly in front of her.

CHAPTER 24

With the doctor and the children gone, the time passed painfully slowly. While she wandered around the empty house, Neela found herself thinking about the doctor's wife, Sarita, the absent person in this family whose presence was nevertheless everywhere. She imagined Sarita as the mother in a picture-perfect family, a loving wife to Dr Vikas, a devoted mother to the children. Neela had witnessed the doctor mourning her, missing her and longing for her, still in love with this woman who had left a great hole in the fabric of his life. How would it feel to love someone like that? How would it feel to be loved by someone? What was love? It was while she was meditating on these matters that one day she put her hand on the doctor's bedroom door and was surprised to find that it swung open. She had expected it to be locked. She knew it was wrong, but she began to walk into the room. Then her conscience pulled her back. She told herself firmly that she was only a servant in that house. Remembering her place, and respecting the doctor's privacy, Neela bit back her questions, and turned and walked away.

Days passed. Lazy, unfilled days. Most of the time, Neela watched television and read the children's story books and wrote letters to her parents. Still the empty time stared at her, bringing back all the bitter memories to her mind. She was surprised to realise that when she was with the children nothing had come into her mind. She was content in their presence. But now the absence and silence were so unbearable that she began counting the seconds for their arrival. Only the hope of returning to work soon kept her going.

As the day of the arrival of Dr Vikas and the children drew near, Neela rediscovered her joy of living. With a lightness of step, she crossed the city, looking forward to getting the house ready for their return. She changed the bedding, went shopping for food, and prepared a meal for them. She even arranged flowers and candles on the table to welcome them home. Finally satisfied, she went upstairs to freshen up and to change into a clean sari. As she combed her hair she heard a crunching sound on the gravel and ran to the window. A taxi was pulling up on the driveway. Throwing the comb on the table and twisting her hair into a chignon, she ran down two steps at a time and opened the front door. She looked out, squinting against the sun, searching for Rahul and Pallavi's cherubic faces. But their agile feet didn't run to her nor did their arms reach out to hug her. Instead she saw Dr Vikas paying the taxi driver. His hair was blown by the wind and he looked thinner. But where were the children?

'Hello, Neela. How have you been?' Dr Vikas greeted her with a smile.

'Fine, thank you sir. Did you have a nice journey, sir?' Not waiting for his answer, she peered into the back seat of the cab, but it was empty.

'Where are the children, sir?'

'The children . . . they are still in India,' he replied, obviously tired.

'Still in India?'

Without another word, he brushed past her, placed his suitcase in the hall and climbed the stairs.

Neela sat at the table, numb. She heard the shower being turned on upstairs, then off again. Eventually Dr Vikas came back down.

'I am sorry, Neela, I should have let you know before, but the children are not coming back.'

'Not coming back?' Neela repeated his words.

168

'I think they are happier there. We have big, loving families on both sides and they managed to persuade me that it would be better for the children if they stayed in India. After a lot of thought, I came to the conclusion that they were right. If we stay in this country, they only have me, but there they have two sets of grandparents, aunties, uncles and plenty of cousins to love them.' He stared out of the window. His voice was low and husky. 'I am hoping that even though no one can replace their mother, at least being with their relatives might make their grief a little easier to bear.' Neela nodded silently but her throat was tight with emotion.

'After a lot of thinking, Neela, I have decided to resign from my job and go back to India . . . I have only come back for a couple of weeks to sort things out at the hospital before I move there for good.'

'Yes, sir,' said Neela, struggling to hold back her tears.

Neela bought a small toy plane for Rahul and a pretty doll for Pallavi and wrapped them in glittery paper. On a card with a teddy bear holding a bunch of balloons, she wrote:

> 'My *dear Rahul and Pallavi, thank you for you like me. I missing you more. I no forgot happy time you give me. I wish you very luck and happy in the world. I love both you lot and lot.'*

As she signed her name at the bottom of the page, she burst into tears. Some fell onto the card, smudging the ink. With a lump in her throat, Neela packed the children's clothes, books, games and toys. It was hopeless. She sniffed, and blinked back tears, and had to keep stopping to wipe her eyes. Finally she gave up, went in to the bathroom, shut the door, held her sari *pallu* over her mouth and sobbed her heart out.

The day before his journey, Dr Vikas disappeared into his room to pack and did not come down for either breakfast or lunch. Neela prepared something light for him and waited downstairs. By eight, he still hadn't come out of his room so Neela went upstairs and hesitantly knocked on the door. He didn't respond immediately but after a few minutes he called, 'Come in.'

This was unexpected. He had never allowed anyone into that room. She waited outside for a few seconds before calling softly, 'Are you sure, sir?'

'Yes. Please come in,' he said.

All the walls were covered with his wife's pictures. It was like a shrine. The only other painting, hanging on the wall above the bed, was of the divine lovers, Lord *Krishna* and *Radha*. Below a large portrait of Sarita there were fresh roses in a vase. The four-poster bed looked huge and empty, its silky peach bed linen flat and uncrumpled. Dr Vikas was sitting in the middle of the floor surrounded by heaps of his wife's clothes. There was an empty, open suitcase in front of him. He looked as if he didn't know what to do and so he was sitting there, staring at it.

'Sir?'

Had he noticed that she was there?

'I am trying to pack . . .' he murmured, looking up at her. He was lost. Lost in his thoughts, and lost to the present and the future. She tried to understand what it must be like packing away his wife's memories, and she knew that it must be an impossible task for him. She stood beside him, not knowing what to do or say.

'Could you please pack them for me?' he finally asked.

'Yes, of course, sir.'

She took the first sari from the heap and began folding it.

He got up slowly then and left the room. She put out a hand in an attempt to call after him and to remind him to have his evening meal but she stopped, knowing that there was no space in his mind for thoughts of food.

Neela folded silk, chiffon and cotton saris, smoothing the creases gently with her fingers and palms. She put every sari with a matching underskirt and a blouse, as if she were making it easy for someone to find everything and get dressed. While she sorted and folded the beautiful clothes, she made herself forget that the woman who owned them would never again unfold them and put them on. The woman was dead.

When the suitcases were full, she stared at them and understood finally that love – an emotion that was fine and strong yet delicate – really could and did exist between a man and a woman. She blinked back her tears as she closed the last lid.

The time had come for Neela and the doctor to say a final goodbye. Of course there was no hiding her distress and sorrow.

'You know, Neela, my children told everyone in India with pride about how wonderful you have been with them. They really enjoyed your company so much. Thank you very much for being here for us. We were desperate and I can't imagine what we would have done without you. I really appreciate all the help and kindness that you have shown us.'

His praise embarrassed her, and she wanted to say so much in reply, but couldn't. 'No . . . sir, thank you, sir . . . I am grateful, sir.'

'You know, Neela, any child would be very lucky to have a mother like you. I hope you have your own children soon.' He picked up one of the suitcases.

'Don't you know, sir, that I won't ever have any children because . . . I am a widow,' she blurted.

A bewildered expression wiped the smile from his face as he put the suitcase down. She noticed him looking at her, really staring. The red *kumkum bindi* that married Hindu women wear was absent from her forehead and that confirmed the harsh truth.

'My God, not you too?' He sat down on a chair. 'I am so sorry. Forgive me for my ignorance. I didn't realise . . . how selfish of me.'

Why should he have noticed when he was so immersed in his own sorrow? His distress now made her feel guilty and she realised that she had made a mistake in revealing her situation. She forced herself to speak cheerfully.

'I am all right, sir. I have many relatives and friends who care for me.' She turned away so that he would not see the lies in her eyes.

'You will be remembered and missed affectionately by all of us, Neela.'

The taxi outside hooted. Neela watched him walk towards it, his footsteps heavy and deliberate.

Chapter 25

It was if Neela had been hanging by a thread which now snapped and dropped her down a deep, deep hole. The days dragged. Each morning she woke up with an empty feeling which she knew was loneliness. It had enveloped her ever since Dr Vikas and his children had left for India. She had no desire to do anything and nothing excited her. She tried to read books but the sight of them reminded her of Rahul and Pallavi.

'Look at the state of you,' cried Anita when she came to visit Neela one day. 'I didn't believe it when Gill told me, but now . . . I can understand how much you are missing them but . . . who are you to those children anyway? Life is like a train journey. You meet people, talk to them and travel with them for a while, but you have to leave them at their destination.' Anita dragged her chair nearer. 'If you care about those children, be happy that they are with their grandparents and are getting lots of love and support.'

'I *am* happy for them,' Neela said, sitting up on her bed, 'and they deserve it . . . but . . .'

'But what?'

'What shall I do with myself every day and where shall I go?'

'How long are you going to stay like this? You have to live your life. Come on, girl! Get out of that bed and go and look for another job.'

Anita was right. What alternative was there? And so the job hunt started all over again. She tried the job centre, the local shops, and a nearby factory but all in vain. Everyone asked about her experience and she struggled in her broken English to convince them all that she was employable. But as days turned into weeks and then a month, the worry of being out of work ate at her.

It was Gill who came to her rescue. She told Neela one day that the factory where she worked was expanding and that they needed extra people. This kind friend was thrilled at the prospect of helping her house-mate.

'Go for the interview, who knows? They might take you,' she said, pouring beer from a can into a glass.

'You think so?' Neela asked doubtfully as she continued rolling a chapatti.

'Yes, why not?'

'But . . .'

'I know, I know . . .' Gill put out a hand to stop Neela. 'You don't need to speak excellent English but you do need to be able to work quickly and efficiently. And another suggestion . . . of course you can go for the interview in your sari if you want but it's easier to work if you wear trousers or a tracksuit and it will stop people staring at you.'

Feeling self-conscious and very silly in her tracksuit, Neela set off for the interview.

'SUPER PACK.' She read the board aloud.

'Yes, this is it.'

They entered a crowded, noisy room filled with women, all seeking work. Cigarette smoke filled the air.

'Look how many people are out of work and want a job,' Gill said, lighting up.

'Yes, but the vacancies, do you think they have?'

'Shhhh,' whispered Gill as a petite, middle-aged woman with tightly-permed hair, dyed blonde, entered the room. She was wearing a jacket over a short, black skirt and knee-length boots. As she tapped her pen on her notepad, the room fell silent, and she introduced herself as Pat Peterson.

'She is the supervisor,' Gill whispered.

'Now this might not be your cup of tea . . .' Pat began.

'What is she saying about tea?' Neela asked.

"Doesn't matter what she says, you have to make this your cup of tea.'

'Oh, I don't mind making tea.'

'Shh. Listen!'

With Gill's help, Neela filled in the application form and Pat agreed to offer her a trial period of one month.

At first, Neela felt strange and out of place working with so many English people. The factory floor was much bigger than in Rusheed-*bhayya*'s clothing factory and the thundering machines looked more complicated than the humble sewing machines she had been used to. Her first week was easy; her job was packing children's story books and audio tapes. But in the second week she worked with four other women sealing batteries. The machine sounded louder than a lorry and looked like a heavy metal circular table with an engine under-neath. There were three slots for the metal jigs, so it required three women to work on it. The table rotated allowing the first person to place a plastic mould into a jig while the second put in the batteries and the third person added the cardboard lid. It was a syncopated dance for three pairs of hands and it had to work smoothly. The mould that contained the batteries and the lid would then fuse together as it passed through a heated tunnel. The women, much more experienced at this, set the machine to run slowly at first then gradually increased the speed. Since they were paid by the number of batteries they packed each day, the faster they worked, the more cash they would take home. Whenever one of them missed her turn (and it was always Neela) the other women would swear under their breath. She found herself apologising repeatedly for holding them up. In the end they became exasperated with her and asked for her to be moved so that they could get on at a decent pace. Neela was teamed up with Rose packing the finished product at the other end of the room.

After collecting and counting the batteries, Neela divided them into sets of ten and packed the sets into small cardboard boxes. Rose packed ten of the small boxes into a larger one, and sealed it with wide sticky tape. Neela was relieved. Not only was the work easier but Rose seemed friendly and approachable.

At the end of the day, she was surprised to see how much they had done. All the women gathered round the boxes to count them while the men carried them onto wooden pallets then fork-lifted them into the lorries that waited ready for departure. Pat Peterson wrote the names of the workers and the details of their work in her book. Every Friday they would be paid their weekly wage and if they earned more than the week before, they would cheer noisily and buy doughnuts or cakes from a van that was parked outside the factory.

'Are you married, love?' Rose asked Neela, shouting against the deafening drone of the machine.

'No.' Neela was surprised by her own answer. She felt guilty for lying but was thankful that Rose did not ask any further questions. Discussing her past life was unbearable.

'Lucky you, you don't have to put up with a lazy bastard like my husband. Don't look at me like that, it's true.' She gestured at the women at the machine. 'In fact most of the women have a man like mine in their lives. You know, that's why they have to work here, to make ends meet. Actually some of them are the only bread-winners in their families.'

'Really!'

'Yes, of course. Some of us are living a day at a time with our lazy, good-for-nothing husbands. Others are either divorced or single parents.'

It surprised Neela that in a country like Britain, there were people struggling with poverty.

Chapter 25

'But I don't think life here is as hard as it is in India.'

'Isn't it?'

'No, in this country even the poorest of the poor get something. They don't starve. At least here people don't die because their diseases go untreated like they do in India.'

'Aren't there any doctors in India?'

'Yes, but no doctor will see a patient if he or she can't pay the fees. At least here you have the National Health Services for free.'

'For free! Who said it is for free?' Rose waved to the other women and shouted,' She thinks that the NHS is free.' Then she looked at Neela. 'No, love. We are paying for it out of our wages. Don't you know how much they deduct? Go and look at your pay-slip. Income tax, national insurance . . .'

That evening Neela took out all the pay-slips from her suitcase and looked at them properly for the first time. She felt foolish for not taking an interest in them before.

'How was work this week?' Gill asked Neela that evening. 'I thought of coming to see you at lunch-time but then I felt lazy and didn't want to walk to your department in the rain.'

'Oh, don't worry, Gill. It was good,' Neela said, placing the cups of tea and a bowl of Bombay Mix on a tray.

'So you like it! What about the girls?'

'Oh, they are nice.'

'That's good to hear.'

'Rose, who works with me, is very nice. She talks to me all the time. She said she has four children and a good-for-nothing husband.'

'Oh!' Gill laughed.

'And Tina, she is very young and pretty. Rose feels sorry for her.'

'Why?'

'Because she is unmarried and had a baby recently.'

'Yes, that happens,' Gill shrugged.

'I know. Just like that letter in the problem pages in the women's magazine.'

'See, reading magazines and working in a factory are definitely improving your knowledge.'

'But Laura seems happy all the time,' Neela continued. 'Rose thinks her partner must be very nice.'

'Well done, Neela! You have already researched all their biographies,' laughed Gill.

Time, the greatest healer of all, eased the sting of missing the doctor's family, and the new routine filled Neela's days. She was so exhausted that she slept soundly at night, and the evenings and weekends passed easily enough either in Gill's jovial company or reading. She began to take a particular interest in the problem page of the magazine she now read regularly. It was like discovering a whole new world that she didn't know existed and was poles apart from her own.

To her pleasant surprise, Neela met two more Asian girls, Reshma and Kajal, at the factory. As she got to know them, her instincts told her that Reshma might have been going through similar problems to her own. She was quiet and subdued. Neela could tell that Reshma was another prisoner in her own home. The issues the women wrote about in the magazines seemed so trivial compared with those that women like Reshma dealt with, living in fear and never knowing the kind of freedom the average English woman took for granted. Neela came to the conclusion that the only way for these women to retain their freedom was to get themselves an education. And to find more courage. Kajal, on the other hand, was bubbly, confident, assertive and extremely entertaining. Neela didn't know if Kajal was dealing with similar problems, but if she was, she had developed strategies for dealing with them without her getting hurt. Neela enjoyed Kajal's company. Just being with her was like a tonic. One day she might ask her how she coped so well and how she managed to remain so cheerful.

CHAPTER 26

Christmas was approaching again and the jolly mood in Super Pack reminded Neela of the Christmas she had spent working in the clothing factory. But with the good memories came shocking ones as she relived the way she had been accused of having an affair with Mr Rusheed: false claims that led to her eventual resignation. Thank God, at least now she was free to do whatever she liked. She loved everything about the festive season. For the first time in her life she went Christmas shopping, grateful for the unexpected thirty pounds bonus that she found in her wage packet.

Neela enjoyed the music they played in the shops, loved the smiles on the faces of the little children surrounding Santa Claus, and she adored the twinkling lights on the big tree in the town centre. She bought a pack of greeting cards in the market hall, and enjoyed choosing boxes of chocolates for Rose, Kajal and Reshma, and bottles of perfume for Anita and Gill. Finally after careful consideration she bought herself some loose trousers and a jumper in C&A. Lately she had discovered that trousers, western tops and tracksuits were much more comfortable than her flowing Indian clothes, especially in winter. Gill was right. It was possible to pass through a crowd almost unnoticed and she hadn't heard any racial remarks for some time. Even the children downstairs had stopped calling her 'Paki'. Perhaps they had become tired of the game, or maybe they accepted her more in her European clothes.

On Christmas Eve, because they finished work early, Kajal invited Neela and Reshma for lunch.

'I don't know . . .' Reshma hesitated. My mother-in-law might make a fuss.'

'Tell her it's Christmas.'

'Uh, you think she cares? She would say, we *Hindoos* and *Musleems* don't celebrate *Chreestmas*,' Reshma mocked.

Although Neela wanted Reshma to stay, she also understood just how much trouble she could get herself into.

'Tell her to mind her own business. Who cares about in-laws! Now we are in England!' Kajal said.

'Yes, you are right. Like they say, be a Roman in Rome.' giggled Reshma.

The Christmas tree sparkled in the corner of Kajal's living room, and the girls soon forgot their troubles and shrieked with excitement. After eating some hot stuffed *parathas* for lunch, they watched Laurel and Hardy on television and laughed till they ached. Neela found herself enjoying the girls' company and they decided to meet whenever possible. Neela wanted to have them back to her room, but the walls of her block of flats were covered in graffiti and the staircase stank of urine. And they all knew it was impossible for Reshma to invite them to her house. So that left Kajal's flat as the only possibility. Although it was small, it was clean, near their workplace, and had all the local amenities they needed. Most of all though, for these three women, it was a sanctuary.

They began meeting regularly on Friday afternoons since that was their half-day at work. Sometimes they would listen to Bollywood songs on cassette tapes, or rent a Hindi video to watch. Otherwise they just amused themselves gossiping about their neighbour and work-mates. If the weather was nice, they would go for a walk in the park. Neela and Reshma both admired their friend Kajal for her courage in standing up to her in-laws and for dragging her husband out of their clutches. It was a frequent topic of conversation.

Chapter 26

'If only every Asian husband was like Kajal's,' Reshma said one day.

'I don't think he is that wonderful. Actually he is an idiot.'

'Doesn't matter if he is an idiot, the important thing is he listens to you,' Reshma replied.

'Yes, that's because I keep him under my thumb by playing on his own weaknesses.'

'What weaknesses?' Neela looked at her friend, mystified.

Kajal laughed, tilting her head to one side. 'If he misbehaves, that's it. My bedroom door is locked for days and weeks on end until he apologises and begs for my forgiveness. How else are we to tame the chauvinistic Indian male?'

While Neela fell silent, Reshma clapped and cheered.

'That's a good idea, isn't it . . . but my husband isn't soft . . . he would leave me if I did that.'

'What do you mean, he would leave you? You should be the one to leave him. Why not? You are earning half the finances and you can look after yourself, can't you?'

'Oi, oi, calm down,' Neela tried to lighten the situation.

Since Gill was going away for Christmas to her sister's house, Neela decided to accept Anita's invitation to go to her place, and for New Year Kajal had already asked her and Reshma to be her guests. Christmas passed peacefully and New Year arrived, giving everyone the opportunity to make New Year resolutions about changes in their lives and new hopes. The three friends waited together for the stroke of midnight when they opened a bottle of lemonade, squirting it around like champagne before they poured it into wine glasses. They then sat back and watched the celebrations on the television from all over the world. Afterwards they played an Indian board-game called *carom* until they were relaxed and tired. They talked into the early hours, telling one another about their lives, sharing their sorrows and fortunes. Part of the fun was mocking and mimicking their silly husbands and in-laws until at last dawn broke and Reshma got up to leave.

'If I don't go now and prepare breakfast the whole house will go wild.'

'I am so glad you left your mad house,' Kajal said to Neela.

'Well . . .'

'You don't have to go now. Have some tea first.'

'What about your husband?'

'Oh,' Kajal dismissed the idea with a wave of her hand, 'knowing him, he will be completely drunk by now and snoring on someone else's floor.'

She yawned as she went into the kitchen.

CHAPTER 27

Neela was the first to hear a key in the lock of the front door.

'See, Neela,' Kajal shouted from the kitchen. 'Speak of the devil! Here he is.'

The door opened and Kajal's husband came in. With a single glance Neela was rooted to the spot. Her head felt that it might explode. The man before her stared back, his mouth open in disbelief. Then a wicked smile played on his face.

'Well, well, well, who is this?' he whispered. 'Allah is great! The bird has come to my roost at last!'

He stepped forward, never taking his eyes off her. Neela felt sick with fear. How could it be possible that her brother-in-law's friend, that monster Tariq, was Kajal's husband?

Having made her excuses, Neela left as quickly as she could. Back in her room, she sat trembling on her bed as she repeatedly relived the recent encounter from hell with Tariq. She couldn't believe that the old nightmare had resurfaced. She knew how lucky she had been to escape from him the first time. But now that he was revealed as her friend's husband, what would happen? She was horrified. How could an evil person like Tariq be blessed with a wife as lovely as Kajal?

She spent the whole day agonising until Gill came home in the evening, but she couldn't face her - not yet - so she stayed in bed pretending to be ill. She couldn't even swallow the soup that Gill made for her because her throat was so tight with anxiety. She struggled to stay calm but couldn't rid herself of the memory of Tariq's gaze.

The next day she reluctantly went to work. As much as she prayed she might avoid Kajal at lunchtime, it didn't happen.

'You went very shy yesterday,' her friend teased. 'Why did you run away like that as soon as Tariq came home? He is all right, you know, he doesn't mind me having friends back. In fact Tariq said we should invite you for dinner.'

Neela said nothing. What could she say?

Stress took its toll, making Neela ill for the next few days. Every morning she struggled to get up intending to go to work, but Gill scolded her and sent her back to bed with a cup of tea and Paracetamol. With Gill's compassion as her security, she drifted off to sleep again.

Startled by a buzzing noise Neela woke and assumed that what she heard was her alarm clock. She forced her eyes open and looked at its face. Six in the evening. She was confused for a moment but finally realised it was the door bell, and it was still ringing. She got up, her head spinning. The door bell rang once more and thinking that Gill must have forgotten her keys as always, she opened the door. It was Kajal. And tall behind her, Tariq.

'How are you?' Tariq's eyes glinted.

Neela felt as if a thunderbolt had struck her.

'Gill told me you are ill and Tariq suggested that we should come and see you. Can we come in?'

'Oh, of course . . . forgive me . . .' Neela faltered as she opened the door wider.

'I brought some chapattis and curry for you.'

Kajal placed the Tupperware boxes on the coffee table.

'These are for you too,' Tariq winked as he handed her a bag of grapes.

Neela looked at them blankly.

'Where is the kitchen? I will warm up the food for you.' Kajal said setting off in what she hoped was the right direction.

'No, no, please don't bother . . . I am not hungry . . .'

'Gill said you haven't eaten anything for the last couple of days and that's not good. You need energy. At least have a bit.'

There was no strength left in Neela to protest. The visit lasted at least an hour and in spite of Kajal's affection it was torture because Tariq watched her like a hawk. Now that he knew where she lived, Neela feared that nothing would stop him. She sensed a storm was brewing above the serene skies. Would her lifeboat survive?

Although her temperature had subsided after a couple of days, she felt physically and mentally drained. Her stomach grumbled but she still could not eat because her mouth tasted metallic and she had no appetite. A couple of months passed which for Neela were like living on a cliff edge. Most Fridays she made excuses not to go to Kajal's house but couldn't avoid her friend altogether. To her relief, Tariq didn't appear again. Slowly her fears began to fade as she argued that he probably wouldn't do anything now. Surely he wouldn't risk losing his lovely wife? Day by day she began to relax.

It was a Sunday evening and Gill had gone out with her boyfriend, Mark, leaving Neela alone in the flat. After spending the whole afternoon trying to teach Gill how to make spicy rice and *raita*, Neela didn't feel hungry. Instead, she took a *guava*, or as Gill called it 'an alien fruit,' from the bowl.

'That alien is making the whole flat stink,' her friend frequently complained.

'It's not alien, it's a *guava*, and that's not a stink, that is fragrance,' Neela would laugh.

That evening, as darkness descended, Neela felt uneasy and wished Gill was there with her. Recently the old unpleasant episodes with Ajay and her in-laws had been resurfacing in her memories and made her feel uncomfortable. Was it to do with the unexpected re-encounter with Tariq? The metallic taste was in her mouth again and she shook her head vigorously. What was wrong with her? Why was she thinking about him? Couldn't she control her own thoughts? Frustrated and annoyed with herself she flicked through the TV channels in an attempt to erase the painful images from her mind.

After watching the ten o'clock news, she switched the television off. She felt lethargic and wanted to go to bed. As she went to close the curtains, she heard the screeching sound of a car in front of the building and peered through the window. Her heart stopped and she gasped. Was she really seeing Tariq or was it her feverish imagination? She leaned forward, making sure she could not be seen. The street lamp made everything clearly visible. She saw him lock his parked car and stride slowly towards her block. She wrenched the curtains shut, ran to bolt the front door, switched off all the lights, and ran to Gill's room which she thought might give her more protection than her own. Neela got into Gill's bed and hid under the bedding. She knew it wasn't difficult for Tariq to climb over the gate and steps to reach her flat. Her heart pounded as she heard the dreaded tapping on the front door. Rigid with terror, she curled into a ball and mentally braced herself. He was calling her name. The taps on the door became a repeated banging. Then there was a pause and Neela heard people's voices from the other flats.

'Can't you see no one is there in the flat?' She recognised her neighbour's stern voice.

'But she is in there. I saw her.' Tariq replied impatiently.

'Who are you anyway? We have never seen you before.'

'If you don't go now, we will call the police.'

'You are disturbing the whole block, man. Come on, get out.'

At last some one seemed to have physically forced him away because she heard the heavy footsteps stomping angrily down the stairs.

Neela remained in the same foetal position for a long time until her startled mind settled a little. She was so grateful that the people who lived in her block had intervened. She got up. He must have gone by now. Without making any noise she went to the window and looked out. Once more she caught her breath. He was still there, leaning on his car, smoking. At that very moment he looked up and she knew he had seen her. Pressing her hand over her mouth to stifle the scream, she ducked under the window. What if he came back again? The bolt inside the front door was hanging on two screws instead of four, and there was no guarantee that he wouldn't break the door down with one more blow.

The only solution was to get out fast before anything happened. Panicking, shaking with fear, she draped an overcoat around her shoulders and unbolted the door with unsteady hands. She would be safer outside than being trapped inside her flat. Thinking that at least she could run and hide somewhere, she headed for the fire exit and stepped out onto the metal stairs. She took off her shoes and climbed down the back of the building. Grateful for the moon-less night, she pushed the old heavy door open a crack to check that Tariq wasn't there. She quietly squeezed herself out.

The empty street, lulled by the dark night, stretched in front of her. Checking right and left, she pulled the hood of her top over her head. If she walked quickly, she thought, she could reach the tube station in ten minutes and there was still time to catch the last train. It would take only an hour to reach Anita's house and she would be safe there.

The roads were deserted. Neela ran, not looking behind her, and at the end of the road turned right. It wasn't far, only another five minutes and she would be mingling with other passengers. A van drove past. A motorbike whizzed by. She breathed a sigh of relief when she saw the Underground sign.

A car screeched to a halt behind her at the kerb. She kept her head low and pulled her hood down to hide her face. The car door slammed and foot steps behind her quickened. Not daring to look behind her, she broke into a run. A firm hand grabbed her shoulder and pulled her to a stop. She knew who it was and screamed.

'Shut up,' he hissed, covering her open mouth with his right hand. 'Where do you think you are going?' Tariq was panting. His breath was hot and laboured. His left hand was tight around her slim waist.

'Come on, my darling, come with me.'

He whispered other endearments while he dragged her towards his car.

She struggled but he was too strong. He opened the car door with his fingers while keeping a tight hold on her. That's it, Neela thought. My life is coming to an end. There was no escape. She wished she could lose consciousness completely so that she didn't have to feel the agony. She wanted to die.

Chapter 28

She was about to give up and let her body go limp when the hard grip around her body loosened, allowing her to float back to life's surface. She gasped for breath. She heard faint voices, shouting, and then a thud. She tried to look but her eyes weren't focusing properly; everything was blurred. Unable to stand up, she leaned against the car, gasping, but a pair of hands peeled her away. She heard the car roar. She heard it speeding away.

'Are you all right?' a voice asked.

She looked up.

'It's OK. You are safe now.'

She saw a kind face, full of concern.

Was this real or was it her shocked mind playing tricks on her?

'Here, take a sip.'

The stranger was holding a bottle of water to her lips. Grateful, she took a few sips. Her lips were parched.

'Don't be afraid. He has gone now. Were you on your way to the station?'

She nodded.

'No trains are going from this station.'

'No trains! Why?' she asked, puzzled.

'They just announced that there is some engineering work going on and all the trains are stopping here.'

'Oh, no!'

'I'm afraid so. We're all going to have to catch the bus. You had better go home.'

'Home . . .?' she gasped. How could she go back there?

'Where do you live?'

She pointed in the direction of her street.

'Come on, I will walk with you.'

She hesitated but where else could she go at that time of night?

'Thank you, sir . . . sorry, sir . . . for the trouble,' she stammered, following him.

'No, no, not at all.'

He waited outside her block until she was safely in.

'Be careful, it's not safe to go out at this hour.'

'Thank you very much, sir,' she said, going inside.

'Take care,' he said, as she closed the door behind her.

It must have been late in the morning when Neela became aware of the phone ringing.

'She hasn't woken up yet,' she heard Gill say.

Hearing her come into the room, Neela turned away and pulled the blankets over her head.

'Someone says it's urgent, love.'

Gill gently tapped Neela on the shoulder but Neela's hands shook as she took the receiver.

'Neela, my darling! Sorry, my *pyari*, that rogue spoiled our fun last night. He came like a demon between us. I will kill him if I see him again . . .'

Of course it was Tariq. He did not give up that easily. She banged the receiver down.

Gill was shocked by Neela's angry response.

'Are you all right, dear?'

She came and sat on the edge of the bed. Neela looked at her with her eyes full of fear.

'What is it? You look awful.' Gill asked.

Chapter 28

Hiding her face in her hands, she shook her head.

'Oh Gill, it was horrible. I don't understand why this is happening again and why he can't leave me alone.'

'Who? Tell me what's going on.'

Neela sobbed, unable to utter the name that sounded ugly to her ears.

'OK, OK,' said Gill, putting an arm round Neela's shaking shoulders. 'Don't worry, love, you can tell me later. I'm going to make a cuppa for you first.'

Gill's soothing presence and a steaming mug of tea calmed Neela's nerves a little allowing her to take a deep breath and tell the whole story of the previous night.

'Oh, Gill, I can't explain how I felt, it was like ... as if I was drowning in to the murky waters of the dark river,' Neela said, holding her breath as if she really were drowning. 'I wished I was dead.'

'How dare he behave like that? Who the hell does he think he is? You should go to the police.'

'No, Gill, please, I couldn't do that to Kajal.'

'I don't understand you. You are worried about Kajal after what her husband has done to you?'

'She would be devastated.'

'I think she deserves to know the truth.'

'I can't break Kajal's heart, Gill.'

'You can't just leave him on the loose, Neela. Can't you see, the man is sick!'

'I will definitely do something, Gill, but I need some time to think.'

'Actually you should report your in-laws to the police while you're at it,' Gill fumed.

Neela smiled wryly.

'Gill, I think I will take a few days off. I will go and see Anita.'

'That's a good idea. She might drill some sense into you.'

CHAPTER 29

'Come and sit here,' Anita said, patting the sofa, then waited quietly until Neela was ready to speak.

'You know,' Neela began, 'Gill said I should report the incident to the police.'

'Did she? Good.'

'Yes, but how can I? My name will be dragged through the mud along with his. You know how people look down on you once you get involved with the police!'

'I know but we are not in India, Neela. It's different here.'

'But even here it isn't very different in our own community, Anita-*behn*. And I doubt anyone would believe my side of the story.'

'I know what you mean, but isn't it sad that for centuries women have kept quiet and suppressed their true feelings? They just silently bear injustice because they are frightened of society judging them.'

'Yes, it is sad but . . .'

'No buts, I think Gill is right. You should report him to the police,' Anita said.

'Why don't you take a couple of days off work?'

'Yes, but . . .'

'It's all right, Neela. Dinesh won't be back from his sister's house in Nottingham for another couple of days. So you can stay here and it will be nice for me to have your company.'

'Gill, could you please let Pat know that I am not coming in to work today as I am ill.'

'All right, love, I will.'

'Hope she doesn't mind.'

'No, she won't care. If you don't go to work you are the one who won't get paid, not her.'

Neela was grateful for that.

'Take care, love.'

'I am sorry, Gill, it's . . . just . . . I still don't feel safe in that flat when you are not there.'

'I know, love, but I have some good news for you.'

'What is it?'

'The police came yesterday to take a statement from you.'

'Really, how did they find out?'

'You know that kind gentleman who came to your rescue? He reported what happened to the police.'

'But how did he know Tariq's name?'

'Apparently he noted down Tariq's car registration number.'

'Oh!'

'Anyway, was he handsome?'

'That's not funny, Gill.'

'Well, was he? The kind stranger?'

'I don't know. I don't remember. It's not important . . .'

'Was he English or Asian?'

'I have no idea.'

Neela was irritated now. She couldn't remember anything about the man who helped her except the reassurance in his voice and the kindness in his eyes.

'I gave Anita's address to the police so they might visit you today. Don't be afraid. Just tell them everything. Let them tackle Tariq once and for all and then you can have some peace,' Gill said firmly.

Having rested and restored her strength, Neela went straight from

Anita's house to Super Pack, but as she walked through the gates, the working men whistled and cheered loudly at her. She smiled shyly, thinking it hadn't been *that* long that she had been away so why were they doing this?

'Hey, how is business going?' one of them called out.

'What business?'

Neela noticed a wicked and not very pleasant glint in his eye.

'Do we have to make an appointment or can we just turn up?' another called.

'Can I come over tonight please?'

'You won't charge us, will you?'

'Is it a free service?'

She didn't understand what the men were saying but she didn't like their manner, nor the way they burst out laughing.

Things felt very wrong as Neela walked across the floor of the factory. Why was everyone looking at her so oddly? As she walked inside, she felt distinctly uncomfortable. Some of the women were whispering behind her back. Some looked at her as if disgusted. Why was there such a peculiar change in everyone? It was like walking under flood lights. Unsure which section she was working on that week, she walked towards Pat's office to look for her name on the board. Reshma was already in the office. Neela felt relieved to see her.

'Hello, Rhesma,' Neela said, smiling, but Reshma fled as if she had seen a ghost. What had happened to everyone? She turned to the door and spotted Kajal walking past.

'Kaj . . .'

But before she had could complete her sentence Kajal rushed at her.

'You slut!' She shouted. 'I trusted you as a friend but look what you have done! Why are you after my husband?'

Her voice screeched with anger and her eyes narrowed with disgust.

'What are you talking about, Kajal? I want to talk to you . . . listen to me . . .'

Neela put out a hand but Kajal ran to join Reshma who was waiting for her at the far end of the corridor.

Bewildered and troubled, Neela walked as fast as she could to the other building to find Gill. Gill remained quiet while Neela told her what had happened.

'Go home, Neela,' she said gently. 'I will come and see you later.'

Neela waited restlessly for Gill to come home that evening, going over and over what had happened at the factory. She paced up and down, winding and unwinding a corner of her sari *pallu* around her index finger.

'What is it, Gill?' Neela asked, the minute she opened the door to her friend. 'Why is everyone behaving like this? Is it because I signed the police statement?'

'No, it isn't,' said Gill. 'Sit down, Neela.'

'Then what is it? Didn't I tell you that Kajal would be devastated? Did you see the state she was in? She was like a mad woman when she saw me.'

'Come and sit here and try to calm down.'

Gill took her hand and pulled her down onto the sofa.

'It's not the end of the world but it's going to be difficult to sort this one out so just take it easy.'

'What is not the end of the world? And why do I have to take it easy?' Neela cried.

'Neela, it's not because you reported Tariq to the police. It's nothing to do with that. It's because someone has played a cruel joke on you.'

'What joke?'

'Someone placed some cards advertising your name in some phone boxes and public toilets around town.'

'Advertising . . . my name . . . for what?'

Gill gave her a long, sympathetic look.

'As a call girl.'

Neela went quiet. It took a while for the words to sink in but when they did, she felt the ground beneath her crumbling. She was falling.

'Don't worry, the police will catch them, whoever it was.'

Neela sat with her head in her hands, sick and dizzy with disbelief.

'If I am not wrong,' Gill said, 'I think you have an idea who did it, don't you? Will you agree now that the nice stranger did the right thing, reporting him to the police?'

Neela nodded.

'How could Tariq do it if the police arrested him for questioning?'

'He might have done it before he was arrested, maybe that same night.'

The next morning, the police came to take a statement from Neela.

Neela felt very nervous as she offered a seat to a big burly police officer and to a woman constable who accompanied him.

'Please sit down,' the police officer said.

Neela sat down at the edge of the seat, wiping her sweaty hands on her sari *pallu*. After confirming her name and address and other details, he asked, 'Do you know a person called Tariq Khan?'

'Yes.'

'For how long?'

'For . . . for . . . perhaps eighteen months.'

'How did you come to know him?'

'He . . . he is my brother-in-law's friend.'

'Did he show any interest in you before?'

'Yes . . .'

'What made you think that he was interested in you?'

'Because . . . he . . . he . . .'

Neela was unable to finish the sentence.

'Relax. Don't worry. Take your time,' the woman constable reassured her.

Neela's heart was pounding hard in her chest and for a few minutes she couldn't continue.

'He . . . he . . .,'

As she tried to explain the previous encounter with Tariq, her voice shook and her eyes filled with tears. She struggled to express herself in English. The woman officer looked at her with sympathy.

'Don't worry,' she said, before turning to her colleague. 'Perhaps we need an interpreter.'

'I think that would be a good idea. We will come back tomorrow with someone who can translate for us.'

After they left, Neela sat motionless for a long time, her head in her hands.

The next interview with an interpreter present was much easier, and Neela found she could tell her story quickly. The police were sympathetic and assured Neela that the cards would be taken down and discarded immediately.

Tariq had created hell on earth for Neela and once again she couldn't face going to work. Even though the police had taken down all the cards, the nuisance phone calls from random people continued until Gill changed the phone number. It was the ultimate humiliation for Neela. What little confidence she had gained over the past months was destroyed.

She heard that Tariq was given a suspended sentence but this gave her very little consolation.

The weeks went by agonisingly slowly as Neela's shame ate into her. She stopped eating and stopped taking care of her appearance. She became lethargic, hardly bothering to get out of bed.

'I think you had better come and see her,' Neela heard Gill saying to Anita on the phone. Her voice was anxious.

Later that day, Neela watched as the two women, her friends, came into her room. She barely greeted them.

Anita pulled back the curtains and let in a flood of light. Neela turned away and pulled the blanket over her head, but not before catching a shocked look in Anita's eyes. Anita stared at Neela's hollow cheeks and dark sunken eyes. Her knotted hair was spread across the pillow. Neela wasn't asleep but Anita had to shake her gently before she could face them.

'Neela, you are torturing yourself,' Anita said softly. 'What crime have you committed to deserve this? Nothing happened, you know. Actually it could have been worse if that gentleman hadn't saved you at the station.'

'I know..but you know . . . what everyone thinks of me?'

'Of course people gossip. Sometimes they weave stories out of nothing. So what?'

Neela turned her face to the wall.

'We do know how much this is hurting you,' Anita continued. 'Gill and I know what happened and we understand what you are going through.'

'Come on, love. You have to pull yourself together,' Gill said, helping Neela to a sitting position while Anita smoothed her tangled hair and plaited it.

'Why can't you find a nice man for her, Anita? That will shut everyone up,' Gill said, shocking Neela. But Gill always spoke her mind.

Anita stopped plaiting Neela's hair and raised her eyebrows.

'Gill, it's hard enough for an unmarried girl to get married so you can imagine how hard it is for a widow or a divorcee. You know almost every Indian man wants a virgin bride, even if he isn't a virgin himself,' Anita said.

'To hell with them and to hell with arranged marriages. We don't need them. Why can't a girl have a partner in her own community without all that nonsense?'

'Because morals and traditions are fed to us with our first drink of mother's milk, and it is a sin for a girl to even look at a man. But of course it's fine for a man to get married within three months of his wife's death and there is a guarantee that he will get a brand new virgin,' Anita replied.

CHAPTER 30

The concern and kindness shown by both Anita and Gill during this painful period moved Neela on many an occasion. She wondered what stroke of fate had brought them into her life when she most needed them. The man who had married her was supposed to love, cherish and care for her but had treated her with cruelty. Her in-laws, on whom she depended, had deceived and discarded her. But these two women, one an immigrant herself, the other a divorcee, showed her love and compassion while she struggled to pull herself together, and expected nothing in return.

It had been three months since she had left her job in Super Pack. So far she had been managing with the money Dr Vikas had paid her when he left for India but she knew that it wouldn't last much longer. At times Neela was tempted to have a glass of wine at Gill's house to drown her problems, but then she recalled images of the drunken Suraj and Tariq and turned away from the temptation.

It was the Sunday morning in the month when the landlord was due to collect her rent. Neela asked him to give her more time because she didn't have a penny in her purse. He didn't take her request too kindly but after a lot of persuasion, he agreed to wait another couple of weeks.

What would happen if she was unable to pay?

'You will end up on the streets, love, if you don't find a job soon,' Gill told her.

'Maybe I had better give up the struggle and go back to India?'

The same old idea crossed Neela's mind but this time it didn't seem to excite or interest her. It seemed irrelevant.

A fortnight passed and the rent due was mounting. The landlord came back again with an ultimatum. If she didn't pay the rent by the following Sunday, he said, she would have to find alternative accommodation.

There was nothing for it but to try once more to find a job. On Anita's suggestion, she tried asking for work in the local grocery shops, but with no luck. Not knowing what to do, and after wandering aimlessly around town, she climbed onto the first bus that pulled up at the stop, and, without even looking at the number, was pleasantly surprised to find herself being driven along a familiar route. Without any particular plan, she got off at the stop by the hospital where Dr Vikas had worked and walked the streets, remembering the peaceful and happy months when she had worked for his family. She wondered how they were doing in India. Would they still remember her? On automatic pilot, her legs took her through the gates of Number 28. She was almost tempted to ring the bell but no, someone else would be living there now. She looked at the house fondly as memories flooded back. Nothing had changed. Everything was the same as before, even the colour of the door and the potted plants on either side of it. The evergreen conifers and the tall silver birch trees were still there swaying in the wind to one side of the house. It was like stepping back into the past; she could still hear the laughter of the children mingling with hers. She could still picture them playing hide and seek around the house and in the trees. Neela stood there for a long while until a car drove up to the house and stopped outside. Neela turned on her heel and quickly walked away.

She called in at the newsagents shop close by and again she was reminded of the times when she used to accompany the children there to buy sweets and ice-cream. Mr Patel was serving customers as usual, smiling politely at each one. As he didn't have any children of his own, he had adored Rahul and Pallavi. She went to the shop window to see if there were any advertisements for jobs. It had become a habit lately and a daily ritual.

'*Namaskar, kaise hai aap?*' Mr Patel greeted her.

'I am all right, thank you, Patel-*bhayya*. How are you?'

'Fine, fine. I haven't seen you lately.'

'No, there is no reason for me to come here since the doctor and his family left.'

'Yes, I heard.' There was a moment's hesitation. 'Maybe it's better for the children and for the doctor too. At least they will have their relatives there.'

'Yes, of course. I am sure they are happy there.'

'I still remember Mrs Vikas. She was a lovely lady. She used to come in every now and then to buy these magazines.' He gestured at his display. 'Where do you work now?'

'Nowhere, *bhayya*. Actually I am looking for a job at the moment.'

'I see. What sort of work are you looking for? Child minding?'

'I don't mind doing anything,' she shrugged.

'Wait a minute, don't go.' He went to serve a customer and came back. 'Come and look at this.' He pointed at a card displayed in the other window. 'I put it up just this morning.'

'Neela read it out loud. Woman needed for housework and looking after a toddler.'

'Are you interested?'

'Yes, definitely.'

'Then phone this number and try.'

Thanking him, she noted the number down.

Once she was at home she steeled herself to ring the number. She knew that jobs like these don't hang around for long.

'Hello, could I speak to Mrs Helen Sagar, please?'

'Yes, speaking,' the lady's voice on the other end of the phone sounded soft, mature and friendly.

'My name is Neela . . . er . . . Pattwar and I saw your advertisement for a childminder in the shop window . . .'

'What did you say your name was? Neela . . .'

'Neela Pattwar.'

Helen repeated her name, asked her a few more questions and, to her surprise, suggested an interview.

'Would you like to come and see me tomorrow morning at nine so that we can talk properly and you can meet my grandson, Krishna.'

'I would love to, Mrs Sagar. Thank you very much.'

At last here was a possibility of life starting up again. A job looking after a child – and with her past experience and the doctor's references, she thought she had a chance of getting it.

Neela rose early the next day and, after deliberating whether to wear a sari or trousers and a top, she eventually decided against the trousers. Wearing a simple, light blue sari, she arrived at Gideapark station clutching a piece of paper with the address. She followed the directions that Helen had given her and arrived in a pleasant, leafy area.

It was a fine-looking bungalow, painted white with leaded bay windows on either side of the dark oak door. The arch of the door frame was adorned with climbing roses and at the side of a small step were potted flowering plants. In one corner, at the far end of the luscious green lawn, there was a scattering of poppies, cornflowers and wild grasses. In the morning sunshine, the glowing whiteness of the bungalow brought out the contrasting colours of reds, pinks and yellows of the flower beds. The air was filled with the sweet scent of the flowers and Neela inhaled deeply. Pushing her niggling doubts and uncertainties aside, she lifted the latch of the gate and, wearing a brave smile, she knocked on the door. It was opened immediately by a woman in her late sixties with grey hair. Even though her face was lined, the traces of her previous beauty were still there. Her blue eyes were smiling.

Chapter 30

'Mrs Pattwar?'

'Yes, madam . . . I am Neela.'

It always felt strange when she gave her name as Mrs Pattwar. She still hadn't got used to being called by her married name and she disliked using it.

'I am Helen, Helen Sagar,' smiled the lady, stretching her hand out to Neela.

'How do you do, Mrs Sagar?'

'Very well, thank you. Please come in.'

Neela was surprised that this English woman had an Indian surname.

'My husband Vidya Sagar was from India,' Helen said, reading Neela's thoughts.

Neela stepped into an immaculately clean lounge filled with light cane furniture. Green and pink cushions, scattered on the sofas, matched the curtains at the open windows.

'How long have you been here, Mrs Pattwar?' Helen asked, handing her tea in a rose-patterned china cup.

'Just over three years, Mrs Sagar.'

After answering all Mrs Sagar's questions, Neela took from her handbag the envelope that Dr Vikas had given her on the day he left for India.

'Mrs Sagar, I used to work for Dr Vikas. Would you like to see the reference letter?'

Helen smiled as she read the letter.

'That's very good. So you looked after his children for quite some time.'

'Yes, Madam, about fifteen months, and then they went to India for good.'

'So I heard from Mr Patel. Actually he recommended you to me.'

'Oh,' Neela replied with a shy smile.

'You see, Mrs Pattwar, my grandson Krishna – we call him Krish for short – will be five next month and starts school in September. I used to work as a headteacher. I am retired now, but still teach at a private school nearby. You can see I am getting on in years and it's becoming quite a chore for me to look after Krish. He is very active and demanding. He needs someone young like you,' Mrs Sagar explained.

'Thank you so much, Mrs Sagar. You needn't worry, I will do my best to look after him.'

'Before you decide, you should meet the little devil himself,' Mrs Sagar said, smiling at Neela's enthusiasm and beckoning Neela to follow her.

They stepped into a brightly-painted bedroom with cartoon murals on the walls. A car-shaped bed dominated the room. Krish was sitting on the carpet surrounded by his toys. He was making a 'broom, broom' sound, while he pushed a toy car forward and backward. Neela could see only a mass of curly hair because his face was down-cast.

'Here he is, Mrs Pattwar, this is my grandson Krish.'

Hearing his grandmother's voice, the boy lifted his head and Neela suppressed a gasp. He was the most beautiful child she had ever seen. He had an angelic face with enormous, sparkling dark eyes. A few curls fringed his forehead, complementing his milk-mixed-with-honey skin.

'Krish,' Neela said, smiling.

'This nice lady's name is Neela,' Helen said. 'She has come to see you. Say Hello to her.'

'Hello,' he said shyly from under his long lashes.

'How are you?' Sitting down on her knees beside him, Neela took his little hand in her own.

What a gorgeous child.

Unable to believe her luck, Neela arrived home feeling ecstatic. She couldn't resist phoning Anita straightaway.

'It's a miracle, Anita-*behn*. I got the job.'

Chapter 30

'Miracles do happen, *puglee*,' Anita laughed. 'Now do you believe in that saying, "Where there is a will, there is a way"? And you got it without anybody's help. Congratulations!'

Neela waited restlessly until Gill came home to share the good news with her too, and they celebrated the success with a take-away pizza, cola, and ice-cream.

Just before Neela left for her first day at her new job, she went to the small bronze figure of Lord *Ganesh* on the shelf in her room and prayed.

'Oh, God, please bless me to do my job well and let Mrs Sagar and her grandson like me and my work. I will come to your temple on Saturday and offer you coconuts and bananas.'

She bent her head and touched the deity's feet.

She took her handbag and was about to leave when she stopped and turned back again to the Lord *Ganesh* to give him a warning.

'Don't you dare make me lose this job too, or else I will never, ever, come to your temple in my life again.'

Neela's first day of work began in much the same way as at the doctor's house. Krish was much younger than Rahul and Pallavi, so she had to bath him and dress him as well. Krish was very quiet and obedient in front of his grandmother but whenever she was out of sight he would glance at Neela with a wicked look and give her a mischievous grin. Since it was Neela's first day, Helen stayed at home to show her everything. Together they got Krish ready for school and went together to the school gates.

'He seems a bit cheeky, but Krish is a lovely little boy,' Neela told Gill that evening. 'And the school isn't far, only ten minutes away.'

'That's good, but don't you get too attached to him,' Gill told her with a smile.

'Oh, no, I won't, I promise.'

CHAPTER 31

Neela quickly learned the ways of Helen's house. Krish was a real handful and it was much more tiring looking after him than the doctor's children. Every morning, getting him out of bed was a battle, and bathing and feeding him was a real challenge for Neela. He listened only to his grandmother.

'Where are you, Krish?' Neela called, looking at an empty chair. It was only a minute ago that she had sat him at the breakfast table but when she had turned her back to fetch the milk from the fridge, he disappeared. She called him again while she poured milk into a bowl of Coco-Pops, but there was no answer. Wiping her hands on a tea towel she went to the lounge to look for him but he wasn't there.

'Krish, where are you? Please come quickly otherwise your Coco-Pops will go soggy,' she pleaded, going into his room. Krish was there, sitting in front of his desk, dipping a piece of chalk into an ink bottle and scribbling all over his scrapbook.

'Oh, Krish, what are you doing? That's your grandmother's ink bottle. Why did you bring it here?'

He looked up at her, grinning.

'Oh, my God, what have you done?' she screamed.

His freshly ironed white shirt, his hands and his cheeks were all covered in blue ink.

'You can't go to school like this!'

She screwed the lid back on the bottle and lifted him up from the chair and took him into the bathroom. It took a while to get rid of all the ink stains from his face and hands, but Krish enjoyed the attention and played with the water. After washing him clean, and putting a new shirt on him, she took him down to the kitchen.

'Come on, eat your breakfast quickly otherwise you will be late for school.'

'I don't want this. It's gone soggy.'

'OK.'

She brought him a fresh bowl of the cereal.

'No, I don't want this,' he pushed the bowl away. 'I want toast.'

'But you said you wanted Coco Pops.'

'I don't want it now.'

'Oh, Krish!' Neela sighed as she put a slice of bread in the toaster and made some strawberry milkshake for him.

At last he was ready for school. It was only a ten minute walk but he made it last half an hour, by taking two steps forward and one step back. Neela had to force him to hold her hand and dragged him to school where they arrived only just in time. She didn't want to complain too much to Helen as she was desperate to manage him on her own.

A couple of months passed, and then one evening when Helen was at home, she asked Neela to come into the lounge because she wanted to talk to her. 'I had heard a lot about you from Mr Patel, but now I have seen your patience and care with Krish for myself. I do appreciate what you do, Neela.'

'Thank you, Mrs Sagar, but he is only a little boy.'

Neela was secretly delighted with the praise.

'He is a little devil,' Helen chuckled, 'but I can see you are taming him nicely.'

'Thank you, Mrs Sagar. That's very kind of you.'

'I was thinking . . .' Helen paused. 'I mean, if it's all right with you of course, my sister lives in the south of France and she has invited me to go there.'

Chapter 31

'That's nice.'

'Since I haven't had a break for nearly five years, she thinks I should go and visit her in the half term holiday.'

'That would be a good idea, Mrs Sagar,' Neela agreed again.

'Would you like to stay here for a few days and look after Krish while I am away?' Helen asked tentatively.

'Of course I will look after him,' Neela replied, without thinking twice.

'I will give you my sister's phone number just in case but I will ring you every day.'

'That will be fine, Mrs Sagar, you don't need to worry,' said Neela.

She was surprised and delighted at Helen's trust in her, and happily prepared herself to shoulder the responsibility she had been given.

And so it was settled that Neela should live in the house and take care of Krish on her own. Helen made sure that everything was in order. She filled the fridge with plenty of food and left numerous useful telephone numbers, including the doctor's, on a pad on the table. She made her grandson promise to behave with Neela, before she went on her much-needed holiday.

'When is Nan coming back?' Krish asked, sitting in his chair at the dining table.

'On Sunday,' said Neela, placing a glass of milk in front of him.

Helen always insisted he should have milk every evening.

'How many more days?'

'Today is Thursday, that means only Friday and Saturday, just two days in the middle and she will be back on Sunday.'

'Why didn't she take me with her?'

'Because she wouldn't be able to look after you there.'

'Then how could she look after her sister?'

'She is not going there to look after her sister,' laughed Neela. 'Her sister is big like your Nan, she doesn't need to be looked after.'

'Then why did Nan go there?'

'To see her. They need to spend some time together.'

He looked at her thoughtfully, cupping his chin with his hands, and said suddenly, 'I don't like you.'

'Why?'

'Because since you came here, Nan doesn't do anything for me any more,' he shouted.

'Well, you are a big boy now, so with you going to school and your Nan teaching, she needs my help to look after you.'

'I don't need your help,' he said, scowling at her. 'Because of you, Nan didn't take me with her. It's your fault.'

'You think so?'

'Yes, because you are lonely.'

'Who said I am lonely?' Neela was taken aback.

'No one. I just know,' he shrugged.

'Really, you are very clever then . . .'

'I love my Nan very much.'

'Of course you love her,' she ruffled his hair.

His mischievous eyes stared at her for a few seconds then he pushed his glass of milk to the edge of the table.

'Please don't play with it. Please drink it.'

'I am going to break it.'

'Oh no, please be careful,' she put her hand out. 'You are a good boy, aren't you?' She gently placed the glass back in the middle of the table.

'No.'

His hands sprang forward and before Neela could stop him, the glass fell to the kitchen floor. As it crashed into pieces, she put her hands over her ears and looked helplessly at the shattered pieces of glass in a big puddle of milk.

'Look what you have done!' she cried. 'Please don't move, stay there, otherwise you will get hurt. Put your feet up until I clean the floor properly.'

Even before she had a chance to fetch a brush and mop, he disappeared.

'Oh no,' she panted. 'Krish, where are you? Are you OK?'

What if he had stepped on the broken glass and cut himself? Her heart pounded in her chest as she frantically searched for him in the dining room, bedrooms and the lounge. She finally found him in the conservatory, watching cartoons with a wickedly innocent expression on his face. Hurriedly she checked his feet. There wasn't a scratch to be seen.

'Oh,' Neela collapsed breathlessly into a settee. It was beginning to get really tough because she couldn't predict what he would do next. In front of his grandmother, of course, he was an angel but the child was testing her patience and many times she felt on the verge of losing her temper. Then she reminded herself to be tolerant and sympathetic if she wanted to do her job well and win him round. She remembered her promise to Helen when she had asked her whether Neela could cope with Krish's tantrums.

'Of course, Mrs Sagar, I looked after two children before.'

But two children were far easier than this one, naughty little boy.

Yet it was very difficult for Neela to deal with Krish's hyperactive behaviour and his constant challenges to her authority. Neela tried her best to be friendly with him, but at times he would refuse even to talk to her. He was a different child from the one who behaved so well with his grandmother. In the evenings he would tell her all about his day at school and his friends, but he never once mentioned Neela's name. If Helen mentioned her, he would just nod Yes or No in answer.

That evening Neela served Krish's dinner, macaroni-cheese and a few boiled vegetables in a melamine plate. As she feared he didn't complain about the food but ate very little. While he played with the rest of the food and cutlery, Neela deliberately ignored his cheeky glances. Deciding not to say anything, she finished her dinner in silence.

While she was getting him ready for bed, Krish asked, 'Why are you not talking to me?'

'Do you want me to talk to you?'

Krish went quiet for a moment thinking, then said, 'If you want to.'

'I would love to talk to you.'

'Can you read me a bedtime story?'

'Of course.'

After tucking him in his car-shaped bed, feeling glad that he was calming down a bit, Neela sat in a chair to read *Ugly Duckling* at his request.

The next morning Neela and Krish walked side by side to school. After many fights and attempts to upset her and challenge her authority, Krish did seem to be accepting her slowly, and even warming towards her. They walked at a pace to suit his small strides, and stopped to look at the many-coloured flowers that adorned every front garden. Suddenly Neela let go of Krish's hand and stopped in her tracks.

'My God! It's one year!'

'What?' Krish looked up at her.

'It's one year exactly since I first came to see your Gran for the interview.'

'What is one year?'

'Twelve months.'

'That many,' said Krish, counting the months on his fingers. At school, he was just learning the names of the days and Neela was teaching him how to count days into weeks and months.

'Nan said my dad isn't coming back for another two weeks. That means how many days?' Again he counted on his fingers.

'Why is he not back for two weeks?'

'Because he is going to a conference in Paris.'

'Oh! Did you have a nice time with him last weekend?'

'Yes, we went to the zoo and I saw all the animals. Monkeys were funny. My dad bought me ice-cream and we had loads of fun.'

'That's good.'

'I love my dad so much. I wish he lived here with us.' His little face clouded.

'Why don't you ask him then?'

'I did, and my Nan did as well, but he said he can't.'

There must be some reason then, thought Neela, saying goodbye to Krish at the school gates.

On the way home, thinking about Krish, Neela felt that she had finally achieved something. At last he was talking to her. Remembering their conversation, she thought again about his mysterious father. It was strange that Helen never mentioned her son. Whenever they had spoken, Helen had seemed to understand quite a lot about Neela's culture and that was very unusual for an English woman, but then her husband was Indian . . . Oh, she must remember to put the book that she borrowed back on the shelf before Helen returned home.

Helen came back refreshed and happy, and she was pleased with Neela's rapport with Krish.

'Without your help it wouldn't have been possible to visit my sister, *dhanyavad*, Neela.

'*Dhanyavad?*' Neela looked at her, astonished. 'How did you know that word?'

Helen smiled. 'I know because I lived in Ananthpore, in southern India.'

Neela's eyes widened with fascination.

'I was born and lived there for 16 years, when my father was serving in the British Raj,' said Helen.

'Didn't you mind all the dust and heat?'

'No, not at all. I loved Ananthpore,' she closed her eyes as if seeing the place.

'Could you understand the language?'

'Many of our Indian friends spoke English but since our servants couldn't, my parents and I picked up a few words of Telugu, the local language.' She smiled at the memory. 'It was fun surprising our friends by speaking in their own language. They used to love that. And appreciated our efforts.'

Neela smiled too, but was thinking how easy it is to please Indian people.

'It was a long time ago, but I still remember a few words like *paalu,* milk, and *neellu,* water.'

'After so many years, Mrs Sagar?'

'Yes, I can still see the place. I always dreamt of going back and visiting it, but I never had the opportunity.' She looked thoughtful for a moment, then brightening up said, 'I might go back one day. Who knows?'

'Really?'

'Yes, of course I would love to. I still have some friends over there who write to me regularly.'

'Oh, that's nice.'

'OK then, off you go. You need a weekend rest after the hard work you did for the last few days.'

CHAPTER 32

Neela spent her weekends alone, mostly reading. The local library had become her favourite place and the books were her companions. After finishing each book she felt an enormous sense of achievement. She was able not only to understand the language, but to understand the complexity of the stories. She related the characters to people she knew, and it helped her to understand them a little better. Analysing the characters helped her to understand human nature.

One Sunday, when Gill was out with her boyfriend, Neela was in her room reading the last pages of *The Black Velvet Gown* by Catherine Cookson. The sun was setting by the time she finished the last chapter and she reluctantly closed the book and traced the letters on the front cover with a finger. It was like that every time, when she read the last sentence of a book. She felt she was saying goodbye to a dear friend and she would miss the characters that had come alive and lived with her until the last page. Thinking about the book reminded her of her friend Anita. Every time Neela said she had finished reading a book, Anita would ask her about the plot and listen with interest. Neela wished Anita would read the books but her English was too limited. She hadn't seen as much of her recently because Anita had taken a job at a local supermarket and had been working weekends. Feeling the urge to talk to her, she looked at the clock and guessed that her friend would be home by now, so she placed the book back on the shelf and reached for the phone.

'How are you, *puglee*?' Anita answered, as soon as she heard Neela's voice.

'Fine, Anita-*behn*. It's been so long since I have seen you.'

'I know. We have both been so busy. Anyway, how is that little tiger boy that you are looking after?'

'Oh, don't ask me about Krish. He is a sweet little thing but the naughtiest boy I have ever known,' she laughed.

'It's good in a way; at least it might prevent you from getting attached. Remember what happened the last time when the doctor's family left.'

'Um, maybe you are right, Anita-*behn*.'

How could she explain to anyone that she longed for any bond that offered affection? Wasn't it worth risking pain for the possibility of happiness?

'So you still haven't met the boy's father? And you don't know what happened to the mother? And you don't know why Helen is looking after the boy?'

'No, I haven't seen his father because he only visits them at weekends, and I haven't even seen a photo of his mother. Having said that, actually I have seen Krish's father's photo on the mantelpiece. I mean, I guessed that the person who was holding baby Krish was his father.'

'But he could be anyone.'

'I think I could tell.'

'Where does this mysterious father of Krish stay then? And why does he leave his son with his mother?'

'Apparently he lives in Edinburgh but is always travelling to other countries for his work. He phones occasionally, usually late in the evening. But Helen has never mentioned Krish's mother, and I don't really feel comfortable asking.'

'You are right. Sometimes it's better not to ask too many personal questions.'

'I have no intention of stepping over my boundaries, Anita-*behn*. If she wants to tell me, she will in her own time.'

Chapter 32

Neela did not tell Anita that she often wondered if there was some mystery that surrounded the family, but she didn't want her friend teasing her for having too vivid an imagination nor for being too emotionally involved so she decided to keep her thoughts to herself.

The warm sunshine through the window woke Neela. It was Sunday so there was no need to get up. She leaned back on her pillow and looked through the window at the cloudless sky. The morning was very quiet and because it was Sunday, there was no noise from the traffic outside. She listened to the chirping birds in the trees and smiled. She felt at peace. Lately, her mind felt freer. Maybe it was a question of time. Time does heal everything, she mused. And the summer weather was working its magic. She couldn't believe the power of nature. It could make a person miserable on a dark winter's day, yet it could lift the spirit on a beautiful sunny day.

The phone rang, breaking the tranquillity of the moment.

It was Margaret, Helen's neighbour.

'Neela, can you please come over here at once,' she said breathlessly. Helen is not very well and I may have to go to the hospital with her.'

'Oh, no! I will come now.'

She hurriedly washed, dressed and rushed out to catch a train.

An ambulance was parked outside Helen's house. Her heart pounding, Neela ran towards it and asked one of the paramedics what had happened. Inside was Helen with an oxygen mask over her mouth.

'Mrs Sagar,' called a devastated Neela.

Helen opened her eyes and waved one hand towards Krish who was standing very still beside Margaret.

'Don't worry, Mrs Sagar. I will look after him,' Neela assured her.

When the ambulance left with its emergency siren screaming, Krish started to wail pitifully for his grandmother. Neela, still in shock, stretched her hands towards him and he came to her, his little face crumpled with distress. Her heart went out to him as she hugged him tight.

'It seems that Helen had a heart attack,' Margaret told Neela. 'She rang me and when I went to the house she couldn't even come to open the door. This little fellow opened it for me.'

'Heart attack, oh my God!' Neela put her hand over her mouth.

'Could you look after him so that I can follow the ambulance to the hospital?'

'Of course, Mrs Morgan.'

'I have already phoned Alex, you know, Helen's son, and he is on his way.'

'How long will it take him to get here?'

'Not long, an hour perhaps. Luckily he had already flown from Paris this morning and he is still in London now,' she sighed. 'Anyway you had better take the boy inside and give him some milk or something. Poor child! He must be terrified after seeing his grandmother like that, and if you need anything please don't hesitate to call me. I will come back here as soon as Alex gets to the hospital.'

'Thank you, Mrs Morgan', Neela said. 'Helen will be all right, won't she?'

'Let's hope so,' Margaret replied.

Neela made some hot chocolate for Krish and some tea for herself. She took both cups into the lounge and put some cartoons on the television for him to watch.

'What happened to Nan?' asked Krish between sips.

'She is not feeling well, so they took her to the hospital.'

'When is she coming back?'

'Soon. When she gets better.'

Once Krish was engrossed in the cartoons, Neela allowed herself to think about Helen. She had looked fine when Neela had left on Friday evening. How could she become so ill in just two days? How awful for her son, Alex. Judging by Krish's comments here and there,

Neela could tell Alex didn't visit Helen and Krish as often as they would have liked.

It was past lunchtime and Krish was getting agitated. Poor boy, thought Neela, he has done nothing but watch television all day. Although he wanted to play snakes and ladders with her, he soon got bored and repeatedly asked for his grandmother. Neela took him in her arms.

'Grandma is sick so she went to the hospital to get better. She will come home soon.'

'But she promised to take me to the museum in London today and she said we could see my dad as well.'

'I know. Please don't worry. I'm sure they will take you as soon as your grandmother gets better.'

His face crumpled as if he was about to cry.

'That's why we got up early this morning and then Gran felt sick.' His enormous eyes looked troubled. 'And the ambulance came . . . pee-paa, pee-paa . . . but Margaret wouldn't let me go with her.' His lips quivered and his eyes filled with tears.

'Please don't cry. Come here,' Neela said, scooping him up in her arms. 'Shall we go and see if Margaret has come back from the hospital?'

He nodded and she patted his back as he laid his head on her shoulder.

Neela had been watching from the window for Margaret's return, and as soon as she saw her coming towards the house, she rushed to open the door.

'How is she?' Neela asked.

Margaret's face was ashen.

'She is dead, Neela. She died.'

It took a good few minutes for Neela to digest the news and when she finally took it in, she let out a loud scream.

'No, it can't be true.'

'Yes, my dear. It's true. At least her son managed to reach her in time.'

Krish was playing on his own in his room as if nothing had happened. He had not heard the exchange between Neela and Margaret in the hall. How could she tell him? A few hours passed in which Neela tried to hide her emotional turmoil from him. Then Margaret was at the door again.

'You can go home, Neela,' she said. 'I will take Krish with me now. His dad is asking for him.'

'How is he?'

'Alex? Oh, he was in such a state, poor boy.' Margaret shook her head. 'I think seeing his son might help him. It's a good thing that they are both going to stay with a friend tonight. I will call you if we need you again and I will let you know about the funeral.'

When she returned home, Neela sat on the bed in her darkened room for a long, long time. She felt sad for Helen, for her son Alex, and most of all for little Krish. She could still see Helen's eyes looking at her from the ambulance. She could still hear Krish's distressed wailing and see his tearstained face. She could feel his anguish when the ambulance left. His weeping and his little outstretched hands when Margaret took him from her touched her deeply. A surge of pity and deep concern welled up inside her. She wanted to be there for him, to hold him, to console him, and to comfort him. She felt restless and helpless. How could she go to him, she who was an outsider? She was only a servant and she had no place in their family, and no role in their affairs, especially after something as serious as a death. But perhaps at least she could go to the funeral when she knew where it would be held.

Two days later, wearing a black sari, as Gill had suggested, Neela went to Helen's funeral. There were already quite a few people gathered in the church. She entered hesitantly, and stopped at the entrance realising that she didn't know anyone. Then she saw Krish at the very front and her heart ached. He was dressed in a black suit and looked small and vulnerable. She wondered how much he was aware of what was happening. Next to Krish was a smartly-dressed man who kept hold of his hand. Although he did not look exactly the same as the man in the photo, Neela guessed that this was Krish's father, Alex.

Feeling scruffy and out of place in front of so many well dressed people, and not wanting to intrude on their private sorrow, Neela remained at the back and stared at Helen's coffin. She offered a prayer from where she stood and then left quietly, wiping tears from her eyes.

CHAPTER 33

Neela felt agitated and claustrophobic in her small flat, waiting and waiting for Margaret's phone call, but then she decided she might as well do something useful since she had nothing else to occupy her so she got out the vacuum cleaner out and cleaned the flat from top to bottom. Gill would be so pleased. Then she cooked *poories* and *palak-paneer* curry and waited for her friend to come home. Gill came in the door sniffing.

'Oh Heavens, that smells delicious.'

'Good, you are not complaining like Yamini. If she were here she would say, "The flat stinks of curry."'

'Why didn't she like Indian food?'

'She liked the food but hated the overpowering aroma of spices.'

'So, how are you?' Gill asked, taking off her coat and going through to the kitchen.

'I can't get thoughts of Helen out of my mind. I can't believe she died suddenly like that,' Neela replied, immediately tearful.

'Don't you upset yourself, dear. That's life. We all have to go when our time comes.'

'But I wish at least she had gone to India before she died. Remember I told you, she was born there in Ananthpore.'

'Oh yes, I remember.'

'She said she loved that place so much and wanted to go and see it again.'

'We all want to do so many things in this life and wish for so much but you never know what's going to happen tomorrow. At least she didn't suffer much.'

'True. In India they say that death without prolonged pain comes only to good people. But now she is gone and I don't know how Krish will take it.'

'He will be fine. His dad is here to take care of him.'

'I hope so. Anyway, how is work?'

'Uh, you know how hard we have to work for measly peanuts! But it's fun. You know how Pat gets worked up? And some of the girls drive her up the wall all the time.'

Neela smiled, picturing the workplace.

'There's a good film on TV at nine. Would you like to watch it?'

'Oh, yes please, Gill.'

Neela loved watching films with Gill who would get so absorbed in the plot and would laugh, cry and scream along with the characters. Afterwards, they often discussed it late into the night.

That was one evening taken care of, but time still passed slowly and Neela began to think about the implications of Helen's death for her own position. She continued to wait restlessly for Margaret's phone call, increasingly agitated about her own future. What would happen now? Would Helen's son take Krish away with him? If so, what would she do? God had always shown her a flicker of light in the darkest moments of her life, but this time she had so hoped that the brightness would last and last. Neela's mind wandered aimlessly. If she lost this job, what would she do? She couldn't possibly go back to Super Pack. The mere thought reminded her of Tariq.

Neela looked out of the window and saw a group of children running around the tall conifer tree near the gate. There were little yellow marigolds underneath the tree reminding her of the ones in her back garden in India. They used to bloom in abundance. She remembered that she and Suji used to compete to make the longest garlands. They would decorate their hair with the remaining flowers and in the evening take the garlands to the temple near the Manjeera. She wondered if her parents were still planting them. She would ask them in her next letter, she decided. Thinking of India made her feel better. Her longing for home had never faded in her heart but her circumstances had taught her to live with it.

The phone call Neela had been waiting for finally came.

'Could I speak to Neela Pattwar, please?'

'Yes, speaking,' answered Neela, puzzled by the unfamiliar male voice.

'This is Alex. Helen's son.'

'Hello . . . er . . . sir,' Neela replied, immediately nervous.

'I haven't seen you but I've heard so much about you from my mother,' the man said, his voice catching on the word. 'And from my son. I just want to . . . thank you very much for all your help.'

'Oh, not at all sir . . . it is . . . fine, sir. Actually . . . I should say thank you to your mother for giving me this job, sir . . . and Krish . . . he is a lovely boy, sir.'

She knew she was chatting inappropriately but she didn't know what else to say.

'Thank you. Actually, Mrs Pattwar, I would like to ask you another favour. Do you think you could look after Krish for a bit longer?'

'Of course, sir. I would love to,' Neela replied, barely suppressing her joy.

'Would you be able to come over tomorrow, Mrs Pattwar, or is that too short notice?'

'Yes, I can, sir.'

'It's just that I have to leave for Milan this evening. I am leaving Krish with Margaret tonight. I will need you in the morning to collect him from Margaret and take him to school. Is that all right with you?'

'Of course, sir. I will do that willingly, sir.'

By eight the next morning, Neela was at Margaret's house ready to collect Krish.

'Look at him. What sort of a father would leave a small son like Krish and go away like that? It's not even a fortnight since his grandma died,' Margaret complained. 'He should have taken his son with him. Krish is too young to be left alone. I know you and I will look after him, but that's different, isn't it?'

Neela didn't know what to say.

'Is his father returning this evening?'

'Who knows? He might not be back for days now because you are here to look after his son.'

Alex phoned that evening and, as Margaret predicted, said that he was sorry that he wouldn't be back for another two days and could Neela kindly stay and look after Krish?

'Yes, sir. That's no problem, sir.' Neela answered politely.

But that night Krish was unusually quiet and Neela felt for him. He must be feeling insecure and upset separated from all his loved ones. His beloved grandma had gone for ever and, if she was correct, his estranged father had abandoned him with a childminder that he himself hardly knew.

'What are you looking at, Krish?' Neela asked quietly.

'Nothing . . . just searching for an empty space . . .'

'Why are you searching for an empty space?'

'Because, when I asked my dad what he was looking at, he said, "Nothing, just an empty space" so I am looking for it.'

Neela was silent.

'When are they coming back?' he asked plaintively.

She knew perfectly well whom he was asking for but was afraid to talk about Helen.

'Are you missing your dad?' she asked, trying to divert his thoughts.

'No,' came the definite reply.

'But why are you so quiet today?'

He didn't answer but just stared at her.

'Are you OK?'

He nodded.

'You are very quiet today, Krish. What's the matter? Why don't you tell me, please?'

'Grandma left because I was naughty and noisy, but now if I am good and quiet, will she come back?'

'Who said that?' Neela went up to him and gently took him in her arms.

'No one. I just know.'

Neela pulled him to the sofa and sat him down on her lap. Putting her arms around him, she said, 'Krish . . . Grandma won't be coming back . . . because . . . because she went to God.'

Krish lifted his head, his eyes full of concern.

'Why did she go to God? Doesn't she like me?'

'She loves you very much,' Neela replied, kissing his forehead.

How could she tell him the cruel truth? How could she possibly protect his young heart from so much hurt? Scolding herself for not knowing the right words in English, she tried her best.

'Grandma loved you so much and she would never be angry with you. She just got so sick and God took her to Heaven to look after her. It's not your fault at all, Krish, and Grandma will be very upset if you think like that.'

Krish listened attentively.

'OK? Now you mustn't blame yourself. Grandma wanted you to be happy.'

He looked as if he understood everything, but soon he was sobbing again.

'I want my grandma. I want my grandma.'

Clenching his fists, Krish began to punch the sofa, then jumped up and ran screaming from room to room, throwing things on the floor. Neela followed him helplessly. What could she do to comfort this child?

Worried that he might hurt himself, she ran after him and at last grabbed him and held onto him.

'Stop it, Krish. Stop it,' she shouted.

The loudness of her voice surprised him and he stopped wriggling in her arms. He went floppy and inert. She kneeled on the carpet and held him tight. Krish was breathing hard.

'Why can't I go to God?'

'Oh, Krish! Listen, I will take you to God's house tomorrow and we will pray together and ask God to give your message to Grandma, all right?'

Krish wiped his tears with his fists.

'Promise?'

'Promise,' she crossed her heart, just like he had taught her. 'I promise. I will take you there.'

That was the first night in many days that Krish slept undisturbed but when he woke he immediately remembered Neela's promise.

'Are we going to give Grandma a message today?' he asked as soon as he was awake.

'Yes, Krish, we shall go to the temple. After you have had your bath and breakfast.'

'OK,' he said.

There were no fights and no arguments that morning.

Neela took him to the temple by train. Krish sat quietly throughout the journey thinking about his message to his grandma and listening quietly while Neela explained all about the temple and the gods. After they got out at East Ham, Neela bought a coconut and some bananas at a small Indian grocery shop.

'What are they for?'

'They are the offerings to God.'

'Does God eat them?'

'No, the priest distributes them to the people in the name of God.' Neela stopped walking and looked at him thoughtfully. 'Actually in India, in the olden days, this was one of the ways to feed the poor.'

The temple was situated on a turning not far from the station. It resembled nothing like any temple in India. Neela could tell it had been converted out of a three-bedroomed house. All lower walls inside had been knocked down to create a huge hall which was spread with a bright red carpet. The walls were covered with red and gold striped wall paper. It was without doubt an inferior substitute for the beautifully carved stone temple in her village. It housed at least a dozen idols of the gods in separate alcoves. The main shrine, a gold-plated, three-walled canopy, decorated with flowers and oil-lamps, was dedicated to Lord Vishnu, the protector, and his wife Lakshmi, the goddess of wealth.

'We have to take our shoes off,' Neela said, and bent to loosen the laces from Krish's trainers in the porch just inside the main entrance.

'Why?' asked Krish, staring at the rows and rows of shoes on long wall-mounted shelves.

'It's a mark of respect to the place, and also so that we don't bring in the impurities from the streets outside.'

'Is this God's house?' Krish asked wide-eyed.

'Yes, it is.'

'Is this a church?'

'No, this is a temple, but it's like in church. God lives here as well.'

'Who is that?'

Krish pointed to a garlanded statue of Lord *Ganesh*, carved in black granite, just inside the main entrance.

'Remember I told you a story about the Elephant God, *Ganesh*? That's him.'

Taking his hand in hers, she pointed to a huge mural on the wall behind the statue. 'Those are his parents, Lord *Shiva* and Goddess *Parvati.*'

Krish nodded, looking at *Parvati*'s bright red sari and staring at *Shiva*, who had a third eye on his forehead, wore leopard skins and was adorned with a snake around his neck.

Neela led Krish to the main part of the temple where she lifted him up so that he could reach the temple bells which were hanging from the ceiling. Krish was excited when he found he could ring them.

'Look, look,' he said while she put him down. Animated, and pulling Neela forward, he said again, 'There is Lord Krishna! His name is my name.'

'How do you know that?'

'I came here with my dad . . . a long time ago . . . and my dad said my name is the same as Lord Krishna.'

'Yes, it is,' she smiled, bending to put her arms around him. 'Krishna is a beautiful name and you are very beautiful, just like him.'

'But why doesn't Jesus Christ live here?' Krish asked, ignoring the compliment.

'He does, but you can't see him. Here he looks different, in many forms, like those,' she gestured to all the deities in the alcoves. 'People use different names for him but it doesn't matter, does it?'

'No,' he slowly shook his head. 'My Nan used to take me to church.'

'We could go to the church too if you want, but I don't know how to pray there. We could ask Margaret and she might take us.'

Neela bought a one pound ticket for the *pooja*. The priest lit the oil lamps, incense-sticks and, chanting the *Vedas*, performed a prayer in Helen's name. Krish watched the *pooja* silently and smiled shyly at the priest, then he stepped forward to offer the coconuts and bananas and asked Lord *Krishna* to give his message to his grandma. 'Please tell her that I am not naughty any more and I will be good from now on.'

Chapter 33

'Your message has already been delivered to your grandma,' the priest told him, placing the *prasadam* in Krish's cupped hands.

Afterwards, as is traditional, Neela and Krish folded their hands and circled round the main shrine three times. Before they left, they sat down on the floor leaning against a wall, and listened to the devotional songs, shared the *prasadam* and watched the other visitors for a few minutes.

In the morning, after Neela dropped Krish at school, she felt the absence of Helen keenly. Her files and books were still on the table in the hall and her shoes remained underneath the desk as if she were still about to step into them. But Alex had removed her coat from its hook by the door. The hook looked abandoned and the empty space stared at her. For some strange reason she wished the coat was there. She still felt that Helen would walk through the door any minute, calling for Krish. Neela's heart became heavy as an image of Helen ruffling Krish's hair affectionately came to her mind.

Alex was due on Saturday. On Friday Krish waited and waited for his father's phone call but it didn't come until late at night, after he was in bed and asleep.

'Hello, Mrs Pattwar. I am sorry to phone you this late but there was a crisis at the office which I had to deal with. Is everything all right? How is Krish?'

Neela heard the tiredness and anxiety in his deep voice.

'Krish is fine, sir. He is sleeping.'

'I hope he is not being too much of a trouble.'

'No, no, he has been really good, sir.'

'That's good to hear. Thank you, Mrs Pattwar. I will see you in the morning.'

'OK, sir. Thank you, sir.'

Again Neela didn't sleep well. Although she had been in that house every weekday for the past year, she had never stayed overnight, and it felt strange sleeping in the spare bed in Krish's room. She lay awake, worrying about Alex. She didn't know how to receive him or what to expect of tomorrow. This was only the second time he had spoken to her and then only on the phone. She had seen him at Helen's funeral but only for a few minutes, and from a distance. All she could remember was a tall lean figure in a dark suit, like a silhouette.

CHAPTER 34

Krish woke early on the Saturday morning, excited that his father was coming. He was obedient and finished his breakfast without making a fuss. After ironing his favourite Mickey Mouse shirt and red trousers that he had asked for, Neela filled the bath and squeezed his favourite bubbly suds from a frog-shaped bottle.

'Your dad might take you somewhere nice today,' she said, soaping him.

'Yes, he said he'll take me to see the ducks in the lake. Do you know how many I saw last time? This many.'

He stretched both arms wide.

'Really?'

'Yes. Little baby ducks this big,' he said, placing his thumb and index finger together and narrowing his eyes. 'And Mummy Ducks and big Daddy Ducks this big.' He stretched his arms wide. 'Have you ever seen a real duck, Neela?'

'Oh, yes, plenty, in India.'

'Do you have . . .' he stopped in the middle of the sentence, looking around. 'Where is my duck?'

'There?'

'No, not that one, the white one.'

'Oh, you mean the swan? Where is it?' she looked around the bathroom but couldn't see it anywhere. 'It's not here. It must be in your room. I will look for it later.'

'No, I want it now!' Krish punched the water with his hands.

'OK, OK, don't splash,' she wiped the drops off her face.

'Now promise me you won't jump up and down while I am gone.'

'OK, I won't.'

Neela searched his room, his toy-box, the whole house. 'Sorry, Krish,' she said, returning to the bathroom, 'I can't find it anywhere. Do you remember where you put it?'

His face creased, his bottom lip quivered, and he screamed, 'I want my white duck, I want my white duck . . .'

He was standing up now, stamping his feet, splashing water everywhere. He was a bundle of nervous energy, out of control and beyond Neela's soothing words. She grabbed him and tried to hold onto him as he jumped up and down in the tub. Still he splashed and sprayed the room with water. What could she do with him to calm him?

'Please, Krish,' she pleaded, kneeling down beside the tub. 'Please don't cry. Oh, no, stop chucking water on the floor. Please be a good boy. Remember you said yesterday that you wouldn't be naughty any more.'

'But . . . I . . . want . . . my . . . white . . . duck,' he howled between violent hiccups.

'Look, Krish, look at me,' Neela held his chin and turned his face towards her. 'Look, I can make a swan out of my hands.' She crossed her palms and linked her thumbs and her fingers wide. She placed her swan-shaped hands in the water and fluttered her fingers in a swimming motion. 'Quack, quack, Krish. Krish, the swan is coming to tickle you . . .' she sang softly, touching Krish's tummy and shoulders. The howls ceased. His face creased in a smile. He burst out laughing.

There was loud applause, making the pair of them jump out of their skins. Neela let out a scream.

'Dad!' yelled Krish.

Neela quickly scrambled to her feet, stunned at the sight of a tall male figure in the doorway.

236

'That was the most beautiful swan I have ever seen,' he laughed.

'Oh . . .,' Neela was embarrassed, confused, aware of her wet sari. She straightened her sari *pallu*.

Leaning against the door frame of the bathroom, he smiled at her. Neela noticed his long lashes and dark eyes which sparkled when he laughed. His hair was slightly wavy and his complexion was a shade lighter than Krish's. From his colouring she could tell that he was of mixed race.

'I'm sorry I startled you,' he apologised. 'I am Alex. Krish's father.'

He stretched out his hand. Neela was aware of feeling terribly shy. She wiped her wet hands on her sari again.

'Sorry, sir . . . my hands are . . . wet.'

'That's all right.'

'Yes, sir, I am . . . Neela.'

'Nice to meet you, Neela.'

She saw recognition then puzzlement.

'I did knock on the door . . . but obviously you couldn't hear it with this little rascal howling his head off.'

'We . . . I . . . didn't notice you, sir. Sorry about the mess, sir . . .' she gestured at the wet bathroom floor.

'It's all your fault, Krish,' Alex laughed.

She tried to wipe the drops of water from her face with her forearm and at the same time pushed the damp tendrils of hair off her forehead.

'I will take him,' Alex offered.

Noticing his suit, Neela handed him a towel.

'I am sorry he was giving you such a hard time.'

Alex lifted his son from the bath and wrapped the towel round him.

'Oh, no, sir, we . . . we lost his swan, sir,' Neela said, following them out of the room. 'But otherwise he has been very good.'

Krish was looking over his dad's shoulders, smiling at her mischievously.

'Oh no, I've just remembered . . . I'm sorry, Neela. This is all my fault,' Alex said sheepishly. 'I gave the duck . . . I mean the swan . . . to Margaret. I left it with her in case Krish wanted it.'

'Oh!' Neela laughed.

There was something familiar about Alex's voice. Where had she heard it before?

That night, back in her own flat and in her own bed, Neela remembered Alex's earlier suggestion that she should go back on Sunday afternoon to discuss her job. Now that Helen had died, she wondered whether he would still need her help. Or would he take Krish with him? Was she going to lose yet another job? Not daring to hope or wish for anything, she closed her eyes tightly and tried to get some sleep.

On Sunday afternoon Neela returned to the bungalow to find Alex looking refreshed and relaxed in casual clothes. He offered her a seat on the sofa.

'I heard so much about you before . . . from my dear mother.' For a moment he lost his composure and looked as if he was fighting back tears. 'And now I've heard more . . . not only from Krish but from Margaret too. About how good you are with Krish, and I have already seen for myself how much care you take of him. I am so grateful to you.'

'Thank you, sir. I am just doing my job, sir.' Neela was not expecting such praise. Looking up, she saw that he had more to say to her.

'I am worried about Krish, Mrs Pattwar . . . sorry Neela . . . do you prefer to be called by your first name?'

'Yes, sir.'

'And please call me Alex. As I was saying . . . I don't know what I should do with Krish . . . I can't change my job just like that,' he flicked his fingers, 'and move here. But right now I can't even take him with me as my work demands a lot of travelling and there's nobody to look after him. But I know I have to do something and very soon.' He sighed. 'It will take me a good few months to decide what to do and in the mean-time, as I said, I can't have him with me, or leave him here alone.' He took a deep breath. 'The only solution I can think of for the moment is to ask you to look after Krish but . . .'

'Don't worry, sir I can do that. I will look after him until you decide what to do.'

'That's all very well, Neela, but I am thinking of nights too. I can't come home every evening.'

'Oh . . .' Neela was about to say that she could look after him during the night as well, but wondered if he had other plans.

'I can't leave him at Margaret's all the time,' he said, rubbing his forehead.

'If you like, I can stay nights too, sir,' she said quickly.

'Are you sure? Is it all right with your family? Won't it be an inconvenience for you?'

'Don't worry, sir. It's no problem for me, sir.'

'Thank you very much indeed. You've no idea how much I appreciate that offer. Where do you live, Neela?'

'It's about a half hour's train journey from here, sir. Flat number 18, Victoria House, 124 Martin Road . . .' she blurted out her whole address.

'You live in one of those blocks of flats behind the station?' he asked, shocked.

'It's not that bad, sir. The rent is very low in that area. That's why I live there.'

'You know, I think I have seen you there,' he looked at her thoughtfully. 'If you don't mind my asking, was it you that night near the station?'

Something jolted her memory. She heard again a strong but gentle voice telling her that she would be all right. Of course . . . of course . . . she put her hand over her mouth.

'Was it you, sir? That night . . . near the station? You saved my life and . . . and . . . I am extremely sorry that I didn't recognise you.'

'You were so distressed, you could hardly speak or walk.'

'I can't thank you enough for rescuing me,' she said, placing her palms together in a praying position. 'You did so much for me that night.'

'No, not at all. Anyone in my place would have done the same. I hope the police took my complaint seriously.'

'They did and I signed the statement,' she shuddered at the memory.

'That's good. That man is a danger to any woman on the street.'

'Yes, of course, sir,' her voice trembled.

'Please relax,' he said, noticing that she was very agitated. 'Would you like some coffee? I am going to have one.'

'I will make it, sir,' she said, jumping up.

'No, you sit down for a change and let me make it for you.'

Neela didn't dare disobey but sat down on the edge of her chair and listened to the sounds from the kitchen – the clatter of mugs and the kettle boiling. Then Alex returned carrying two mugs.

'What an amazing coincidence,' he said.

'Isn't it?' she replied.

'Anyway . . .' he said, changing the subject, 'we were talking about Krish, weren't we? I must ask you if the arrangements we have agreed on will be a problem for you and your family . . .'

'No problem, sir. I live alone. I can stay here as long as you need me to.'

'Thank you, Neela. It will be at most for a few months.'

'Definitely, sir. I am more than happy to do it.'

'Thank you so much. That's an enormous help and I will have peace of mind knowing that you are here taking care of my son.'

Neela couldn't believe her luck, in fact she was trying not to grin with sheer joy. She hadn't expected this at all. What an enormous relief after all the worrying!

'Since you are only renting that place, would you like to vacate it and move in here?'

Neela was speechless. It was much more than she had hoped for. He observed her long silence and looked at her enquiringly.

'There's no hurry. I took leave on compassionate grounds until next Sunday, so take your time and think about it some more, and you can tell me later.'

'There is nothing to think about it, sir. I would be delighted to move in and look after Krish.'

Back at the flat, Neela couldn't contain her excitement. She phoned Anita and also told Gill. She told them both the whole story, how her job had worked out, and how, incredibly, her employer had turned out to be the kind gentleman who had saved her from Tariq.

'I can't believe it. Are you sure?'

'I am indebted to him for life and I am glad that I am at least being useful to him by looking after Krish,' she kept repeating.

Both her friends teased her mercilessly about 'the kind-hearted stranger' coming into her life again.

'That's why they say, life is stranger than fiction, *puglee*,' Anita laughed.

Gill said she was sad that Neela was moving out, and that she wouldn't see so much of her in the future, but she knew it was the right thing for her friend to do.

'I wish you the best of luck,' she said.

'Thank you, Gill. I seem to have had as much luck as I deserve already.'

'Don't put yourself down, love. If anyone deserves a bit of luck, you do.'

Yes, thought Neela. Perhaps she is right.

Though she had hated living so close to Tariq, nevertheless Neela felt sad when the time came to pack up her things and empty her room. She had grown to like her little place and was fond of the conifer tree near the gate with the little flowers underneath it. Even the noisy children on the second floor had become part of her everyday life and she was going to miss them too. But the worst part was saying goodbye to Gill who had become so close to her over the past two and a half years.

As she boarded the taxi, Gill hugged her affectionately.

'Take care of yourself and please keep in touch.'

'Oh Gill, I am going to miss you so much.'

'Ready?' the driver asked.

'Yes,' Neela replied, slamming the door. Gill had gone inside so that she could wave from the balcony, and Neela's last image was of her friend with her arm waving and waving as the taxi drove away.

The taxi turned right at the end of the road and a phase of her life disappeared behind her.

CHAPTER 35

Krish and Alex were waiting for her at the bungalow and helped her out of the taxi and inside with her bags. They accompanied Neela to the spare bedroom next to Krish's. She had been inside this room before when she had been cleaning the house, but it was transformed. The white walls were painted in magnolia like the rest of the bungalow. The new bedlinen and curtains had a pink and green floral print. Standing against the wall, opposite the window, was Helen's gilt-edged mahogany wardrobe with full-length mirrors on each door. There was a small table beside the bed with a reading lamp on it, and a dressing table with an oval-shaped mirror neatly fitted under the window. She knew that Alex had prepared this room for her. She had always admired the elegance and beauty of the bungalow, but now she was actually going to live in it. She smiled to herself, savouring the luxury. She didn't want to sit on the bed for fear of creasing the clean, soft bedlinen. It was luxurious beyond anything she had experienced, and that night, as she folded back the covers, she felt nothing but gratitude to Alex for what he had done for her. This bed was such a far cry from all her previous beds which had been old and used and creaky, their springs poking through lumpy mattresses. As she slid into the clean sheets and felt their silky texture against her skin, she determined to stay awake for a long time so that she could savour the new sensations and really appreciate them. But within minutes she was deeply and peacefully asleep.

Early on Monday morning Alex left for Edinburgh but not before thanking Neela profusely for all her help. As he finally took his leave, he took her to one side.

'Please look after Krish. I will phone regularly. I have left all my personal numbers in the address book, including the family doctor's and other useful numbers you might need. If there is anything . . . anything at all . . . please don't hesitate to phone me.'

'Please don't worry about Krish, sir. I will look after him.'

Alex lifted his son and hugged him tightly.

'Be a good boy and listen to Neela,' he said.

Krish nodded, but clung pitifully to his father.

'Please come back soon, Dad,' he wailed.

'I will come back soon, son,' Alex whispered, kissing him gently and unwinding the boy's arms from his neck.

Then he shook hands with Neela.

'I have to go to Denmark for a month to provide training,' he told her quietly. 'I will try to come back by Friday night, and if not, definitely by Saturday morning.'

Krish whimpered as Alex climbed into the car. Wiping his tears and holding him in her arms, Neela stood beside him at the front door while Alex drove down the drive and turned onto the road.

They both watched and waved until his car disappeared.

Gradually, increasingly, Neela devoted more and more time to Krish and he, in turn, seemed to settle well with her. Even though her accent and pronunciation made him laugh, he loved her to read bedtime stories to him, so most nights she bribed him to do his homework by promising him one of her age-old Indian stories. Krish enjoyed the tales of wise elephants, cheeky monkeys, selfish foxes, fearsome lions and lovely, brightly-coloured birds. And in return, Krish brought a new meaning to Neela's life because looking after him gave her a purpose. However, the little boy still missed his father, and as the days and weeks passed he became more fretful. By the time they had reached the third week of Alex's absence, Krish was pining for his father and Neela consoled him by counting the days that remained.

'There are only four days left,' she told him.

Or, 'Look, two days left, Wednesday, Thursday, and he will be here on Friday!'

Towards the end of Alex's absence, Neela was walking home after dropping Krish at school, when she saw Margaret with Pam, the lady who lived two houses down the road. They were standing on Margaret's doorstep talking. Neela greeted them with a smile. Ever since she had moved in to look after Krish, Margaret had been particularly helpful and had advised her on all sorts of things from making sandwiches for Krish's packed lunch to weeding the lawn and pruning the rose bushes.

'Good morning,' they said together.

'I was just telling Pam how good you are with Krish,' Margaret said.

'Krish is a lovely little boy,' Neela replied.

'You make it sound easy, Neela, but I know that parenting is very difficult especially if the child is not your own. Margaret keeps saying how well you are coping.'

'Thank you. Actually Krish makes my job easy. He is such a lovely boy. And he's been through so much. He is missing his grandmother and at the same time he is trying to adjust to me. It can't be easy for him.'

'Of course,' sighed Margaret, 'and poor old Helen too, bless her soul. She was everything to him. He must be devastated.'

'I wonder what happened to his mother,' Pam shrugged.

'She has always been a mystery. Helen never liked to talk about her,' Margaret replied.

'Have you seen her?' Neela asked.

'No, dear. Helen moved here when Krish was only three months old. For a long time Helen kept herself to herself and it's only recently that she started opening up to me, talking about her childhood in India, and her marriage to Mr Sagar, but she never ever mentioned Krish's mother.'

'What is Alex planning to do about Krish?' Pam asked.

'I don't know. Has he said anything to you?' Margaret looked at Neela.

'No, only that he needs some time to decide.'

'I think he should move here or take his son to live with him,' Pam said firmly. 'My heart goes out to him, poor little kid. He has suffered enough!'

'It is difficult for Alex too,' Margaret said. 'How can he look after Krish on his own? His job is too demanding and he has to travel all over the place. Yes, as he said, it will take time, whatever decision he may take. He is a fine young man and I know he won't abandon his son.' She looked at Neela, 'Without you it would have been impossible for him.'

'God bless you, dear,' Pam added.

Embarrassed by the compliments, Neela smiled modestly and took her leave. The fact was that it didn't feel like a duty. She enjoyed looking after Krish and it gave her an immense sense of fulfilment. She wondered whether it had always been inside her, this need to be needed. Since his grandmother's death, Krish's tantrums had subsided and he had grown gradually closer to Neela. After school he liked to do things with her like going to the park or playing in the garden or just staying at home playing snakes and ladders.

Eventually Alex phoned, confirming that he would come home, as promised, on the Friday night. Neela felt oddly anxious about his arrival, but as she often did when she was nervous, she busied herself with practical jobs, and made chapattis, rice and two vegetable dishes for Alex. On Friday evening, she gave Krish a bath and fed him, but Krish was far too excited to go to bed so they waited up together until finally at ten o' clock they heard the chink of the metal knocker. They both ran to the door. Neela opened it while Krish jumped up and down, shouting at the top of his voice.

'Dad! Dad!'

'How is my little tiger?' Alex laughed, swinging him up in his arms.

'Hello, Neela, how are you?' he asked, carrying his son into the lounge.

'Fine, thank you, Mr Sagar,' she said shyly.

While he went into the bathroom to have a shower, Neela set the table with Krish talking at her nonstop about the plans he had for his dad for that weekend.

'Have you eaten?' Alex asked his son, when he finally sat down at the dining table.

'I have, but Neela hasn't,' said Krish, climbing on the chair next to his father.

'I am sorry. You shouldn't have waited for me,' he said.

Then noticing that only one place was laid, he leapt up again and went into the kitchen to bring a plate for her.

'Do please join me.'

'I will have it later, Mr Sagar.'

'It's already late. I am sorry. I didn't realise. Please,' he gestured at the chair opposite his.

'Dad, Neela has told me so many stories.'

'Has she? You like stories, don't you!' he ruffled Krish's hair.

'Dad, do you know the story of the wise elephant?'

'No, I don't.'

'I like it so much. It's my favourite. The second best one is The Cheeky Monkey. Remember, Neela, how he stole the bananas from the man? And third,' Krish said, stopping to count on his fingers.

Neela smiled, grateful for his appreciation.

'This is delicious.' Alex helped himself to more *okra* curry.

'Thank you, sir. Oh sorry . . . Mr Sagar.'

'Just call me Alex, It's simpler. I know from my mother that in India you don't call people by their first name but here . . . everyone uses Christian names, employers and employees, young or old.'

'OK sir, but can I call you Alex-*ji*?'

'All right. If it makes you comfortable,' he laughed.

On Saturday morning Alex told Neela to take the rest of the weekend off because he was going to take his son out. So she took the opportunity of visiting both her friends. Neela was pleased to learn that Gill was still happy with her boy-friend, and Anita had planned a holiday along with her husband in Rome.

'*Shahabash!*' exclaimed Neela, because she knew how hard the couple usually worked all year without taking a day off. This was indeed a rare event.

'You know this is our first holiday abroad since we got married,' Anita confirmed, reading Neela's thoughts.

'Really! So it is your honeymoon, after twenty years,' Neela teased.

By Sunday evening, Neela had caught up on both her friends' lives.

On Monday morning, Alex was still at home and seemed to be waiting for Neela so that he could tell her what he had arranged. He told her that he would open a bank account in her name so that she could draw as much money as she needed.

'No, Alex-*ji*,' she protested, 'I can't accept this. You have already given me so much. Free accommodation and meals and . . . of course I will never forget what you did for me on that night. You saved my life. Please don't do any more. It makes me uncomfortable.'

'It's not only for you, Neela. It's for my own convenience as well. Suppose I'm stuck somewhere and Krish needs money for something. I can easily transfer some into your account and you can write a cheque.'

'Yes, I see that,' Neela agreed.

They went together to the bank, and for the first time in her life

Neela had her own cheque book. Again she was astonished at how much trust the family placed in her. Her hands shook when she took the cheque book from Alex and she gratefully listened very carefully while he explained her how to fill in a cheque and where to sign it.

Although Alex continued to phone regularly, almost every evening, he only visited his son about once a month. He would try to make up for lost time by taking Krish out for dinners and picnics, to the park and the zoo, but Neela increasingly wondered why he hadn't sorted out his job and made a decision about Krish. On one occasion he was away for more than six weeks, and often changed or postponed the dates of his return. This meant disappointment for Krish as time and time again he was let down.

It was the last Friday of the school term. Neela wondered why Krish wasn't smiling as he usually did when she collected him from school. His face was grave and he was unusually quiet.

'How was school today?' Neela asked, desperate to break the silence between them.

'All right,' he shrugged.

'What's the matter, my tiger?'

He gazed at Neela silently, pursing his lips tightly. The pain in his eyes was obvious; of course he was missing his father. Not wanting to upset him more in the middle of the road, Neela walked silently beside him until they reached home. Krish let her help him out of his school uniform, and into his casual clothes, but still he remained silent.

'Would you like to go to the park?' she asked.

'Do you want to watch Tom and Jerry on TV?'

'No! Leave me alone!' he snapped.

Krish remained in his room and refused to come down. Neela made his favourite strawberry milk shake and took it to him. He was lying across his bed, face down, looking small and vulnerable. Placing the glass on the table, she gently lifted him onto her lap.

'Do you want to talk about it now or after your milk shake?'

His face crumpled and his bottom lip quivered and he turned his face away.

'What's the matter, Krish? Are you missing your Dad?' she cajoled.

Krish lifted his long, wet eyelashes and looked at her.

'Why are you upset, my baby?'

As she hugged him to her, he buried his face against her chest and sobbed. Neela rocked him gently and patted his back.

'Daddy doesn't love me,' he said at last between sobs.

'That's not true. He loves you very much.'

'Then why doesn't he live here with me then like all the other dads? And why don't I have a mummy?'

Distress shook his voice, melting Neela's heart. Still hugging him, she took him into the lounge and sat him down on the settee. His body was jerking with sobs which in turn made him hiccup. Understanding the pain of separation for such a tender young heart, Neela waited until his sobs subsided.

'Shall we phone your dad? Do you want to talk to him?' she asked.

Krish nodded and wrapped his arms around her neck. She kissed him, lifted the receiver on the phone, and dialled his father's number.

CHAPTER 36

When Alex answered the phone, she nudged Krish and whispered, 'Go on . . . talk to him.'

'Dad, when are you coming home?'

Neela leaned in closer so that she could hear Alex's reply.

'Soon, son.'

'I am missing you, Dad.'

There was a pause then.

'I am missing you too. I am sorry Krish. There is some important work I have to do but I will try to get home next weekend.'

'Dad?'

'Yes, my Tiger,'

'Do you love me?'

'Of course I love you, more than life itself. You are everything to me.'

'Then why don't you live here with me?'

'I will. Soon. I just have to sort a few things out and then I will be there with you all the time.'

'But Dad . . . in my school everyone has got a mummy and . . . and why don't I have one?'

There was a longer silence at the other end of the phone, and then Neela heard a long sigh.

'I will talk to you when I come home, Krish. I will phone you again tomorrow.'

'Dad, can you come home for my birthday?'

'Yes, I hope so, but . . .'

'What, Dad?'

'Listen, Krish, I will try, but I can't promise, but don't worry because we will celebrate at the weekend.'

Seeing Krish's overwhelming disappointment, Neela couldn't contain herself any longer. She took the receiver from him.

'Forgive me for interfering, Alex-*ji*,' she said, 'but you haven't seen Krish for more than six weeks now and I hope you understand how upsetting this is for him?'

She waited for a response but there was only silence.

'He has been crying the whole evening for you. Couldn't you at least come home for his birthday?'

The other end of the line fell silent for even longer and Neela feared that she might have overstepped the mark.

'I am sorry for interfering but . . .'

'No, not at all, I am glad you are being honest and I appreciate the way you care about Krish.'

She was relieved that he wasn't angry. On the contrary, his voice sounded upset and guilt-ridden. He sighed.

'The only thing is, it is on a Wednesday, isn't it? Can I ask you a favour, Neela? Can you arrange a party for him for Wednesday?'

'Certainly, Alex-*ji*.'

She smiled at Krish who was close at her side, and passed the phone back to him. 'Listen, Krish. I will come home on Friday evening and we will celebrate on Saturday,' Alex told his son.

'OK, Dad!' Krish answered, finally brightening up.

That night, after putting Krish to bed, Neela's thoughts turned to Krish's mother. She was feeling uneasy about her. She had worked in this house for nearly eighteen months and had been living here now for six, but Krish's mother still remained a mystery. Where was she? Was she even alive? No one talked about her. Only Margaret had suggested some time ago that Krish's mother must be separated from Alex and that's why no one mentioned her name. How could a mother live without seeing her child for so long? If she was alive, surely she would have claimed Krish by now.

On the Sunday Neela sat with Krish at the kitchen table planning his sixth birthday party. He had already sent out the invitations to his ten best friends and had taken great pleasure writing name cards, and filling party bags, and making the shopping list for his special menu.

Neela bought him a remote-control car. Margaret helped her to make a tennis-court cake, complete with tiny little sugar figurines of the players. In the evening, Helen's bungalow grew noisy and lively as boisterous children played games, and popped balloons and blew shrill whistles. The party was a success and Krish was happy. At the end, when everyone had gone, he gave Neela a big hug and told her how much he loved her. Turning away, she hid her tears.

Friday finally arrived and Krish's excitement knew no bounds, affecting Neela too. After dropping him off at school, she unlocked Alex's room to tidy it up. It was tastefully decorated. Two magnificent paintings hung on the walls, one a sunrise and the other a sunset, both depicting mountains and water with rippling orange reflections. Neela had seen them many times before, but every time she marvelled as if seeing them afresh. Wondering who the artist was, she peered in the corner at the signature and was amazed to read *Alex*. She had no idea that he could paint so well. She marvelled at his modesty and his talent.

The sound of a key turning at the main door made her jump. She straightened her sari, pushed back the stray strands of her hair, and went to the door. There was Alex, tall and handsome, smiling broadly at her until she felt both foolish and nervous.

'Can I come in please?' he asked, grinning.

'Oh, I am sorry . . . I didn't expect you at this time,' she apologised, moving aside. Without Krish there between them, Neela was keenly aware of his physical presence and could feel the banging of her heart. In an attempt to gain control of her emotions, she busied herself in the kitchen, preparing tea. When she was more composed, she took the tea on a tray through to the lounge.

Taking a cup, Alex looked at her and said, 'I promised Krish I would buy him a bicycle for his birthday.'

'I know, he told me,' she replied, avoiding eye contact.

'I am thinking of taking him straight from school to the shops.'

'That's a good idea. He will love that.'

'Why don't you come as well? If you are free.'

'Me?' asked Neela.

'Yes, Krish would love to share the fun with you as well.'

'Thank you. I would love to.'

Neela couldn't hide her excitement.

They parked the car and took the lift into the shopping centre. As the steel doors opened, Neela gasped. There, in front of her, was Yamini, holding shopping bags and waiting to take the lift down.

Neela stood stock-still and looked as if she had seen a ghost. Yamini seemed just as surprised but she was the one to break the ice.

'You look well,' she said, rolling her eyes. 'And I see you have a new family.'

Yamini's tone was snide and ironic and Neela could see she was looking Alex and Krish up and down. Alex took Krish and stood at a discreet distance, waiting for Neela to finish her conversation.

'How are you?' Neela asked, struggling to find something to say.

'How can you ask me that after everything you did?' Yamini jeered.

'What did I do?'

'We heard about everything from Tariq, you slut,' Yamini hissed.

Neela turned and ran. She didn't want to hear.

'Are you all right?' Alex asked, puzzled and following fast behind her, dragging Krish by the hand.

Chapter 36

'I am sorry . . .'

'Come and sit here,' Alex said, gesturing to a bench.

It took a while for Neela to gather herself. She was visibly shaken.

'I am sorry,' she repeated.

'Stop apologising. It's all right. Would you like a drink?'

'No, I am fine now . . . thank you.' She stood up. 'Shall we go to the shop? It's already four-thirty. Come on, Krish, you have one hour to choose the bike. What colour are you going to choose?'

Neela was aware she was chattering about nothing but she had to hide her anger.

'I want a red bike, Neela,' Krish answered, unaware of her distress.

'That's your favourite colour, isn't it?'

'Yes.'

Neela put the bitter encounter behind her, at least for now, and tried her best to join in Krish's excitement. Why let bitterness about the past spoil things for this little boy?

Until she saw Yamini, she thought she had laid her ghosts to rest for good but now she realised that they were still there, lurking in the recesses of her heart.

When they got home, of course Krish wanted to get straight on his new bike. Neela watched with interest as his father fixed the stabilisers to it and then supervised his son up and down the pavement. Up and down, they went over and over again until Krish could confidently ride on his own. Then, utterly exhausted with all the excitement, Krish suddenly went limp and did not argue when his father suggested it was bedtime. Alex read him a bedtime story, tucked him up, and then came into the kitchen to help Neela wash the dishes.

'Oh, no, Alex-ji, please.'

'It's OK. Please don't feel bad.' Alex took a plate from the draining board and began to wipe it with a tea towel.

Once again Neela was very conscious of being alone with him but

255

as Alex continued to talk about Krish, she began to relax. For a while they stuck to safe subjects. She asked about his work and his trips abroad and he asked about her home in India and how she had come to England. She recounted the incidents briefly, omitting details where she felt they were inappropriate.

'So . . . what about your husband?' Alex finally asked, noticing her reluctance to say anything about Ajay.

'He has passed away.'

'Oh, I am sorry to hear that.'

He watched her with obvious sympathy while Neela quietly finished rinsing the dishes.

'Would you like some coffee?'

Without waiting for an answer, Alex reached for the kettle, and when Neela went to the cupboard to get the cups he stretched out his hand and blocked her.

'Please relax. Since you cooked dinner for us, it's only fair that you let me make you coffee.'

'OK,' Neela laughed.

'Do you mind if I ask who that woman in the shopping centre was?' Alex asked, when he came through with their coffee.

'She was my sister-in-law. I am really sorry about that . . .'

'But why were you so upset?' he asked her gently.

Neela looked down but could not speak.

'I am very sorry,' he said. 'I don't want to make you feel uncomfortable. You don't have to talk about it.'

'No, no, Alex-ji. I can tell you . . .

And without saying anything much about her husband Ajay, Neela told him the story of her in-laws. When she came to the part about Tariq, she had to stop to fight back tears.

'I can't believe that he was your brother-in-law's friend, and I can't believe that you didn't go to the police sooner.'

Neela's throat felt tight with pain.

'It's hard to believe people like that exist. How much you have been through. A hell of a lot,' he said.

'I am fine now, Alex-*ji*,' she smiled. 'Your kindness . . . and I can't thank you enough . . . that night . . . . without you . . . I can't imagine . . .'

'I don't think you should keep thinking about that incident,' he interrupted. 'I am sure that rogue is behind bars now.'

'I am so indebted to you . . .' she began, but again he interrupted her.

'It's shocking that it's still going on, even today. I mean, in-laws treating their daughters-in-law in this appalling way.'

'I know other girls who are suffering in silence, Alex-*ji*, like Reshma.'

'But even if it is only one in a hundred, it shouldn't be happening. Our system of arranged marriages is wrong. When a girl gets married, she marries her husband's whole family.'

'Exactly.'

'I think people in India should know what goes on over here.'

'But no one tells them, Alex-*ji*. Over there they just believe that life here is perfect and easy.'

'Maybe someone like you should speak up and let them know.'

'Me?'

'Yes, because not only do you have firsthand experience, you have compassion.'

'But how can I? And would they believe me?'

'Yes of course they would, especially if it's dealt with through the media. Why not write about an article about it and send it to some magazines in India?'

'Me? Write for a magazine?' she asked, incredulous.

'Yes. Why not?'

'I can't even write a few words properly. How can I possibly write articles, Alex-*ji*?'

'I am sure you can, Neela, You are the right person and who knows, you might be the first person to draw attention to these issues. Why not? You can write in your own language.'

'Alex-*ji*, but . . . I don't think I can write something as big as an article.'

'Don't you write letters to your friends? Just begin as if you are writing a letter to a friend.'

'I will think about it.'

Neela was far from convinced. She had never written anything weightier than family news.

'Good, from tomorrow, after dropping Krish at school, your job is to write, and to write with devotion and conviction. It doesn't matter if you don't do the housework for a few weeks. By the time I come back next time, I want to see your article ready to be published.'

'Oh, no!'

'Seriously, Neela, think about it. If you can prevent one girl like you from experiencing misery, it would be worth the effort, wouldn't it?'

'Of course. Thank you, Alex-*ji*.'

CHAPTER 37

Neela couldn't begin to imagine how to write an article for a magazine but still the suggestion fascinated her. Every so often Alex reminded her of it so an idea that had been seeded began to germinate. She attempted a few scribbles on pieces of paper but it was a struggle and soon the bin was overflowing with screwed-up paper. But eventually an idea seemed to grow on its own and at last the words flowed from her pen and an article was born, in the shape of a letter. She wrote it as Alex suggested, to a friend. When it was finished, she told Alex but expressed her doubts.

'I don't know whether you can call it an article. It's only a letter.'

'That's great. That's how it should be. So that the readers will identify with it and it will feel more personal.'

He suggested that she should send it to one of the leading Hindi magazines in India. After rewriting and editing it carefully, she gave it the title 'A letter from London' and sent it to *Saheli*, a woman's magazine in her area of India.

'Congratulations!' Alex exclaimed, as soon as he came home for the weekend.

'You actually wrote the article and sent it!'

He extended his hand to shake hers.

'Thank you,' she said, aware of the touch of his warm hand. 'I've noticed that you enjoy reading, don't you?'

'Yes, I do,' Neela replied, chiding herself for feeling so much emotion.

'Come and see this then.'

He led her to his mother's room and pointed at the bookshelves.

Neela had always been fascinated by Helen's book collection and in the past she had peered at the shelves whenever she came into the room. She didn't realise that Alex had noticed her interest.

'My mother used to collect books. She was a voracious reader. You are very welcome to read them. My mother would be pleased to know that someone is enjoying them.'

'Thank you, Alex-*ji*, but I don't think I understand enough English. Most of the time I just read children's books and I've read one Catherine Cookson novel. I read with difficulty.'

'If you can understand children's books, I am sure it won't be difficult for you to read some of these.'

Alex ran his hand over the spines, reading out the authors' names.

'Look, Neela, *Anita Desai, Geetha Mehtha and RK Narayan.* They are all fantastic writers. I think their books might interest you because of the writers' reflections on India. Their subjects are very simple and delicate, yet very effectively written.'

Neela listened attentively.

'And,' Alex gestured to another shelf, '*Catherine Cookson, Iris Gower, Emily Bronte* and *Charlotte Bronte*. You must read *Jane Eyre*, I read it when I was at school and I will never forget the characters.'

'Wow!' she said, wide-eyed.

'And of course these are my father's favourites,' he added, taking down a different book. 'Here is the great Indian philosopher . . . You must have heard of J. *Krishnamurti*. He is renowned as a world teacher.' Alex flipped a few pages. 'Look what he says, '*Without goodness and love, you are not rightly educated.*' He looked at Neela and said, 'You said you are not educated. What do you say now, Neela?'

Neela smiled shyly as he moved to put the book back.

'*Rabindranath Tagore's Geetanjali*,' he read out, pointing at another one.

260

Chapter 37

'I read the translation of that book when I was in India.' Neela said and suddenly one of the sweetest poems came back to her:

> *When thou commandest me to sing it seems that my heart would break with pride; and I look to thy face, and tears come to my eyes. All that is harsh and dissonant in my life melts into one sweet harmony – and my adoration spreads wings like a glad bird on its flight across the sea.*

'Then try the English version. You might find it easy to understand. He is one of the greatest poets of all time and someone I greatly admire,' said Alex.

'Me too,' Neela's eyes shone with delight.

'So, I expect you to read them all! It will help you now that you are embarking on a writing career,' he smiled.

'It's only a short article, Alex-ji, and I don't know whether they will like it. Please don't make too much of it.'

'I am certain they will like it.'

His faith in her ability to write was kind and encouraging, but she thought he was just helping her to occupy her time and was not really serious. She had enormous doubts but she was fascinated by the challenge. And it was something that had grown between the two of them and for this reason alone she would try to see it through.

A whole new world opened up for Neela as she began on a programme of reading. She was very committed and if necessary would read the same page again and again until she understood it. Whenever Alex came home, he would ask about the book that she had just read and they would discuss it, often late into the night. Neela found their discussions wonderfully stimulating and was surprised by the strength of her own opinions. Sometimes they would debate the philosophy of life and human nature. His deep emotional insight into so many subjects amazed her and she felt that her life had taken on a whole new dimension. Alex had a gift for showing her new meanings. Sometimes it only took a few words and she saw things in a completely new light.

At first Neela was somewhat reluctant to air her opinions but Alex always put her at ease and so immersed her in their discussions that she would lose herself. He was an enthusiastic listener and always commented or complimented her views. As she talked more freely with Alex, her respect for him only grew. Now she too would count the days and hours, like Krish, as they waited for him to come home, and his visits became the focal points in her life too. While his absence made her feel empty, she came to life in his presence.

One evening, Neela was sitting quietly reading when the phone rang. It was Alex. He had remembered that there was a parents' evening at the school and had forgotten when it was.

'It's on the fifteenth, exactly a week from today, Alex-*ji*,' she said looking at the calendar.

'I need to know the dates . . . because I am about to book a ticket to India.'

'To India?'

'Yes, Neela. I am thinking of going soon, probably after the parents' evening.'

'How long are you going for?'

'A fortnight, maybe.'

'But . . . you promised Krish that you would move back here by the end of the month!' Neela could not hide her dismay.

'I know, but it is important that I go. I will explain everything when I come home.'

That night, after Krish went to sleep, Neela settled in her bed, switched on the lamp to read, but after just a few pages, she heard Krish calling her.

'What is it, Krish? Did you have a dream?'

Krish was sobbing. Neela ran to him and knelt by his bed.

'No . . .' he shook his head. 'I want Daddy,' he wailed.

'Oh, Krish . . .' Neela said, hugging him. 'He is coming next week . . . for your parents' evening.'

'But why doesn't he live here?'

'He said he will . . . soon.'

'He always says that . . . but he never will!'

Krish was more distressed than Neela had seen him for a long time, and she made up her mind to talk to Alex next time he was home. It was not fair to Krish to make promises he did not keep. She fetched Krish a glass of water and stayed with him, stroking his forehead, until he fell asleep. For the first time, she felt angry with Alex. He was not being fair to his son. When she returned to her reading, she found herself turning the pages but nothing was sinking in. She was pre-occupied with anxiety about Krish and Alex and could not shake off her anger. Why was he going to India now? It was six months since Alex had promised Krish that he would consider a job in London, so that he could move home by the end of the month. But for some reason he kept postponing it and Krish was getting increasingly agitated. Neela couldn't understand why someone with such integrity did not keep his promises to his son. It didn't make sense. Alex never missed an important event. He was there for Krish when he won the singing prize at school, and when he played Jesus in the school play at Christmas. But these were one-off events. Neela understood that what the boy needed was the steady, regular presence of his father in his day to day life. Krish received a daily phone call when what he needed was his father in person. Neela couldn't understand any of this. It just didn't make sense. It wasn't that Alex didn't consider his son's feelings, and he clearly loved him dearly. There was something else and she couldn't put a finger on. It nagged at her and puzzled her. Neela decided to confront Alex, for Krish's sake.

Alex came home in time for the parents' evening and was pleased to hear that Krish was making good progress at school. Then, on the

Saturday, after a tiring trip to an amusement park, Krish was ready for bed early, so Alex and Neela could look forward to a long, quiet evening to themselves. Neela stayed in the lounge, listening to the familiar sounds of Alex putting his son to bed, and made up her mind. When Alex came in, Neela stood up, ready to confront him.

'Please, Alex-*ji*, can I talk to you?'

He could see that something was wrong.

'Of course, please . . .,' he gestured at her to sit down.

'I am worried about Krish. He misses you so much,' she said, plunging straight in without any preliminaries.

'I know.'

'Alex- *ji* . . .' Neela's voice was steely.

'Please relax. What's the matter? Is everything all right?' He looked at her, searching her eyes for some unreported crisis.

'I know I am only a housekeeper and a child-minder and I shouldn't interfere, and we have discussed this several times before, but Alex-*ji*, don't you understand how much Krish misses you and longs for you. He was desperately disappointed when you didn't move here last month, as you said you would, and he woke up in the middle of the night asking for you and I didn't know how to console him.'

Alex flushed.

'Forgive me for expressing my thoughts, Alex-*ji*, but Krish is just too young to be left all the time without his father. Please don't misunderstand me. I say this for his sake.'

Alex rubbed his forehead and sighed.

'No, no, you are right to say this. I know it's important for Krish, and also for me that I should be here with him and I feel terrible that I haven't done anything about it yet.' Alex's voice was serious. He stood up abruptly and went over to the window where he stared out at the darkened sky for a long time. Neela knew not to interrupt.

The darkness swept away the faint light that had lingered in the room and Neela could see only Alex's profile and his white shirt.

Chapter 37

Though she couldn't see the expressions on his face, it was obvious that her words had stirred him. Should she have opened her mouth and taken such a liberty with him? After what seemed an eternity he moved away from the window, switched on a lamp in the corner of the room and paced slowly up and down, up and down. Finally he sat in his chair. He looked hard at Neela until she turned away.

'Have you ever wondered what happened to Krish's mother?' he asked.

Neela looked up again and returned his gaze.

'No one talks about her,' she replied. 'I have often wondered . . .'

'I haven't talked about it so far to anyone, except my mother, but I think now you should know since you have become so close to Krish, and . . . well . . . I feel that you deserve an explanation. I think you will understand.'

CHAPTER 38

'You know, Neela,' Alex began while she looked at him and concentrated on his every word. 'It's a long story so I beg your patience.'

She nodded her head slowly.

'I am an only child and my parents taught me everything. They gave me the confidence I needed, and the courage to face life. They showed me how to enjoy modest things like country walks, the beauty of nature, the fragrance of flowers, and they encouraged and supported me all through my schooling and university years. When I graduated with first-class honours . . .' he stopped and smiled, 'you know, their faces lit up and they were so proud of me. When I got my first job in Leeds, I bought them gifts. At last I could show them my appreciation and I went home so excited.'

He paused, closing his eyes. Neela saw pain in his expression.

'But my father had a brain haemorrhage and died just minutes before I reached there. It was a devastating blow to me and my mother. I couldn't possibly leave her on her own, so I changed my job and moved here so that I could be with her. We found solace in each other's company and we slowly recovered. At first we couldn't talk about my father because she ended up in tears and her pain was unbearable. But we slowly began to find the strength to talk about him and to reminisce about the little things.'

Alex paused, then picked up the story again, all the time looking at Neela.

When my father was alive, he used to go to the temple every Saturday. You know, the same temple that you take Krish to, and my mother always used to go with him. I still remember her in her sari. She was so beautiful. I used to think she looked like a goddess. Every Hindu festival there was a big celebration in the temple and it usually ended with some sort of religious show ... a concert or a dance performance. My father was a great lover of the Indian classical arts, especially music. He didn't sing but he recognised every *raga* and *tala*. When I was little he used to send me to music lessons once a week in the temple, and I used to accompany him to concerts. But as I grew up, my studies and social life took up all my time and I eventually gave up the music lessons. Gradually my visits to the temple decreased and finally stopped.

'On the third anniversary of my father's death I went with my mother to the temple to perform the yearly ceremony. We missed him so dearly. We sat on the carpet under the marble arch, leaning on the pillars, in front of the shrine, to watch the *pooja*. The priest served us the *prasadam*, the offerings.

'When he announced the dance programme, the familiar beat of the *mridangam* started, very slowly at first, and then the *veena*, flute and violin joined in. The divine music moved us hugely. *Vatapi ganapatim bhaje.* As the vocalist started the prayer, the whole temple vibrated with the beat of the ancient south Indian *karnatic* music. The melodious voice of the singer and orchestra produced waves of *swaras* and *ragas* that gently stroked the dark marble of the temple walls and resounded in every corner. The whole atmosphere was exquisite.

'The prayer finished and the dancer graced the stage with her ankle bells jingling. She was wearing a traditional amber-coloured dance outfit with all the temple jewellery. I was mesmerised by her beauty. She did the *namaskaram* – a greeting of respect for the God and for the audience – before starting her dance called *Bharatnatyam*. Her first step and the first expression on her face were engraved on my heart. I lost myself in her beauty. The sparkle in her eyes, the grace in her dance, and the emotion in her expression merged into a single, enchanting experience for me. I couldn't resist. I applauded so loudly that several people turned to look at me, but my mother just smiled, knowing how I felt.

'Time stood still for me until the *thillana*, the finale. I watched her exit the stage as gracefully as she entered. And then I just sat and watched the door for her to re-emerge. My ears heard nothing more of the music. At last the dancer, whose name was Ragini, came out of the green room wearing a sea-green sari; I remember thinking that she looked like a mermaid. Her hair was loose and she didn't have her dance makeup on any more, but she was more beautiful than before.

'She sat at the side of the stage, leaning on a pillar. Her eyes skimmed over the audience and reached mine. She then closed her eyes and began to sway gently to the music. At the end of the show, my mother took me to greet all the artists. She already knew most of them, but not Ragini. I enthusiastically introduced myself to her, and congratulated her on her exquisite performance.'

Alex had shut his eyes as he thought back, but now he opened them and looked at Neela.

'I am talking a lot about myself. I'm sorry. I hope I am not boring you?'

'Oh, no, Alex-ji, Please carry on.'

'Anyway,' he sighed, 'I found out afterwards that Ragini was a student at the London School of Economics. I confess I made enquiries and discovered that she lived near the temple in a shared flat with some other students, and I assumed that she would travel to college by tube like me. I was surprised that I had never seen her before. To be honest, I was already trying to work out how I could bump into her.

'Wherever I was and whatever I was doing, I thought about Ragini. I had never felt this way before. Her name was on my lips all the time. My eyes searched for her everywhere. I even used to get off at her station, or walk up to the temple in the hope that I might just catch a glimpse of her. When my father was alive he used to encourage me to read translations of Indian mythology. Now all those beautiful celestial damsels came alive in her form. I couldn't imagine beauty beyond Ragini.

'Then one day I saw her sitting opposite me in the tube. I couldn't believe my eyes. All those days when I had imagined meeting her exactly like this, and had even rehearsed what I would say to her, and there she was and my mind went blank. I was so nervous that I couldn't even say Hello. She must have known I was staring at her because she lifted her eyes from her book and smiled at me. I wanted to say so much, but all I managed was to return her smile.

"I think I saw you in the temple," she said.

Where I had failed, she succeeded.

"Yes. I came to see your performance. It was superb ... so beautiful."

I was speaking so fast.

"Thank you," she replied with a smile.

'I conquered my nerves and asked her about her studies, and so we began a conversation that by the end of our journey was as easy as if we had been friends all our lives. I found out that she had come to the UK only a few months previously from Hyderabad, for her studies, and was in her first year at the college. When we got off the tube, and took our leave, I plucked up the courage to ask her if I could see her again.

"Why not?" she replied.

'Occasional meetings at the temple became regular meetings, and soon we were going to the theatre, to the park, to the cinema together. We became good friends, and of course it didn't take long for our friendship to develop into something more intimate and beautiful. To my surprise she revealed that she had felt the same about me as I did about her, right from the very beginning. We became inseparable. Time raced by, a delicious haze of always being together. After a year, I asked her to marry me. She said that she would not marry me without her parents' permission, and she was doubtful that they would give it. I was so impatient. So desperate to be with her. I suggested that we go to India together, to convince them. But she didn't like the idea and asked me to give her more time to think.

'We were young and naïve and so much in love. Inevitably, Ragini became pregnant. She was very scared, but on my insistence, she agreed to marry me. We had a simple Hindu ceremony at home with a priest, because that was all she wanted. No big wedding, no registration and no guests.'

Thinking Alex needed a break from this long story of his past, Neela went to make them both coffee. When she returned, one question was on her lips.

'What about your mother? Was she happy about you marrying Ragini?'

'Of course,' said Alex. 'She was over the moon but at the same time she was concerned and keen that Ragini should let her parents know. Somehow Ragini convinced my mother that it would be better if she told them in person.'

'She must have been terrified.'

Neela imagined the scandal in India of an unmarried pregnant girl.

'We understood that, and respected her wish. We knew that she intended to tell them after her exams. The baby would be born by then.' Alex paused, remembering.

'After the wedding Ragini moved in here with us.'

Neela nodded, trying to imagine a pretty girl sitting next to the handsome Alex Sagar who right now was pouring his heart out to her.

'I thought I was the luckiest person on earth to have such a wonderful girl as my wife and I assumed she was happy too.'

'Assumed?' Neela looked at him, puzzled.

'I was overjoyed that she was pregnant, but one day Ragini shocked me by saying that she wanted an abortion.'

'Oh, no!' cried Neela.

'I thought it was only natural for her to be worried. After all she was still young and only a student.'

'Of course, but . . . .'

'At last I managed to talk her out of it and reassured her that everything would be fine once the baby was born. My mother tried her best and looked after Ragini like her own daughter but for some reason Ragini remained distant. Anyway, just a month before her final exams, she gave birth to our beautiful son. You know we named him after *Krishna*, the lord who preached *Bhagavad-Gita* to *Arjuna* in the *Maha Bharata*.'

'Yes,' Neela replied.

'He was so beautiful and I couldn't believe Ragini and I had together created such a wonderful creature. I had a whole new purpose in life.'

'How did Ragini manage to cope with her studies as well as the baby?'

'My mother looked after Krish.' For a moment Alex was lost in thought. 'Well, Ragini got through her second year but instead of relaxing, she seemed unsettled. She avoided any conversation concerning India or her parents, yet I knew she kept in constant contact with them because I saw the letters. Assuming she must have told them, I approached her one evening, and suggested that we book flights to India.'

Alex looked at Neela. 'Do you know what happened?'

'No, what happened?'

'Ragini couldn't even look at me. Slowly I prised out of her the fact that she hadn't told her parents that she was married, let alone that we had a child. I was speechless. She said she was scared of breaking the news to them. I did understand her fears and said I wouldn't let her go on her own and that I would be there with her. I put my arms around her and tried to reassure her. But there was devastation in her eyes and she pushed me away. She said that she needed to go on her own. Finally she convinced me that she needed to break the news gently, when she judged the time to be right.'

There was a long silence again while Alex looked back at the past. A good few minutes went by before he spoke again.

'She said she loved me and couldn't live apart from me.'

His face clouded over and he looked at Neela as if he were searching her face for answers. 'I just don't understand why she behaved like that.'

Neela's heart beat faster as he went on.

'Ragini just kept repeating that she wanted to go alone to India. I wasn't quite sure what she meant, and when I asked her, she said that she wanted to go without Krish. Of course, I thought I had misheard. She begged me to let her go, just this once, so that she could talk to her parents. She said that then she would send for us and we would go out and meet her parents.'

Alex closed his eyes and leaned back on the chair.

'Even now I cannot understand how a mother could even think of leaving a baby who was barely three months old. But my mother, more familiar with Indian culture, seemed to understand Ragini's situation and supported her. Ragini left, promising that she would write to me as soon as she reached India and I believed her.'

Neela frowned, dreading what would come next.

'Anyway,' Alex was staring into the darkness outside the window, 'parting from Ragini was very hard and without her, life became mean-ingless. Regardless of my mother's love, and my little son's smiles, I felt lonely.'

'And?' Neela asked, unable to bear the pauses and the suspense.

'Almost a month passed,' Alex began again, 'but I didn't hear from her. I couldn't wait any longer and my mother was also worried. In the end I decided to go to India.

'I left Krish with my mother. It wasn't difficult for me to find Ragini's parents' home and, clutching a piece of paper with the address, I hired a taxi which stopped in front of the gates of a huge house in Jubilee Hills. When I saw the grandeur of the houses in that area I was stunned. The house, or shall I say the mansion, was at least fifty times bigger than this bungalow here. I was stopped by a guard at the big white gates.'

'Really?'

'Yes, I had to plead and even bribe him to take a note to Ragini. While I waited with hopes and dreams in my heart, I noticed the magnificent front garden through the trellised gates. There were all sorts of trees: jackfruit, almond, neem, tamarind and coconut. A snake of pink concrete separated the lush green lawns and led up to the marble steps of the mansion.

After what seemed like ages, the gate-keeper came back and, without even opening the gate, handed me a piece of paper. I opened it and read the contents. My mind refused to take in the words she had written and I read the note again and again to make sure that my eyes weren't misleading me. My mouth went dry and my legs felt weak. I felt dizzy. I leaned on a nearby tree for support.'

Neela's eyes narrowed as she tried to guess what was in the note.

'The hot afternoon sun and my emotional turmoil made me sweat profusely. I told myself that it could not be true. The crumpled paper was fluttering in my hands and the letters in blue ink were smudged with my sweat. I read them again. It still said, "Please forget everything and go away. Kindly don't ever try to contact me again."

'Can you believe that, Neela? Ragini, my own wife, who said she couldn't live without me, wrote that I was not to contact her again?'

Neela was dumbfounded. For a while there was silence.

'Maybe it wasn't Ragini who wrote the note.'

'No,' he shook his head. 'Even though she didn't sign her name, it was her. I knew her handwriting.'

Alex continued, 'While I was standing there, dizzy and sweating and in shock, the gate-keeper was shouting "*Ja-o, ja-o,*" in Hindi "Go, go," he said. "GO!"'

To my shame I begged the gate-keeper to please let me in. That's how desperate I was. But the gate-keeper shouted at me again and I had to leave.'

'Oh God!' cried Neela.

'How can I tell you how I felt? There are no words to describe what I was going through. I returned to my hotel. I spent the whole night agonising. The whole thing was a mystery. In the end I must have dozed off but I remember waking up with a throbbing headache. I didn't have the strength or the energy to get up, but I had to. I had to see Ragini. I buzzed for a strong cup of coffee and forced myself out of bed. I decided that I was not going to leave India without seeing her and finding out what had happened. I would go to her house again but this time I was prepared to break the gates or make a scene if I needed to. I wanted to shout to the world that I was Ragini's husband and had come all the way from London to claim her.'

'Good!' said Neela.

'I don't even remember whether I had my coffee. I do remember feeling sick and hot, and very unwell.

'The next thing I remember was being woken by a swishing noise. The sweeper boy smiled at me and greeted me with a good morning. He told me that I had been ill for nearly a week! Certainly my own voice sounded weak to my ears when I responded.

He explained that I had been very ill. Apparently it was heat stroke.

'There was a knock on the door, and the doctor himself came in with the manager. He came and sat down on a chair near my bed and checked my pulse and my temperature. Then he smiled at me and said, "Well, Good morning! You are finally on the road to recovery."

I thanked him and the manager for their kindness.

"You English have a bad habit of going out in the sun but not here in India, young man. In summer the heat is so unbearable that even a crow wouldn't go out in the midday sun."

Although I was physically very weak after such a long period of ill health, nevertheless the next morning I summoned a taxi to continue with my mission. Once again we entered the grand Jubilee Hills. We drove along wide roads with magnificent houses and spectacular gardens. But a few yards before Ragini's house, the taxi stopped, The noise of drums interrupted my deep thoughts, and ahead we saw that a wedding procession blocked the road. People came out on to their balconies to take a look while young men and women danced in front of the bridal car First came the red and black uniforms of the band. Then the fancy cars, shining in the blazing sun. Finally a gold Rolls Royce, decorated with fresh flowers and twinkling coloured lights. It passed deliberately and slowly so that everyone could take a good look at the couple inside. Though I wasn't interested, the atmosphere was magnetic and I too was curious to see the newly-weds. I looked. Sitting next to a suited, booted, and garlanded bridegroom was . . .'

Alex could not continue for a moment as he struggled to control his emotions.

'Dressed exquisitely, the bride . . . can you believe who it was?'

'Oh, no!' Neela put a hand over her mouth.

'Yes, my Ragini.'

'Even though she was clearly visible through her thin veil, I could not read her expression. She sat motionless next to the groom, her head bowed, her eyes down-cast. As if she knew I was there. The procession moved past in slow motion and I didn't even blink. My vision was blurred, and my throat tight. I thought I was going to faint.'

Neela looked at his worried face.

'Was I dreaming or was it my imagination? Had I mistaken some other girl for my Ragini?'

Neela shook her head in pity.

'The taxi driver asked me if I was one of the guests. I didn't reply.
I was thinking hard. Either Ragini had not told her parents about
her commitment to me as she had promised, or her parents had
condemned it, leaving her no other option. The idea of her being
forced into a second marriage made my blood boil.'

Alex walked to the cabinet to pour himself a drink and took a few
minutes to calm down.

'Do you know any more now? Do you think Ragini was forced into
that marriage? Neela asked.

'I don't know, but I wanted to believe it.

I stayed for another week in that hotel room, drinking and crying
like a mad man. It was only my mother's phone call that brought me to
my senses. I wanted an explanation from Ragini, but my bruised pride
wouldn't allow me to pursue the matter. I agreed with my mother to
leave India, and returned home with emptiness in my heart. At first I
couldn't look at my mother or my son. Somehow I felt I had let them
down. But then one day my mother put her arms around me and I
sobbed my heart out on her shoulder like a child. I couldn't stay here
in this house either; this place was filled with memories of Ragini.
It was too painful even to look at Krish because he reminded me so
much of her.'

'Was that the reason you moved to Edinburgh?'

'Yes, I submerged myself in my work. I wanted to forget the past.'

'And have you?' asked Neela.

Alex looked at her.

'I almost succeeded. I mean during the day I managed but the
nights were cruel. I could almost see her and feel her next to me. It
was mental torture.

'One weekend when I came here for a visit, my mother saw the tell-
tale signs and told me gently that only a weak person would drink to
drown his sorrows while a wise person would accept life as a mixture

of pain and pleasure. She said it was only natural to crumble under a storm, but a wise person still survives.

'She used to say if we can't get over it, at least we should try and learn to live with it.

'Eventually I did. I learned to live with it. But one question remains unanswered. Why did she do it? Perhaps it will remain a mystery for ever. And you are right. Krish is my responsibility and I know I have neglected him. Before my mother died, I knew he was safe in his grandmother's loving care and now . . . well, I am sure he is in equally capable and caring hands.'

Neela, bowed her head modestly. The dim light cast a shadow on the left side of his face, making him look vulnerable. She wanted to take him in her arms and comfort him. Horrified that she could even have imagined such a thing, Neela quickly composed herself.

'Did you try to contact her again?'

He shook his head.

'Neela, I have decided to accept the job in London. I will be moving in soon after I come back from India.'

'Oh! Alex-*ji*,' Neela exclaimed, 'that's wonderful news. Krish will be thrilled.'

CHAPTER 39

A week had gone by since Alex had left for India but thoughts of him stayed constantly with Neela. She was baffled by the events in his life. She had read about drama like this in books and seen it in films but she couldn't believe such things happened to real people in real life. Dr Vikas had managed to make her re-evaluate her opinion of men, and now Alex was doing the same. Both of them offered proof that true love was still alive in the world.

Although Neela now knew the facts about Krish's mother, she felt that there were still layers of mystery and questions that perhaps would never be answered. She wondered if Ragini had ever cared for Alex who loved her so much? And what about her baby? Had she been forced to part with him? Questions piled on questions. Although Alex hadn't said anything to her, it was obvious to Neela there was more to his visit to India than he was revealing. Would he go in search of Ragini? If the woman he loved so much declared that she was still in love with him, would he bring her back? How would Krish react to his estranged mother? Images of another woman becoming close to Krish and Alex made Neela so angry and upset that she dropped the spoon into her soup. Pushing her bowl away, she felt a twinge of jealousy for the woman she had never seen.

'Neela, Neela, there is a letter for you.'

Krish came racing in.

'What is it?' she asked, dragging herself away from her painful thoughts. It wasn't the usual blue aerogramme that she received once a fortnight from her parents or from her friend Suji, but a white envelope, and instead of her name and address being handwritten, they were typed. She looked at it, puzzled, and spotted the name *Saheli* on the top corner of the envelope. With her heart pounding, she tore open the envelope and tugged out the contents. It was from the editor of the magazine. Her fingers trembled as she read the words. They had accepted her article for publication. She grabbed a chair and sat down, staring at the letter. She read and reread it until the words were etched in her mind.

'What is it?' asked Krish, tugging at her sari *pallu*.

'Oh Krish!' she exclaimed. 'They are going to publish my article.'

She lifted him up and kissed him hard on both cheeks.

'Wow!'

Krish clapped his hands. They both cheered and jumped around the kitchen for joy.

Neela couldn't eat or sleep that night. How could a simple village girl like her not just write an article but have it accepted for publication? As the news slowly sank in, the first person she thought about was Alex. Without him she would not have written a word. Her heart swelled with gratitude towards him and she realised how much she missed him. How she wished he was there to share the news with her and how happy he would have been hearing about it.

She was awake almost the whole night. She was trying to make sense of the fact that her heart fluttered at the mere sight of Alex and that she felt strange and restless when he wasn't here. To distract herself from these uncomfortable thoughts, she switched the light on and picked up the letter from her bedside table. Leaning back against her pillows, she traced the name *Saheli* and allowed herself to feel a delicious sense of achievement. Then she got out her writing things and composed two letters, one to her parents and the other to Suji, giving them the good news. It was almost dawn when, elated and exhausted, she finally drowned in a deep sleep.

When Alex arrived back from India, he didn't come home from the airport. To the immense disappointment of both Neela and Krish, he travelled on instead to Edinburgh. They waited every weekend but Alex made excuses about being too busy tying up loose ends before he moved to his new office in London. When he did finally call, Neela was desperate to ask whether he had seen Ragini but feeling that it would be presumptuous of her, she bit back her questions.

'How was your trip?'

'Yes, it was fine, thank you.'

The rest was left unsaid.

A few days later Alex phoned again and this time asked her about the article. Neela was touched that he remembered but before she could say anything Krish grabbed the phone from her and blurted out that it had been accepted.

'Congratulations! Why didn't you tell me before? I am really proud of you and we must celebrate,' said Alex when Neela finally got the phone back.

'Thank you.'

The long awaited Friday night came, bringing Alex home. Although he seemed tired and had lost weight from his trip, he looked as handsome as ever. It was a lovely coincidence that the next morning, Neela received in the post a copy of the magazine *Saheli* from the publishers. The whole of the centre page spread was given over to her article with her name in big letters across the top. Sharing this event with Alex simply added to the excitement. Although he couldn't read Hindi, he looked at every sentence closely, and traced her name with a smile.

That evening, after Krish had gone to bed, Alex asked Neela to read the article to him. She felt uncomfortable at first but agreed, translating every sentence into English. At the end Alex applauded.

'What can I say? It is superb and very thought-provoking and well written.'

Neela accepted his praise modestly and thanked him.

'It was you, Alex-*ji*, who gave me the inspiration and encouragement to write. Without you I would never have put pen to paper.'

'Well, you wrote it. See, you shouldn't hide your talent. Well done!'

'Thank you, Alex-*ji*,' she smiled.

Over the next three weeks Neela was inundated with congratulatory letters from her family and friends in India. But her parents and Suji wrote worried letters, in case she herself had gone through all the misery she wrote about. She decided that she wanted to put their minds at rest, to stop them worrying so she answered diplomatically, explaining that it was a reality that was happening to many girls who, like her, came to the UK. Her cousin Shankar sent her cuttings of reviews and letters from *Saheli* readers. They were a mixed bag; some criticised her for upsetting unmarried girls by questioning age-old traditions and subjecting them to unnecessary fear about marrying men in countries outside India. But most were complimentary and thanked her for giving them insight into the subject.

Neela translated all the letters for Alex when he came the following weekend.

'That's very good. Now do you believe how effective your writing is? Look how you have provoked so many readers.'

'But the angry ones worry me.'

'Why? That shouldn't put you off. On the contrary, you should write more.'

'Sometimes they confuse me,' said Neela, leafing through the letters. 'I mean these old traditions and religious values.'

'In what way?'

'If they are no good, then why did our ancestors practise them?'

'I don't think it's a question of good or bad. A religion is only a way of life that people choose to live. I am sure the traditional preachings were written by men because women weren't educated in those days. It's obvious that women just accepted them without question and suffered in silence.'

She nodded in agreement.

'Now, times have changed,' said Alex. 'Women are being educated and they don't just accept the old rules any more.'

'Yes, I think you are right.'

'But people in India, especially in the villages, are still in the dark. So it could help them if you continue writing articles like this, especially since you have experienced so much yourself.' Alex paused. 'I am sorry. Maybe I shouldn't bring this up. It can't be easy for you.'

'It's OK, Alex-*ji*.'

'Instead of allowing the awful events in your life to damage your spirit, you have come out triumphant. I admire your strength and spirit.'

'Thank you, Alex-*ji*, but . . . do we have to go through such unpleasant experiences to learn these lessons and to become wise?'

'Not necessarily . . . but don't you think that what you go through determines who you are?'

'Maybe.'

Neela was the last person to see how much she had changed.

Alex was looking at her with admiration in his eyes. Feeling shy, she looked away.

Finally, finally, Alex moved home permanently. Krish was thrilled and excited, but Neela felt more ambivalent because she did not know if Alex would still need her help. She waited for him to introduce the subject, but he said nothing. Unsure whether she should begin looking for another flat and another job, she just had to mention it herself.

'No, no, Neela. Of course not. We still need your help and there's no need for you to move out.' He looked at her. 'Unless of course you feel uneasy with my presence here.'

'Oh, no, no,' she said, again torn by conflicting emotions.

While Neela's routine did not change much, Alex's presence added something potent to her day-to-day life, even though he left early in the morning for his London office and came back late in the evening. She anticipated with joy the occasions when he would ask her to join him for coffee in the lounge and they would quietly discuss the news, or a book one of them had read.

His job continued to include a lot of travelling and sometimes that meant he was away at the weekends. On these occasions, not only did Krish miss him but Neela did too.

It was on a Tuesday afternoon that Alex phoned from Paris.

'Could you do me a favour, Neela?' his voice sounded urgent. 'Could you go into my room and check if there's a black book on my desk please?'

She went into Alex's room as instructed and saw the book there; she picked up the extension and said, 'Yes, the book is here, Alex-ji.'

'Could you find the page with today's date, please?'

'Yes,' she said, opening it.

'Good. Now there should be a list of appointments; could you read them out for me, Neela?'

The call ended after she had given him the information he needed, and she was about to close the book when she spotted the photo. It was tucked inside the transparent pocket of the inside cover. Neela stared at the photo. Alex was in a suit, as handsome as ever, but it was the tender expression on his face that mesmerised her. A pretty woman was leaning on his shoulder. Neela's hands shook as she realised that this was Ragini, the woman who had stolen Alex's heart and then left him. She looked from one lovely face to the other for a long time, until she could no longer bear to see Alex next to that other woman. Quickly she put the book away on the desk and busied

Chapter 39

herself straightening the room. It was her way of calming down. She noticed a shirt lying across the bed and remembered it was the same white shirt that Alex had worn when he told her the long story of his past. Remembering that night, she smoothed the creases and felt the softness of the material. Overcome by strong emotions, she hugged the shirt to her and breathed in the faint traces of his after-shave. She didn't know how long she stood there like that, holding the shirt as if it were him.

At first she was oblivious of the phone ringing.

'Hello? Neela?' It was Alex again.

She threw the shirt onto the bed as if he could see her hugging it.

'Sorry, Neela, I was in a hurry earlier. I couldn't talk much.'

'That's all right . . .'

'I am just phoning to say thank you. You have saved me so much hassle. The appointments today are crucial. I didn't realise I had left the book at home. I don't know what I would have done if you hadn't been there. Anyway, how are you?'

'Fine . . . thanks,' she said collecting herself and feeling rather foolish. 'Krish is fine too. He is at school and I am going to collect him in half an hour.'

'Good, good. I am taking an early flight on Friday and don't forget, we should plan to celebrate this weekend.'

'Celebrate?'

'Yes. Your publication.'

'Oh.'

After putting the phone down, Neela felt ashamed of herself. She didn't understand what had come over her. It was a strange feeling that she had never experienced before. Lately, thoughts of Alex pre-occupied her and time stood still in his absence. What was more, she was shocked to find that she felt a growing hostility towards Ragini. It was all so bewildering. Unsure how to deal with the complexity of her feelings, she waited restlessly for Alex to come home.

CHAPTER 40

As Neela hadn't travelled further than the suburbs of London, Alex and Krish decided that they should celebrate Neela's success with a trip to the Lake District.

'You will love it there. Apparently poets and writers like you go there for inspiration.'

'I don't think I am a writer or a poet . . .'

'Oh, what is this then?' Alex said, pointing at the magazine that was on the coffee table.

'That was like an essay from a school child's notebook.'

'Don't be so modest, Neela. You know you have already drawn the attention of *Saheli* readers and now, who knows, they might invite you to India to give them some talks and when that happens . . . I hope you won't forget us,' Alex teased.

'Oh please, Alex-*ji*,' she protested.

Neela was thrilled with their plan. She had been longing to see the Lakes ever since she had heard about them from Yamini years ago. And it was only recently that she had read a biography of *William Wordsworth*, which she found among Helen's books. She loved his poetry, so gentle yet with so much emotion.

Alex had suggested that they should start their journey very early, before the dawn broke, so that they would reach Windermere at least by lunchtime. Neela decided to pack everything the night before. She looked in her wardrobe and sighed at the row of white, grey and khaki saris. Ever since Ajay's death, she had been wearing only those colours. As a widow, it was the custom to wear those colours but even after she left her in-laws' house she had carried on wearing them. But now, accompanying Alex to a new and beautiful place, she felt them to be inappropriate. She stared into the wardrobe for several minutes before firmly shutting the doors. Her hands shook as she reached under the bed for her suitcase and opened the lid. The reds, oranges, yellows, pinks and purple filled her with joy. She longed to wear these vibrant colours again. Lifting them out, one after another, she filled her travel bag with shades of the sun and the sky, the earth and the grass.

Neela knew that the countryside around the Lakes would be beautiful but it surpassed even her wildest dreams. Krish spotted white sheep with little paint splashes of red and blue. She watched them too as they fed on the lush green grass, a gentle picture whose backdrop was thick forest, rocky hills and waterfalls. Neela wished the farmers wouldn't paint the sheep red because it made them look injured. Through the car window, she squinted against the sunlight to look up at the hill. She wondered how on earth a lone sheep managed to climb up so high.

'How will it get down, Dad?'

It was her own question too.

'It will come back the way it climbed up,' Alex assured his son.

'This is Lake Windermere,' Alex announced as he slowed the car and pulled into a parking space. Krish spotted a restaurant that displayed illustrated menus, and he immediately forgot the sheep and demanded food. How quickly a child's attention can jump from one thing to another, Neela thought.

'Yes, why not?' Alex turned the ignition off.

It was a beautiful spring day with interludes of sunshine which made the lake glitter silver. A breeze created ripples in its otherwise still waters. There were people on the banks surrounding the lake, walking, cycling and having picnics. Others were jet-skiing and surfboarding on the water. As they walked on a path along one side of the lake, Neela took off her cardigan and carried it on her arm.

'Look at those trees and those daffodils. They remind me of Wordsworth's poem, *Beside the lake, beneath the trees,*' Alex said quietly, as if musing to himself.

'Yes, exactly,' she smiled. It had been her thought too.

'The colour of your sari . . .' he began, but stopped mid-sentence and looked away.

She looked down at her sari. Yes, it was the exact colour of the daffodils. She was flattered that he had noticed what she was wearing. ·

'Please come and stand under the tree so that I can take a photo,' Alex asked.

'Oh . . .'

Feeling extremely self-conscious, Neela was about to object but she didn't want to cause a scene so she went and stood under the tree at the edge of the water as directed. The water tickled her feet, and the sound of the waves lapping against the shore was music to her ears. After taking several photos of her and Krish, Alex showed her how to operate the camera so that she could take some of father and son. At Ullswater, Alex stopped again to take photographs. Down by the lake, he wiped the surface of a rock with his handkerchief so that Nela could sit on it. Neela was flattered. No one had ever taken pictures of her before. But she was also embarrassed by Alex's attention.

They drove around the lakes and hills until the sun dropped below the horizon and then headed for the hotel: another new experience for Neela. She stepped into a carpeted lounge and sat on a leather sofa beside Krish while Alex collected their keys. She gazed at the paintings of lakes on the walls, the flowers in stone vases on the polished reception desk, and the girl behind it. She stared at the chandeliers that hung from the high ceiling.

They took the lift up to the third floor and went first to Neela's room where Alex showed her how to open the door with a card and then left her to settle in. It was a single room with pale green walls and matching bedlinen and curtains. Neela was particularly taken with the huge picture window that filled one entire wall. And the view when she pulled open the curtains! Opening the double glass doors, she stepped out to the balcony and stood mesmerised. In the evening mist, the mountains, woods and lake looked as if they were hidden by a veil.

The next morning when she went down for breakfast, she noticed that Alex's eyes lit up at the sight of her. He offered her a seat next to Krish and Neela sat down shyly. The elderly waitress who served them smiled at Alex and remarked on his beautiful family.

'Thank you,' Alex replied, glancing across at Neela.

Catching the mischievous twinkle in his eyes, Neela blushed and lowered her gaze.

'What are we doing today, Dad?' Krish asked, interrupting the looks that were passing between the two adults.

'Would you like to go on a boat trip across Lake Windermere?'

'Oh yes. That would be great,' Krish replied.

'And what do you say, Neela?'

'Yes. I would enjoy that very much.'

Neela couldn't hide her excitement as they boarded the boat. Even though she had lived very near to River Manjeera, she had never travelled on the water before. The sun came up as the boat gently moved forward. Holding the rail for support and standing next to Krish at the back, Neela watched the yellow and red of the sun broken into a thousand mirrors on the bow waves.

'That sari suits you very well. It is the colour of the sunrise.' Alex said, for once answering Krish's questions half-heartedly without taking his eyes off Neela. 'Yes, a sunrise sari.'

She felt the heat rise to her cheeks.

Lying in bed that night and thinking through the day's events, Neela smiled as she recalled Alex's compliments. 'Sunrise sari' she whispered to herself, turning to look at her orange sari, draped on a chair. And was there a glint in Alex's eyes earlier or was she imagining things? Did he also have feelings for her? She took a deep breath and shook the thoughts out of her head. The magic of the Lake District must have done something to her.

It was already nine in the evening when they began the long drive home. After an hour Krish became tired and restless and asked to sleep on the back seat. Neela swapped with him and got in the front. It was a star-lit night and the road was deserted. Every so often she glanced sideways at Alex. He was driving the car with ease and seemed to be lost in his own thoughts.

She wondered what was going on in his mind. Suddenly she knew. It was as if Ragini were sitting between her and Alex. She stirred in her seat, troubled by the image, and upset at the turmoil she felt when she should be content.

'Are you all right, Neela?'

Neela was annoyed with herself for allowing her imagination to get out of control. 'Yes. Thank you.'

'Have you enjoyed the trip?'

'Yes, of course. Very much. It was beautiful! I will never forget this trip. Thank you Alex-*ji*.'

'My pleasure,' he laughed at her enthusiasm. 'We are leaving the Lake District now.'

Neela looked back as the car sped along the motorway but darkness had fallen and she could see nothing.

CHAPTER 41

The following Monday, Alex left for Edinburgh to attend a conference. After dropping Krish at school, Neela arrived home feeling really
dejected and empty. She was staring into her cold mug of tea, and
trying desperately to understand her own feelings, when an inner voice
whispered *It is love! You are in love with him!* No, it wasn't true. Of course
she liked and respected him, but love? She told her inner voice to shut
up. *Then why are you always thinking about him? Whenever you close your
eyes you see his image.* Yes, she couldn't deny that. There must be something wrong with her. No, there was nothing wrong with her because
what she was feeling was very appropriate – just gratitude and respect
and admiration. Nothing more. *Oh, is that all?* Again that prying inner
voice. OK. OK. She admitted it. Yes, she was in love with Alex. But
for her to feel love was inappropriate and hopeless and stupid. She was
shocked and angry with herself for spoiling everything that she had
worked so hard to achieve. It left her with only one option.

In tears, and already planning the next inevitable stage, she decided
she would at least tell him the truth. After all, what difference would it
make now? She found a piece of paper and a pen, and wrote:

'Dear Alex-ji,
I don't know what this feeling is, but I can't imagine life
without you . . .' she paused for a long time looking at the
words. Unable to think of anything else to say, she left it at

that and folded the pink paper. She went to Alex's room, searched for a suitable place to leave it, and slipped the envelope between the papers in a blue folder that looked like an office file.

Neela watched with a mixture of horror and inevitability as Alex picked up the file on his way to work.

For the next few days, Alex arrived home late saying that he had been very busy. Then he said that he had to go to Milan for a conference. Usually these trips caused him little anxiety, but this time he seemed stressed. Neela wondered whether his unusual behaviour was anything to do with her letter. And he had gone to Milan very recently so why he was returning so soon? Neela began to wonder whether he was using the trip as an excuse to get away from her. It was agony not knowing what he had made of her letter, and she regretted her impulsive action. She scolded herself too for getting above her station and for not remembering her place. She trembled whenever she was in his presence and an awkward silence settled between them where before there had been ease and relaxed conversation. How had she let her heart rule her head? Why hadn't she nipped her feelings in the bud? He was the master and she was the servant. They were like the sky and the earth. How could they possibly come together? She felt awkward. She felt a fool. She wished she had never met him.

> *'Isn't life strange?' wrote Neela in her notebook. 'You never know who you are going to meet in your life and to whom you will feel close. Why do you get attached to one person and not another? Fate plays its own mysterious part. Whether you like it or not, sometimes fate decides that you must leave those you love and go your own way.'*

As she closed the notebook, her tear-filled eyes looked at the bronze figure of Lord Ganesh on the shelf.

'Why do humans develop such huge emotional attachments to one another?' she asked him.

Not knowing what to do with herself once she had made up her mind, Neela turned to Anita as someone she could talk to and who never criticised her. And so it was to Anita that she first confessed her plan to return to India.

'So why are you crying, *puglee*? You should be happy. Haven't you waited a long time for this moment?' Anita asked. 'Now you are completely free, I mean, more confident, more knowledgeable, you speak good English, and you seem to have become a writer overnight. I expect that financially you are managing too?'

'Yes.'

'Your parents will be very proud of you.'

'I know. I am longing to see them. It's been so long, almost nine years. But I have become attached to this country . . . I mean the people . . . especially Krish, you and Gill . . .'

'And Mr Alex Sagar,' Anita teased, but stopped abruptly when she saw the expression on Neela's face. 'You are only going to visit your parents, right? And you will be coming back, won't you?'

'No, Anita-*behn*, I won't be coming back . . . because I want to stay with my parents for the rest of my life.'

'What do you mean, the rest of your life?' Anita exclaimed. 'I know how difficult it's been for you and I can imagine how desperately your parents are waiting to see you, but the rest of your life? Be realistic, Neela. What about your own life? Have you thought about your future?'

'Yes, I have. I've thought about it a lot. Remember I always wanted to go back,' she smiled weakly at Anita.

'What does Mr Sagar think? How is he going to manage without you?'

'I haven't told him or Krish yet. I expect they will look for someone else.' Neela's voice trailed away. 'Krish is twelve now and I don't think they need a live-in-nanny any more.'

'But . . . you must come and visit us.' Anita was wiping away her own tears now.

'I can't thank you enough for your support through all these years, Anita-*behn*. I will miss you.'

Neela found it much more difficult to reveal her decision to Krish than Alex. After deliberating for a few more days, eventually she decided to break the news to Krish first. Up in his room, she told him she wanted to talk to him, and, as he always did when they had something to say to one another, he moved over in his bed to make a space for her. She looked at him as if she were seeing him for the first time. She couldn't believe that the little mischievous boy was already developing into a handsome teenager. He had inherited his father's good looks and had grown so tall that she had to lift her head to look at him. How quickly time had passed! How could she leave him after six years of being together? He was the son she had never had and she believed that Krish loved her as much as she loved him. How could she possibly hurt him by carrying out her plans?

'Krish I am thinking of going back to India,' she finally said.

'India?' Krish repeated. 'What for? A holiday?'

'No, for good.'

He stared at her in silence, his eyes wide.

'Why?' he asked, not hiding his dismay.

'Because I think it's time for me to go and see my parents. You are a big boy now and . . . and since your father is living here with you, I am sure you can manage without me.'

'What do you mean, manage without you?' There was shock in his voice.

'I mean at nearly thirteen you can manage without me but my parents are getting old and they need me.'

'I understand that,' he replied. 'But do you really have to go?'

'I have to, *beta*,' she said, stroking his hair, 'otherwise I don't think it's fair on my parents. You know they have been waiting for me for so long.'

'I know, but you will come back for Christmas, won't you?'

'I don't know, Krish.' Neela looked away because his eyes were so full of hope. 'I think it might be difficult for me.'

'Promise me you will come for Christmas,' he said.

'I am sorry, Krish. I can't promise you anything. I love you, Krish.'

'I love you too, Neela. I wish you didn't have to go.'

'I wish the same.'

Once she had broken the news to Krish, her idea became a reality and she realised there was no turning back. Waiting for Alex to return from his trip was torture. She was afraid that any delay might weaken her resolve and she wouldn't have the strength to carry out her decision.

'Are you sure that's what you want to do?' Alex asked when she told him. He was as astonished as Krish.

'Yes, Alex-*ji*,' she lowered her eyes to hide the pain.

'I never thought you would leave us like this. Of course you have to go and see your parents . . . but . . . if you change your mind and want to come back, please remember you are more than welcome here.'

Hearing the genuine warmth and affection in his voice, her heart fluttered with hope but it was brief, and vanished when she remembered that he hadn't even mentioned her letter. Once again the ghost of Ragini was there next to him, laughing at her and telling her not to be a fool.

The two suitcases that she had brought from India all those years ago were still there in the loft, tattered and worn. Alex refused to let her use them and bought her a new suitcase with wheels which seemed big enough to hold the contents of the whole house. It reminded her of the time all those years ago when she had packed Rahul and Pallavi's clothes for their India trip. She didn't know at the time that they were not coming back.

As the time for her departure drew nearer, she tried her best to hide her feelings for Krish's sake, and almost succeeded. She noticed how awful Alex looked. His eyes were bloodshot and it was obvious that he wasn't sleeping properly. She controlled a strong urge to run to him and embrace him.

At the airport, Krish found it very hard to say goodbye and clung to her as she made ready to take her leave. Their farewell was emotional with both of them in tears. Neela couldn't even look at Alex in case he saw what she was feeling, but as he gently wiped the tears from her cheeks and took both her hands in his, she looked up at him in surprise seeing in his eyes the tenderness and pain she herself was feeling. Each step she took put more distance between her and them until their faces disappeared and mingled with a hundred other faces into the crowd. She boarded the plane not knowing if she would ever see them again.

As the aircraft took off, she lifted her hand and placed it lightly on her cheek where Alex's last touch was still warm. She wiped away the flood of tears with the end of her golden daffodil sari.

CHAPTER 42

As the plane approached Bombay airport, Neela forced her thoughts away from Krish and Alex, where they had remained throughout the long journey, to her dear parents. In a few hours they would see her again and Neela knew the joy and happiness they would feel. Her heart ached with longing for her parents and for her village. She had struggled to suppress these feelings, hoping that one day the time would be right for her to return. It was that hope that gave her strength through the worst times, but now when the moment had almost arrived, it didn't seem to comfort nor excite her as much as she had anticipated.

Neela stepped out of the aircraft to be greeted by warm air filled with the scent of sun-baked earth. Taking an *auto-rickshaw*, she reached the main bus-station and boarded a bus to her village. As she travelled, staring out of the window, her deep love and respect for the land where she had been born, and where she belonged, filled her heart. Nine long years melted away. She was home.

The bus approached her village, cruising smoothly along a newly-built cement road. Time slowed down and she experienced the end of her journey in slow motion. She smiled at the old, bumpy mud road, which was now peppered with pebbles, thorn bushes, and wild flowers, and she noticed the old dusty pathway in the middle that used to be the only main road to her village and was always a cloud of red dust as rickshaws and bullock-carts danced along its bumpy trail. It seemed a lifetime ago that she had trodden that path. The lush, green rice fields on either side of the road swayed in the breeze and welcomed her. She craned her neck through the window, and there it was, surrounded by glistening sandy banks, the River Manjeera. She gazed at its liquid gold shimmer in the evening sun.

Brakes squealed and the bus-driver shouted, 'Gangapoor, Gangapoor.'

She watched the doors open and the rush of people pouring out of the bus like a flood.

Neela waited until the bus was almost empty, then slowly climbed out onto the dusty pavement. There were her parents waiting.

'Maa . . .' she called, and fell into her mother's arms.

'How are you, my *beti?*'

'How long it's been, *beti.*'

As the three of them hugged and clung to one another, their tears washed away the nine years of separation. Neela became a little girl again, staring at her parents through misted eyes. But time had moved on and she was not a little girl. Nor were her parents young. Their hair had turned grey and they were much thinner. She saw that her parents were growing old.

Neela was overwhelmed with guilt as she walked slowly with them to the house and stepped over the threshold. How could she have stayed away from them for so long?

Two years ago, she had sent enough money for them to be able to buy back their old house but how small it was, and how quickly it had fallen into decay. There were unsightly cement patches on the walls, the tell-tale signs of mice and rats scraping away to create the cavities for their dwellings.

Her mother had rearranged Neela's room so that it looked and smelled exactly the same as when she had left it all those years ago. She walked to the window sill and was amazed to see her *Asoka talcum powder*, a small pot of *Eyetex-kajal* and a box of bangles waiting for her return. It was the same, her very own room, but at the same time, strangely unfamiliar, as if it no longer belonged to her.

300

Chapter 42

Her arrival in her village brought the same excitement from the neighbours as her wedding day had done nine years previously. Many people came to see her, bringing little gifts of fruit, sweetmeats and flowers. She was a girl from their village who had returned from England after nine years and was therefore their celebrity. Their affection moved her deeply and she understood that the people in her village hadn't changed at all.

The days passed quickly for her at first because she was caught up in local events and was indulged in her parents' affection. But the nights were long and uneasy. Sharda cooked a variety of dishes every day, including all Neela's favourites, but often Neela would eat them through her tears, as she remembered the days when she endured cold and hunger and the violence of Ajay.

'What is it, Neela?' Sharda asked, noticing her daughter's distress.

'Nothing, Maa,' Neela smiled. It's only because I haven't seen you for so long.'

'Now you have returned, the house has come to life, *beti*.'

Her father looked at her fondly.

'I wish I had come earlier. I have missed you, Bapu.'

'Never mind, *beti*, at last you have come.'

It was not long before Suji came running in to embrace her. She had put on a lot of weight and had an air of maturity about her. Maybe motherhood was the reason, thought Neela, fondly looking at her friend and the children who hid shyly behind their mother's sari.

'Hello, Neela, my *dost*, my writer friend! How are you?'

'Oh, Suji! How long has it been! I can see these are yours!'

'Yes.'

Suji pulled the children to the front.

'Oh, they are so cute. Come here.'

But as Neela hugged Suji's children she thought of Krish, and again her eyes misted. She scolded herself for being so emotional.

'You look really nice, Neela. Your skin has become smoother and lighter. Maybe the water and the weather in England suited you.'

'She hasn't put on any weight though,' said her mother, coming out of the kitchen with two steel tumblers of tea.

'Oh, Maa . . .'

'It's the fashion to be slim, Aunty.' laughed Suji. 'Much more so in England than here.' She examined Neela from head to toe. 'You haven't changed much, apart from cutting your hair a little short, and wearing high heels. Remember how Kitty and Bablu teased you about wearing mini skirts and stick heels in England?'

They both laughed at the memories.

'But having said that, I must congratulate you on writing such an amazing article.'

'Thank you, Suji, but it was . . .' she paused, wanting to tell her friend that Alex had been her inspiration, but she couldn't talk about the man she loved, even to her childhood friend.

'I got the letter you sent me before you left England, Neela. I think it's an excellent idea of yours to set up evening classes here in the village to teach women to read and write. It will make such a difference to them.'

'With your support, Suji, I hope it will work.'

'Of course it will work. Most of the women here can't even read the alphabet and I am sure they will be grateful if someone like you takes an interest in them.'

'Then in that case shall we start planning and ask the priest if he can allocate the outer buildings of the temple to us? Maybe we should also ask the head of the village to provide a small grant towards the project.'

'Yes, why not? The sooner the better. We'll go tomorrow!'

Suji was full of enthusiasm for Neela's plans.

During the daylight hours, Neela threw herself into organising classes at the temple and planning how to pull her ideas together. But at night when she was alone in her room, thoughts of Krish and Alex engrossed and preoccupied her. She felt hollow inside with longing for them. She dreaded the future and hated being left with nothing but a few books and pictures to connect her with the man and the child that she now knew she loved.

One evening, Neela was sitting on a rope-woven cot under the tamarind tree in the backyard while her mother combed her hair smooth, freeing the tangles just like when she was at school. She looked up to see her father hitching the swing back into its place on the veranda for her. How she had missed such love and affection. She had missed the small joys she felt out here, like the air in her hair while going up and down on the swing, or walking to the river banks with her friend Suji, and picking and eating fresh berries from the fields.

'What did the priest say about giving you space in the temple building?' Sharda asked.

'He is happy, Maa. He said it's a fantastic idea and also said it will give them an excuse to renovate the old buildings for a good cause. But Maa. . . the head of the village turned my project down. He said he could not give us any money.'

'What did he say?'

'Oh, he gave me a long list of things that he was trying to do for the village and in the end he confirmed that he couldn't even afford a small grant towards the project.'

'I am not surprised,' said Sharda. 'Why would any politician care about the poor when they can earn millions in corrupt money? They send their children to private colleges and universities.'

'In that case the only way I can do this is to buy a small number of books, notebooks and pencils myself to set us up.'

'You have to think carefully before you jump into it though,' warned Sharda.

Within a couple of weeks the old building was ready to use. Neela and Suji arrived with a blackboard, chalk, notebooks and pencils and waited for the women to come.

On the first evening only a couple of women turned up but once news of their campaign spread, the group gradually grew to fifteen.

Apart from the evening teaching when Neela worked with the other women, she retreated more and more into herself and barely noticed what went on around her. She tried her best to be sociable, but she felt no desire to communicate with anyone. Late every evening, she went to the River Manjeera and sat alone, lost in the past. Her memories haunted her day and night until she found it hard to eat or sleep. For the millionth time she wished she had never written that silly note to Alex and spoilt the settled, happy life they had had together.

In the village, nothing had changed. Time had stood still while she had travelled on through years of conflict and turmoil, hope and fear, despair and happiness. She wondered how she could live here as if nothing had happened to her. Slowly and sadly it dawned on her that finding peace in her childhood home would be impossible. While others saw the same Neela, she knew she was a different person, yet it would be hopeless to try to explain her feelings to anyone because they could not begin to understand her situation.

She was sitting lost in her thoughts under the *banyan* tree near the river when she heard the voices of a group of female *coolies* going home after working in the fields, where they harvested the pulses, ground-nuts, maize, vegetables and fruits. All of them balanced cane baskets on their heads, each filled to the brim with okra, *karela*, long snake-gourds and rounded bottle gourds, as well as *sitaphal, guava* and *sapota*. Some carried their babies on their backs too in slings. Their colourful saris hitched high up to their knees and their sari-*pallu* tucked around their waists tightly, they walked at a leisurely pace with a smile on their faces. Neela watched them as they passed and heard the jingle of their anklets and toe rings. How simple and uncomplicated their lives were here in the village. If she had remained here, she too would not have changed and perhaps she might have found contentment here.

Chapter 42

Neela knew that Sharda had been watching her closely since she had come home and was well aware that her daughter was upset about something, so it did not come as a surprise when one day she spoke up.

'It's been eight years, *beti*. It's time to let go. Please try and pull yourself together.'

Neela guessed that her mother assumed that she was grieving for her dead husband.

'I am all right, Maa,' Neela lied.

For her parents and everyone else in the village, she was still a mourning widow. How could she tell her mother that she wasn't mourning for Ajay, but was yearning for another man and his child.

'I am only thinking . . . Maa . . . whether I should go into town to find a job,' she said.

'You don't need to, *beti*. You have already worked so hard. You even bought this house back for us.'

'Don't be silly, Maa, that wasn't hard work at all. In fact these last few years I never felt I was working . . .'

'In a way I was hoping that you would stay in England,' Sharda murmured. 'You might have had a chance of marrying again there.'

'Maa!' Neela was surprised.

'Yes, Neela, that's what I have been thinking. What hope is there for you in this village? My heart is breaking because we can't get you married again.'

'I don't need to get married to be happy. That's not the only destiny for a girl.' She smiled at her mother. 'Don't worry about me, Maa. I am fine. You should see how many girls live independently in England. Didn't I tell you about my friend Gill?'

'Yes, but that's in England, Neela. You know how it is here for a girl who lives on her own.'

'Times are changing, Maa . Someone has to be the first to challenge society and I am sure many women will follow. Only then will our communities treat women as equals.'

'It may take centuries,' sighed Sharda.

'Maybe, but it is still worth trying.'

Whenever Neela walked through the streets, the people in the village either looked at her pityingly or commented on what they saw as her impossible situation.

'*Hai Ram! Beti*, we never thought you would end up like this when you got married,' cried an elderly woman when Neela went to fetch the drinking water from the well that was two streets away.

'What can anyone do? This is her *karma* that she has to endure in this life. God only knows what sort of sin she committed in her past life,' a younger woman answered.

'Look at her though. She is so young and pretty. My heart is melting to see her without a *kumkum bindi* on her forehead,' sighed another.

Hearing those painful comments, Neela wondered why such damning rules were made in the first place. Why was a woman punished like this but not a man? Neela looked at her coarse white sari and couldn't help but smile at the thought that these women did not know what was going on in her mind. She was acting for their sake. They did not now that she had worn her daffodil and sunrise saris not long ago and had been admired by a wonderful man.

Frustrated rather than comforted by the women's comments, Neela began to wonder how on earth she was going to be a *sanyasini* if she couldn't calm her mind and accept her situation. She felt suffocated by the well-meaning but jaded attitudes of the people in the village, who saw her as a failure and as someone whose life was in the past.

Neela spent the early mornings in the temple, collecting flowers or lighting lamps. Every auspicious day, she accompanied her mother to attend the devotional and philosophical preaching of *gurus* and *sadhus*. But however much she tried, she could not concentrate and nothing banished the thoughts of Alex and Krish. It was clear that she would never become a *sanyasini*.

Chapter 43

It was exactly six weeks later when the postman brought a letter from England.

Neela immediately recognised the neat handwriting on the pale blue envelope. The feel of the paper reminded her of Alex's firm handshake and the gentle touch of his fingers wiping away her tears at the airport. Clutching the letter, she ran to the banks of the river.

Trembling with anticipation, she seated herself in the shade of a huge *peepal* tree and took a deep breath. Her hands shook as she slit open the letter and pulled out the folded blue sheets of paper. She stared at the words and traced the initials embossed on the bottom corner of the pages.

Dear Neela

How are you? Hope you are well and enjoying the company of your parents. We are fine here but missing you very much. Life is not the same without you and I couldn't help but write this letter to you.

'Oh, Alex-*ji!*' she sighed.

Neela, I can't tell you how many times I have tried to write to you but, never mind, at last here are the words from the bottom of my heart.

I am sure you remember the day I told you about my relationship with Ragini and you know too how much I agonised over what had happened, and that eventually I decided to go back to India to find out the truth.

When I returned, I waited for you to ask me what had happened while I was out there, but strangely, you didn't. And I was too bitter to talk about it. Many times I wanted so much to tell you, but somehow I never found the right opportunity. Perhaps deep down I was afraid of losing the closeness that I felt with you by talking about Ragini again.

You probably guessed that I had to see Ragini once more to find out what had gone wrong so that I could stop agonising over the past. But I also wanted to know how I would react, when, or if, I saw her. I couldn't remember how I felt about her any more because the cruel reality of my situation, like poison in Lord Shiva's throat, had soaked into me. Many times I relived the relationship with Ragini and in hindsight realised that there had been signs that I had chosen to ignore. Only looking back did I begin to understand that she hadn't really understood me nor had she loved me enough. I had always pushed such doubts away, reluctant to judge her too harshly.

The other reason for going back to India was to do my duty by Krish. One day he will need to know what happened to his mother. If I didn't have an explanation myself, how could I possibly help Krish to understand?

Anyway, when I reached India, I went straight to Ragini's father's house. The gate-keeper wasn't there and the gate was locked. I enquired in the neighbourhood, and fate was on my side because I met one of Ragini's friends, Seema. She told me that Ragini's father had passed away, and that her mother had gone to live with Ragini somewhere in Madras. She didn't really want to give me Ragini's address, but when I explained that I had come all the way from England, she relented.

Chapter 43

I took the next available flight to Madras, got straight into a taxi and got out a few yards from her house because I wanted to walk and clear my head. Her home was as huge as her father's. While I was staring at it, a car drove through the gates into the front courtyard. I thought I saw a glimpse of Ragini. I went closer, hiding behind the compound wall, and peered through the grills of the gate. The woman who got out of the car was unmistakably Ragini. I would recognise her from a mile away and it wasn't difficult to guess that the well-dressed man beside her was her husband. A little girl, who was playing with her ayah on the veranda, ran towards them. Ragini lifted the child up and hugged and kissed her. Then the man took the child in his arms. Ragini smiled at him affectionately as he put his other arm around her waist and drew her closer to him. To anyone else, that glimpse of a beautiful family would have brought pleasure, but for me it was agony.

Seeing her with her family didn't give me all the answers I wanted. I still needed to talk to her. That night I sank into my hotel bed, tired and disturbed. The next day I waited until mid morning before setting out again, hoping to catch Ragini alone.

As I hoped, Ragini was by herself, seated in a cane chair, reading a book on her front veranda. I opened the gate and she looked up at the sound. The book in her hand fell to the ground and she jumped to her feet. A look of shock was etched on her face as she stared at me open-mouthed. A long silence stretched between us as I struggled to control my emotions.

I was the first one to break the silence. I asked her how she was. She looked like a frightened deer confronted by a hungry lion. Slowly her lips parted and she whispered my name.

'So you remember my name?' I said.

'Why have you come here?'

'Why did you leave me?'

309

'Get out!' she hissed, glancing over her shoulder as if afraid someone might see or hear.

'I'm not leaving until I have an explanation,' I told her.

'Explanation!' she exclaimed. 'Surely I have already given you one. Couldn't you see that it was over?'

'Ragini, how could it have been over when we created a child together?'

'But I never loved you, Alex. Don't kid yourself. I was infatuated with you, that's all.'

I looked at her long and hard.

'I am surprised that you are only telling me this now.'

'Go away. Leave me alone.'

There was fear in her eyes, and distaste. I didn't know what made me ask the next question but I couldn't help it.

'Do you love your husband?'

'Yes. In fact I was already betrothed to him when I met you.'

I was stunned. 'Why did you betray him then? If you loved him . . .?'

Her face turned crimson and she went silent.

'I suppose I didn't know what I was doing. It was all a mistake.'

It took me a while to control my anger.

'Please, Alex . . .'

She gave me a tentative smile.

'I was very young and immature. I fell in love with you because you were so handsome.' Her tone was casual, as if she was talking about a dress that she bought because it was colourful.

I think this was the point when I understood that she could not hurt me any more. She had already inflicted as much damage and pain as she could. What enraged me was the fact that she hadn't once mentioned her son. I felt in my pocket for his photo but then stopped. What was the point? It dawned *on me that for her Krish was probably nothing more than the product of her lust. I had been trying to break down the solid wall that she had built between us but now there seemed to be no point.*

As I walked back to the hotel room, I tried to understand how a mother could cut one child out of her heart while loving another. I had always believed that a mother would do anything not to lose her child. But Ragini had changed many of my beliefs, and now had obliterated all my feelings for her. What remained was disgust and many bitter memories.

Neela took a deep breath as she turned the page.

You do understand, Neela, don't you, that I needed to travel that far not just to discover the harsh truth but to confirm and believe it. I can't tell you the relief I felt afterwards. It was like a peaceful death after a long illness. I feel so free now.

A cool breeze ruffled Neela's hair and she smiled as she tucked a strand of it behind her ear. She continued reading.

Neela, as I flew back home, I couldn't stop thinking about you and your affection for Krish. I don't think you ever realised how much your love for my child moved me. I relish your many fine qualities and I have nothing but respect for you. I realised then, on that flight over the ocean, that you are the mother that Krish never had. Your sensitivity, your compassion, your delicate way of understanding others are qualities that have inspired me count-less times. And, Neela, you might not believe this but it was you who healed me and made me sane. As time went by, I thought ours was a wonderful friendship but I must admit that my feel-ings for you grew into something much deeper.

I will never forget our trip together to the Lake District. At first I feared that it might bring back memories of Ragini, but no, it was only you who filled my thoughts. I felt at peace with you in that beautiful place.

Neela couldn't read another word because her eyes were full of tears and the sentences became blurred on the page. Impatiently, she wiped them away and carried on.

You looked so beautiful in your golden daffodil sari. Neela, can you feel how my heart is still racing as I think about you. Did you know how much I wanted to call your name and hear it echo in the mountains?

And then out of the blue you decided to go to India. It was so unexpected and I was devastated. You have no idea how I felt when I heard your decision! Gradually it dawned on me that I had taken you for granted, believing that you would be here for me and Krish for ever. I should have revealed my feelings to you there and then, but I didn't want to oppose your wish or impose myself on you. Now Krish misses you dearly. Not a day goes by without him talking about you.

I miss you too, Neela, miss you with every breath of my life. Your departure took the light away and plunged me into darkness. I am lost without direction.

Your ever loving,
Alex

Neela was sobbing loudly. Her tears dripped onto the blue paper and smudged the precious words.

CHAPTER 44

Dear Alex-ji,

I too am lost without you. Since I have come here, I have struggled hard to settle with my parents but it has been impossible. Many times I tried to convince myself that I only felt friendship for you but the truth is that each time I saw you, my feelings grew stronger. My conscience told me that my dreams of you were unreachable. Confused and scared, I scolded myself for losing my heart to you so recklessly.

In the end it was very difficult for me to live under the same roof as you in case I gave away what I was feeling. I was confused. Conflicting thoughts made me take the drastic decision of leaving you. I may have departed in haste, and with a troubled mind, but I left my soul with you.

With all my love,
Neela.

Every evening, on the banks of the River Manjeera, Neela read and reread Alex's letter savouring each and every word until darkness swamped the place. The knowledge that Alex loved her made life beautiful and worth living, and she waited eagerly for his reply.

One evening, perhaps two weeks after she had received his letter, she walked the now familiar path to the river and sat on its banks. The sky was darkening fast and the sun was sinking below the far horizon. Peasants and cowherds on their way home from work kept up a stream of chatter and sang their age-old songs. The tinkling of bells round the cows' necks told Neela that they too were ambling home. As the hustle and bustle of the day's ending faded, Neela watched the moon rise and spread its soft shimmer over the water. Everything looked completely different in this silver light so that even the rocky hills on the far side of the river melted into the clouds, their outlines softened against the darkness. The tall palm trees became silhouettes against the sky, and the branches of the huge banyan tree cast dark reflections in the water. The only noise was the rustle of leaves.

But then the breeze quickened and a sudden gust lifted the sari *pallu* from her shoulder. She crossed her arms to pull the spare fabric around her but it caught on something. She tugged at it but it held fast. Exasperated, she spun round to free it.

But someone was bending to release her sari *pallu* from a thorny bush where it had snagged and was holding it out to her. She stared at the man in utter disbelief.

'Alex-ji?'

He smiled.

'When . . . when did you come?'

It was as if she were meeting him for the first time.

'I'm sorry that I couldn't let you know that I was on my way but there is no phone in this village . . .'

For a moment neither said another word.

'I can't tell you how happy I was to receive your beautiful letter and I just couldn't wait. My reply was to fly out to you.'

'Where is Krish? Did he come too?'

Neela did not know where to look or what to say. The only way she could cope with her emotions was to avoid his eyes and look steadily at the path.

'I left him with your mother.'

Chapter 44

'It's beautiful here . . .'

'Neela, look at me,' he finally said.

He handed her a piece of paper which of course she recognised.

Dear Alex-ji, he recited out loud, *I don't know what this feeling is, but I can't imagine life without you . . .* Neela, I only read this note a short time ago. I didn't find it until long after you had left.'

Neela looked down, embarrassed.

'It was safely hidden in that blue file until a few days ago,' Alex said.

'Oh no!'

'If I had found it sooner, we might never have been separated.'

Words could wait. Half-voiced thoughts fell silent. Two shadows merged into a single night-coloured shape. They were aware only of each other as the cool, evening breeze blew from the River Manjeera. The future had begun.